# Burning Bridges

## FRANK F. WEBER

ISBN: 978-1-63821-356-7
EISBN: 978-1-63821-363-5

Published in partnership with
BookBaby
7905 N. Crescent Blvd.,
Pennsauken, NJ 08110

And
The Story Laboratory
www.writeeditdesignlab.com

Published by
Moon Finder Press
500 Park Avenue,
P.O. Box 496, Pierz, MN 56364

I would like to thank John Prine for the numerous insights his music brought to me. Thank you Oh Boy Records, Warner Chappell, and Downtown Music Publishing, for giving permission to use quotes from his songs at the beginning of each chapter of the book. There are some people you can't replace.

A special thanks to Michael Lewandowski, a retired police investigator and owner of Priority Investigations, for his contributions to this novel.

MICHAEL D. LEWANDOWSKI
Priority Investigations and Protective Services LLC
Lic# 1012  Licensed/Bonded/Insured
priorityinvestigationmn.org

I would like to thank Brenda for loving me so dearly through an almost life-ending experience in 2021. I'm appreciative of her kindness and am humbled by the grace offered by so many people I now consider friends.

Thank you to my editor, Tiffany (Lundgren) Madson, for her commitment to detail, her grasp of the English language, and her insight into the development of true crime thrillers.

A special thanks to Krista Rolfzen Soukup, of Blue Cottage Agency, for always being positive and her guidance with making my work available to so many, in so many different formats.

There are a number of players involved in this true crime who were included to keep it true to the story, so here is a reference page:

## List of Characters

Jon and Serena Frederick . . . . . . . . . . . . . INVESTIGATORS

Nora and Jackson. . . . . . . . . . JON AND SERENA'S CHILDREN

Victor Frederick . . . . . . . . . . . . . . . . . . . . . JON'S BROTHER

Harper Rowe. . . . . . . . . . . . . . . . . . . COLLEGE STUDENT

Kali Rowe. . . . . . . . . . . . . . . . . . . . . . . HARPER'S MOTHER

Jeremy Goddard . . . . . . . . . . . . . . . HARPER'S STEPFATHER

Greg Peterson . . . . . . . . . . . HARPER'S SIGNIFICANT OTHER

Billy Blaze . . . . . . . . . . . . . . HARPER'S BIOLOGICAL FATHER

Connie Berg. . . . . . . . . FORMER PARTNER OF BILLY BLAZE

Steve Berg . . . . . . . . . . . . . . . . . . CONNIE BERG'S HUSBAND

Carter. . . . . . . . . . . . . . . . . . . . . . . . . CONNIE BERG'S SON

Tony Shileto . . . . . . . . . . . . . . . . RETIRED INVESTIGATOR

Vicki Ament. . . . . . . . . . . . . . TONY SHILETO'S ROOMMATE

Loni Thompson. . . . . . . . . FORMER LOVER OF BILLY BLAZE

Fats Gangl. . . . . . . . . . . . . . . VICTIM OF WEAPONS THEFT

Moe Brown . . . . . . . . . . . . . . VICTIM OF WEAPONS THEFT

Deb ZionBILLY. . . . . . . . . BLAZE'S MATERNAL HALF-SISTER

Cayenne Tiller. . . . . . . . . . . . . . . . . . . . . . . DRUG ADDICT

Paula Fineday . . . . . . . . . . . . . . . . . . BCA INVESTIGATOR

Moki Hunter . . . . . . . . . . . . . . . . . . . . . . . . . . . . . CHEF

Chimalis Bena . . . . . . . . . . . . . . . . . . Restaurant owner

Mara Barrera. . . . . . . . . . . . . . . . .Billy Blaze's ex-wife

Phoenix Blaze . . . . . . . . . . . . . . . . . . Billy Blaze's son

Cheryl Wicklin . . . . . . . . . . . . . . . . . . . . . . Drug addict

Curtis Wicklin. . . . . . . . . . . . . . . . . . . . Chery's husband

Darko Dice. . . . . . . . . . . . . . . Blaze's partner in crime

Gunner Black. . . . . . . . . . . . . .Billy Blaze's best friend

Rachel West. . . . . . . . . . . . . . Gunner Black's daughter

Margo Miller . . . . . . . . . . . . . . . . . . . . . Lover of Blaze

Randy Vogel . . . . . . . . . . . . . . . . . .Veteran and addict

Andri Clark. . . . . . . . . . . . . . . . . Randy Vogel's fiancée

Nellie Ellison. . . . . . . . . . . Former lover of Billy Blaze

Trisha Lake . . . . . . . . . . . . Former lover of Billy Blaze

Gwyneth Porter . . . . . . . . Former lover of Billy Blaze

Keith Stewart. . . . . . . . . . . . . . . High level trafficker

Riezig "Zig" Ziegler . . . . . . . . . . . . . . . . . . . Trafficker

Nitika Brown . . . . . . . . . . . . . . . . . . . . . . . . Sex worker

Lilly Pengilly. . . . . . . . . . . . . . . . . . . . . . . . .Sex worker

Jada Anderson . . . . . . . . . . . . . . . . . . . . . . . . .Reporter

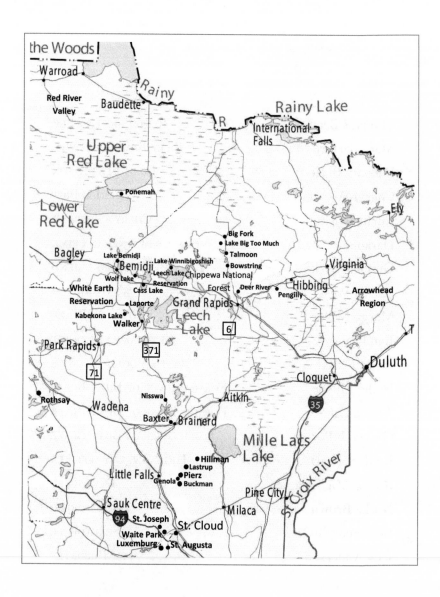

the Woods

Warroad

Red River
Valley

Baudette

Rainy

Rainy Lake

R

International
Falls

Upper
Red Lake

Ponemah

Lower
Red Lake

Ely

Bagley

Big Fork
Lake Big Too Much
Talmoon
Bowstring

Lake Bemidji
Lake Winnibigoshish
Bemidji
Wolf Lake
Leech Lake Chippewa National
Reservation
Cass Lake
Forest
Deer River
Virginia

White Earth
Reservation

Laporte

Grand Rapids

Pengilly

Hibbing

Arrowhead
Region

Kabekona Lake
Walker

Leech
Lake

6

Park Rapids

371

Duluth

71

Cloquet

Rothsay

Wadena

Nisswa

Aitkin

35

Baxter
Brainerd

Mille Lacs
Lake

Hillman
Lastrup
Pierz
Buckman

Little Falls
Genola

Pine City

St Croix River

Sauk Centre

94

St. Joseph

Milaca

St. Cloud

Waite Park
Luxemburg

St. Augusta

*Pay attention to the name under the John Prine quote, as the chapter is told from this character's perspective.*

*Chapters 2 & 4 are intense and, at times, may seem ridiculous, but this is true crime and I felt the reader deserved to experience actual events. Chapter 4 is this man's true to life charges. A recorded assault, an insane criminal history, comments you wouldn't expect a victim to make, a murder weapon tossed in the Platte River in Royalton . . . Enjoy!*

*Truth is stranger than fiction,*
*but it is because Fiction is obliged*
*to stick to possibilities; truth isn't.*
—MARK TWAIN

# 1

*Shoot the moon right between the eyes*
*I'm screaming*
*Take me back to sunny countryside*
—JOHN PRINE, *CLOCKS AND SPOONS*

## JON FREDERICK

9:00 A.M., THURSDAY, APRIL 9, 2020
BIRCHMONDT DRIVE NORTHEAST,
WEST SIDE OF LAKE BEMIDJI, BEMIDJI

At twenty years old, Harper Rowe reminded me of an abandoned fawn. The willowy, baby blue-eyed woman had long blonde hair, brush-stroked away in waves, reminiscent of impressionist art, like Renoir's *Girls at the Piano*. With her long legs crossed, she sat in front of me in a cushioned wicker lounge chair, in her grandparents' four season porch.

In a soft-spoken tone, Harper wove the tapestry of her sad tale. "My mom, Kali Rowe, was a buyer for Macy's and was in New York for work. And now she's dead."

"I'm assuming not from natural causes."

"Most unnatural." Her eyes welled with unshed tears. She shared, "My mom had the dubious distinction of being one of the first coronavirus deaths in New York."

My heart ached for Harper. She was in the same boat as the loved ones for the victims of homicides I'd investigated, back when I worked for the BCA. No hugging or kisses good-bye—*just gone.*

The dam burst and Harper took a moment to gather her composure. Wiping away tears, she wearily continued, "My mom used to call me every day. And I'd act like taking her calls would be that final prick that would burst my sanity." She could barely get the words out. "It's a bridge burned, now. Did you ever wish you could have one more conversation with someone?"

"Yes." I also wished my wife, Serena, was here. She would know what to say. Sterile, taciturn data, devoid of any ability to comfort, ran through my brain. I tried my best, "I'd bet your mom was similar, with her mom, and *your* daughters will treat you the same—no matter how great of a parent you are. It's just a part of growing up."

With heartfelt sincerity, Harper warned of the burden she carried. "Before she went into the coma, my mom told me, 'I love you and I want you to know there is nothing that I wouldn't forgive you for. You have been my pride and joy. I'm hoping you will forgive me, too, even for things I never told you.' That's a hard line to let go of." The weight of her grief had the potential to create unforeseen challenges.

"I'm so sorry for your loss. Kali sounds like an amazing person."

"She was."

I felt so useless. "I would hug you, but . . ."

Harper understood. "I appreciate your boundaries. Everything is so weird. It's my junior year of college. Instead of spending Saturday night with friends, we're online live streaming. Instead of enjoying a romantic meal with my boyfriend, Greg, we're Snapchatting. I'm already sick of social distancing, but I don't want to die. It just sucks!"

I cringed inwardly, a bit, by her use of "boyfriend," when referring to an adult male. I never referred to any adult as *girl* or *boy*, due to the history of sexism and racism associated with those terms. It bothered me that there were so many books about adult women, *Girl on the Train, Gone Girl, Girl with the Dragon Tattoo*, etc. that referred to women as girls. I never used *girlfriend* or *boyfriend* when discussing adult relationships. When I was with the BCA, and an offender would talk about his *girlfriend*, I would respond, "Isn't it illegal for you to date girls?"

While Harper regrouped, I decided it was a good time to clarify the reason I was there. "Why do you need an investigator?"

After blowing her nose, she said, "I want you to find my dad." She paused momentarily, and then anxiously purged information. "Well, he's not my *dad*. Jeremy Goddard is technically my stepdad, but he's my rock. He's Dad, as far as I'm concerned. He hugs me whenever I need a hug and loves me. I could never have the heart to tell him what I'm doing today; he might think he failed me. After Bemidji State went completely online and my roommates moved home, I moved in with my mom's parents. I want to learn as much as I can about her life."

"Your grief speaks well of you and your love for your mother. Viktor Frankl said, 'Everything can be taken from you but one thing: the last of the human freedoms—to choose your attitude in any given set of circumstances, to choose one's way.'"

"Thank you. I appreciate that."

Harper straightened out of her melancholy and got back to business. "I need to find my biological father." She handed over her birth certificate. "I needed this for a passport last year. My mom told me where to find it in her file. I didn't bother to mention to her my father's name was on the certificate, since she was reluctant to give me any information about him. I Googled him, but couldn't find anything under the name, William Blaze."

The birth certificate identified Harper's father as Billy Blaze. Billy might've been his legal name.

I left the Bureau of Criminal Apprehension (BCA) one year ago; I was finally picking up my first case as a private investigator. I performed construction work for a local company, until our architect came down with COVID and everything came to a halt. Serena asked me to take this offer and, since she was handling our finances, I was going to. The family farm on which I was raised fell to bankruptcy. I, for damn sure, wasn't going through it again.

I said, "You were born in St. Cloud."

She nodded, "He granted me power of attorney when I turned eighteen. He apparently knew someday, I'd come looking for him. And that's all I know."

My first thought was that her father had a criminal history. Career criminals eventually needed someone on the outside, during their incarceration, to take care of their affairs, so it was a pretty common practice to give a sired adult power of attorney. There were also a number of legitimate reasons people wanted another to have a power of attorney, such as career military involvement or poor health.

Harper blew unruly strands of hair out of her eyes. "My mom took the time to help a lot of unsavory characters, but she never let them in my life. I'm assuming my bio-dad fell into that category. My mom wasn't crazy. I'm sure there's a reason she deflected any questions I had about him."

My obsessive brain took a brief tangent. When it comes to food, *savory* is salty rather than sweet, but an *unsavory* person is a *salty* person. So, a sweet person, like Harper, was the opposite of both savory and unsavory.

I asked, "Who is paying my wages?"

She cleared her throat and said with shaky confidence, "I am."

"A college student is paying me two thousand dollars a week and covering medical expenses for my family?" I doubted it.

Embarrassed, she admitted, "Okay, it's not me directly. An anonymous professional is putting the money into an account and I'm forwarding it to you."

I said, simply, "Explain."

Harper scratched one of her long legs by rubbing the other over it. "After my mom's funeral, a woman contacted me and told me she'd cover the expenses for an investigator to find Billy, if I promised to keep her name out of it. She gave me your name. Do you want the job or not?"

It wasn't a matter of wanting it. My family needed the money.

YESTERDAY WAS MINNESOTA'S BIGGEST INCREASE, TO date (+85 new cases), of the coronavirus. By the Governor's "stay at home" order, businesses had been shut down and people were advised to isolate. Serena was taking this order seriously, protecting our children—Nora, age five, and Jackson, one. She had confined herself to the home with them. We were hammered with news that the pandemic was worse, daily.

After leaving Harper, I called a friend and retired county investigator, Tony Shileto. Tony was paralyzed after being shot on the job, but still occasionally took on laborious work for investigations, such as viewing camera footage or going through files. He agreed to see what he could find on Billy Blaze. I then contacted a St. Cloud police officer I knew and asked if he'd ever heard of Billy Blaze. I thought it was good fortune, at the time, that this officer had interviewed him back in 1997. The interview had been recorded at the police station. It was three years before Harper was born, but I felt watching Blaze interact and speak would at least give me some sense of what he was like.

5:15 P.M. WEST ST. GERMAIN STREET, ST. CLOUD

THE ABANDONED DOWNTOWN OF ST. CLOUD was reminiscent of a Twilight Zone episode. Sergeant Jason Nelson's squad car was the lone car parked on Germain Street. Normally, traffic would be backed up, with agitated people honking horns, as they scurried to leave work from the neighboring courthouse and social services buildings.

The stocky officer stood six feet from me, wearing a white mask—a restriction resulting from the COVID-19 pandemic. His voice was muffled. "I can't talk about this, but here's the interview." Jason extended his gloved hand to offer me a DVD.

Surprised, I asked, "On a DVD? From 1997? Not a lot of folks had access to DVDs then—they'd only just become available earlier that year."

Jason explained, "It was originally recorded on a VHS tape; we've since converted all VHS evidence to digital versions. Saves on storage space."

"Well, I don't have a VHS player, so this is perfect. Thank you."

He continued, "The scratches you'll see on Blaze's face are from his lover—Connie Berg."

"What was Connie like?"

"Hard to read. When I arrived on the scene, Blaze was sitting at the kitchen table with a bottle of tequila; Connie was alone in the bedroom and oddly tranquil. No puffy eye or bleeding lip—just a red mark on each wrist. She was so calm it was eerie. I didn't know what to make of it."

I asked, "His legal name is Billy Blaze?"

"Yeah. Honestly, I didn't think she had much of a case. Blaze told me that, a couple weeks later, he pled guilty, 'just to get it over with.'"

"Do you have an address for Connie?"

Jason huffed behind his mask, "You're not BCA, anymore. You helped us with the Kaiko Kane case, so I'm returning the favor." He pointed to the disk I was holding. "Destroy it when you're done . . ."

## 9:45 P.M., PIERZ

SERENA LAID BACK ON THE COUCH with her knees bent across my lap, as I massaged her feet and legs. Her tender heart, green eyes, long brunette curls—all so lovable. Serena and I had yet to clarify where the investigation ended and our home life began. When I was with the BCA, I practiced strict professional boundaries. Now, in private practice, I was working with my lover. It was easier to assign tasks to someone for whom you didn't have deep feelings. The upside was Serena wanted to work investigations and she was the most insightful person I knew.

With a devilish grin, she said, "I know you, Jon. You've spun yourself into a knot over something."

"I'm hoping that working a case together doesn't make you love me less."

Her eyes scintillated. "Our love can handle this—I promise." She kissed me, "Before you, my head was full of what-ifs. Now, it's *what's next* for us. You've had the key to my heart for—maybe forever. At thirty-five, we're starting our own investigative agency—together. I'm so excited to solve our first case!"

"I love you, Serena. Don't hesitate to ask me questions."

She glanced upward, pursed her lips, and said, "This might be a criminal justice one-oh-one question, but why do most people commit murder?"

"Narcissistic injury. The victim said or did something the killer's ego couldn't handle. It's the most common reason men kill women and women kill men."

As I worked the muscles in her legs loose, we watched Officer Nelson's recorded interview of Billy Blaze. There was a cocky assuredness with which Blaze entered the room. He had a dense black, military style crewcut. Bloodied scratches marred his face.

Serena flinched, "Ooh, the poor guy. She must have had some nasty nails."

"We'll see."

Serena commented on his tight, black t-shirt. "The man's a body builder. You don't get that build just from hard work."

Seated in a stark interview room, Officer Nelson, in full uniform, asked Blaze to explain the alleged assault against Connie Berg.

Blaze told him, "I had too much to drink—I admit that." He looked down, "It's hard to get over Connie's cheatin' She slept with my best friend." He picked up a Styrofoam cup of water and took a large swallow, his bulging Adam's apple jittering in his thick neck.

"How do you explain the red marks on her wrists and strands of duct tape on the floor?"

Billy scrubbed a hand over his bristly hair. "You know how it is when you're angry and jealous—and drunk. I told her I needed to know exactly what she did with that bastard, one more time. She said we'd gone over it enough. When I told her it wasn't enough for me, she came at me, scratchin' like a wildcat. So, I taped her wrists together to stop her. What's she sayin' I did?"

"Connie said you hit her in the head, repeatedly, and punched her in the stomach."

Blaze shook his head with a smirk. "And you *always* believe the woman. If that's her story, where are the bruises?"

"She had a red mark on her forehead."

"When we were wrestlin' back and forth, we butted heads. That wasn't my fault." He challenged, "What did you get from the rape kit?"

The officer paused, "She didn't say you raped her, so we didn't test."

Blaze considered this before suggesting, "Well, maybe you should. The argument was over her cheatin.' You know how angry people get when you catch them in a lie. Do the kit. I'd like to know who's DNA is in her. Do the swab, or do a polygraph, or whatever you do. You'll see what I'm dealin' with. She broke my heart."

Officer Nelson leaned back in his chair and asked, "Why don't you just leave her?"

"I love her. As miserable as she makes me—I still love her . . ."

Serena's inviting emerald eyes met mine, "Do you believe him?"

"No."

"Why not?"

"I'm not sure. I don't like him. Either he's naïve to the way it works, or he knows it like the back of his hand. I have a feeling it's the latter. He suggested the officer do two things to verify his story that the officer can't do. He can't subject a victim to a lie detector test or a rape kit without an alleged rape. And, right after he said he was angry over the affair, he took a large swallow of water. People get a dry mouth when they lie."

Serena mused, "I wouldn't have known they wouldn't automatically test a victim, either. And as for the water, he was hungover."

"True."

She suggested, "My gut feeling is the truth lies some-where between her statement and his. Honestly, I feel kind of bad for the guy. He's hurting . . ."

Unexplainable details lingered in my brain long after they were disclosed. In this case, it was the spontaneous generation of duct tape. How did duct tape magically appear in Blaze's hands, in her bedroom, if this wasn't a premeditated assault?

# 2

*He proved he could run, twice as fast as the sun*
*By losing his shadow at night*
—John Prine, *Billy the Bum*

## JON FREDERICK

### 10:00 A.M., GOOD FRIDAY, APRIL 10, 2020
### RIVERSIDE DRIVE SOUTHEAST, ST. CLOUD

Today, Christians commemorate the crucifixion and death of Jesus Christ. It was a day of fasting and penance. Due to COVID, all churches were closed. I observed my Good Friday tradition of listening to *Jesus Christ Superstar*, during my drive to St. Cloud to meet Connie Berg. It put my worries back in perspective. Being requested to quarantine was still a hell of a lot better than getting crucified.

Connie's stucco, cottage-style home offered a beautiful overlook of the east bank of the Mississippi River. Connie was my first successful effort at a face-to-face interview. I had called ahead of time to let her know I was looking for information on Blaze. She asked if I'd been tested for the coronavirus. I assured her I lived in one of the few counties in the state that still had no confirmed cases. Connie agreed to meet, but insisted I stop over when her husband, Steve, wasn't home. I wasn't sure what she'd have to offer, since Blaze's assault on her happened more than twenty years ago, but it was a start.

Connie informed me she had been a recluse since the stay-at-home orders came forth and preferred to go without masks. We would social distance, keeping six feet apart, as was the recommendation of the CDC.

Before allowing me in, Connie looked through the sidelight window by her door, and then on tiptoes, clad in white Converse sneakers, scanned passed me and beyond. Her frightened hazel eyes were lined with worry, reminiscent of some rugged years but, in her forties, there was still something bewitching about her. After surveying my surroundings and satisfied I was alone, she ushered me in.

Connie ran nervous fingers through her long, strawberry blonde hair, shaking her natural waves off her shoulders and down her slim back. Her petite frame was snugged into a plain white t-shirt and distressed jeans clung perfectly to slender legs, a fraction of tanned ankle showing between the hem and her sneakers. The extent of her accessories consisted of a thin silver chain around her neck, with a heart-shaped pendant she slid back and forth across the chain as if the gesture summoned protective spirits.

Once inside, Connie dug a pack of cigarettes out of her bag. "I haven't smoked for a year. All it takes is the *mention* of Billy Blaze and I have to pick it up again." She tapped a cigarette out of a pack and lit it, the simple silver ring on her thumb dancing as she flicked the lighter to life. She took a long drag and exhaled from the side of her mouth, closing her eyes while savoring the process, then snapped them open and addressed me. "What do you need to talk to me about?"

"I'm just starting to gather information. I got your name from a 1997 domestic assault charge Blaze caught."

She expelled an angry trail of smoke. "Are you here to question if it really happened, like the last investigator?"

"No." Based on her reaction, there was no doubt in my mind Blaze had assaulted her. "Any idea where I'd find him, today?"

She snorted, "Don't know and don't care, as long as he stays away from me. I'd been divorced from Carter's father for about a year when I became involved with Billy. We didn't officially live together, but we spent a lot of nights together. I was in a bad spot—lonely, depressed, drinking too much." She shook away the intrusive memory. "But I'm with a good man, now."

"When's the last time you saw Blaze?"

"I haven't seen him since the assault, but he's visited me, just the same. After I filed the charge, he broke into my store and trashed it. I knew it was him, but I couldn't prove it. Nothing was taken; the only items broken were things he knew were important to me—an antique clock from my grandpa; a collection of glass roosters from Grandma. The items weren't nearly as valuable as the memories that went with them. If you pissed Billy off, he would find something that meant a lot to you and destroy it. Another Blaze tactic was to bring up the most shaming thing you ever shared with him and use it like ammo against you, every time it suited him. He is pure evil."

"On the night of the assault, what was the argument over?"

Connie uttered sardonically, "Do you mean, what did I do to provoke him?"

It wasn't what I meant, but I didn't respond, as she deserved the opportunity to vent. The prevalence of domestic abuse in an educated country like the United States was disturbing. There were twenty thousand domestic abuse calls every single day. More than five hundred women were murdered each year by their lovers. There were ten million victims annually, which worked out to be one in every seventeen women in the U.S.

Connie continued, "Billy was an ass when he drank tequila. I called him at the bar to see when he was coming home. I could tell by his tone it was going to be one of *those nights*. So, I set up a camera to record him. I thought maybe if he saw how obnoxious he got, he'd get sober. But it ended up worse than I anticipated—real bad." She let out a deep, exhausted breath, her hand trembling as she brought the cigarette to her lips for comfort.

"The investigators never mentioned a recording."

Connie aggressively stubbed out her cigarette. "I didn't tell them I *had* it. If they would've confronted Billy about the recording, he would have killed me. I was going to hang onto it until he was incarcerated and a court date was set. When he pled guilty, I hid it, thinking I'd need it when he tried to slither out of his consequences."

"Do you still have it?"

"I kept it as a reminder to make certain I never considered doing anything for Billy, ever again. He can be charming." She stood up quickly and waved for me to follow her to the living room, as if on a mission. "My husband's never seen it and he never will. Only the attorneys and I viewed the recording. If you're looking for Billy Blaze, I want you to truly see the piece of shit he is. He charms people and people think he's smart, but he's just a bully."

She rummaged through drawers in the credenza that held her TV and components, as I silently sat on the end of the couch. She pulled out a VHS tape and slid it into an outdated player. I was surprised she still had one. It reminded me that much has changed since that assault in 1997.

The video began with Connie briefly on-screen, turning the camera on. She piled clothes around the camera, and then disappeared. I noticed the narrow hall on the screen, outside the bedroom, was similar to the hall I'd just passed. "Was this recorded here?"

"Yes."

I asked, "Where are you?"

"Hiding in the closet. There were times if he couldn't find me right away, he'd just give up."

*Blaze came stumbling into the bedroom, holding a roll of silver duct tape. He sing-songed in a lecherous, Jack Nicholson tone,*

*"Where are you, Connie? Daddy's looking for you!"* He laughed to himself. *Blaze tossed the duct tape on the bed and pulled his t-shirt off, turned away from the camera, revealing a grisly tattoo of the grim reaper carrying a sickle, which covered his back.*

Connie sneered, "If you didn't pick up on the icon, the words, *GRIM REAPER*, are tattooed across his shoulders." She attempted to be hard, but the zip, zip, zip of her heart pendant across her necklace gave her uneasiness away.

*Blaze undid his belt, dropped his jeans, and proceeded to strip completely. He called out, "Here I am, baby, in the raw. Come and get it!" He dropped into a squat and glanced under the bed. After a brief scan of the room, he walked out, his glutes clenching in syn-chrony with the raging muscles in his back. The reaper deferred to him, contorting with his movements.*

*When he returned, Blaze was agitated. He stepped out of sight for a moment, then the sound of a door opening and ruckus of bodies wrestling could be heard.*

I could hear Connie begging, *"Please, just go to sleep. Let go. You're hurting me. Let GO!"* *When they came back into view, Blaze was dragging Connie toward the bed by her hair. Bent over, she was desperately holding his hand to her head with both of hers, to keep her hair from being ripped out.*

*Blaze barked, "Hide from me, you stupid bitch? Get your ass in bed."*

*Still folded in half, Connie pled, "You're drunk. Please, just leave me alone. Maybe tomorrow night."*

*Blaze abruptly kneed her, hard, in the head.* I winced, as he could have knocked her out. *He hoisted a dazed Connie onto the bed.* There was no mention of the infidelity story Blaze gave the officer.

I turned to Connie, who was now looking away from the TV and out the window, a fresh smoke burning between her fingers. Her shoulders were hunched in self-protection, as if reliving the assault.

Having no desire to re-traumatize her, I paused the video and asked, "Do you want me to shut this off?"

She shook her head, "No. Billy's attorney argued that the recording was too traumatic to watch—for *him!*" She aggressively tapped ashes from her cigarette, missing the ashtray. "So," she continued in frustration, "Billy never had to watch it. Can you *believe* that? He terrorized me, but don't you dare hold him accountable. It's too *traumatic* for him," she said with dripping sarcasm. "I was so angry!"

"Blaze pled guilty."

"Yep, he did. His attorney told me I'd be better off if Billy didn't know about the recording. He convinced Billy to take a plea and get it over with. If you want to know about Billy—*really* understand him—I'm going to make you watch all of it."

I was about to hit play when she reached out to warn me. "Have you ever seen someone raped?"

"Unfortunately, I have. Every once in a while, we get assaults caught on a recording and we have to go through them, to clarify the exact charges. Believe me, I get no pleasure from it."

She nodded, "Play it."

*Blaze was telling her, "Call me Master."*

*"Not so loud," she pled. "Please, don't wake Carter up."*

*He slapped her hard across the face, her head snapping back. "That's all up to you."*

*Connie tried twisting her body to escape, but he punched her ferociously on the side of her head. "I can't hear you . . ." She whimpered quietly and he hit her again. "How do you address me?"*

*Voracious for validation, Connie summoned the courage of a survivor and fought back. She scratched desperately at his face and tried pushing him off.*

*Blaze again pounded on her head, just beyond the hairline—no marks.*

*After several terrorizing minutes, Connie stopped resisting. Exhausted, she conceded, "Okay," and meekly placed her hands in front of her face.*

*He grabbed the duct tape and bound her wrists together.*

*"Just don't hit me again." Her voice was plaintive. She forced out, "Master." It was clear she'd played this game before.*

*"Spread your legs, whore."*

*"Don't call me that."*

*He jabbed her in the stomach, "I'll call you whatever I want."*

*The wind briefly knocked out of her, Connie gasped to catch her breath. She curled up, "Please, don't tie me up. I'll just go along."*

It was sickening to watch.

Apparently calloused to the abusive video, Connie tiredly explained to me, "He passed out after the last time he taped me up and I spent two hours working myself free, so I could be dressed before Carter got up. I didn't want to go through that again."

*Blaze roughly ripped off her pajama pants and underwear, as he said with exasperation, "Why do you gotta make it so difficult? Maybe next time you work late, I'll just have that nice piece of ass, Chantel."*

I asked, "Who's Chantel?"

"My babysitter—who was fourteen, at the time. Her parents are good friends of mine. They'd die if they heard him saying this."

*Blaze continued brazenly, "You've seen the way she looks at me."*

Connie whispered, "She's scared to death of him. After I reported the assault, Chantel's parents insisted Carter came to their house when she watched him."

*Blaze began having sex on her.*

I will never use the word "with," as it would suggest she consented.

*He added, as he pounded his dominance into Connie, "Maybe I'll have Delores, too."*

I turned to Connie with a questioning look and she explained, "Delores is my mom. She's also scared to death of him."

Blaze was really a piece of work.

Connie studied me, "What are you thinking?"

I didn't offer thoughts yet, but continued watching the nightmare.

*Blaze was now detailing the sexual things he could do to Chantel and Delores, while he continued to violate Connie.*

I turned the volume down. "I guess my first thought is, did you ever think of killing him?"

She offered a sad laugh. "You bet I did—and in so many different ways. Any sane person would have," she shrugged. "But I wasn't that strong. I had a hell of a time working up the courage just to leave him."

He'd already done and said a hundred things that would result in any healthy person leaving him, but I knew why she struggled to leave. Over seventy percent of all domestic homicides occurred after the woman ended the relationship. She was afraid he was going to kill her.

*The same nauseating dialogue went on and on. Blaze was struggling to bring himself to orgasm and was becoming progressively more demeaning and violent.*

I asked, "Do you mind if I fast forward?"

Connie nodded and handed me the dusty remote. She quietly contemplated, "When he was sober, I'd tell myself maybe it wasn't as bad as I thought." Continuing to stare out the window she said wistfully, "A perfect body, wasted on such a jackass."

The ridiculousness of that statement struck me. After he'd threatened to rape everyone who helped Connie and her children, she could still find him attractive?

Connie rendered, "I got tired of fearing for my life. Nothing can make up for the degradation." She waved to the recording. "Keep fast forwarding until he leaves the room. I just want you to hear him when the cops arrive. To me, that's the most telling."

I forwarded through Blaze turning her over and taking her dog-style. Connie's aggrieved misery was painful to take in.

She interjected, "If you look close, you can see he's making me lick the mattress like a dog."

Shuddering inwardly, I continued to fast-forward until Blaze left the bedroom.

*Connie rolled to her side in pain. She then bit the duct tape with her teeth and peeled it off her wrists. She slowly got up and found her phone on the dresser. This had to be where she dialed 911. She slipped her pajamas back on and sat dejectedly at the edge of her bed.*

Connie narrated, "He's is in the kitchen drinking, at this point."

*A small boy entered the bedroom, yawning widely. Connie quickly pulled him into a protective hug and escorted him out of the room.*

She spoke without emotion, "He woke Carter up, so I brought him back to bed. The boy had bad dreams."

Not surprising.

I paused the recording and asked, "Where is Carter, now?"

She smiled with pride. "Whidbey Island, Washington. He's served eight years in the Navy and I don't see him leaving any time soon."

My first thought—data—Whidbey Island is the fourth largest island in the U.S. Instead, I said, "It's a beautiful area and a commendable path. I can see you're proud, as you should be." I let her have a moment, and then gestured to the TV, looking a question at her. She nodded and I pressed *Play* again.

*Connie returned, slid her phone under the dresser, and dug through a dresser drawer. She removed a pack of cigarettes and a lighter, and then returned to the edge of her bed to smoke.*

She continued her commentary, "I didn't want Blaze to smash my phone again."

Sounds of the police officers' arrival were followed with Blaze talking to them in the next room. His tone was a dramatic departure from what I'd just witnessed. He was now respectful and contrite.

We heard him saying, *"I just got home from the bar and right away, she starts raggin' on me. We exchanged some words. I should've been more considerate—I admit it. She called you guys just to make a point. We're fine, now. I'm sorry she bothered you."*

The officer could be heard saying, *"Sit at the table with my partner, while I do a walk through."*

*An officer entered the bedroom and asked Connie, "Are you okay?"*

*She stared absently into his eyes without responding.*

*He studied the bright abrasion on her forehead. She turned her wrists to expose the red lines in her skin around them.*

*After glancing down at the duct tape on the floor, the officer proclaimed, "We're going to haul Blaze to the back of the squad car, and then I'll return and get a statement."*

*She nodded. When the officer left, Connie was seen approaching the camera. Her eyes were vacant and she was likely in shock. As a shaky hand reached into view, the recording ended.*

I commented, "You didn't report the rape."

"I thought the assault would be enough to get him sober and in a domestic abuse program. Neither happened."

"He was ordered to."

"Yeah, but you know how it goes. Me and a thousand other domestic abuse victims have the same experience. He found a slimy attorney who kept putting it off and getting second and third opinions. I had to close my shop, over and over, to appear in court. But I stood strong. I had the recording to refresh my memory. Running the shop over the years has helped me maintain my sanity. I never backed down. And finally, when Billy couldn't postpone his consequences any longer, he disappeared. His final message to me was, *You can't make me do anything, bitch!*

"The assault was twenty-three years ago. Do you honestly think it's still significant to him?"

"Billy fought me in court for twenty years and lost. Billy doesn't lose."

"Where do you think he is?"

She visibly shuddered, "During the day, I can convince myself he's found some other poor soul to torment and he doesn't care about me, anymore. But at night, I can feel his eyes on me. He's out there, just below the radar. Some Saturday mornings, when I'm doing yardwork, I've seen his footprints by my bedroom window. Guys like him don't go away."

I handed her a card with my number on it. "Call me the next time you see either him or the prints. Do you have a security system?"

"Yes. And I double-check the locks on the doors and windows every night. It's ironic that *I'm* the one who's locked up."

"Do you have a DANCO in place?" A DANCO is a Domestic Abuse No Contact Order.

"Yes. That's one thing the court gave me, with no questions asked. It's not that easy for most victims." For a moment, I saw those same empty eyes I'd seen in the video. "But you know as well as I do, that paper isn't going to stop him. I'll pay. It's just a matter of when. You never get the best of Billy Blaze. It'll come when his newest distractions end and he has time to think about me again . . ."

# 3

*All the news just repeats itself*
*Like some forgotten dream, that we've both seen . . .*
*You know that old trees just grow stronger*
*And old rivers grow wilder every day*
*Old people just grow lonesome*
*Waiting for someone to say, "Hello in there, hello"*
*So if you're walking down the street sometime*
*And spot some hollow ancient eyes*
*Please don't just pass 'em by and stare*
*As if you didn't care, say, "Hello in there, hello"*
—JOHN PRINE, *HELLO IN THERE*

## JON FREDERICK

### 7:15 A.M., SATURDAY, APRIL 11, 2020
### PIERZ

I needed to put in a long day again, today. As a private investigator, I didn't have the access to records and resources I had when working for the Bureau of Criminal Apprehension. I was fortunate to have maintained some trusted friends.

This morning, Serena rested peacefully, with her long chocolate curls splayed across her pillow, as I lay next to her, planning my day. I heard the patter of feet belonging to our precocious daughter, padding down the hall. Giving me a conspiratorial smile, Nora pounced on Serena.

Accustomed to the wake-up call, Serena pulled Nora into a loving cuddle.

Nora, a curly-haired and vibrant, smaller version of Serena, gave her a quick hug and tried wiggling away.

Serena hung on to her, "Honey, I need a full, one-minute snuggle."

"That *was* a minute," Nora argued.

"No, that was ten seconds—at best."

Nora whined, "Well, it felt like an hour."

Serena laughed, "You can snuggle a little longer."

Nora lay stiff and, in mock pain, grumbled, "How *long* is this going to go on?"

After giving her one more hug and a kiss, Serena proclaimed, "You are free to roam, my princess."

Nora hopped out of bed and yelled, "C'mon Dad," as she ran downstairs.

Serena reached over and put her hand on my bare chest. "Can I sleep ten more minutes?"

"Of course."

"Wake me when you need to leave."

As I dressed, she added, "I know we need the money, but if you don't want this case, we can just hunker down and barely survive for a while."

I kissed her and headed to Jackson's bedroom. Our one-year-old was just waking up. Jackson needed to be held for a bit before he oriented to a new day. Cradling him against my chest, his chubby arms wrapped tightly around my neck, I put Serena's tea water on the stove and started breakfast. I loved that my little ones demanded what they needed. Even though it was trying at times, it was far better than being emotionally repressed. It was my task to teach them how to regulate their raw emotions.

I was raised in a family where you were shamed anytime you expressed an emotional need. My mom would give me a story of how Jesus had it so much worse. My dad—well, you just didn't bring up emotional things to him. It would be like seeking solace from someone suffering from a migraine headache. At best, you'd get yelled at.

Serena eventually meandered downstairs and, after hugging each of the kids, made her tea and sat at the kitchen table. Nora approached her with a children's book, snuggled into Serena's lap, and they read *Little Duck*, by Rosetta Weber.

I smiled at the loving kisses Serena gave to Nora between pages. While Serena intended the pecks as loving, I could see Nora was becoming progressively more annoyed with them. Nora had Serena's beauty, but had my limited tolerance for being touched by others.

Frustrated, Nora finally turned and grabbed Serena's cheeks in both hands, and aggressively kissed her, all over her face before challenging her, "There. How do *you* like it?"

Serena and I enjoyed a good laugh, before she finally asked me, "How long are you going to be working today?"

"All day," I sighed. "Tony got me the cold case box for one day. I'll lock myself in the music room for the day and go through the entire file, so we can spend Easter Sunday as a family, tomorrow."

She nodded, "We're painting and dying eggs today."

It tore at my heartstrings to miss moments like this with my kids.

Feeling my pain, she whispered, "I understand. It's the nature of the beast. You can make up for it tomorrow."

RETIRED INVESTIGATOR, AND CLOSE FRIEND OF mine, Tony Shileto, was helping the Drug Enforcement Agency get caught up with their paperwork. The DEA was in the process of developing a criminal case against Billy Blaze, when he went off the grid. Tony was giving me access to the file, sub rosa, for one day. The name of the undercover informant involved in the Blaze investigation was redacted from the file.

I wasn't going through the case at Tony's, because Serena felt it was too much of a risk for me to enter his home. Tony's paraplegia required healthcare workers to be in and out of his home, every day. COVID-19 was rampant among healthcare workers, which was concerning for Tony, as he was both vulnerable and in need of their care.

I called Tony, primarily to vent over all the reports in small print in the file. Vicki Ament, a twenty-nine-year-old, former meth addict, answered the phone. Vicki and her daughter, Hannah, shared Tony's home.

After we exchanged hellos, Vicki complained, "I may have to take a math class before COVID is over, just to buy toilet paper. Being it's limited, I have to stand there using the calculator on my phone to figure out which one to buy. A big roll equals two regular rolls, a giant roll is two and a half rolls, and a mega roll is four rolls."

I teased, "I could make you a conversion chart."

Vicki laughed. "Isn't that what they use to make people not gay?"

"That's conversion therapy. They used to call it shame."

"Next time, I'm just calling Tony from the store." Vicki said, "I assume you called for him."

Tony didn't have much time to talk. A nursing assistant was there to massage his legs, to assist his circulation. Serena had been a great friend to Tony when he struggled with accepting that he would never walk again. He asked about her and I shared, "I worry about Serena being home all the time. I'll never convince her otherwise, but I still think sometimes, you need to step away, even if it's just to go for a drive."

Tony warned, "This COVID crap could kill any of us. They're saying five thousand Minnesotans will die from COVID before the year ends. She's the only one who seems to have it in perspective."

The numbers quickly ran through my head. This would be one in every thousand Minnesotans. The reality ended up worse than the dire prediction. One quarter of the deaths would occur in Hennepin County, primarily in Minneapolis. The added stress to this community would prove to be significant as the year progressed.

I made a note to call Tony more often. Like all old investigators, he lived for conversations about cases.

# 4

*Your flag decal won't get you*
*Into Heaven anymore*
*They're already overcrowded*
*From your dirty little wars*
*Now Jesus don't like killin'*
*No matter what the reason's for*
*—John Prine, Your Flag Decal Won't*
*Get You Into Heaven Anymore*

## JON FREDERICK

10:00 A.M., MONDAY, APRIL 13, 2020
BIRCHMONDT DRIVE NORTHEAST,
WEST SIDE OF LAKE BEMIDJI, BEMIDJI

Serena had us all dress up for our Easter meal, even though we didn't go anywhere. Our Nora was proud of her cream-colored, cotton dress, with a tulle underlay and bunnies dancing along the hem. Our poor little Jackson had to wear khaki trousers, a V-neck sweater, and a bowtie.

Nora was a sponge for new information. She caught me reading an article about how President Trump was considering pardoning Charles Duke Tanner. Charles received two life sentences, after being caught with possession of cocaine in 2004. I explained how a leader could pardon a person who was judged unfairly. When we finished our Easter egg hunt, Nora announced, "Eggs, you don't have to hide anymore. The Sister, Nora, pardons you."

It was a heartwarming family day, even though we managed to end up one egg short. Unfortunately, the hunt was inside, due to the half-foot of snow we received. Together, we searched every nook and cranny—although, I wasn't sure what a *cranny* even was. Deep down, both Serena and I were convinced the other must have hidden that one. I guessed we'd smell it, eventually. My dad used to set Easter eggs in a bowl on the kitchen table and eat them days later, but he did a lot of things you couldn't reason him out of.

THE MORNING NEWS ANNOUNCED THAT, YESTERDAY, once again, we experienced the highest increase in new coronavirus cases in Minnesota (+194). While it was typically better to have information, I hated knowing Serena was being hammered with bad news every time she turned on the TV.

I had the unenviable task of going over the information I received on Billy Blaze, with Harper. Being naïve wasn't all bad—it simply meant you hadn't been exposed to all of the terrible things people did. Harper's innocence would be abandoned after our conversation.

Back on her grandparents' four-season porch, Harper nervously covered herself with a blanket and sat with a pen and legal pad, waiting for the verdict.

I began, "If I was in your shoes, I'd want factual information, rather than opinion, so I've prepared a timeline of Billy Blaze's adult life. He was born in 1973, so he is now 47 years old." I held up a thick stack of papers, "This is what I've unearthed so far, from 1991 to the present."

"I'm ready."

I wanted to tell her, *No, you're not,* but instead, offered, "You don't have to take notes. I've printed you a copy of what I'm presenting. Just sit back and ask questions." I started by handing her a picture.

She relaxed as best she could, in her cushioned wicker chair. "Thank you." Harper studied the photo of her biological father and commented, "Well, he's not bad-looking—kind of has that rugged look of Jason Statham in *The Mechanic*. He's built like a professional athlete."

I took a deep breath and started. "On March 11, 1991, Blaze was ticketed for Driving While Intoxicated. He then joined the military and was stationed in Iraq after Desert Storm. Blaze ended up being shot in the hip by a sniper. This fueled open resentment toward Muslims, so the Army elected to give him a medical discharge, rather than allow him to return to duty. For the next six years, he worked at the Grede Foundry, in St. Cloud, and lived a relatively quiet, civilian life."

Harper smiled hesitantly, "Okay, he served our country and he drinks a little. And maybe he has some unresolved anger to work through."

"On August 22, 1997, he pled guilty to Domestic Assault. The victim, Connie Berg, reported he struck her in the head multiple times. Blaze had scratches on his face."

She asked hopefully, "Do you think it was it one of those he-said, she-said, lovers' quarrels, that just got out of hand?"

"No," I said softly. "The incident was recorded. He raped her violently and brutally assaulted her. She scratched his face trying to fight him off. One week later, he vandalized the bridal boutique Connie owned. Even though there was an eyewitness, she elected not to press charges."

I continued through the disconcerting timeline of her father's life. "The next day, Blaze leapt from a moving car on Highway 15, on a busy stretch where it crosses the Mississippi Bridge in St. Cloud. His heart had stopped, so he was given mouth-to-mouth resuscitation. He had a seizure after he came to. He had used both heroin and cocaine intravenously."

Her eyes shone with unshed tears. She pondered, "He must have been tormented with guilt."

"On October 22, 1997, while intoxicated, Blaze assaulted a Muslim man after leaving the Red Carpet Nightclub. The man was simply driving by. Blaze asked, 'How are you doing?' and the man remarked, 'Better than you,' in reference to Blaze's intoxication. Blaze pulled the man out of his car through the open window and beat him."

Harper looked disappointed but, still looking for a silver lining, she commented quietly, "He must be strong."

"That he is. By the way, unless I say otherwise, all of these crimes occurred in St. Cloud. On January 1, 1998, Loni Thompson returned home to find her front door had been kicked open, leaving a size ten shoeprint right next to the door handle. Her collection of crystal was smashed on the floor. The only items taken were a key to her home, alcohol, and jar of change. Prior to coming home, she had a verbal argument with Billy Blaze at the Lincoln Depot Pub. The bartender had kicked Blaze out of the bar for being obnoxious, an hour before Loni left. Blaze denied breaking into her apartment and described Loni as 'a drunken broad I picked up once,' adding, 'She was just pissed I wouldn't do her a second time.' Loni told the officer she was afraid of Blaze and preferred not to press charges."

Harper didn't respond, so I went on. "On February 27, 1998, Blaze was charged with Disorderly Conduct. He was leaving a house party when he said to a couple entering, 'Now there's a gross-looking woman.' The woman tried to deflect the comment, responding, 'You're drunk.' Quoting the police complaint verbatim, Blaze threatened, 'Bitch, you have no idea who you're messing with.' When her partner intervened, Blaze kicked him in the shin and then ripped the woman's blouse open. Both were very frightened of him."

I glanced up while Harper sat back in shock. "On April 1, 1998, police responded to a fight that was reportedly instigated by Blaze at an apartment complex. When Officers arrived, the fight was still going, but Blaze was gone. He didn't receive any charges. Three weeks later, he received his second DWI, after it was reported he was swerving his IROC-Z Camaro through traffic on St. Germain Street in St. Cloud, yelling obscenities out his open window, targeting minorities. Blaze tried to provoke the officers who responded into hitting him, but neither did."

Harper asked, "What's an IROC-Z?"

"It was a muscle car named after the International Race of Champions—sold to guys who never left the county of their birthplace. I asked my dad about the IROC and he said it had no street cred, because it always lost to Mustangs in street races or takeoffs from stoplights. It was a poor engine choice; the chassis was too heavy and it was overpriced—but it looked nice. My dad isn't a politically correct guy. He suggested IROC stands for *Italian Retard Out Cruising.* The one Blaze was driving had to be close to a decade old, as General Motors stopped making them in 1990."

"Please tell me you're done with 1998."

"On July 11, 1998," I continued dispassionately, "a couple complained to police that Blaze was yelling from the window of his IROC at a woman working the drive-thru at Panera. When the couple stepped over to his car to ask him to stop, he hopped out, undid his pants, and exposed his genitals to them." I decided not to use exact words, "He suggested they perform oral sex on him."

Harper was so overwhelmed, she now tried to make light of it, "Winnie the Pooh style—shirt, no pants."

"On October 1, 1998, a man who met the description of Billy Blaze fired a shot from a IROC-Z on Highway 10, into a trailer home in Sherwood Manor. The witness couldn't confirm with certainty it was Blaze, so no charges were filed. On October 6, 1998, Ricky Walters reported Blaze had stolen his .308 caliber, pump action, Remington rifle. The next day, a bartender at the Old Brick House Pub said Blaze walked in and pointed a .308 pump action Remington rifle at this head. The bartender wrestled it away from him. Blaze claimed he was bringing the rifle to the bar to give to a man he owed money. He was charged with Aggravated Assault and Theft, but all of the charges were dismissed."

Harper was surprised by this. "That doesn't make any sense. Why would they dismiss charges when his guilt was so obvious?"

"This is a situation I plan on revisiting. My guess is Blaze gave up evidence on a major drug dealer. The DEA is given a lot of latitude with witnesses when they're going after a major player. When I worked for the BCA, I helped send a rapist to prison that had four previous Criminal Sexual Conduct charges dismissed, in exchange for his testimony on drug cases."

She huffed in frustration, "Didn't it seem like they were making deals with the wrong guy?"

"It sure did. But he ran out of rope with me."

Harper stuttered, "Did Blaze—Dad—ever show any remorse?"

"Not really." Realizing she was struggling with calling Blaze *Dad*, I stated, "Jeremy is your dad, Harper. Blaze is just a guy your mom was with for a short time." She seemed to appreciate the opportunity to separate herself from him.

I cleared my throat. "Moving along, on February 26, 1999, Blaze and his friend, Gunner Black, stole a 30-30 Winchester, a Crossman 33 Air Rifle with scope, a Smith and Wesson nine-millimeter handgun, and a Chrome plated Colt .45 pistol, from 'Fats' Gangel and 'Moe' Brown. The pistol was unusual, as it had a shiny chrome grip. Blaze and Black's vehicles were impounded and searched, but no weapons were found. After the vehicles were released, investigators realized neither Blaze nor Black had a valid driver's license. No charges were filed. Within two weeks, they crashed a house party and Blaze, with a chrome-plated Colt .45 in hand, made everyone hand over their money."

"Did he get charges, then?" Harper's expression was a mixture of hope and dread.

I shook my head, "No. There were lots of illegal drugs present, so none of them wanted their names in a criminal complaint. The incident was documented by an undercover DEA agent in the home and the DEA wasn't ready to give up his cover. One week later, Blaze was charged with Aggravated DWI."

Harper considered, "Do you think the DEA tipped off the police to make sure he was charged with something? Maybe even give them opportunity to search his car for the guns?"

I smiled, "It happens. On March 17, 1999, Blaze's sister, Deb Zion, told police Blaze had been calling her and threatening to kill her. No reason reported. No charges filed."

"Zion? That's an odd surname."

"It's one of the most common surnames in the world. It was her birth name. Half the people with this surname live in Africa."

"Is his sister black?"

"I would guess so. Her race wasn't in the file."

Harper sat up, "I never even considered this, being I'm," she waved a hand across her blonde hair and vanilla skin, "very white—is Billy Blaze of mixed race?"

"No. He's white and so is the majority of his cohort."

"How do you know their race, if you don't know his sister's race?"

"They have criminal charges, so that information is available through the Department of Corrections." I stopped and considered, "I believe it was sometime in March or April of 1999 when you were conceived, correct?" Tony Shileto had run a background check on Harper for me. Her record was clean.

"Yes." She queried, "Did you come across my mom's name anywhere?"

"No, I didn't—and that's a good sign. It means she wasn't involved in all the illegal stuff Blaze was into."

Hopeful, Harper asked, "Do you think it's possible Billy Blaze isn't my father?"

"I believe Blaze is your father. Kali wanted you to stay away from him. If there was any possibility he wasn't your father, he wouldn't be on your birth certificate."

She slumped in consternation, but dropped the line of questioning.

I continued, "Meanwhile, back in St. Cloud, on May 3, 1999, Blaze showed up at Linda Michael's home looking for her husband. He threatened, 'He better be home in an hour.' Fearing for her husband's life, Linda called the police. That night, she received a call and was told, 'You called the cops. Now you're a dead bitch.' Even though she absolutely believed the calls were from Blaze, law enforcement wasn't able to trace the number, so no charges were filed.

"On July 16, 1999, Jeff Anderson was found badly beaten in the parking lot of the La Playette Bar in St. Joseph. Jeff reported he was assaulted by Billy Blaze, but he refused to press charges. On August 5, 1999, Dominique Romano called the police and stated Blaze threatened him at the White Horse Restaurant and Bar in St. Cloud. Once Dominique was safely escorted home, he refused to press charges. He stated it would only make things worse."

"It's all so crazy."

"The next one's a little lighter. On August 14, 1999, Kaplan's Dentistry on Northway Drive, in St. Cloud, reported Billy Blaze was in for a checkup. When he left, they realized two cans of cola were taken from the fridge and a CD was stolen from the boom box. They decided it wasn't worth filing charges."

"Did they say what the CD was?"

"I'm a Barbie Girl, in a Barbie World—Aqua."

Stunned, Harper asked, *"What?"*

"I'm kidding. Sorry. That song's been branded into my brain from taking my daughter to arcades and waterparks— back when we could. They didn't record the title of the CD."

I wasn't finished. "Okay, Deb Zion let her brother stay at her home for a couple days in August of 1999. On August 29, she called the police and reported she realized checks were being forged from her account. That night, her son, Lenny, received a call from Blaze telling Lenny to stay in the basement, as he was going to shoot up the home in retaliation for Deb calling the police."

"Nice brother," Harper said flatly. "Very appreciative of her kindness."

"On October 2, 1999, Blaze and Black broke into the St. Cloud Animal Hospital and stole boxes of disposable syringes. Police responded to the silent alarm and Blaze was arrested leaving the building. He was released pending a trial. Three days later, Shari Kramer called the police, reporting Blaze entered her home and threatened her friend, 'Chief,' with a rifle. Chief apparently owed him money. Blaze fired the rifle in the home and then handed Chief the shell, stating, 'The next one's in you.' Blaze then walked down the street to the Press Bar and Parlor and fanned the gun across people sitting in the bar. A bouncer approached him and he aimed the rifle at the bouncer's head; the bouncer wrestled it away. Blaze pled guilty to two counts of Terroristic Threats and was sentenced to two years in the Minnesota Correctional Facility in Stillwater. He was released from jail for Thanksgiving weekend, to get his affairs in order before going to prison. On Thanksgiving Eve, he rolled his IROC numerous times, after driving at high speeds down I-94, south of St. Cloud, and that was the end of the IROC-Z. Blaze was found unconscious and didn't recover consciousness until the next day. For the rest of 2000, until 2002, he was in prison. He lost his good time as a result of fights in prison."

"Please tell me prison turned him around." She added sarcastically, "It is a *correctional* facility, right?"

"Shortly after his release, on May 3, 2002, Blaze was ticketed for public urination. The reporting officer said Blaze was standing shirtless, in the Perkins parking lot at 1:30 a.m., with his jeans open, and a woman named Cayenne Tiller was on her knees in front of him, performing oral sex on him. Blaze argued he was just peeing and the woman had knelt down by him because she felt sick. The officer thought he'd give him a break and just write him up for public urination. In return, Blaze wanted to fight the officer, but the officer just walked away."

Harper was trying to find some sad humor in this. "So, this time, it's a Smokey the Bear scenario—wearing jeans but no shirt."

I smiled, "We seem to have a cartoon bear theme going."

She grimaced, "I'm sorry. It's just so preposterous!"

"Honestly, I wouldn't know what to say, myself."

She added, "And cartoon bears have an apparel problem. Yogi and Fozzie bear both wear a hat and a tie and no other clothing. Bears seem to struggle with understanding the purpose of clothing."

"I can't argue with the evidence."

Harper seemed to be recovering from being shell-shocked with bad news. She asked, "Are there any positive events?"

I optimistically offered, "He had an American flag decal on the rear window of his new Corvette." I pointed out, "Keep in mind all of my information is from law enforcement files. With COVID-19, I can't simply go door-to-door. I've made some phone calls, but these people aren't easy to find and, when I do find them, they're reluctant to talk.

"After his release from prison, Blaze had a couple visits from a young woman with what appeared to be her two-year-old daughter."

Harper was momentarily stunned with the realization it could have been her. Dazed, she said, "I don't remember."

The hippocampus, which processes memory, isn't fully developed until age four, so few people have memories from before then. I said, "Someone we talk to will know who the woman was." I paused, then got back on track. "Let's see. Blaze married Mara Berrara in July of 2002."

"Is it Mara or Marra?"

"It's spelled M-A-R-A, but it's just more fun to say M-air-a Barrera, so that's what I'm going with until I hear otherwise. On August 2, 2002, the night manager at the Travel Host Motel in St. Cloud called the police asking them to remove an unruly resident. Blaze had deep lacerations on his right wrist and forearm from smashing in the driver's side window of Mara's vehicle with his fist. The manager said Blaze was smearing blood on the motel counter. He told the clerk he left his wife's car undrivable. He was incarcerated for forty-five days on a probation violation." I glanced up to make sure she was okay. "You have a half-brother. Blaze fathered a son with a Mexican woman when he was fifteen."

Harper perked up. "Tell me about my bro."

"Your *bro*—Phoenix Blaze—is thirty-two, now, but back in 2002, he would've been fourteen. On October 1, 2002, concerns were expressed that Blaze was harboring Phoenix. Phoenix had an outstanding warrant for car shopping."

"Car shopping?"

"Going from car to car to steal items. Blaze claimed he hadn't seen Phoenix but, on November 17, 2002, Phoenix was arrested after stealing a car only a block away from his dad's home. Phoenix went on to become a major drug dealer for the Latin Kings. He's currently serving an eight-year prison sentence in Oak Park Heights—the only maximum security prison in Minnesota. It's underground."

Harper shook her head, "I won't be visiting my bro. This is like a horror movie you can't shut off until you've seen the end."

"Getting back to Billy Blaze, on November 6, 2002, Mara Berrara refused to let her husband into her home because he was intoxicated and he was a mean drunk. Billy pulled a bat out of his trunk, smashed in all the porch windows, and then threatened to 'bury her' once he got inside the house. After a physical altercation with the police, Blaze spent the night in jail. Mara reported she was deathly afraid of Billy."

"How long does this go on?"

"A while."

Harper shivered. I wasn't sure if this was due to the cool breeze wafting through the porch windows or from the chilling tales of her father. Last week, the temperatures were in the fifties. At this moment, in Bemidji, or "Burr-midj," as the locals called it, it was a chilling eighteen degrees. She got up and retrieved another blanket.

Expelling a deep sigh, she beckoned, "Keep going."

"In 2003, the DEA took a special interest in Blaze when Curtis Wicklin called them from the Stearns County Jail and reported his wife, Cheryl, was being supplied with drugs by Blaze. On March 3, 2003, officers performed a welfare check and found Cheryl with slurred speech, bloodshot eyes, and needle marks all over her arms. She claimed it was because her doctor, whom she referred to as 'bobble dick,' always had to try numerous times when he drew blood. Cheryl claimed it was all a big set-up and her husband was just trying to make her look bad."

"Bobble dick. Now that's a nice nickname."

"It turns out her doctor's name is bobble dick."

"Bob L. Dick?"

"No, it's spelled, B-O-B-E-L-D-Y-K. They contacted Dr. Bobeldyk, who indicated he hadn't seen Cheryl for over a year, and he'd never had difficulty drawing blood from her.

"On April 28, 2003, Blaze was arrested for trespassing when he was intoxicated and refused to leave the Ultimate Sports Bar and Grille, in Waite Park. And the drama at home heated up when Curtis Wicklin was released early from jail. Curtis found his wife in Blaze's bed, grabbed Cheryl by the hair, and dragged her out of the home. She managed to dial 911. Cheryl claimed Curtis told her, 'I'll kill you, bitch,' and her good friend, Billy Blaze, witnessed the threat. Curtis pled guilty to Assault."

"Unbelievable."

"On July 30, 2003, Blaze reported his home was robbed. Even though he said he was face-to-face as he fought off the burglar, he couldn't identify him. There was no forcible entry noted. Police questioned if the home was actually robbed. Blaze filed a claim to his insurance. Later that day, a report came in that Blaze had made a threatening phone call to a six-year-old girl named Rachel West."

"Who is she?"

"Her name wasn't in this report because she was a child. After cross-referencing a number of interviews, I discovered Rachel is Gunner Black's daughter. Blaze was pissed at her for not passing a message on to her mother."

"For God's sake, she was a small child."

"I know—it's insane. Rachel's name comes up again. On August 2, 2003, Mara Berrara filed for divorce and she was granted an Order for Protection against Blaze. She reported that, in the little over a year they'd been married, he'd punched her in the stomach, choked her, and dragged her around the house by her hair. She reported being terrified and knew he was watching her when she was in the community. There were times she'd opened the curtains to find him standing right outside her window. She couldn't sleep at night and didn't even feel like eating."

"I think I'm okay with never meeting my bio-dad, but I have to hear how this ends."

"On October 28, 2003, Chris Parker reported hearing glass breaking. Police arrived and found Billy Blaze on the street with a baseball bat. Blaze said he was also awakened by glass breaking and stepped out to check it out. All of the windows had been busted out of a home that was set to be demolished. Blaze said he saw teens jump in a car and take off. No charges were filed. And then, Blaze was off the grid for over a year. The rumor is he became involved with a wealthy divorcee and was traveling the world."

"I didn't see that coming."

I paused and asked, "Are you okay if I use the exact wording for the upcoming complaints? We have too much to cover to try to rephrase what he said in politically correct terms." I also felt that the exact wording gave a clearer picture of this guy.

Harper said, "It would be my preference. I want to hear what you have, not what you think I should know."

"By April of 2005, Blaze was back in St. Cloud. On April 14, 2005, he was charged with violation of a DANCO—a Domestic Abuse No Contact Order. After they listened to Mara Berrara's phone messages, he was also charged with Terroristic Threats. Blaze was recorded saying, 'You think you're so fucking smart by not answering. I'm killing your motherfucking ass, bitch! And fuck you and everybody in this world. I'm killing you! You got that, bitch? Fucking cunt. Answer that phone or I'm blowing up your house.' After a half hour passed, Blaze called again and, in his most pleasant voice, left a new message, 'Hi pretty. I'm horny and I want only you, babe. I want to taste you. You know what I'm talking about. How about answering the phone? Okay?'" I felt like I needed a shower just reading those words aloud.

Harper laughed at the ridiculousness of it. "Just ignore the last call. In the mood for romance?"

"When police informed him that, this time, they were able to trace the calls to his home, Blaze stated, 'Maybe it was my son.' Now, you get a break. Blaze was sent to prison from 2005 to January of 2008. He executed his sentence, so he was a free man when he was released."

Harper furrowed her eyebrows, "What does it mean to execute a sentence?"

"Offenders often do some time, and then are released early with the agreement they spend years on probation. People typically want to get out of prison as soon as possible, so they take the deal. But Blaze did the full sentence, with no early release, so he wouldn't have to worry about probation.

"Once released, he dropped off the radar for a full year. The next we hear of Billy Blaze was on January 31, 2008, when he got his fourth DWI, in Ohio. He disappeared until September 28, 2008, when he popped up, back in St. Cloud. A man in a vehicle waved down a police officer saying he just picked up a man with broken arm who smashed up a Corvette. The 'Vette had veered into the parapet of a bridge and, after crossing it, left the road and rolled. The police officer recognized the injured man as Blaze. He refused to go to the hospital, saying he didn't have insurance and couldn't afford the bill. The officer pointed out that Blaze was too intoxicated to be driving. Blaze told him the car was driven by a friend and, since the accident, he couldn't remember the guy's name or where he lived. Co-owners of the Corvette were Billy Blaze and Margo Miller. Blaze was charged with driving without insurance."

I shuffled to the next page. "Then he was gone again for over three years. The rumor is he was running drugs in Florida. On May 22, 2011, Blaze was arrested for a hit-and-run in St. Cloud. He followed a woman's car into the Hobby Lobby parking lot and bumped her car from behind, in an apparent effort to get her to talk to him. She said when she stepped out of the car and he saw she was eight months pregnant, he swore at her and drove off. She was furious."

Harper was lost in thought. "What do you think he's doing that he keeps dropping below the radar?"

"Honestly, I don't know. It's hard to believe it's something legal. On November 30, 2011, fifteen-year-old Rachel West called the police and told the officer that Blaze was standing in the trailer court, looking in her window, watching her. Rachel feared he was going to kill her. On the counter, she found an envelope marked, 'Give to Connie.' The message inside read, 'Billy Blaze is coming to kill you.' Rachel asked the officers if Blaze was going to kill Connie Bloom. She had been with Connie earlier in the day and Connie told her Blaze had threatened to 'shut that big mouth, permanently.' The officers told him they believed he was referring to Connie Berg."

"How many Connies did he threaten to kill?"

"At least two. And then something changed. Up to this point, he was consistently getting out of charges. Now, the police seemed to be paying closer attention to him. On July 20, 2012, Blaze apparently had a woman bent over the trunk of a car, with her skirt pulled up, in the Grand Central parking ramp in northeast St. Cloud, taking her from behind. When a police officer told them to go home, Blaze threatened the officer. Blaze was charged with Disorderly Conduct. Two weeks later, on August 3, 2012, he interfered with an officer's attempt to test a woman who was driving erratically. Blaze was a passenger in the vehicle. Blaze received a ticket for Obstructing the Legal Process, while Margo Miller ended up being released without charges."

Harper sucked in a quick breath, looking on the verge of saying something, but clamped her teeth down hard on her bottom lip. Anxiety rippled across her features, which I attributed to the loads of disappointment I was heaping into her lap. I gave her a moment to gather her thoughts. With a simple, *come here* gesture, she invited me to continue.

"I think he got Margo out of a DWI. On July 6, 2013, Blaze got his fifth DWI. Woops—missed one. On February 24, 2013 he was picked up for suspicious activity."

"What is suspicious activity?"

"Typically, you see this in the record when they suspect someone is selling drugs, but somehow he ditched the product, so they didn't have enough to charge him. The following day, Blaze was picked fup or threats against Randy Vogel, reported by Randy's partner, Andri. Randy refused to press charges. My guess is Blaze believed Randy ratted him out and found him. Two days later, on February 26, Blaze was charged with Domestic Assault and Felon in Possession of a Weapon, after he threatened a woman with a handgun. When the police executed the warrant, they found Blaze walking down Lincoln Avenue with a large bolt cutter up his sleeve. He didn't have a weapon on his body, but they were able to photograph the imprint of handgun on his waist, where he is known to carry a gun. A Colt .45 caliber handgun was found five feet away. When they searched him, they also found blank checks belonging to Clara Lebowitz. Clara reported she'd never met Blaze and didn't know how he got her checks."

"To put it mildly, it's unnerving to know my genes are half psychopath. Is it psychopath or sociopath?"

"It's the same thing. Generally, the term, psychopath, is used in forensics. And your genes aren't half psychopath. You're not born a psychopath. You become one through life experience and lack of guidance."

"Thank you," she breathed in relief.

"Blaze's name was now tagged in the police data, so when his name came up on a call, they were directed to always send at least two officers. On May 23, 2013, Blaze was charged with Terroristic Threats against Robert Johnson. Blaze was taken in for a couple days by Craig and Irene Foley. He decided to take a nap on Craig's recliner in their living room, bare chested and pants open—because he ate too much. Rob was a friend of the Foleys' and he thought Blaze was being rude, so he set a cold beer on his chest. Blaze hopped to his feet and put a loaded gun to Rob's head, threatening to kill him. When interviewed, Blaze denied having the gun. He told police, 'Robert's on drugs. That punk mother fucker. Why are you pullin' this on me? I could give a fuck less about a fuckin' drug addict mother fucker. I hate drug dealers and I want to nail 'em all.'"

"But wasn't Blaze a drug dealer?"

"Yes, but he likely felt pretending he hated them was better cover. When you threaten and beat up this many people, without charges, it's always because the victims are into something illegal and they don't want an investigation. The most interesting part of this story is that Craig and Irene had taken Blaze in when they found him, badly beaten, in the alley behind the Press Bar. His eyes were black and blue, and he had marks on his face from punches thrown by someone who was wearing a ring with skull on it. Blaze claimed he fell. He had a pocket full of pain meds, but they were all prescription. Craig told police he took Blaze in because he wanted to help out a former vet. Irene wasn't happy about it. She described him as 'pure evil.' Irene said if anyone did something Blaze didn't like, he'd pat the gun on his waistband to intimidate them. During the police interview with Irene, she revealed that Blaze violently raped her friend, Cheryl Wicklin, just a few months ago. Irene hadn't told her husband, as Cheryl swore her to secrecy. Craig's statement revealed Blaze had told him he was a Desert Storm vet who was shot in the stomach, the head, and in the leg. Blaze told Craig his dad was mafia and was murdered."

Harper interjected, "Is any of that true?"

"I have no idea. I need you to sign releases so I can review some records."

"It's the first time I've heard him lose a fight."

"He's not the kind of guy who would call the police if he was beaten. But I do think you have a point. Something changed. Now he doesn't have any money."

"You said Cheryl Wicklin's name, earlier."

"Her husband called the police and told them Blaze was shooting Cheryl up with drugs a decade ago. Blaze was her witness when she reported her husband had assaulted her. Cheryl eventually got clean, but Blaze managed to find her and felt she owed him."

Harper sighed, "If he does you a favor, he cashes it in heavy, doesn't he?"

I nodded in agreement. "The charges he compiled in 2013 sent Blaze back to prison from 2013 through most of 2015. On December 12, 2015 and January 11, 2016, he was arrested for Check Forgery. On February 2, 2016, Margo Miller reported her Corvette was stolen. When Blaze was pulled over in it, she told police it was just a misunderstanding. On February 5, 2016, it was reported Blaze stole cash from a residence. On May 16, 2016, he was picked up for busting the heads on garden gnomes with a baseball bat, in the middle of the night, but the victim, Nellie Ellison, declined to press charges. On October 3, 2016, Michelle Evens reported suspicious activity in Blaze's basement. He threatened Michelle by calling and saying, 'Goodbye sunshine; hello darkness.' Michelle was advised to get an OFP against him."

Harper commented, "Now dear old dad's finding his rhythm again."

"On October 12, 2016, the police were called as Blaze was being obnoxious in Taco John's. He wouldn't leave. This was right across from the police station, by the way."

Harper laughed. It was all she could do at this point.

"On October 18, 2016, Nellie Ellison called the police. Blaze had told her that her daughter better leave town or he would come over and teach her a lesson. Nellie was advised to get a restraining order against him."

"Do you have the daughter's name?"

"No. It wasn't in the report. On November 24, 2016, Blaze was charged with Assault in the Second Degree, after he beat a cabdriver with a crutch. The cab had picked him up at the MC's Dugout Bar and Grill. Blaze lit up a cigarette in the cab and the driver asked him to put it out. Blaze got angry. When the ride ended, Blaze threw his money on the floor of the cab. When the driver bent down to collect it, Blaze beat him in the face with his crutch."

"Why was he on crutches?"

"It didn't say. Fortunately, a guy named Riezig Ziegler—aka, 'Zig'—witnessed this and intervened. He yelled, 'Fucking Blaze, just settle down!' When Blaze attempted to strike the driver again, Zig hit Blaze so hard he dropped to the tar. Blaze then wanted to fight Zig, but Zig just laughed and told the cabdriver to call the police, but to leave his name out of it. Fun fact," I noted, "In Pierz, we called a mountain of a man 'the Rock.' In Germany, they'd call him 'riesig.' It means massive or colossal. Sorry for the trivia, it's how my brain's wired. Anyway, the cab driver told the police, 'Blaze is always bad when he drinks tequila.'"

"I don't think tequila completely explains his behavior."

"On New Year's Eve of 2016, Blaze was intoxicated and swearing in the VFW in St. Cloud. When the bartender refused to serve him any more alcohol, Blaze threatened the bartender, Jolyn Anderson, 'I know where you live. I'll hunt you down and will fucking kill you.' Three weeks later, Blaze was considered a suspect in a financial card fraud case, but there wasn't enough evidence to charge him. On February

24, 2017, an undercover agent reported he overheard Blaze planning a robbery. The pharmacy was warned and they amped up security.

"On March 17, 2017, Randy Vogel was found in Cloverleaf trailer park, shirt soaked in blood, bleeding from his face and the back of his head. Vogel reported Blaze punched him and stabbed him with a screwdriver. Blaze reportedly went to Vogel's home with a biker named Darko Dice. The door was locked, so Blaze used a screwdriver to force entry. He grabbed Vogel off the couch, punched him, and stabbed him. Vogel reported Blaze accused him of leaking information about a robbery. He swore he didn't and he was telling the truth. Vogel didn't want to press charges, stating Blaze had beat him up before, and 'he told me if I ever press charges against him, he'll kill me.' The state felt there was enough evidence to proceed with charges of Assault in the Second Degree against Blaze, even without Vogel's cooperation. Randy Vogel disappeared before the trial in March of 2017, and hasn't been heard from, since. His fiancée, Andri Clark, filed a missing person's report and told police Randy wouldn't have willingly disappeared without her."

I paused to let this sink in, before I shared, "Now, this is the time you're turning 18. Blaze filled out papers that gave you power of attorney over his affairs, should he become incarcerated. Your mom made you promise you'll never seek him out."

Harper shuddered and, under her breath, said, "Thank you, Mom."

"On April 3, 2017," I powered on, "Terri Connor was parked at the Kwik Trip in St. Cloud. She was about to back away, when a car pulled up behind hers, driven by Darko Dice. Blaze shouted out the passenger window, 'Hey, hot stuff,' followed by additional remarks about her body. Terri asked him to knock it off and let her leave. The car bumped her vehicle. Carrie Nelson observed and asked, 'Did they just hit your car?' Blaze stepped out of vehicle and shouted at Carrie, 'Fat bitch, get your ass back in your car.' Blaze and Dice continued to yell insulting obscenities at Carrie, while keeping Terri blocked in. Both women thought they were going to be assaulted. Eventually, Darko backed the car away and Terri took off. Fearing for Carrie's safety, Terri called the police. When the police found Darko and Blaze cruising Division, Darko was charged with DWI. Blaze was initially charged with Disorderly Conduct, but both women refused to follow through with charges."

"I thought you were going to say he pulled his pants down again." Harper pulled the blanket tightly around herself. "Blaze apparently recovered from whatever he was struggling with and is scarier now than ever."

I gave her a single nod of agreement. "On June 3, 2017, Alissa Larson stated she saw a shirtless man, with a large tattoo of the Grim Reaper on his back, bust into her neighbor's apartment, which was directly across the hall. Alissa watched through the safety of her peephole. She gave an exact description of Blaze, down to the tattoos. But once she told her neighbors about it, she was warned of Blaze. She refused to participate in a photo lineup, out of fear of retaliation. Now here's an interesting twist. In July, Blaze was seen with a woman who was described, and I quote, as a 'dark rooted, platinum-haired bombshell,' named Trisha Lake."

"It sounds like a name from a talk show."

"That isn't the weird part. A DEA informant, whom I'll refer to as 'Joey,' went to a crack house in Minneapolis with Blaze and Trisha. They hadn't spotted Blaze in crack houses, prior to this time. Trisha was in her forties and was a college student at St. Cloud State. I don't know if this was a field trip for her, or a new venture for Blaze. Blaze told Joey and Trisha to walk around for a bit while he disappeared, and then they left. Joey admitted that, on a night Blaze was out of town, he slept with Trisha. She told him that she was not officially *with* Blaze. Her exact words were, 'I thought I'd party with him for a bit, stay at his house awhile, and then goodbye, good luck, I'll see you later.' Joey was pulled from the undercover operation, as his colleagues felt Blaze was in love with Trisha, and he was going kill Joey when he found out about this."

"So, was Joey the informant all along?"

"Yes. During his exit interview, Joey revealed there was another woman, Gwyneth Porter, who fell hard for Blaze at this time. Gwyneth was a successful businesswoman in St. Cloud from a respected family; she didn't want anyone to know she was involved with Blaze. She was a Rotary Club member and lived in a nice house over on Cooper Avenue South in St. Cloud. Joey had asked Blaze about Gwyneth, but Blaze pretended like he didn't hear him. And then there was drama with Cayenne Tiller."

"Now, where did I hear her name earlier?" Harper added, "Cayenne? Is she a spice girl?" She chuckled at her own joke.

"She's the one with Blaze when he got the public urination charge. Cayenne was in front of Blaze's home a few times during the summer, ranting and raving in a drug-induced rage. On August 17, 2017, when the police picked her up for disturbing the peace, she claimed Blaze hit her. But she was so nonsensical, they didn't do anything with it. On August 18, the house next to where Blaze was staying burned down. When police were investigating the fire, the neighbors shared there was lots of foot traffic, at all hours of the night, at the Blaze home."

Harper asked, "Is this story coming to an end? I think I've heard enough."

I smiled and tapped the multiple sheets of paper into a clean pile. "I'm done."

Her eyes widened, "What do you mean, you're done? You've got three years left to cover."

"A week later, there isn't hide nor hair of Blaze to be found."

"If the DEA was thinking of prosecuting him, they must have some information on him."

"Here's the last report. On August 22, 2017, Blaze was seen out with Trisha Lake at Legends Bar and Grill in St. Cloud for jazz night. He made it home, as a neighbor heard an argument involving Blaze and a man and woman at 2:00 a.m. It wasn't unusual, so she went back to sleep. The Corvette was sitting there the next morning, but no one was home. Gunner Black returned the next afternoon with a badly bruised face. Billy Blaze was never seen or heard from, again. Eventually, Margo Miller came and got the Corvette."

Harper pondered for a minute. "What do you think happened?"

"No idea. Do you want me to keep looking for him?"

She gazed out the window as she answered, "I don't think so. I stopped caring about him ten minutes ago. But the ending bothers me. Give me the night to think about it. I just wonder how my mom ever ended up with that rakish degenerate."

"Kali was young and I've heard Blaze could be charming."

Harper was not satisfied with the answer, but tried to appease me. "Yeah, maybe. My mom used to say, 'There are some guys you can't save.' Maybe Blaze taught her that lesson."

# 5

*In a cold and gray town, a nurse says, "Lay down*
*This ain't no playground, and this ain't home"*
*Someone's children, is out having children*
*In a gray stone building, all alone . . .*
*While unwed fathers, they can't be bothered*
*They run like water, through a mountain stream*
—JOHN PRINE, UNWED FATHERS

## HARPER ROWE

6:45 P.M., MONDAY, APRIL 13, 2020
BIRCHMONDT DRIVE NORTHEAST,
WEST SIDE OF LAKE BEMIDJI, BEMIDJI

Jeremy Goddard, my handsome, six-foot, two-inch dad, visited me tonight with the gift of a Rafferty's Pizza. My grandparents' home, in Bemidji, was a long way to deliver a pizza from Brainerd. Jeremy had a neatly cut head of thick, red hair; he was a few years younger than my mom. He worked hard in the print shop at Central Lakes College. He was a gentleman and an ex-marine, who could clearly take care of me in Mom's absence.

Grandpa was unusually respectful of me tonight. He didn't interrupt me once. And, come to think of it, there was none of Grandma's anxious chatter. I attributed this to the awkwardness of getting together without Mom. When my grandparents exited the kitchen and Dad remained seated at the table with me, I braced for bad news. Had he heard something about Greg?

I asked, "Who has the coronavirus now?"

Dad's nervous smile suggested I was off track. "This is about your mom. Remember how she thought I liked potatoes au gratin?"

"You *do*," I said, confused. "You told her how much you loved it every time she made it."

"I did—but I don't. Sometimes you say something that's not entirely true, because you just want to make it better for someone else."

Incredulous, I asked, "Why would you pretend you liked potatoes au gratin?"

"When your mom and I were dating, we had a hell of an argument. We were at that point we either had to take it to another level or break up. I absolutely did not want to lose her. Kali invited me over and had made potatoes au gratin from scratch. Cooking was never her forte, but I appreciated the work she put into that meal. It was sweet of her. If she'd have made mud, I would have loved it."

I smiled, my eyes stinging with familiar tears.

"I never had the heart to tell her. If I had to eat potatoes au gratin for every meal—for the rest of my life—just to have one more day with her, I would."

"She was lucky to have you. Okay—so, Grandma and Grandpa had to leave the room so you could admit you don't like potatoes au gratin?"

"You told me they put the wrong birth year on your mom's tombstone." He looked a little sheepish. "Well, they didn't."

Dumbfounded, I ran numbers through my head. "If that's true, she would have been sixteen when she had me."

He nodded. "When she was fifteen, your mom fell for a slick adult named Keith Stewart. He romanced her and convinced her that her parents were treating her like a slave, when she was ready to be an independent adult. He wasn't your typical trafficker. Stewart had a big, beautiful house, just south of St. Cloud, which was an attraction to teenaged girls who were full of angst and wanting it all."

"Mom was sex-trafficked?"

"That's what I'd call it. I don't know if there's a number you need to reach to meet the definition, because your mom was only with one guy—Billy Blaze. Let me explain."

I was stunned.

He said, "Stewart first met Kali at the mall in St. Cloud and stepped up his seduction of her until he talked her into running away from home. Once he had her isolated from her family, Stewart convinced her he needed a big favor. Up to that point, he was treating her like a princess and Kali thought they were in love. He told her it was vital that she have sex with Billy Blaze. He needed something to hold over Billy's head or Blaze was going to send him and his friend, Zig, to prison. Stewart's charm and insistence wore her down. After she gave in, Kali realized this must be how it starts for all girls who are trafficked. This would be her life, from now on, unless she did something about it."

My heart ached at the image of my mother so vulnerable, so young.

"Kali made an error in judgment, but she was smart, even at fifteen. She convinced Stewart that everything was fine. She told him that, for a reward, she wanted to buy some new clothes the next day. While at the Crossroads Mall, Kali managed to get away from Stewart long enough to call her parents. She demanded they leave the police out of it, because she felt both Blaze and the trafficker were dangerous. Kali kept trying on clothes until friends of her parents' marched right into the dressing room and walked out with her."

My mom was so strong. It was hard to imagine her needing to be rescued by anyone.

"Kali was incredibly ashamed," he continued, "and her parents were upset, but they pulled together and moved on. After things had finally settled, some, she realized she was pregnant. When she refused to adopt you out, it all heated up at home, again. Your grandpa warned her they weren't going to help. But your mom was a trooper. She gave birth to you without the support of family. Kali's always said, 'The only person I really needed to show up was my baby.' She thanked God every day for you."

Dad smiled warmly and put a rough hand over mine. "I should also point out your grandparents came around. Your grandma picked you and Kali up at the hospital and she cared for you until Kali finished school. After you were born, your mom focused on being a great mother and a successful professional—overcoming obstacles with grace and class."

I took it all in. "But why the lie?"

"Kali had all of the statistics. Daughters of teen mothers are more likely to drop out of school, more likely to use drugs, and more likely to be teenaged mothers, themselves. It went on and on, and I didn't feel it was my role to argue. Your mom was afraid that, as a teen, you'd glorify her past, instead of realizing she barely dodged a bullet. She insisted we tell you she was three years older and she got pregnant while in college. Afraid you'd discover the truth, Kali was always at your side when you visited Bemidji."

I wish Mom would have been honest with me. I had so many questions. "But why hide it from me?"

Dad shrugged, "Your mom loved you—from the moment she knew you existed. She put Billy Blaze's name on your birth certificate, just in case something happened to you and you needed stem cells or something only your biological father could provide. Your welfare took priority over her peace of mind. But she always worried that, someday, Blaze would find you. Now that you're staying with her parents, you're going to hear stories. I wanted you to hear the truth from me, first."

I wished I could tell Mom how much I loved her. Would I have handled it differently? It was hard to say. I pensively spun my mom's wedding band on my right ring finger.

Something was still bothering Dad.

His voice became even more serious. "The news reports are saying COVID-19 is going to be widespread among healthcare workers. I admire Greg's decision to complete his nursing practicum at the Hennepin County Medical Center, but it also means you need to stay away from him until it's safe. If he loves you, he'd want that for you."

I continued to fiddle with Mom's ring. Greg cried when he warned me he'd have to stay away from me. I had to see him—I'd take the chance. I couldn't lose everybody. But he believed it was the moral path and I finally acquiesced. He promised we'd make up for the lost time, someday, with greater appreciation of our time together.

I told Dad, "Greg and I have already addressed this."

I started to feel guilty over finding comfort in Mom's ring. It had once belonged to Jeremy's grandmother. I was of no blood relation. Did he resent that I had it? I reluctantly slipped it off and handed it to him. He was hurting, too, and I didn't want to be selfish. "I'll stay away from Greg—for now."

Jeremy gently placed the ring back in my palm and closed my hand around it. "It's your ring, Harper. Kali insisted you have it after she passed. *I* want you to have it. My grandmother loved me and asked that I only part with it when I met someone I loved as much as she loved me. She didn't give it to me when I was first married—only when I met Kali. This ring isn't about blood—it's about altruistic love. There was a note with the ring. What did it say?"

"You only wear this as a wedding band when you meet someone you love more than me," I paused, and then added, "and more than Greg." I looked at my dad, questioning, "What did she have against Greg? He always told me how great she was. Greg is one of our amazing healthcare heroes. You couldn't ask any more of him." Greg was the commencement speaker when he graduated from St. John's University. With his unwavering commitment to success, he was more like my mom than anyone I knew. But now, I wondered, *did I really know Mom?*

"It's not that Kali disliked Greg." He added carefully, "She said Greg got the solos and you were second chair in your relationship. Greg's flattery grated on Kali, because she felt he complimented her to manipulate you. If you were frustrated with him, he'd talk about how amazing your dying mother was."

I interrupted, "That's not fair. Greg was just being kind."

Jeremy held his hands up in retreat, "I'm just the messenger. You asked and I told. Greg is your call. Just know—I raised you from the time you started school and I couldn't love a biological daughter any more than I love you. You and the boys are everything to me. I will respect the man you're with—provided he respects you—because of my love for you."

I bustled around the kitchen table and hugged him hard, from behind, across his sturdy shoulders, kissing him on his cheek.

Dad squeezed my arms tightly, hanging on a bit longer. His voice was thick with emotion, when he said, "I love you. I need you to be safe."

9:30 P.M.

IN THE BIBLE, MATTHEW 7:15, MATTHEW wrote, "Beware of false prophets, who come to you in sheep's clothing but inwardly are ravenous wolves." This phrase ran through my mind when I thought of Margo Miller. I had no reason to dislike her. But her showing up right after Mom's funeral, to help me find my father, was disconcerting. I was ashamed of

my biological father and Margo's love for him brought me
no comfort.

I sat on the bed typing her an email.

*Margo,*
*I can't thank you enough for your agreement to fund an*
*investigation to find my father. I met with Jon Frederick*
*today and he's nice enough. He has a ton of information*
*on Billy Blaze, but it's all disturbing. I don't want to be*
*a part of your search for him.*
  *Thank you again. I wish you the very best.*
*Sincerely,*
*Harper Rowe*

It wasn't long before I received a response:

*Harper,*
*I wouldn't draw you into this if it wasn't essential. We*
*may be saving a man's life. You have power of attorney*
*to access resources that can provide answers. Your father*
*is an exciting and vibrant man, capable of great passion.*
*But he traveled in circles with dangerous people. My*
*concern is that he got himself into a situation he can't*
*get out of and he needs our help. He wouldn't have gone*
*this long without contacting me if it was at all possible.*
*You must have some sense of justice.*
  *Please reconsider.*
*Margo*

I wrote back:

*I'm sorry. This is just a bad time for me. It doesn't feel right.*

Margo responded:

*Please open attached video.*

When I opened the video, I was horrified. It was an Instagram video of me, lying topless in bed, that I had sent to Greg late one night when we were both lonely. After positioning the camera, I laid back. I hoped that by some miracle the recording didn't catch the rest. No such luck . . .

Aghast, I shut it off and sat in silence. I typed:

*I thought you couldn't record Instagram.*

Margo responded again:

*I can record your Instagram messages if I'm online as Harper Rowe. That's all a hacker needs to do. Please open attached video.*

I didn't want to open it, but I did. It was a naked Instagram of Greg that he had sent to me. *What had I gotten Greg involved in?*

Margo followed the video with an email:

*Harper,*
*Your father taught me if you want to get what you desire, you have to be willing to use all your resources. So, here's the deal. If you don't agree to help in any way possible, I'm sending the video of you to all of your dad's friends and your grandparents. Let them see how you're following in your mom's footsteps. The video of Greg will go to everyone he works with. If you don't believe I can do this, call Greg and check in with him.*

*How much do you love Greg? Are you willing to cost him his practicum and possibly ever working in a hospital again? For what? All I'm asking is that you help me find your father. It's neither a malicious nor an unreasonable request. I'm not asking you to personally find him. You simply need to do everything in your power to assist the investigator. If you don't call Jon Frederick and beg him to do whatever it takes to find Billy Blaze, within an hour, you and Greg will soon be internet stars.*
*Margo*

I sent:

*How do you know my mom? I need that answered first.*

She responded:

*I have no ill feelings for your mom. She was with Billy long before I was in the picture. I spoke to her in Macy's in 2017, when I was with Billy. I remarked how knowledgeable and approachable she was. Billy told me, 'She had my baby years ago. We agreed to cut it clean and go different directions.' I have to admit, I was a little surprised when I learned your age, but it was decades ago. We're all stupid when we're young.*

*Stop wasting time. You're down to 58 minutes. You'd better hope Jon is available, because I'm signing off and won't be responding further. In 58 minutes, I'll be coming back on and I better see an email to you, from Jon, indicating you're 100% in this case. Imagine your study group hashing out that video of you . . .*
*Margo*

Greg called and I immediately answered, "Are you okay?"

Without preamble, he blurted, "Did you send a message to my coworkers, asking, 'How well do you know Greg?' It was sent from you."

"No. Absolutely not. Was there anything attached?"

"No, just that question. What's going on, Harp? You know how hard I worked to get this practicum—don't blow it for me. Do you have a jealous ex?"

Flustered, I responded, "No. I'm sorry. Greg, can I call you back? There's something I have to address quick. I love you!"

His "I love you, too," trailed off as he hung up.

I considered Margo's motivation for finding my father. Her intentions could be far more malevolent than she divulged but, after hearing Blaze's history, it was hard to believe he didn't warrant her nastiness. I needed to protect Greg and my grandparents. I wasn't wild about my unveiled image being public information, either.

I scrambled to find Jon Frederick's card. Where had I left it? It wasn't in my jeans pockets. I dumped my purse on the floor and quickly dug through my possessions—not there. I ran downstairs and frantically shuffled items around on the kitchen counter.

Grandma heard the ruckus and came around the corner, concerned. She asked, "For God's sake girl, what's gotten into you?"

"There was a business card with Jon Frederick's name on it." I continued rifling through the mess of junk mail that had accumulated on the counter.

Grandma stood silently, spindly arms folded across her sinking chest, observing me coming unhinged. "What do you need a private investigator for?"

Restive, I turned, "Grandma, please. I need that card. Did you find it?"

"I think I deserve an answer."

There was no way in hell I was sharing my predicament with my grandmother. For a moment, I couldn't think—and then it came to me. "In my criminal justice class, we have to interview investigators. I just realized there are some questions I missed and it's due at 10:30 tonight!"

In no hurry, she dawdled away. I worried saying anything would slow her further.

I bit my lip as I waited for her to return. When she came back, she was carrying her jacket. "I threw it in the garbage and your grandpa has already hauled the garbage out."

As I raced out of the house, Grandma yelled, "Good lord, girl, put some shoes on!"

I dumped the garbage bag onto the garage floor and pawed through it. We just *had* to have leftover spaghetti for lunch.

Grandma soon joined me. "Have you lost your marbles?"

My eyes prickled with frustration as I recklessly tore through the trash. I whined, "It's not here."

She studied me. "Get a grip." She casually plucked a foil garlic bread bag out of the pile, pried it open, and pulled out the card.

I snatched the card from her frail hand and told her, "Thank you! Leave the mess; I promise I'll come back and clean it up."

She pursed her lips. "Just write your paper. I'll clean it up."

I DIALED JON FREDERICK AS I RACED back to my room. It rang and rang. "Come on!"

He finally answered, "Harper. Have you made up your mind about the investigation?"

# 6

*The water tastes funny*
*When you're far from your home*
*But it's only the thirsty*
*That hunger to roam*
*The clock played the drums*
*And I hummed the sax*
*While the wind whistled down the railroad tracks*
—JOHN PRINE, *ROCKY MOUNTAIN TIME*

## HARPER ROWE

8:30 A.M., TUESDAY, APRIL 14, 2020
PIERZ

I drove two and a half hours south, to Pierz, to meet with Jon and Serena Frederick. They lived in a large, two-story house in the country, surrounded by maple trees. An old fashioned, steel-wheeled cart rested against the garage, surrounded by wooden wine barrels. Comfortable outdoor patio chairs encircled a fire pit. If you couldn't relax here, you couldn't relax.

Serena gave up her isolation to work with Jon and me in finding Billy Blaze. I'd tested COVID clean and hadn't been social, since. At five-foot-three, Serena was a petite and vibrant beauty, with big green eyes and long dark hair with an enviable natural curl. She was so positive and accepting of me. She must've been a great mother.

A beautiful music room surrounded us from floor to ceiling in rustic barn wood. Guitars and a keyboard were neatly set against the wall, as it was now our command center. Jon locked us in the room, while their two children ran about the house under the supervision of Serena's parents.

We each sat at a folding table, which would serve as our desk. Jon stated we all needed to share information if this was going to work, so our materials were to be in the open on the table tops. We just had to be respectful of leaving each person's table as we found it.

Jon asked, "What made you change your mind about finding Blaze?"

"Morbid curiosity." To avoid further questions, I put it back on him, "What drives you?"

Jon leaned back and casually shared, "Shame. But marriage has taught me purging my humiliation might make me smarter."

Serena gave him a glance, "I believe I said sharing our difficult moments brings us closer and allows for greater insight."

He responded, "Exactly. That, and a low tolerance for bullies. When I was a kid, I biked into town, four days a week, for baseball practice. On Wednesdays, our coach was always late because he went to Flicker's Bar on Tuesday nights. This allowed the bullies time to exert their dominance over the pack. Like me, many of the boys stood by their bikes until the coach arrived, to keep them from being damaged. My bike was the compilation of a bunch of trashed bikes. I painted it black with some old paint I found in the garage to make it look like it could have been one bike, and I was proud of it. A lot of us were in the same boat. Our bikes were our only way off the farm. If you wrecked your bike, no more baseball, fishing, or adventures with friends."

Mom and Jeremy married when I was six and we moved to Baxter. As a girl who had friends just down the street from my Baxter home, growing up, I hadn't fathomed that level of isolation.

Jon continued, "One of the bullies was ranting on and on about how the Platte River Bridge was exactly halfway between Little Falls and Pierz. The boy next to me, Everett, told him it wasn't. The bully repeated his declaration and Everett again said, 'It's not exactly halfway.' Everett was right, but I warned him to stop talking, as I knew this would end badly. Today, Everett might be diagnosed with a high functioning form of autism, but back then it was just called *not knowing when to shut up*. The bully was soon in Everett's face, ready to give him a beating. I intervened and explained, 'He isn't calling you a liar. He's simply stating what he believes. He could be wrong.' Everett, of course, wouldn't stop saying, 'I am not wrong.' I postponed the physical altercation by making light of it. The coach finally arrived and, for the moment, the crisis was averted. I found out the next day the bully had trashed Everett's bike after practice and Everett's dad wouldn't let him play baseball anymore, because he didn't take care of his things."

I could feel a lump in my throat, "That's terrible."

"I've thought a lot about that moment," Jon said sadly. "The bully was a kid who was being beaten by his father. He eventually straightened out and became a decent man. Everyone has a reason to be an ass—even you. But some choose not to be. I thought of Everett all summer, alone on the farm. I was too young and stupid to go talk to his dad, and I'm not sure Everett would've wanted me to. Instead of smoothing things over, I should have supported him and ended the situation right there—even if I was pummeled for it." Jon snapped into the present. "I'm going to find Billy Blaze and stand up for whoever he's bullying today."

I asked, "What does Everett do, now?"

"He provides Christian ministry to convicts in prison. Being social didn't come natural, but with guidance from a loving sister, he managed it."

I wanted to tell him not to be ashamed, but I didn't want to be a hypocrite. I shouldn't be ashamed, either, yet my shame over that video had me working the case. I appreciated his honesty.

Serena broke our silent pause by getting to the business at hand. "Harper, let's have you sign releases to cell phone companies. Once we identify Blaze's provider, we can figure out where his phone is being used. I'm emailing agencies for Release of Information forms. We'll have you sign them and send them immediately back. I think a couple of places to start would be the Veterans Administration Medical Center in St. Cloud and CORE Professional Services in Sartell. With Blaze's criminal history, it's likely CORE has done a psychological assessment on him."

Jon pointed out, "We need to determine which county Blaze resided in. St. Cloud is in three—Stearns, Benton, and Sherburne Counties. Once that's determined, we should get releases to review the Pre-Sentence Investigations completed by corrections agents."

Serena nodded, "Okay." She added, "The frustrating piece is, with COVID-19, how many of the agencies will be responding to records requests? Most of the county buildings are shut down."

Jon shared, "Harper and I can start calling the phone numbers I pulled from the file."

I observed Jon and Serena; they wasted no time. I wondered if it was like this for all parents of preschoolers. Even though it wasn't my choice, it still felt good to be part of a team. I slipped the scrunchie from around my wrist and piled my hair on top of my head, then got to work.

Jon gave me a list of people to start calling. The first few went to voicemail.

Jon put his conversation with Curtis Wicklin on speaker so we could listen.

"This is Jon Frederick. I'm looking for Billy Blaze and I was wondering if you have any information related to his whereabouts. Anything you share will be kept in the strictest confidence."

Curtis growled, "Blaze ruined my life. He ruined my marriage. Left my wife an addict. If you find him, tell 'im I've got a bullet with his name on it."

"Do you have any idea where he is, today?"

"Blaze is a rat. I heard he turned state's evidence on someone and is somewhere up in Duluth, in the witness protection program. He torched every life he touched and now we're paying to protect the bastard. Where's the justice?"

Before Jon could say another word, Curtis hung up.

Jon brushed it off, "Okay. Curtis Wicklin doesn't know where Blaze is. The Drug Enforcement Agency knows I'm looking for him. If Blaze was in witness protection, someone would have contacted me and told me to back off."

I began to grasp the difficulty of this task. Jon couldn't go door-to-door because of the state's COVID restrictions. We were trying to get people, who generally didn't cooperate with law enforcement, to give up information to a stranger over the phone.

Jon asked, "Do you want to try Gunner Black?"

As I punched in the numbers, I knew I was going to have to give up something personal to get anything. After several rings, I thought I might have a temporary reprieve.

I was about to hang up when the call was answered with a churlish, "Yeah?"

"Gunner Black?" I asked, nerves jangling.

"Who wants to know?"

"Hi Gunner. This is Harper Rowe, Billy Blaze's daughter. I was wondering if you might know where I could find him."

He gruffly asked, "Who's your mother?"

"Kali Rowe. They weren't together long. It was back in 1999."

Jon wrote on the notepad in front of me, *Put the call on speaker.*

Gunner declared, "Harper Rowe! Well, how the hell is Batman?"

I got this every so often. DC comics introduced a Batman sidekick named Harper Rowe about a decade ago. Her hidden identity was Bluebird, as opposed to Robin. "I think Batman's okay. I'm hoping the same for Dad."

Gunner continued to guffaw, "Baby girl Harper. I remember the day you were born. We were at DB Searles and Blaze was tellin' everyone his girl's having the first baby of the millennium. Have you ever been to DB Searles? They had the best Bloody Mary this side of the Mississippi."

DB Searles was about a hundred feet on this side of Mississippi. I was only in the place once, when I was eighteen. I loved the antique cherry wood bar in DB Searles, but it was just easier to say, "No."

"Well, you missed out, little lady. They closed the doors for good in 2018." Gunner continued, "He got the call a little after midnight, when everybody was hollerin' and toastin' each other."

"My mom—called Blaze?"

Gunner said, "No. Your mom wasn't talkin' to him. He knew a nurse at the hospital who was givin' him updates."

Harper revealed, "My birthdate is December 31, 1999."

"Yeah," Gunner laughed. "You were born at 11:45 p.m. on New Year's Eve. Blaze complained, 'She pushed that baby out early just to spite me.' And maybe she did. It's nothin' against your mom. Blaze was like a wild mustang—you just had to let him run. Nothin' you said or did would get in his way. It's just how he was wired." He paused momentarily, "He knew you'd look him up one day. He said, 'Someday, that girl's gonna hate her mom and run to me—and I'll be waitin'.'"

Jon scribbled on the notepad, *Ask him where you could find Blaze now.*

I asked and Gunner responded, "One thing for damn sure—if he doesn't want to be found, you ain't findin' him. Give me your number and I'll call you if I hear somethin'."

I gave him my number and Jon hurriedly wrote my next question for him. I queried, "Do you think I should hire an investigator?"

Gunner growled, "No—totally unnecessary. Blaze disappears for a while, but he always comes back to St. Cloud. There's some who claim he's never left."

"Who are *they?*"

"Connie Berg, for one."

"Are there others?"

"Mmmm, there have been, but off the top of my head, I just can't come up with the names."

I had to ask, "Did you know my mom?"

Gunner said, "No, not really. Other than Blaze sayin' she was a hot little—" he stopped himself.

Anger overtook me. "Did you know my mom was only fifteen years old at the time?" This was apparently news to Jon and Serena, as they exchanged concerned looks.

Gunner quickly backed off, "Look I don't want any trouble and I'm not causin' any trouble for Blaze." He hung up.

I blew it. I hurt for Mom. She was so young. At fifteen, we were all so stupid. I looked at Jon, "I'm sorry."

Serena walked over and put her hand on my shoulder, "Hey, it's okay. You just need to remember, we're not trying to teach these people a lesson, we're just gathering information."

Her gentle touch felt so comforting. She followed it up with a compassionate hug. I missed being hugged. Mom's parents weren't huggers. Picture the old farm couple with the pitchfork from the American Gothic painting. They were the, *Is that something you'd be comfortable wearing in front of Jesus?* parents. They provided and cared, but weren't much for emotional expression. And as far as Jesus, with his long hair and robe, I saw him more as a hippie than a prude. Mom was affectionate and loving. No one wonder she ran away from home.

Feeling unconditionally accepted with Serena and Jon, I shared how Mom had run away and been trafficked.

Jon noted, "Gunner Black doesn't want to give up much on Blaze. The only name he gave you was someone who had made a complaint to the police."

Serena reminded me of my mom. She was loving, but also was going to be tougher on me. She told me, "You need to call Gunner back. Let's go over what you're willing to share . . ."

Soon, I was back on the phone, telling Gunner, "I'm sorry for getting upset. My mom recently died from the coronavirus and I just want to find my dad."

Gunner was silent for a bit before responding, "I'm sorry for your loss. Blaze was a lot of things, but he didn't chase underage girls. He didn't need to. I just don't see him sleepin' with somebody he knew was underage."

I suggested, "Dad might not have known. I have no desire to get him in trouble."

Jon was writing again; I relayed the information to Gunner. "The statute of limitations is up on that offense now, anyway, so Dad can't be prosecuted for it. I just want to know him."

Gunner cleared his throat and offered, "Your dad lived with me over on Germain, just a couple blocks north of the Library in St. Cloud. My home is nothin' fancy and it's not a great neighborhood."

I could hear Jon whisper to Serena, "Stearns County."

"I've met you. I doubt you'd remember—you were just a baby. Kali stopped over with you a couple times. She didn't say much and she never let anyone else hold you. Billy wasn't much for babies. Nothing personal—he was a busy man."

My stomach churned. *Mom, what the hell were you doing?*

Gunner continued, "Blaze met your mom at Eagles Landing Estates over in St. Augusta. Have you ever seen the houses at Eagles Landing?"

"No."

"Big, beautiful mansions for the rich. Not a place you'd expect to be hookin' up with a teen. Look, I'm sorry for your loss, but I need to go . . ."

Jon and Serena both complimented my effort. They were so kind. I told them, "I want to thank you for never referring to Blaze as my dad. It was hard for me to even say it, but I realize I need to, if we're going to get people to talk . . ."

# 7

*People that are glad, sometimes they wear a smile*
*And people without dreams, they walk the extra mile*
*But all the people who don't fit*
*Get the only fun they get*
*From people puttin' people down . . .*
*So cold, sometimes it gets so cold*
—John Prine, *People Puttin People Down*

## KHARON

5:30 P.M., FRIDAY, APRIL 17, 2020
HIGHWAY 6, OTENEAGEN TOWNSHIP

My phone buzzes and, before I can say a word, the boss asks, "Does my man, Kharon, have the cabin ready? Our filly Lilly is driving me nuts."

"Good to go. I'm headed back—just south of Bowstring on Highway 6. Has Hades found his Persephone, yet?" He loves it when I refer to him as the unseen giver of wealth.

"No—that's where the Greeks got it wrong. I'm not kidnapping some vegan nut out picking flowers. My girls are selling me their souls. You're more the Persephone type. They have their fifteen minutes of fame with me and I'm ready to move on. By the way, I can't have you knocking Nitty out of commission for a week again. Right now, she's a hot ticket. Hands off."

"Alright. You don't have to tell me twice, boss."

"I appreciate your loyalty. Can you cut over to Nisswa and stop at the Chocolate Ox? I need some decadent candies to

70

set out for a client. I'll place the order. You just need to pick it up. I'm assuming you have enough behind-seat storage in that truck for a couple trays—no dead carcasses using the space?"

"No problem."

Something is bothering him. It's okay sometimes to let shit fester. A great tabasco sauce takes years. Disrespecting the coziness of my disinterest, he reveals, "A private investigator named Jon Frederick is digging up information on Billy Blaze."

"Why should I care?"

He grumbles, "It could lead to an investigation of the disappearance of Randy Vogel. And an investigation of you could drag me into the net. No more side jobs for that psycho bitch. I don't want anything dug up that comes back on me."

"I had no qualms with Vogel. There's no reason to question me. We're good." I want to say, *He wasn't buried,* but decide it is best to leave it at that. I haven't given that night much thought. What's done is done. I'm a big boy—I'll work for whoever I choose.

(THREE YEARS EARLIER)
2:30 A.M., MARCH 22, 2017
BUCKMAN PRAIRIES, 83RD STREET,
TOWNSHIP ROAD 328, BUCKMAN

A FREEZING NOR'EASTER WIND PINCHED MY ears and chilled my fingers to the bone. I'd taken a miserable side job that required me to trudge through six inches of snow, in a pitch black coniferous forest. If she'd have told me where we were headed, I would have worn my Sorel boots. Instead, jagged blades of ice cut into my ankles just above my Nike Killshot low tops.

The woman who hired me bragged about the warmth of her cashmere-lined Burberry gloves, but with this polar blast, she had to stop to blow her hot, entitled breath on her hands. The steam from her breath suspended in the cool air for a moment, before vaporizing into nothingness. She waved the flashlight ahead of us, casting eerie black shadows in the distance. We were surrounded by darkness in all other directions.

I used the shovel for a walking stick as we surged forward. We each pulled on an arm as we dragged the heavy body across the frozen tundra.

My chest tightened. Exhausted, I spat out, "I'm dragging ninety percent of the load. I'm gonna have a heart attack and you'll be burying me, too."

Her dark eyes glared at me. "Are all killers this whiny?" Answering herself, she muttered under her breath, "Maybe it's why you're a killer. The ill-temper came first."

As we dragged the load, the lecture continued. "You'd know if you were having a heart attack. I think you need to cut down on your spicy jerk sauce."

She was pushing her luck. I could crush her. But I'd never see the rest of my cash if I permanently shut her up.

Determined, but a little kinder, she prodded, "Just a little further and we're fine."

I barked, "How the hell did you find this place?"

"I was at a party here a couple of decades ago," she gloated. "I wanted some privacy with a man and we found the Pines. Believe me, no one ventures through here."

We stopped and let our departed friend's arms fall to the ground. She shut her flashlight off and stood over the permanently speechless man, in the black, opaque silence. I hadn't even heard a car in the distance since we'd been out here. I knew this guy. He served in the Kulan Valley in Afghanistan. The vets all claimed he'd give you the shirt off his back, but he mainlined meth like he had a death wish. I thought about asking her what he did to deserve his fate, but it didn't make a difference at this point. We weren't bringing him back to life. I paraphrased Alfred Lord Tennyson, *I am not to reason why, I am but to do and die.* Finally catching my breath, I asked, "Was he good—a real livewire?"

She emitted a deep sigh as she glanced down at the body. "Well, he's dead. Why do you think we're dragging him?"

I clarified, "I mean, the guy from the party."

"Are you kidding me? We're about to bury a body."

"It's better not to think about it. Trust me."

With weary disgust, she said, "He was alright. Farm boy—tight, strong back muscles. That V body shape—big shoulders, small waist, tight ass. The excitement of being naked in the woods was as good as the sex." She turned the flashlight back on. "Okay, you can start digging."

I was trying to picture her and a farm boy out here. "You ran through the woods naked?"

"No one streaks through a pine forest. We stripped when we found our spot."

The shovel soon clinked against the rock-hard ground. *What the hell is she thinking? You can't bury a body here.* "It's frozen."

She argued, "The frost went out two days ago."

I pointed out, "Even out here, in a snow-covered forest?"

Instead of admitting she messed up, she explained, "The frost went out twenty days earlier last year. It's been warm for a week. How was I to know it would be freezing tonight? Just keep digging."

I wanted to tell her *Kharon doesn't bury bodies,* but instead, quietly did as I was paid. I chipped away at the frozen dirt. This was going to take all night. "Okay—tell me more about your date."

Her incessant whining resumed, "One time in my life I need to bury a body and I get stuck with a degenerate. I didn't know they made pervs in your size. Okay, he was a gentleman. He let me lay on his shirt."

*Keep pushing your luck with the insults and I'll be burying you.* I set aside my anger for the moment. "Did he put it back on?"

She smiled as she reminisced, "As a matter of fact, he did."

"Did he wear it back to the party?"

Ignoring me, she bent down and squeezed the cheek of our departed friend, taunting him, "At a loss for words? Snitches are like crickets. Chirping loud until you get close. Then they're dead quiet."

Okay, I wasn't spending all night out here with Zelda Fitzgerald or whatever crazy dame she was trying to act like. I frantically stabbed the shovel into the frigid earth, with the goal of exiting the black forest as quickly as possible.

She stood back up and ordered, "That's enough. You're right, the ground's too hard. Leave him for the wolves. Nobody comes out here, anyway . . ."

(PRESENT DAY)
9:30 P.M., FRIDAY, APRIL 17, 2020
ROUNDHOUSE BREWERY,
23836 SMILEY ROAD, NISSWA

THE CHOCOLATE OX PICK-UP GOES SMOOTH and it's time for me to relax. I love this tap room. It's so much more relaxing than sitting in a bar where, as often as not, the guy sitting next to me is looking for a fight. You'd think being large and strong would be a blessing, but it's a curse. There's always some cocky drunk waiting to jump me in the parking lot, so he can brag he knocked down the biggest guy. That doesn't happen in taprooms. No big screens flashing replays and no trashy advertisements. Instead, Johnny Rocker is on the outdoor stage, playing *Folsom Prison Blues*. Folks are sitting around a fire pit, enjoying a frosty cold beverage and laughing. I finish a Coal Train Porter, which is a robust roasted malt beer, with a hint of mocha. I'm treated by staff and patrons, alike, as a friend. It's how the world should be.

But it's not my world. My life is getting the cabin ready for our next deposit into the underworld. I give the bartender a grateful nod as she takes my empty glass. I head to my truck in the dirt parking lot behind the establishment.

As I approach my Silverado, I see a couple passionately kissing in the car parked next to mine. I stand in the darkness and watch. She craves his contact. If she pulls him any closer, he'll be behind her. What would I have to change to be that man, at this moment?

She briefly glances over her shoulder and our eyes meet.

The guy hops out of the car. "Can I help you?"

*Here we go again.* I step out of the dark. Once he sees my size, he retreats back.

I smile, "I apologize. I just don't remember the last time I've seen people genuinely happy. I thought I'd give you a minute before I hopped in my truck."

The woman comes to the man's side and wraps her arm around his waist, sharing, "It's our anniversary."

She's pretty, but not my Persephone. I slap a twenty dollar bill on the trunk. "Have a couple on me." I make good money and have no problem paying for entertainment.

# 8

*Hot love, cold love, no love at all*
*A portrait of guilt hung on the wall*
*They made love in the mountain*
*They made love in the streams*
*They made love in the valleys*
*They made love in their dreams*
*But when they were finished there was nothing to say*
*'Cause mostly they made love from ten miles away*
—JOHN PRINE, DONALD AND LYDIA

## HARPER ROWE

### 10:45 A.M., FRIDAY, APRIL 24, 2020
### PIERZ

I needed to find Billy Blaze for my own sanity. My family was becoming suspicious of my trips and I hated having Margo and those damn videos looming over my head. The daily Minnesota report of "the most deaths in a day so far," was depressing. Sunday was the new record at thirteen—then Tuesday, with seventeen deaths, followed by Wednesday with nineteen, and yesterday, twenty-one.

Greg had been more distant, lately. He missed my calls most nights, as he'd either get stuck working another shift or, completely exhausted, he'd fall asleep. I couldn't honestly explain why I insisted on no more sexting. It was hard to dial it back with a man while trying to convince him that my love for him was stronger than ever.

I went through the side door of Jon and Serena's home, which brought me directly into our command center. Serena wasn't allowing any outsider contact with her kids and I respected that. Jon was already gone.

Serena looked up from her paperwork and read my expression with ease. "Are you okay?"

I opened my mouth to answer, then pathetically broke down and told her how much I missed Mom. It wasn't one specific thing my mom said that pulled me through my hardest times. It was seeing her, with all the stressors of life, and illness, continue to be a loving person to the very end. She was my safety net. I felt so vulnerable without her.

After my much-needed purging of pain and a good cry, Serena and I ended the conversation with a hug. We were ready to get to work when Serena's mom stepped in and said she needed help with Jackson. Her five-year-old daughter, Nora, peeked in the room and told me, "You're pretty." Nora had long, dark curly hair like her mother and those same fiery eyes.

I thanked her but, before I could return the compliment, Serena swept her away from the door.

I walked about the room and peeked at the information on the tables. On Serena's table, there was a note that read, *Blaze's credit cards were used by Moki Hunter, Cass Lake.* On Jon's table, there were three names on a Post-It: *Gunner Black; Rachel West; Trisha Lake.*

When Serena returned, I told her, "Nora is a sweetheart. She looks full of vim and vigor."

Serena smiled, "That Latin phrase is actually redundant. *Vim* means energetic strength and *vigor* means strength and energy. You could just say, 'Nora's loaded with vim.' She's a high octane kid. Jon weight trains in our basement three days a week, and Nora goes with him and does what she calls her 'warrior exercises.' She performs tasks like rolling from a summersault to her feet, and then in one fluid motion will fire a foam arrow at a target."

I laughed at the visualization.

Serena then caught me off guard. "Tell me what you know about Margo Miller."

My stomach leapt into my throat. Had Margo contacted Serena? I stood there mute, even as my bugging eyes were giving me away.

Serena said casually, "Margo is a surgical technician at the St. Cloud Hospital. She's smart and inherited some money." She looked directly at me, "And she's paying us."

I had promised to keep her name out of it. "How do you know?"

"Margo bought Blaze a Corvette. The rumor is he traveled the world with somebody. There weren't a lot of options to consider from the file. The gossip among hospital staff circulates twenty-four hours a day. A friend who works at CentraCare told me Margo received a divorce settlement and took all of 2004 off, which coincides with Blaze's world travels. Jon asked if I could clarify who's paying us and I believe I have."

I considered how Margo had accessed Greg's and my email contacts. She likely knew someone who worked at HCMC with Greg, and I had given Margo my email address. I told Serena, "I promised I'd never give her up." I couldn't afford to have *la loba*—the *she-wolf*—Margo, mad at me.

Serena looked back down at her work, cool as a cucumber. "You didn't. Don't worry about it. Just let me know if she's got more going on than just being lovesick for him. I don't trust anyone around Blaze, including Margo, and I don't want you to get caught up in something, here. Blaze and Vogel both disappeared and others around them died in questionable circumstances. If we're not careful, one of us could end up dead. Jon and I care about you—more than we need to find Blaze."

I forced out, "I'll let you know if I have concerns." I couldn't get myself to tell her. The video was so stupid and embarrassing. Changing the topic, I pointed to the note, "Who's Moki Hunter?"

She smiled. "He's cute—here's his Facebook photo."

Serena handed me a picture of a young, Native man, with straight, shoulder-length black hair, smooth bronzed skin, and warm copper eyes. She said, "Moki's a twenty-year-old male who used Billy Blaze's credit card months after Blaze disappeared, at Reeds Family Outdoor Outfitters in Walker. I found the fraud charge by talking to friends who worked in billing with credit card companies."

Confused, I could feel my forehead tightening. "Is that legal?" I was graduating from college next year and I didn't need legal charges.

"No. But we're going to need to cheat a little, if we're going to pull off a successful investigation in the COVID-19 era. Jon can't legally access data like he did as a BCA agent, and he can't go door-to-door to talk to people because of COVID, so we have to ask friends for favors. We would never use any of the information maliciously. Are you okay with that?"

I reluctantly nodded. "You seem to have friends in the right places."

"I used to work in billing for a hospital. I'm upfront and they know I'm not out to hurt anyone." Serena sighed, "Honestly, I don't feel good about it. We need to be careful of Machiavellianism—of becoming so focused on this investigation that we slip into the dark triad."

I raised a curious eyebrow and she explained.

"Niccolo Machiavelli touted that it was better to be feared than loved. He believed treachery and violence was excused if the intention was beneficial. The dark triad refers to Machiavellianism, narcissism, and psychopathy. All three are associated with being manipulative and calloused."

I thought aloud, "Like Billy Blaze."

She stopped herself, chuckling softly. "Sorry about the unnecessary trivia. That's Jon's influence on me. I enjoy it, but I know some find it excessive." Nervous concern flashed over Serena, as she refocused on the task at hand. She continued, "I received some information on Blaze. CORE Professional Services completed a psychological assessment on him in 1997, after his assault on Connie Berg. Billy Blaze's parents were Ethan Blaze and Angel White; they were never married. Ethan was an alcoholic who was charged with Child Maltreatment for purposely leaving Billy alone in a park when Billy was five. Ethan was physically abusive to Angel and Billy. He died from cirrhosis in 1996. Angel was a sex worker who had four children with four different men. Deb Zion and Billy Blaze are the only two of her kids still in Minnesota. Deb's father, Lionel Zion, was beat to death in prison. He was doing time for an armed robbery."

I interrupted, "Isn't it weird that she gave her kids their dads' last names?"

"Angel White struggled. I imagine she had her own trauma history. Billy was the youngest and Angel maintained custody of only him. She lost her rights to all of her other children and they were adopted out before Billy was born. She was physically abusive to Billy and he frequently ran away from home. He attended a different school every year, until he dropped out in tenth grade. He was also sexually abused by some of Angel's partners. He told Angel about the abuse, but she didn't believe him, because she felt she was meeting her partners' sexual needs."

I felt an incredible sadness for this *father* of mine, and remembered Jon's words—psychopaths are made, not born. I fumbled for words, "So where is my bio-grandma now?"

"Angel died of unknown causes in April of 1997. Throughout the assessment, Billy was swearing about police officers failing to rescue him from his mother's abuse, and then later mad at them for being unable to determine how she died. Angel lived a hard life, with a lot of drug use and body trauma. It's not uncommon for a medical examiner to be unable to determine the cause of death."

I considered, "It's interesting that both of his parents died shortly before Billy went off the rails."

"Sometimes, the death of an abusive parent brings the loss of a loving childhood to the forefront and unleashes narcissistic rage." Serena handed me the assessment to peruse.

Billy Blaze's claim that he never assaulted Connie Berg, when Jon shared that the brutal attack was caught on film, bothered me. Blaze was quoted, stating, "The cops always take the word of the woman." The therapist didn't believe him. Billy was diagnosed with Posttraumatic Stress Disorder, based on his childhood. He was also diagnosed with Narcissistic Personality Disorder, Antisocial Personality Disorder, Alcohol Use Disorder, and Opioid Use Disorder. It was recommended that he complete a domestic abuse program, chemical dependency treatment, and participate in individual counseling, until it was deemed no longer necessary by his therapist.

When Serena saw I was looking at the diagnosis page, she explained, "Narcissistic refers to extreme self-centeredness. Narcissus, in Greek mythology, fell in love with his own image in a pond and drowned in it. Antisocial individuals hurt and use other people. Someone who disregards the rights of others without remorse." She then pointed to the Opioid Use Disorder. "This might be our ticket. If he has a history of abusing Oxys, like the report suggests, I'd like to know where and when he last picked up a prescription. Blaze was shot in Iraq. I have a feeling he was prescribed meds through the VA. Unfortunately, the Veterans Medical Center is slow getting out information, even pre-COVID."

I thought about names on the tables. "Who is Rachel West? There were a couple of different times in Blaze's history when he threatened her."

"I haven't determined if Rachel is a friend or a foe, yet. Your new pal, Gunner Black, is her father and Blaze's housemate, so imagine what it was like for her, having regular contact with those two. Rachel is not interested in speaking to us." Serena pulled up a voicemail on her phone and put it on speaker, "Call me again, Ms. Frederick, and I'm filing a harassment charge."

I had to smile at the young woman's brazen response. I held up the Post-It. "What does Jon have on Trisha Lake?" Trisha was the blonde Blaze was with before he went off the grid.

"Our friend, Tony Shileto, received a tip from a police officer that she's in the Bemidji area."

Surprised, I said, "That's where I live. I can ask around."

Serena cautioned, "I'd prefer you didn't. Let Jon handle this. The FBI listed Bemidji as the most dangerous city in Minnesota—based on the number of violent crimes per population."

"It's because it's squeezed between Red Lake and Leech Lake reservations. Everybody knows that . . ."


9:45 P.M., BEMIDJI

AFTER MAKING THE LONG TREK BACK to said dangerous city, I was exhausted. It was a beautiful drive from Pierz to Bemidji, made more so by the bright greens of spring exploding from the foliage along the way. Unfortunately, a chunk of the trip was on a two-lane stretch where you could easily get caught behind a meanderer pulling a pontoon and have to either settle in, or put your life at risk and pass. On my way home, the former occurred and the latter did not; it was a lesson in patience.

I sprawled across my bed, stretching out my cramped legs. Thumbing through social media and becoming instantly bored, I decided to search for Moki Hunter on Facebook. Moki lived in Cass Lake, another one of the most dangerous communities, on one of the most dangerous reservations in the state. My social work courses taught me that twenty percent of the children in Cass County suffered from hunger. Cass County had a high school dropout rate of over thirty percent. Of course, statistics didn't necessarily apply to any one person. While the FBI claimed Bemidji was the most dangerous city in the state, I was living there and rather bored, at the moment.

So, what did Moki do for fun? I found myself drawn back to his picture. He had the brightest brown eyes I'd ever seen. No pictures with a lover—female, male, or other. The most prominent picture was of Moki with each arm around the shoulders of younger teenagers—I guessed his brother and sister. The remaining pictures surprised me; I swiped through image after image of complicated appetizers and entrées that made my mouth water. Our man, Moki, loved to cook.

# 9

*The sky is black and still now*
*On the hill where the angels sing*
*Ain't it funny how an old broken bottle*
*Looks just like a diamond ring*
—JOHN PRINE, *FAR FROM ME*

## JON FREDERICK

10:25 A.M., SATURDAY, APRIL 25, 2020
4101 WEST DIVISION STREET, ST. CLOUD

I wanted to have a conversation with the last people on record that had contact with Billy Blaze. Gunner Black was no longer taking our calls and had apparently told his daughter, Rachel, to avoid talking to us, too. That left me with Trisha Lake. I wanted to know exactly what happened on August 22, 2017—the last night Blaze was seen alive.

I managed to talk Trisha's son, Baric, into speaking with me, provided the meeting occur in a very public setting. He didn't trust anything related to his biological mother. I needed Trisha's address and hoped Baric, who lived in St. Cloud, might have heard something about Blaze.

The Macy's parking lot outside of the Crossroads Mall was in clear, public view of busy Third Street, and under the watchful eye of surveillance cameras. Not one to waste time, I told Baric I was primarily interested in his relationship with his mother.

Baric was a fit and serious young man, who stood his ground as he shared, "I was raised by my dad and my stepmom, Laura. I spent more time with Laura than anyone. She was a saint. Imagine marrying a man whose previous wife was a beauty queen. Trisha would promise my sister, Saffron, and I a day at the fair, but of course, Trisha would never show. Laura was left to clean up the mess. One day, my dad sat us down and pointed out we had a mother who was right in front of us, loving us every day. From that point on, Laura was my mom."

I asked, "So, what was it like being Trisha's son?"

"She was like a Corvette with a single cylinder engine. Men lusted for her everywhere we went and, when she got attention, we didn't matter. I just wanted a mom. I had no idea how nurturing a mother could be until we gave Laura a chance. Saffron and I got tired of being let down. We talk about contact with our mother, today, the way you might talk about getting a speeding ticket. It's not painless, but it doesn't break us." He smiled sadly. "But you should see pictures of Trisha when she was young—she was gorgeous. She was just a vortex for attention and, when you're a kid, you want some, too. Her biggest problem is she's never had to take care of herself and now, it's like—she can't."

"How did your dad handle her being with Blaze?"

"Didn't concern him. They were long over before Blaze came along. It's always been too easy for Trisha. My dad got a babysitter so she could run errands during the day. Come to find out, the *errands* she performed were all done on her back." Frustrated, Baric's focus sank down to the parking lot tar. "I'm sorry. That's not fair. She isn't evil. Anyway, my dad had already accepted the fact that you can't make somebody love you."

My obsessive brain postulated that "baric" could either be an atmospheric weight or could mean containing barium. Barium was never found in nature as a free element. Like the

Baric in front of me, it needed attachment. I asked, "When's the last time you saw Billy Blaze?"

Without hesitation, he tersely remarked, "July Fourth weekend of 2017. I'll never forget it. I had confronted Trisha about her cocaine use and we argued. I tried to smooth things over a few days later, by stopping over at Blaze's to see if she wanted to go to the fireworks. Like always, I parked in the alley behind the home and walked to the house. As I was walking up to the house, Blaze had my mother bent over by an open window and was doing her dog style—lights on, curtains wide open. He looked at me and threw me a shit-eating grin. I just turned and walked away. When I talked to Trisha a couple days later, all she had to say was, 'You should've called ahead of time.' The kicker is, I *had* called. Blaze took the message."

"Do you have any idea where he has been, since?"

"I haven't heard a word about him. But I haven't spoken to Trisha much, either."

Baric stared over toward the red bullseye above the Target store. Without prompting, he offered, "I thought about killing Blaze. He defiled my mother and left her broken. But what's the point? She'd just find another Blaze. Last I heard, she was living with a guy named Carlos Tavares in a trailer park in Bemidji. Carlos has a half dozen prior domestics. After my dad, each guy got more controlling and abusive . . ."

2:00 P.M. IRVINE AVENUE, BEMIDJI

I'D SPENT THE DAY LOOKING FOR Trisha Lake in Bemidji. Downtown Bemidji featured a classic red, brick government building, erected in 1902, in the Beaux-Arts style. When I headed east on Irvine Avenue, an eerie sadness settled over me, as if the cumulative pain of past inhabitants still haunted the air.

The east side of Bemidji was once home to the thirty-two acre, Beltrami County Poor Farm, which consisted of a four-story barn, a granary, a pest house, a smoke house, and a house with a root cellar. Poor folks who suffered from the epidemics that originated in lumber camps were shipped off to the farm. The pest house held those with contagious diseases, particularly diphtheria, smallpox, and typhoid. It had its own graveyard. People segregated away from society to die—like COVID victims, today. After the logging era passed, the farm became a detention hospital that housed people in extreme poverty.

When today's pandemic ended, one of the tragedies would be the money wasted—while so many suffered. Our legislature built a $6.9 million morgue for COVID-19 that would never hold a body. Harvard, a college with a $40 billion endowment, received $9 million in taxpayer aid from the federal government. I couldn't let my thoughts proceed further into the COVID labyrinth. It was all negative and there was nothing I could do about it.

Getting back to the case: It was hard to believe Trisha's new partner, Carlos Tavares, could be worse than Blaze. All it took was a casual conversation with a police officer to get steered in his direction.

Carlos Tavares once lived in the Hillcrest Manor trailer park on Irvine Avenue, but had moved to a mobile home he rented in the Sylvan trailer park, in Northwest Bemidji. The history of the Bemidji trailer parks was less than stellar. Just four years ago, a child porn creep named Jacob Kinn murdered Melissa Norby and kidnapped the five-year-old girl she was babysitting, in Hillcrest Park. Diligent, around-the-clock work by the BCA and the Bemidji Police Department led to finding the little girl in a camper, hidden in the woods near Bigfork. The poor thing was duct-taped, but still alive. She was delivered, smiling, safely to her mother.

No one responded when I knocked on the door of Carlos's ramshackle, partially burned mobile home. As I waited, I heard someone inside, but the movement soon stopped. An unsettling feeling rushed through me. I stepped back and noticed a slight movement of a window curtain. Someone was behind it and this wasn't good. My phone buzzed and I quickly answered it. Harper was in trouble . . .

# 10

*You can gaze out the window get mad and get madder*
*Throw your hands in the air, say, "What does it matter?"*
*But it don't do no good to get angry*
*So help me I know*
*For a heart stained in anger grows weak and grows bitter*
*You become your own prisoner as you watch yourself sit there*
*Wrapped up in a trap, of your very own chain of sorrow*
—JOHN PRINE, *BRUISED ORANGE*

## HARPER ROWE

7:30 A.M., SATURDAY, APRIL 25, 2020
BIRCHMONDT DRIVE NORTHEAST,
WEST SIDE OF LAKE BEMIDJI, BEMIDJI

Greg didn't call again last night and it was driving me crazy. Didn't he understand I was stuck here, thinking about him all day and night?

As I grumbled to myself, my phone chirped with the sweet music of *Gold to Glass* by the Revivalists—Greg's ringtone. *All of my gold turned to glass . . . I need someone to help these hard times pass.* I eagerly wrestled across my bed to grab it. "Greg!"

I barely recognized his voice. He painfully croaked, "Hon, I'm going to be okay, but I've got the 'rona. That damn virus got me. I tested positive yesterday."

Stunned, I felt panic wrap around my vocal cords like a python, crushing any opportunity to even form a response.

He continued, "I've been careful, but when you're work-ing long shifts, you get careless and something I did cost me. I'm running a bit of a temp and my throat feels like it's being shredded with razor blades. But I'm okay—I'll *be* okay. I don't want you to worry about it. I'm young, Harp. I'm in good shape. I'll be fine . . ."

A sluggish wave of despair saturated me. The reality of experiencing love was whirling away in a dark vortex. Well-intended words were chattered that meant no more to me than if the placaters were speaking in tongues. First Corinthians 14:4: *The one who speaks in tongues edifies himself . . .*

2:30 P.M., CASS LAKE,
LEECH LAKE RESERVATION

HELL WITH EVERYBODY! I DROVE DIRECTLY to Cass Lake, aggressively jinking around meanderers. I was going to find Moki Hunter, dammit, and force him to give up Blaze. I needed to make *something* right. *Please God, help Greg survive this.* I needed him.

I was so preoccupied with Greg, I hadn't given a lot of thought to my plan, until I drove by Dreamcatcher Park and St. Charles Church in Cass Lake. I slowed and eventually pulled in front of a rundown, rambler-style house just off of Main Street—Moki's address, in the heart of the Leech Lake Reservation. I gazed over at my notebook on the passenger seat and began reconsidering my reckless decision. I might have been safer in North Minneapolis. After several minutes, a teenaged girl began staring out the window at me, talking to someone out of sight. I couldn't formulate a plan.

What did I know about Moki Hunter? He stole my bio-dad's credit card and he loved to cook. Not an especially sterling resume.

Finally, a Native couple around my age walked toward my car. I made sure my doors were locked and offered a sheepish smile. The guy was an athletic man, with short, cropped hair like Blaze, which didn't ease my anxiety. She had long, satin black hair and was thin as a rail. Both gave me that *What the hell are you doing here?* look.

He suddenly stepped right in front of my car, rested his hands on the hood, and glared at me.

I quickly looked behind me, planning to back away, but now the Native woman was planted directly behind my car. *Son of a bitch.*

I recognized Moki from his Facebook profile as the man walking out of the house, making a beeline toward me.

I scrabbled for my phone and swiped with shaky fingers to call Jon. Thankfully, he answered before the second ring. "Jon, I'm in trouble. I'm in Cass Lake and they're all around my car."

"Give me your exact location."

"Moki Hunter's house." I looked at the address I had put in Google maps. "One-oh-two Lyle Chisolm Drive. It's across the street from Dream Catcher Park."

"I'm in Bemidji—twenty minutes away," Jon calmly assured me. "I'll be there soon. I need to hang up and call the Tribal Police to help you out."

I appreciated that Jon didn't waste time asking why I was here.

As I trembled inside the safety of my car, I took a minute to take in this Moki character. Physically, he was in good shape—potentially dangerous. His arms were defined with muscle, jutting out from a sleeveless t-shirt. He wasn't overly jacked, though. His muscles looked like they were earned by hard work. His hair was thick and wild, reaching to his shoulders.

He signaled for me to roll down the window. I pushed the window button and it started automatically going all the way down. *No!* I frantically jabbed at it until it stopped halfway down. He glanced inside and commented, "Let me guess—Bemidji State University."

I nodded affirmatively.

"And you needed to see how us Indians live. Well, grab a pen, my unpigmented friend," he said with enthusiasm, "because you managed to land one, right on the hood of your car!"

His voice assumed the tone of carnival front man. Moki pointed to his friend and gestured in hushed, dramatic tones, "We are looking for the average, the typical, the norm—a guy whose name probably *is* Norm. His Indian name is—" He flung an upturned hand at the man relaxing on the front of my car.

Playing along, my new hood ornament said, "Tyee."

Moki pranced dramatically to the front of my car and put a hand on his friend's shoulder. "No, we can do better than that." He gave me an affected, grave look, as he said, "We call him *Cracker Jacker*. Not for his love of caramel popcorn, but instead for his propensity for stealing white women's cars."

They both started laughing.

I had no idea where this was going. *Jon, get here before it gets weirder.*

Moki tugged on Tyee's gold shirt, "Let's see, what do car-thieving Indians wear?" He taunted me again as he circled around his friend. "Write this down, now. Laker yellow t-shirts that say *KJ* on them. A team named after all of those Los Angeles lakes. So what," he asked Tyee, "does *KJ* stand for?"

Tyee smiled, "King James."

Moki turned back to me, "Before we got rid of the Indian logos, he was *Chief* James. As a matter of fact, here on the rez, we still read the Chief James version of the Bible."

In spite of my life and current circumstances, I felt my lips twitch in amusement.

Moki caught my half-smile and continued, "Cracker Jacker, do you have a flask on you? Come on, give it up. We've all heard the stories."

Tyee responded, "No, but I did drink a cherry cola this morning."

Moki teased, "Do you think it had anything to do with your *skin color?*" He turned to me again, pointing, "Write that down. Indians love cherry cola."

Tyee had enough. He shook his head at Moki, "You're an idiot."

Unfazed, Moki's narrative became increasingly dramatic, "And what do *Indians,*" he emphasized, "wear on their feet? Nina, what are you wearing?"

She responded by sticking out a foot and rotating her ankle, enjoying the game. "Canvas sneakers, of course."

"How about you, Cracker Jacker?"

"Vans slip-ons."

Moki looked down at his own shoes, which bore the Nike logo. "Well, this won't do. We need to decide on a shoe." He turned to me with a shrug, "Sorry, but I can't come up with any stereotypical footwear that we should be wearing. Let's see, it should be something comfortable. Maybe without laces."

A Native elder came walking by and, after leering at me, told the three, "We don't need trouble."

Moki nodded respectfully, "Understood."

He turned back to me and whispered, "We were fortunate in our field study to catch a live Indian walking by. Write down, 'They all walk in single file. The one we saw did.'"

Nina had now sauntered to the front of my car to join her friends. I leaned away from the window, fearing she'd grab a fistful of my hair.

She threw a hard look toward me and said, "Maybe a better question is, *What can we surmise about white chicks?*"

Moki rubbed the side of my fender. "White women love gray cars. It may be not as vibrant as the other colors, but what can you say? It really goes with everything."

Nina peered in the window at me, "And they *love* their

beachy blonde hair, artificially blown back, like they just got off the sailboat. But they apparently don't talk." She spun around to face Moki, enjoying my humiliation. "What percentage white do you think she is? We have to show our Native percentage. It only seems fair to ask."

I was too embarrassed to share that I didn't even know my biological father.

Tyee commented, "Is that a beaver on her shirt?"

Nina hit him. "That's for what you're thinking."

I offered in a voice I didn't recognize, "Bemidji Beavers."

Tyee gestured toward me, "She won't get out of the car. Maybe she's not wearing pants?"

*Winnie the Pooh style*—I didn't dare say it.

Nina teased Tyee, "Are you thinking fishnet stockings?"

Moki cut in, "No, that would be *our* thing."

Nina jeered at Moki, "You're so stupid."

Ignoring her, Moki toned it down and leaned against my car door as he spoke directly to me, "I have to admit those blue eyes get me. Shimmering like the morning sun on Cass Lake."

Nina punched him in the shoulder, "You're *flirting* with her."

Moki turned his hands up in surrender.

Before he could defend himself, we were interrupted by the arrival of a Tribal Police squad car. The officer quickly stepped out, "Moki, I received a call indicating this young woman is in trouble."

Moki cracked, "She was no trouble at all."

The officer waved me out of the car and I complied.

When Moki and his friends took a gander at my TOMS slip-on shoes, with a neon dinosaur print, they all started giggling.

Under her breath, Nina commented, "Moccasins."

I turned to Moki, "They're a statement about my white-ness. I felt unworthy of wearing the amazing moccasins made by Itasca Leathergoods."

Moki busted out laughing and said, "Bemidji, you are someone I'd like to get to know."

The officer first told Moki to shut up, and then turned to me, "What are you doing here, miss?"

I was embarrassed. "I wanted to talk to Moki, but when they," I gestured toward Tyee and Nina, "approached my car, I got scared and called for help. Nothing happened. I'm sorry for troubling you. I panicked."

For the first time, the officer snickered. "What did you need to talk to Moki about?"

"He used my father's credit card, three years ago, and my father—Billy Blaze—hasn't been seen, since."

Moki defensively proclaimed, "I found his billfold in the ditch."

The officer turned to Moki, "Stop talking. Listen to what she's saying! They may be trying to stick you with a homicide."

I cut in, "No—oh, no, that's not what I'm saying at all." I searched Moki's caramel-colored eyes, "I just want to know where you got it. I'm trying to find my father."

Mercifully, Jon pulled in, tires chirping as he screeched to a halt. I exhaled in relief when he rushed over and asked, "Is there trouble, Officer?"

The officer eyed Jon up and down, "Are you FBI?"

"No."

"Then you have no jurisdiction, here. You need to leave."

Jon turned to me, "What's this about?"

I couldn't look him in the eyes, so stared down at my proclaimed, white-girl shoes. "I wanted to ask Moki where he got Blaze's credit card."

Moki offered, "I can show you where I found it."

The tribal officer was losing his patience. "Shut *up*, Moki." He turned to Jon, "I said *leave*."

Jon tipped his head toward his car and said, "Follow me out." I dropped back into my still-running car and gladly threw the gearshift in drive but, wanting to at least appear composed, forced a smile and slowly rolled along.

I followed Jon on the Paul Bunyan Expressway from Cass Lake, past Little Wolf and Grace Lakes, as we made our way to Bemidjid, I called Jon and explained my intentions for my unauthorized venture.

Jon said politely, "The tribal police officer was right. Anytime a crime is committed between a Native and non-Native on the reservation, the FBI investigates. Neither the tribal police nor the county sheriff's department has any jurisdiction. You need to check with me before you do anything this reckless again." He paused and asked, "So, what got into you today?"

Frustrated, I shared, "Greg has the coronavirus." I could barely finish my thought without my voice thickening with tears. "And I'm just supposed to stay home and wait—like I did for my mom. I need to get this search over."

"You're not alone, here. I'm going to have you set up a FaceTime call to Serena. We need to help each other through this. There are a lot of dangerous players."

"I'm sorry for wasting your time."

"This wasn't a waste of time. I admire your assertiveness. Moki appeared interested in you and he offered to show us where he found that credit card. Talk to him online, if you can, and let's see if he'll assist."

"I'll friend him on Facebook."

Jon said, "Blaze's credit card being found here is an anomaly and I'm not sure what it means to our investigation. I can't sort out what he was doing here. When he's in Minnesota, Blaze doesn't venture far from his home, just off of Germain. He had an incident in Waite Park and another in St. Joseph, but for the most part, his troubles were within walking distance of his home. There are no reports that place him north of St. Cloud."

Shameful possibilities wound through my head. My mom hated Billy Blaze. How did his billfold end up so close to her hometown? How far would Mom have gone to protect me? Her words, "I hope you can forgive me for things I never told you," rang through my thoughts. *Could she have killed Billy Blaze?*

# 11

*I been brought down to zero, pulled out and put back there . . .*
*My head shouted down to my heart*
*"You better look out below!"*
*It ain't such a long drop, don't stammer don't stutter*
*From the diamonds in the sidewalk to the dirt in the gutter*
*And you carry those bruises to remind you wherever you go*
—JOHN PRINE, *BRUISED ORANGE*

## TRISHA LAKE

6:35 P.M., SUNDAY, APRIL 26, 2020
30TH STREET, BEMIDJI

Carlos and I picked up takeout burgers at Bar 209. We enjoyed supper in his truck at Cameron Park, by Lake Bemidji—the juicy burger was delicious and the view of the beaming sunrays over the lake's rippling surface was breathtaking.

But Carlos was in such a mood. He needed to get back to work. He was one of the best diesel mechanics around, but with Knife River Corporation laying off construction workers, he sat at home with me all day, restless and angry—like the coronavirus was somehow my fault. Lately, no matter what I said, it was wrong.

Carlos was a Chicano version of Billy Blaze, tightly wound, spoiling-for-a-fight muscles, and bristly, short dark hair. I never should have left Billy. As we stared across the lake, Carlos took a couple of pulls from a pint of Captain Morgan. When he set it down, I picked it up and gulped down a large swig, myself. We didn't speak—there was nothing to talk about.

On the way home, I joked, "I'm becoming a lightweight. After one drink, I'm ready for a nap."

Carlos's eyes slithered disapprovingly over me, like I was something foul he scraped off the sole of his shit kickers. "Lightweight? You're the queen of the six-ounce shot."

"Well, since you're not working, we can't afford to get my meds filled, anymore." My anxiety had been off the charts since my prescriptions ran out, but I would pay for that remark.

He was seething now and I cursed my smart mouth. I needed to tread lightly to diffuse my careless comment.

The benzos—Xanax and Ativan, especially—let me float through life, but the docs wouldn't prescribe them, anymore. Zoloft and Prozac both worked, if I wanted to still feel, which was always a toss-up for me. But I couldn't afford a doctor visit, so alcohol would have to do, for now. We cruised in silence into the Skyliner trailer park, to the remains of our rented home. I hoped the drive had cooled him down.

Once inside, I slipped off my shoes and shimmied out of my jeans. I really needed to vacuum this floor. Crunched chips and UFOs—Unidentified Fallen Objects—stuck to the soles of my bare feet. I reached under the back of my shirt and unclasped my bra, breathing a sigh of relief as I pulled the straps through the sleeves of my shirt, until I was free of the contraption. I stretched out on the mattress, which was laid out in the middle of our living room.

A couple weeks ago, when I refused to have sex with him, Carlos set my bed on fire. He wasn't trying to kill me—at least I didn't think so. He poured my bottle of Southern Comfort on the floor next to the mattress and tossed a cigarette on it. Carlos thought he was going to get a good laugh as I scrambled to put it out, but I was drunk. I stared at him in defiance and let the flames burn. He turned his back on me and left for the bar. When I realized it was all on me, I struggled to put the fire out. It burned most of the back end of our trailer, so now we live in the front. Served him right, far as I was concerned. The landlord couldn't kick us out because of the cold weather rule.

Carlos crawled onto the mattress beside me and, in his greasy voice, informed me, "Time for some lovin'."

I was tired, but *fine*. Maybe it'd improve his mood. That sweet smell of alcohol sweat and cologne was once arousing for me; it had since become the essence of pain and humiliation. My body tensed defensively before my mind made the connection of what was to come.

Carlos ordered, "Turn over."

"No," I sighed, feebly pulling a ratty quilt over myself, trying for some dignity. "Let's just do it face-to-face."

"I want anal."

*Give me a break.* "I don't *do* anal."

Carlos laughed, "That's not true."

The bastard had taken me anally after I'd passed out more than I'd ever care to admit. I'd wake up feeling like a pipe had been shoved up my ass, sticky and gross. I made the mistake, once, of suggesting maybe he ought to find a guy. The beating I took for that cost me two teeth and more than a handful of hair.

I should've just left, but I didn't have a place to go. And, in my heart, I deserved it. I'd abandoned my kids. I hurt people who actually cared. I was tired. For whatever reason, my soul reared up and screamed in protest—*enough!* I would take my licks figuratively, but I'd had it with being a casualty of Carlos's sick desires. As long as I was conscious, he wasn't sexually abusing me again. I stiffened my body and refused to turn over.

His mouth twisted into a vicious smile as he repeated with menace, *"Turn over."* When I turned away from his glare, resolute in my decision, he said, "Maybe you could listen better if you stopped breathin'." His grimy fingers hooked around my throat, as if he was making a joke. But he wasn't, really.

As I fired all the hate in my soul at him through my eyes, he slowly tightened his grip until I was panicking. Imagine holding your breath for as long as you can, and then being forced to hold it longer. *Well, I tried, anyway.* For a second, everything became a weird green haze; then he loosened his clutch and gave me a reprieve. It sent me into a coughing frenzy as I curled up on my side, heaving and gasping the fetid air in the trailer. After I caught my breath, I rolled onto my back again. I searched his dead eyes for compassion, but found none. Maybe it was never there.

Carlos seethed, "Listen, bitch, where is a piece of white trash like you gonna go if I throw you out?"

"I have friends." Even I knew it was pathetic.

He mocked in a whiny tone, *"I have friends."* Phlegm cracked in his throat as he laughed, "You keep saying that. Nobody's come lookin' for you since I dragged your sorry, good-for-only-one-thing ass here. You're doin' this. And from now on, you're doin' it *every* time I ask. If I tell you I want it, I expect you to pucker up and have your ass waitin' for me."

I mustered up strength from depths I didn't know existed. When I refused to budge, he blasted a thundering punch into my chest. It felt like a wrecking ball had been dropped on me. As I lay there gasping, he slapped me to bring me back to my grisly reality.

Stunned, I squeeze my eyes shut. I was sure bones broke with that punch. Pain radiated from my chest. I tried to buy some time. "Fine—just . . . please, just give me a minute."

"You've said it yourself," Carlos said caustically, "your body's going to hell. I need a little more, you know, *friction.*"

He clumsily wobbled out of his jeans in anticipation and dug his fingers into my hip in a silent demand that I needed to turn over.

Just breathing was painful, at this point. I forced out, "I don't enjoy it."

"Don't be so damn selfish," he berated me, "you ungrateful bitch."

I sadly accepted that he was right. I had nobody—no place to go.

My ex-husband and even my children used to beg me to come home but, at the time, I was a prima donna. After everything I'd pulled, they hated me. Back in 1992, I was a candidate for Miss Teen Minnesota and people in my hometown of Park Rapids were proud of me. I never deserved the pedestal; the cavern in my heart just kept expanding, overtaking the space selflessness once possessed. I had fallen. I was tired of pleasing people and being used.

I wasn't a blowup doll and I wasn't getting flipped prone. Tonight, he'd have to kill me first.

Carlos registered the resolve in my face and moved quickly to quash it. He hovered over me, once again taking my throat in his meaty grip. His black eyes bored into mine. "You can't say you didn't ask for this."

I stiffened my arms against his shoulders, trying to force him back, but my chest felt like it was splitting. I couldn't move him off me. I was seeing stars. *This is how it ends.*

As I drifted into a dream state, I heard an intense, irate voice growl, "Get off of her!"

Suddenly, we weren't alone. Carlos was quick to his feet, releasing his grip and freeing my airway. At the foot of the mattress stood a dark-clad stranger. He was wearing a black mask on his face, covered by a shiny plastic shield. A dark blue windbreaker covered his torso and blue work coveralls with built-in knee pads protected his legs. His surgical glove-covered hands held a gun with a silencer—aimed at Carlos. This man meant business.

Without a care for his state of undress, Carlos warned the man, "I'm only going to say it once—get the hell out of my house."

I recovered my breath and blinked my eyes into focus, trying to make sense of what was happening.

The intruder was lean, strong, and calm—and not going anywhere.

I rolled away and scrambled for my jeans, quickly pulling them on, my fingers fumbling as I tried to button the top clasp. I just gave up and yanked my shirt down over the waistband, looking frantically from one man to the next, wondering about the lesser of two evils.

Carlos was stocky and relatively short, though I wouldn't dare mention it out loud. I was required to wear flat shoes so I wouldn't look down on him when we were out together.

This new player stood at least six feet. He advanced on Carlos, his gaze now angling downward, and informed him with a gesture of his gun, "I'm taking Trisha."

Carlos's voice had lost some bravado, but he taunted his newfound enemy, "Look, germ boy. You ain't firin' that gun. Hell, you're even scared to get your hands dirty."

The man laughed and, in a chilling tone, warned, "Listen dumbass, I'm wearing a mask so I don't get blood splatter on me. I've been hired to take Trisha—by any means necessary— and I intend to do so. Step away, or wait for me in hell."

Carlos's nerves began to show, which gave me secret pleasure. He asked, "Who sent you?"

"Not your business," he responded flatly. "I already have death on my hands, so keep trying me."

Ever the badass, Carlos took a step toward him and started to say, "Get the hell—"

The man fired a shot past Carlos's ear, into the burned

recesses of our home. "You promised me you'd only say that once."

Someone was going to die. He advanced on Carlos in two steps, the silenced gun not wavering from his grip. He said, "I'm not wasting anymore bullets. I'll shoot you and burn the rest of this shithole down with you in it."

I wasn't sure who to side with. I stepped toward Carlos, fearing this masked man could be worse.

Carlos was considering his options. "Okay. You can have her, but it will cost you a grand."

Talk about humiliation. I felt like a hog being marketed. Billy would have killed for me.

The intruder directed me, "Get your shit and we're leaving."

Dejected, I told the stranger, "It will only take me a minute."

When I returned with my sorry, small bag of possessions, Carlos was bargaining, "So, what do I get? I oughtta get something for her." I couldn't believe the conversation. I felt my whole body curling in on itself. *How did I get here?*

"You get a chance to wake up on earth tomorrow," said the man. "Trisha's leaving with me. The only question is, will I be leaving a corpse behind? If you make one more move in my direction," he gestured with his gun, "I'm tenderizing your body with bullets."

Too quickly for my tastes, Carlos decided I wasn't worth the battle. "You know what? Take that ungrateful bitch." He spat in my direction. "She doesn't even earn enough to pay for her smokes and booze. Glad to be rid of her . . ."

I decided I'd take my chances and go with him. When I scrambled into his Ford Taurus, I noted crinkling under my body and found myself sitting on a large plastic tarp.

Without a word, he gunned his getaway ride and we were quickly headed down the road.

After miles of tense silence, I suggested, "You can take the shield off, now. I'm unarmed." I dramatically held up my hands.

He didn't respond and made no moves to remove the shield. As the plastic crunched beneath me, it finally registered. *The hit was on me.*

As my system went into full-on flight mode, my rescuer casually asked, "Are you okay?"

*Am I okay?* I wanted to laugh. I breathed calm into my voice, "I think he cracked my sternum."

We drove in silence as he headed south on Highway 71 out of Bemidji. I finally begged, "Please, take the shield off. It's freaking me out."

He turned to me, "I'm not taking this shield off. I was told you needed help, so I put my life at risk for you. The police aren't coming. You've called the police three times in the last month, but each time then asked them not to stop out."

"What would you say when the cops respond with, 'We can come, but I want you to consider we may be bringing COVID from our last scene'?" I meekly asked, "Who are you?"

"Jon Frederick."

"Where are you taking me?"

"St. Cloud."

Hope flooded through me; my son had reached out for me. "I knew Baric would come for me. He's a great kid."

"Baric is a good guy, but no one asked me to rescue you."

Hope is a nasty thing. I should have known better than to allow it to even flicker.

Jon said, "Your landlord told me Carlos was beating you to death. He didn't want his home to be one more Bemidji trash and burn story. He said you seem to have a death wish. Your landlord's a piece of work, himself. He would've kicked you out but was afraid no one else would rent the place."

"He can't."

"Actually, he can. He can't turn off your utilities between October fifteenth and April fifteenth, but he can evict you for a material violation of the lease agreement—like starting a fire."

It wasn't always like this for me. "Men used to do anything for me."

"Men like Billy Blaze?"

"Yeah. Are you a friend of his?"

"What happened to him?"

I hated when people answered questions with questions. "Ask Gunner Black. I don't really want to talk about Billy. Do you want to hear about Carlos?"

He asked, "How long have you known Carlos?"

"About a year."

"Did Carlos know Billy Blaze?"

"No. What does that have to do—" He shot me a sharp look. "Carlos wasn't even in Minnesota until 2019. Billy was gone by then."

He interrupted, "Then I don't care about Carlos. Tell me about Blaze."

I sighed, robbed of my time to tell of all the atrocities I experienced at the hands of Carlos. "What do you need to know?"

"I want to know what happened that last night you were at Blaze's house."

I gazed out at the lifeless brown ditches and barren trees surrounding us as we headed through the Leech Lake Reservation. "It was Gunner's house," I corrected. "House payments are too much of a commitment for Billy."

Jon was losing his patience.

"Okay, Gunner shouldn't have been home—if I was in the area, he was supposed to spend the night elsewhere." I reminisced, "I love jazz and Wednesday night is jazz night at Legends Bar. After we closed up Legends, Gunner was still home. He still struggles with the loss of his wife." I explained, "She died of cancer in 2015. I know it sounds callous, but it's not like they were together—they were divorced. Anyway, Billy told Gunner he should be happy the whore's gone. He rubbed it in that he had slept with her before she divorced Gunner, and then Gunner and Billy went at it, head to head, like two rams wanting to bang the same ewe. Gunner finally called his daughter to pick him up. Billy was relentless. He amped it up when Rachel arrived. Billy was giving details about Gunner's ex that no daughter should ever have to hear. It was sickening. I had to leave him."

The setting sun was glaring off his face shield, so it was hard to gauge his reactions. "What's Rachel's last name?"

"West."

"What happened?"

"Things got crazy. At some point, Billy broke Gunner's nose. I didn't see it. Once Billy's on a rampage, you don't shut him up. It just runs its course. I spent the next couple days with a friend in St. Cloud, before leaving for L.A. to be with my daughter. My friend was on Judge Judy. Can you believe it?"

He wasn't impressed, so I continued, "The mistake I made was coming back to Minnesota and finding Carlos."

"Have you ever heard of Kali Rowe? She would have been about fifteen when Blaze was with her."

"No. Billy didn't chase younger girls. He loved full-bodied women. If he thought they were out of his league, he chased them harder. If he saw them as below his grade, he treated them like trash."

"Blaze was with Kali at a home with a pool, in a wealthy, but rural neighborhood south of St. Cloud."

"So she's one of Keith Stewart's girlies. Stewart has a beautiful home with a pool in Eagles Landing. It's just south of Kiffmeyer Park in St. Augusta." I studied him, "You're not a cop, are you?"

"No. Just a Good Samaritan offering you another chance."

What was his angle? Men always wanted something. He saved my life—I owed him. "I'm not worried about being prosecuted. I just don't want to end up at the bottom of a lake. This is just between us—okay?"

Unresponsive, Jon stared straight down the road ahead of us.

I couldn't figure him out, but then again, I could win an award for misreading men. I decided to just give it up. "Keith is a major meth dealer, but he doesn't use. It's all about the money for him and he is slick. I was out to his place, once. Billy asked me to deliver some money for him. Keith offered me a glass of wine and gave me a tour of his home. Glasslike marble floors and spotless. We sat on the second floor balcony watching a black girl in a white bikini, swimming in the pool below. She couldn't have been more than sixteen years old. My best guess would be fifteen."

He asked, "How long ago was it?"

"It was back in 2016. I remember because that's when I first met Billy. I was surprised he trusted me to deliver a large amount of money to a man I'd never met. Billy could charm the pants off a girl. He bought me whatever I wanted. Keith, on the other hand, was creepy."

"Why do you say that?"

"He tried to hustle me. Told me I could just stay with him and I'd be safe from guys like Blaze. I could be his liaison to his adolescent talent searches. He wanted to help troubled girls who'd been abandoned by their families. Have you ever been in a place that just didn't feel right?"

"Just a few minutes ago."

I understood and I could appreciate a smartass. "I don't mean trashy or dangerous. It felt like a lie. Like something was going on I didn't understand. I understand drugs. I didn't understand this. When I left, I walked around to the side of the house to take another look at the girl. Keith didn't see me. He said something to the girl and she got out of the pool and removed her swimsuit. She turned in a circle for him. He had her stand there for a bit, even though it was cool and uncomfortable for her. Then he ordered her back in the pool, without the suit. I just left. What a creep!" I trembled involuntarily as the sensation of frigid cold crept up the back of my neck. "There are worse guys than Billy Blaze."

"That isn't a very high bar." Jon sighed audibly and a burst of fog appeared on his shield. He studied me for a second, before returning his focus to the road. "If you want to stay miserable, just keep cultivating your bad habits."

Incredulous, I scolded, "You can't, for one second, believe I *wanted* this."

"I don't think you wanted it, I think you let it happen. Misery is the easiest route. It takes almost no energy."

This man was mean, but he was also fit and sure of himself. I quickly took in his muscular shoulders and long legs, and knew he could protect me. I reached over and put my hand on his leg. "Do you have a place for me to stay, tonight? I clean up nice. You saved my life and I'm grateful."

He glared down at my hand and I quickly removed it. "No."

Jon pulled over and stepped out of the car to make a phone call. Was he going to do me right here? When he returned, he set up a FaceTime call with someone named Serena. He pulled back onto Highway 371 and a pretty brunette appeared on the screen.

# 12

*She may look like a woman*
*But she's still some daddy's little girl*
*And I think that she may be*
*The oldest baby in the world*
—JOHN PRINE, *THE OLDEST BABY IN THE WORLD*

## SERENA FREDERICK

8:15 P.M., SUNDAY, APRIL 26, 2020
HIGHWAY 371, LEECH LAKE RESERVATION

I was pleased Jon had Trisha Lake FaceTime with me. Jon was still angry that he had to go all *Scarface* to rescue Trisha. He anticipated it would come to this and had brought the silencer for extra intimidation. Jon had shared that Trisha had come on to him and, now that I was talking to her, she was very apologetic.

He was taking her directly to the St. Cloud Hospital. I had initially questioned why they'd admit her; now seeing her, I understood. Trisha's skin had a grayish pallor and she looked like death warmed over. She was wearing a low, scoop-necked top that showcased protruding collarbones and defined knobs of her bruised breastbone under a papery layer of skin. She had a split lip and still had the remnants of a hand print on her face from where she'd been slapped. Her left eye was a little greenish, healing from an old bruise. Dark roots streaked with silver ran from her scalp and disappeared into long, lackluster hair that was an unnatural shade of yellow.

Trisha sounded drunk as she rambled on, "I'm sorry. Jon's your guy, I get it. You've got yourself a badass. When he fired that bullet past Carlos, things got real."

Jon hadn't told me he'd fired his gun. No wonder he was upset; he didn't like having to use a gun.

Trisha slumped into a somber sadness, "Please, forgive me. This crap has been with me since I was a kid. I was taught it's how you get guys to help you. My grandpa told me if I followed his advice, I'd never have to work a day in my life."

She closed her eyes for a moment and I thought she was going to fall asleep, before she continued, "Who am I kidding? I talk about my grandpa like he's some sort of benign Valentine. He also told me," she lowered her voice and snarled, "'That purse between your legs is a cash box.' Yeah, he bought me Barbies and a bike. But he also used to stick *things* into me, until I got big enough. And when I told my mom, she blamed me."

Trisha's eyes glistened with tears. She quickly stammered, "I—I'm sorry for saying that. It's gross. It just infuriates me. Since I was little, everybody said, 'You're going to be a heartbreaker.' I didn't want to be a heartbreaker. In fifth grade, I already had high schoolers after me." She reminisced, "I was the star of my class. The attention was intoxicating. But then, you get to high school and people remind you that you really didn't do anything to earn your status. You were just delivered in a pretty package." She looked in Jon's direction, addressing him. "I wish Baric would have sent you." Back to me, she asked, "Do you know what Baric and I argued about the last time we spoke?"

I shook my head.

"He said I would screw anyone for a little attention. I told him, 'Don't you dare talk to your mom like that. It's not right.'"

Jon finally spoke, "How did Baric respond?"

Trisha was eager for Jon's attention. "He said, 'I don't.' How dare he refer to that bitch my ex married as 'Mom.' She wouldn't even let me see my kids. That's why they hate me."

She was as damaged on the inside as on the outside. Maybe worse. I said, "That must have been hard."

She harrumphed, "You don't know the half of it."

"Are you feeling okay?" Her words were slowing as if simply speaking was effortful.

"Tired. Just tired. Where am I going?"

I shared, "The St. Cloud Hospital. You look like you've been through a lot of trauma."

Trisha nodded, "Okay. They can get me my anxiety meds and then I don't have to be drunk all the time."

"Trisha, can you tell me about Billy Blaze?"

She raised her voice, "Big bad Carlos was the one who did this." She gestured to her battered face. "I should've stayed with Billy. I just didn't love him. Billy wanted to marry me. He could have had anyone and he wanted *me*. There's something about being with that guy everybody fears."

It didn't surprise me that Blaze had an abundance of women. Studies show narcissists scored highest at speed-dating events. They could turn on the superficial charm, but just couldn't maintain it. They'd cajole others to meet their own personal needs, as opposed to sincerely caring about others.

"What happened to Billy?"

"Hell—I imagine." She laughed to herself, "He *is* the Grim Reaper."

"Do you think he's dead?"

"Ask Gunner Black or Rachel West. They're the ones who were arguing with him. I left Billy and I never saw him again after that night . . ."

## 10:25 P.M., PIERZ

WHEN JON FINALLY RETURNED HOME, WE went through our routine. He stripped in the back porch, put all of his clothes into a pillow case, and immediately went upstairs and showered. We'd always done this so he could be clean after being at a harrowing crime scene. The danger of the coronavirus made this task additionally important.

I stepped into the bathroom and observed his form through the translucent glass. Jon told me he felt he'd always had too much adrenaline in his system. I'd only seen the consequences of it once, decades ago. When we were in school together, long before we ever dated, Jon took on a bully who was three years older and beat him bloody. Jon had it with the boy picking on his schizophrenic brother and, while I understood, I remembered thinking it was scary. I later learned about the harsh discipline he received from his father and how his anger with it had all been unleashed in that moment. Jon was embarrassed and disappointed with himself. He felt that type of cruelty was unlovable. Tonight brought that all back to the surface for him and he needed to calm his mind.

Hell with it. I stripped and stepped into the shower with him.

## 11:30 P.M.

WE WERE PLEASANTLY EXHAUSTED, RESTING ON the couch in front of our fireplace. My feet were at home in Jon's strong hands and I relished the massages he so lovingly provided. I wondered, sometimes, if it helped him expel tension, as well.

I told him, "I've been trying to get an audience with Mona Dohman, Department of Public Safety Commissioner, in an effort to get you reinstated at the BCA. She's a step above your former boss, Sean Reynolds. We need a backup plan, in case our investigative agency doesn't work out. Your return is going to be hard sell if you shoot someone." Before he could respond, I held a hand up. "Shhh. I'm not shaming you. I know you did what you had to, tonight, but I'd prefer you avoid situations like that."

"I had a landlord tell me Trisha was being beaten to death and he said she's cried wolf too many times with the police, so they weren't responding. From looking at Tavares's history, I knew I'd have to come in full barrel and never relinquish control of the situation, or I was going to have a battle."

"Are you okay?"

He gave me a sad smile. "Much better since you joined me in the shower . . ."

# 13

*Oodles of light, what a beautiful sight*
*Both of God's eyes are shining tonight*
*Rays and beams of incredible dreams*
*And I am a quiet man*
—JOHN PRINE, *QUIET MAN*

## HARPER ROWE

1:30 P.M., MONDAY, APRIL 27, 2020
BIRCHMONDT DRIVE NORTHEAST,
WEST SIDE OF LAKE BEMIDJI, BEMIDJI

Yesterday, Minnesota news announced the most deaths in one day, as a result of the coronavirus. Twenty-eight more families grieving like mine. The news was so devastating—every night.

I was done waiting. Moki Hunter accepted my friend request on Facebook. He and I had been chatting back and forth the past couple of days. I found myself anticipating the *bing!* indicating I'd received a personal message from him. It was a nice distraction when the rest of my world was crumbling around me. Moki was polite and tender-hearted. My only fear of meeting with him alone was catching the coronavirus. Maybe I'd just wear a mask the next time I was with the Fredericks and not tell them. *What am I becoming? Proverbs 19:9: A false witness will not go unpunished, and he who breathes out lies will perish.*

My grandparents packed a lunch and took a drive along the north shore. I hoped someday I'd have a love so intense and committed that going for a drive together was the best possible thing we could do, other than being at home.

I mentioned to Moki that I liked shrimp and he told me he'd make me the best shrimp and vegetable tempura, with eel sauce, I'd ever eaten. Evidently, there was no eel in eel sauce, which is a good thing. I told Moki he'd have to make lunch since my grandparents would be home before dark.

He arrived less than an hour later, with all the groceries to make his shrimp tempura. His hair was pulled into ponytail as he cooked in his white apron. I sat on a stool in the kitchen, watching him work.

I warned, "We need the kitchen to be as clean as we found it."

Moki looked sideways at me, "You didn't tell your grandparents I was coming."

"Absolutely not! They never would have left." I needed to clarify, "This isn't about race. It's about having any new person over in the midst of this pandemic."

He nodded his understanding as he removed a can of beer from his bag of groceries, and asked, "Do you mind if I put this in the freezer for a bit? The colder the better."

I took the can of Bemidji Brewing German Blonde Ale from him and placed it in the freezer compartment of our fridge.

Moki smiled, "The key to a great tempura is to use carbonation instead of water. I've found that a good beer gives it a flavor enhancement."

I teased, "So, does the beer go in me or the tempura?"

"Both, eventually. I'm sorry, I didn't bring any extra to drink."

"I don't need a drink."

He continued with his culinary advice, "Always buy frozen, uncooked shrimp. It's freshest if it's flash-frozen shortly after it's caught and remains frozen until you prepare it. The raw shrimp displayed in Minnesota grocery stores is taken from bags in the freezer section."

I smiled as he went on with his cooking lesson, until I finally asked, "How did you come by your love of cooking?"

"My mom. She makes the best pumpkin soup you'll ever eat."

"I'm not wild about pumpkin."

"Neither am I, but hers doesn't taste strong of pumpkin and it could be served as a delicacy in any exclusive restaurant. It's amazing."

"I'll have to take your word for it."

"Or try it," he added sheepishly, "sometime."

I clarified, "You know I'm in a relationship."

"Yeah. How's he doing?"

"Okay. Horribly sore throat, so we're down to emailing. I wish I could do something for him."

Moki offered, "How about a little Greek mythology humor? After the doc examined the centaur, the centaur told him, 'My throat's not horse, but my legs are.'" He smiled to himself and silently went back to work.

I smiled too, but quickly caught myself. I told him, "Maybe I'm being selfish, but you're the only one who's made me smile in months and I wanted a little more time with you."

"No worries," he said pleasantly. "I needed to get off the rez. It's like any hometown—same old folks still having the same stupid arguments. I loved the metro and being at Le Cordon Bleu in Mendota Heights. When COVID put every school online, it sent me back home. It's so much more difficult to explain the culinary palate presented."

"I never considered that."

"At the school, nobody cares about race. It's about how you cook. We're constantly tasting each other's work and giving each other feedback. I'm lucky to have my mom, but she's only one person and she has a hard time being critical of me."

"Sounds like a great mom." I paused, and then decided to just put it out there. "If this is racist, please tell me, because I'm not trying to be insulting. It surprised me that you didn't have traditional Native foods among the dishes you displayed online."

He grimaced as he considered my comment.

I tried to make light of it, "I guess my ignorance is just a statement about me as a white person."

He rested his hand on my shoulder momentarily, and then apologetically removed it. "My mom said the same thing, basically. 'Be proud of who you are.' But that's not it. Imagine if you restricted your knowledge to only what white people have done in your field. It would be so limiting."

"That's a great point."

"I want to try everything, then come back and establish my own cuisine, which will have a strong Anishinaabe influence." His brown eyes met mine briefly and I felt uncomfortably warm. He smiled, "I'm ready for the beer, now. Believe it or not, I'm generally a quiet man, but I find myself going on and on when you're around."

I retrieved the beer and he poured most of it into a glass bowl with his tempura mix.

Moki said, "Perfect." He handed me the can, "Do you want the rest?"

I took a sip, "I'll share it with you." And then I realized what I'd done. "I'm sorry. I should have poured it in a glass."

"Drink what you wish and I'll take the rest."

I took one more sip. "I'm done, but I won't be insulted if you don't drink the rest." I asked, "So, how did you know Billy Blaze?"

Moki picked up the can and seemed to savor finishing it. "I didn't. I just found his billfold on the Gulch Lake Forest Trail." He looked at me curiously, "You don't call him *Dad*?"

"No. Billy Blaze was a terrible man. I have a dad. Maybe it's morbid curiosity, but I'd like to know what happened to my biological father. Then you can know what kind of bad seed you've chosen to befriend."

He kindly reassured me, "The seeds aren't that different. It's the soil that affects how they grow . . ."

# 14

*I take a walk, I come back home*
*Then I sit a spell*
*Watch the ponies dance around*
*The empty wishing well*
*Night has fallen*
*I've said the things I did*
*The only baby sleeping*
*Is when I was a kid*
*Do you remember*
*When you were my friend?*
*That's the way I'd like things*
*Just like way back then*
—JOHN PRINE, *WAY BACK THEN*

## JON FREDERICK

10:30 A.M., WEDNESDAY, APRIL 29, 2020
PIERZ

Serena and I sat at the command center, hammering away at the suspect list.

Focused, Serena brushed her long curls back, stating, "Loni Thompson doesn't seem like a legitimate suspect. Blaze trashed her place after an argument in the bar in 1998. It's unlikely she came back nineteen years later and killed him over it." She crossed Loni's name off our long list. "And I think you can eliminate Ricky Walters. Blaze stole his rifle in 1998, but Walters ended up getting it back. No further contact."

It was hard separating my love for Serena from our work. I still saw her beauty with the same, love-struck eyes I did as a teenager. But working the investigation had enslaved parts of her that used to share light, meaningless conversations with me. I understood. I was the same way when I started, before I learned the importance of maintaining a balance.

I added, "I found out yesterday that Fats Gangel died of a heart attack in 2015 and Moe Brown was in prison in 2017 for manslaughter. Moe fired a gun in the air at a rave held inside an industrial building. The bullet ricocheted off a beam and killed one of the ravers. Darko Dice ate his gun in May of 2017." Three more names crossed off our list.

Serena bit her lip, "The lives of these people are all so tragic. I'd like to interview Blaze's sister, Deb Zion," she circled Deb's name, "but she told me, the one time we spoke, with everything that's happened in Minneapolis over the last couple years, 'It's a bad time for a white investigator to be asking for help from an African American woman.' She said, 'Come to a Black Lives Matter rally and we'll talk.' I told her I understood, but I'm not going anywhere until COVID dies down."

"I'm not sure Deb has much to offer us. They were estranged for months when Billy disappeared." I offered, "I think I might know which of these characters was our undercover agent."

Serena continued to stare at the list of names. I wasn't sure if she heard me.

She finally turned to me, "Are you going to tell me?"

"There were no conversations between Robert Johnson and the undercover agent. The agent never even quotes him. I think Rob *is* the undercover DEA officer interloping with this group. I shared my theory with Tony, hoping to get a reaction, but he's hard to read over the phone."

Her troubled thoughts remained elsewhere.

I added, "I'd like you to ask Trisha if she ever went to a crack house with Rob. The undercover agent talked about going to a crack house with Trisha and Blaze." I stopped and took her hand. "What are you thinking? I know you well enough to see when something's bothering you."

Serena's green eyes met mine, "It was painful making love with you last night."

"I'm sorry. You should have told me." I remembered the moment. I was going to pull away and she held me close.

"It started wonderful, but then all of a sudden my body just tightened. And I'm sore today."

I softly told her, "I never want to hurt you. Tell me." I felt terrible.

"I honestly thought it would be over in a flash. I think my conversations with Trisha brought stuff back. You know with mirror neurons and all."

We have mirror neurons in our body that allow us to experience what someone is telling us, to varying degrees. Someone as compassionate as Serena likely connects very well with others—in Trisha's case, too well. You couldn't afford to connect too deeply in the moment you were addressing abuse in an investigation, or it started messing with your head. She was referring to the psychological concept of erotic plasticity, or the degree to which one's sex drive can be altered by environmental influences. Sometimes, simply the way something was said could fire a neuron, which connected with other neurons in our brain related to an experience. It has also been called physiological memory or associative memory.

Serena's conversations with Trisha seemed to have taken a toll on her. "Do you want me to deal with Trisha in the future?"

She dismissed this, "There is so much trauma with everyone involved in this case. Anyone I talk to could trigger flashbacks. And we're dealing with this at a time when I fear, every night, you could bring home a virus that could kill our kids, you, our parents, me."

I hugged my wife. She had left me in the past, because

symptoms of her trauma kept coming back. I couldn't lose her again.

She released the hug and said, "Back to work."

I suggested, "Why don't you take a few days off and see how you feel, then."

My phone buzzed.

Tony Shileto shared, "I spoke to the informant and he warned you're wading into dangerous waters. There's a killer in this crew, so tread carefully. Maybe even a serial killer. There was a rumor about some dead girls, but he got nothing but crickets when he asked about them. Along with Blaze, you've got Darko Dice, Keith Stewart, Riezig 'Zig' Ziegler, and Gunner Black—all dangerous. Have you met any of them yet?"

"Not face-to-face, but I know who they are. Darko shot himself a few months before Blaze disappeared."

Tony paused. "Interesting."

I shared, "Stewart was offering up juvenile females and later using recordings of the encounters for blackmail."

"It wasn't just blackmail," he interrupted. "There are pervs who pay up to two grand for a night with clean, under-age girls. It's big risk, but big money. The DEA knows about Stewart, but they've never been able to prove anything. He only has girls there who aren't reported as runaways. There have been calls by concerned citizens, but the girls deny anything illegal going on, so nothing ever comes of it. Our inside guy referred to Stewart's driveway as *Lolita Lane*."

Tony added, "Gunner Black and Billy Blaze had some knock-down, drag-out fights. Blaze always had to one-up Gunner and that had to get old. Blaze eventually treated them all—friends and enemies—like trash. Any one of them could have killed Blaze. It was a dangerous gig and our inside guy was glad to get out."

I asked, "What did he know about Margo Miller?"

"He thought she was a little paranoid—but in his case, I guess it was justified. He described her as the successful, professional female version of Blaze. Cold and callous, but she performed as poised and polite in the presence of the right people. Margo viewed herself as the puppet master, but it was more that Blaze happened to be moving in the direction she desired at the time. He said no one controlled him. He was adept at knowing what women wanted to hear—at least in the short-term."

"Tell me about Trisha Lake."

"Trisha cost him the gig. The informant wanted to save her. Trisha told him Blaze had raped her one night when she was drunk. The next time they spoke, she denied it. His gut feeling was Blaze did rape her, but she found a way to convince herself it was her fault. Trisha wasn't ready to be rescued. Blaze got his hooks into women and the hooks didn't come out until he had destroyed them."

I hesitated before asking, "I need to know who Billy Blaze ratted on in 1998, to avoid the assault and weapons charges. That person was likely back out of prison in 2017."

"Wasn't it in the file?"

"It was redacted. You know I won't let it come back to you."

After a long pause, Tony said, "Riezig Ziegler."

# 15

*I sat there at the table, and acted real naïve*
*For I knew that topless lady, had something up her sleeve*
*She danced around the bar room, and she did the hoochy-coo*
*She sang her song, all night long, tellin' me what to do*
*Blow up your TV. Throw away your paper*
*Go to the country. Build you a home*
*Plant a little garden. Eat a lot of peaches*
*Try and find Jesus, on your own*
—JOHN PRINE, *SPANISH PIPEDREAM*

## JON FREDERICK

### 10:00 A.M., THURSDAY, APRIL 30, 2020
### PIERZ

The COVID-19 numbers were starting to skyrocket. We had a record of new daily cases in Minnesota (+463).

Harper wore a mask into the command center today. I asked her if she thought she had the coronavirus and Serena asked if she visited Greg. Harper responded no to both questions, so we left it at that.

### 1:30 P.M., PAUL BUNYAN STATE FOREST, BEMIDJI

HARPER AND I WERE HEADED TO the Gulch Lake Forest Trail, in Paul Bunyan State Forest South of Bemidji. The trail was located on Leech Lake Reservation near Laporte, Minnesota.

In the early 1900s, Laporte was a prospering small town with a pickle factory and a jail. The pickle factory burned down and the jail only had one inmate, who escaped through the roof. Today, Laporte was less than half its former size, at one hundred eleven people, and I imagined the locals could name them all.

Moki Hunter was late for our meeting, so Harper and I, wearing our masks, stopped at Laporte Grocery and Meats, the Knob and Kettle Restaurant, and the Popple Bar. No one knew of Billy Blaze and he was a guy people tended to remember.

When Moki arrived, he hopped in his car and we followed him to a ditch a few miles away, west of Kabekona.

If Blaze drove here from St. Cloud, this location would suggest he took 71 North, rather than 371. It was faster, but less well known. It was a road someone from northern Minnesota would be more likely to take. I wasn't sure if it meant anything. It was just one of those pieces you stored in an investigation.

Moki was carrying a small notebook and, while studying his phone, waved us to follow him on foot. He apologized for not wearing a mask, "I thought we'd be far enough apart."

We were. I removed mine and said, "What were you doing out here?"

He gestured toward the old logging path. "I was told there were morel mushrooms in this area. There were, so I marked the coordinates in my notebook." He pointed to the base of an old ash tree. With a smile he said, "And they're back." He retrieved a plastic bag from his pocket and eagerly began collecting the sporous fungi.

Harper joined him and studied his find, teasing, "With your knowledge of wild food, your spiritual faith, and your wisdom, you could live an enlightened existence in the wilderness. Walden Three. First Thoreau, then Skinner, and now Hunter."

Moki remarked, "Assuming I'd want to live alone in a shack."

I asked, "Where was the billfold?"

"Right over there." He pointed about six feet from where we stood.

I searched the area, but found nothing else.

Moki and Harper joined me.

Moki said, "There were cash and credit cards in the billfold. I was seventeen, at the time, and I saw the card as a solution to my desire for new hunting gear. It was stupid."

I couldn't help noticing Harper had no questions for Moki. It was as if she already knew what he was going to say.

I asked, "How much cash?"

Moki's eyes met mine, "A couple hundred dollars."

Blaze wasn't robbed. "Have you ever met Billy Blaze?"

"Never."

"How did you get caught?"

Harper interrupted, "Why does that matter?"

"I want to know if Blaze reported the fraud. Credit card companies often call if you make a major purchase far away from your billing zip code."

Moki offered, "I went back to Reeds Outdoor Outfitters in Walker and told them what I did. They appreciated my honesty, but they still had to report it."

I gave him credit. "A man of honor. I respect that."

Harper grinned.

I directed, "Well, let's split up and look around."

Moki's eyes widened with realization. "You're looking for a body . . ."

# 16

*I bought the rights to the inside fights*
*And watched a man, just beating*
*his hand against a storm window*
*While miles away o'er hills and streams*
*A candle burns—A witch's dream*
*Silence is golden till it screams*
*Right through your bones*
*Don't let your baby down*
—JOHN PRINE, STORM WINDOWS

## HARPER ROWE

10:15 P.M., FRIDAY, MAY 1, 2020
BIRCHMONDT DRIVE NORTHEAST,
WEST SIDE OF LAKE BEMIDJI, BEMIDJI

Moki called tonight. I grinned so hard during our conversation, my cheeks hurt. He gave me grief about constantly reminding him of what a hero Greg and all of our healthcare workers had been, during this pandemic. He teased, "So, how are white women doing?"

"Well, I'm sure I can speak for everyone, when I say lonely as hell. But the good news is alcohol sales are up. They are a vital industry."

"Eat healthy. Wash your produce, but eat fresh fruit and vegetables. You must have heard that sage advice, 'An apple a day keeps the doctor away.'"

I added, "An apple a day keeps anyone away, if you throw it hard enough."

"I make an amazing morel mushroom and asparagus dish."

It was always a small trigger that sent my thoughts into a dark place. The neural train in my brain went from looking for morel mushrooms in the woods, to looking for a body, to the possibility of Greg dying, and tripcocked at Mom's death.

I muttered, "I could be a Disney princess."

"Um, what?"

"Almost all of the Disney Princesses have dead mothers."

"Hey, hey, hey. This calls for an emergency dessert. I will deliver it tonight."

"You can't come here tonight. And I have my Greg time, yet."

"I won't come *in*," he assured me quickly. "It'll take me a couple of hours. I'll just leave it on your window sill. Okay, let's talk about something else. What do you think about Columbus?"

I started laughing. "Now that's a nice noncontroversial thing for a Native and a white person to casually discuss."

Moki said, "In a sense, it is."

I decided to play along. "Okay. I honestly haven't done a lot of research into Columbus. The holiday never made sense. There were people living here when he arrived. So obviously, a Native deserves credit for discovering America. If they really wanted to give a white person credit, Leif Erikson landed in Newfoundland, Canada, in 1001, about five hundred years earlier. Other than Jesus, Columbus is the only person who didn't live in the U.S., who has a holiday honoring him, and there's no comparison. Columbus landed in modern day El Salvador and lived in Haiti, if I remember correctly."

Moki agreed with my logic, "All good arguments. Do you want to hear better ones?"

"Sure."

He let me off easy for my ignorance. "Some of this information didn't become available until 2006, when Spain opened up archives. Columbus wrote a letter to a friend describing how he was *given* a Native prisoner to have sex with and, when she fought him off, he whipped her with rope until she complied. He bragged that, when he was done with her, he got her to act like she'd been brought up in a school for whores."

It made me sick to my stomach.

Moki continued, "When his brother, Bartelomo, heard a woman had accused Columbus of being of lowly birth, Bartelomo had her marched through the streets naked and had her tongue cut off. Columbus thanked him for defending the family name. Columbus had a Native man's nose and ears cut off for stealing corn. The stories go on and on. He made the Taino Natives work in gold mines for him, when they should have been harvesting, and a large number starved to death." Moki's voice cracked in despair, as he finished. "Within only decades of his arrival, it's estimated that eighty-five percent of the Taino Natives were dead."

I could only say, "I'm sorry." I wanted to hug him.

"It's not your fault. Can you imagine how hurtful it is to see this man celebrated, year after year?"

"I'm so sorry, Moki, for being so ignorant."

"I just want you to be educated, so you know why I feel so strongly about this."

"Well, now I do, too." I jumped in. "If you don't mind, I'd like to ask if you know why the Native woman was removed from the Land O'Lakes butter logo. I hope I'm not being insulting. I want to understand racial issues better."

"While a Native group applauded getting rid of the stereotypical picture, I didn't agree with it. The drawing was redone by a Native named Patrick DesJarlait, who was one of the very few Native illustrators in advertising. She's on her knees offering butter, with beautiful lake scenery in the background. I was never insulted and never read anything into it. Should women who live by the sea be insulted by the Starbucks logo, or should white people be insulted with companies that feature pioneers? I feel like we have enough real issues to focus on."

"The original Starbucks logo featured a mermaid with bare breasts."

"Okay, maybe you should be insulted."

"They fixed it, so it's a non-issue, now."

Moki cracked, "I tried *I Can't Believe It's Not Butter* on my toast this morning."

"How was it?"

"Unbelievable." He chuckled, "The jokes get better."

"I do understand why North Dakota abandoned the Fighting Sioux moniker. Sioux was a derogatory word meaning *snake*, given to the tribe by their enemies."

Moki was on a roll. "They could've changed the spelling to S-U-E, and named the Fighting Sue after a domestically abusive man, if they wanted a similar level of disrespect."

"Let's be happy they went with Hawks."

I SPENT THE REST OF MY Friday night watching Greg struggle with sleep. His throat was too sore to talk, but I begged him to let me see him. So, he stood his phone up and I watched him suffer while nurses stepped in trying to cool down his high temp. Greg worked in a hospital to give others hope. Now I was hoping and praying for him.

I close-captioned the news, so I could hear Greg's every breath. Another new record for new coronavirus cases in Minnesota (+594). Almost one-fifth of cases in Minnesota, now, were comprised of healthcare workers. As my tired eyes began to give in to the weight of sleep, I caught the glow of a small flame outside. A candle was nestled into a hot lava cake on my window sill. The dark, melting chocolate glistened. Its rich, earthy cocoa aroma and creamy texture enhanced its sweet, heavenly taste. Now, that was a friend . . .

# 17

*I hope you don't*
*Do like I do*
*And ever fall in love with someone like you*
*Cause if you fell*
*Just like I did*
*You'd probably walk around*
*the block like a little kid*
*But kids don't know*
*They can only guess*
*How hard it is*
*To wish you happiness*
—JOHN PRINE, *ALL THE BEST*

## JON FREDERICK

11: 45 P.M., FRIDAY, MAY 1, 2020
RIVERSIDE DRIVE SOUTHEAST, ST. CLOUD

Voice shaking, Connie Berg called me to report a man was lingering on the edge of her property. I immediately raced to St. Cloud.

Dreadful apprehension had exhausted Connie. Her husband, Steve, had returned from his shift minutes before I arrived and was comforting her.

Wrung out, she said, "I don't wish any harm to Billy. I just want to be left alone."

Steve asked me, "If you can stay with Connie for fifteen minutes, I'll shower, quick. I work in a nursing home and we're trying to minimize any cross contamination."

Connie walked outside into the cold night and guided me to the window. It had been damp, but didn't rain today, which made the ground soft enough to leave a full shoe print. I had brought the kit with me and poured the plaster. Fortunately, Blaze had left a size ten shoe print on Loni Thompson's door a couple decades ago.

She sighed, "You know, there was a moment I was happy with Billy. But you only *have* a moment with him, and then it's over. Regardless of how you feel, you can't get that moment back, because the quest is over for *him*. You become something he's conquered. He'll take you out to play with you, once in a while, but don't you dare deny him."

Blaze had a destructive modus operandi. I suggested, "I want you to keep track of every date and time you see the stalker standing here. If he's driving through St. Cloud at a certain time every week, it's possible I might be able to catch him in the act."

Before leaving, I walked Connie back inside.

Steve yelled from the kitchen, "Connie, let me pour you a glass of Pinot Grigio, to calm your nerves."

I knelt on one knee and checked the size of the shoes her husband left by the door—size eight.

Connie looked at me in disgust, "You're kidding, right?"

I'd seen stranger things happen in relationships. I didn't want her to lose faith in her best source of support, so I told her, "This is just a formality. We both know who I'm looking for. I need to be able to say in court that I ruled Steve out. I'm pretty sure my plaster cast is closer to a size ten." I asked, "Can you tell me why Gunner Black won't talk to us?"

Connie shrugged. "Have you tried talking to his daughter, Rachel West?"

"She's not talking to us, either."

"That's too bad. I liked Rachel. She's witty and was the only sane person in that whole scene. Rachel warned me about Blaze. I wasn't ready to hear it."

Her revelation triggered a memory of a comment she made during our discussion of the assault: *Any sane person would have killed Blaze.* Was that a premonition or simply a colloquialism?

# 18

*I once knew a man who was going insane*
*He let love chase him right up a tree . . .*
*Now he has everyone's sympathy*
*I hate it when that happens to me*
*Dog bites man, man loses girl*
*What did he ever do wrong in this world?*
—JOHN PRINE, *I HATE IT WHEN THAT*
*HAPPENS TO ME*

## HARPER ROWE

4:40 P.M., SATURDAY, MAY 2, 2020
PIERZ

Serena comforted Cheryl Wicklin and apologized for having called her, before finishing what appeared to have been an unpleasant conversation. Clearly pained, Serena pinched the bridge of her nose and squeezed her eyes shut, for a moment, as she gathered herself.

I was so grateful they didn't ask me to call rape victims.

Serena finally looked up at me. "Cheryl said Blaze is the reason she keeps a loaded gun by her bed. But she hasn't seen him for three years."

My late arrival didn't help her mood, but Serena presented her angst in the form of an apology. "I'll only have a few minutes with you today, as I need to get back to the kids. Jon spent the day with them while I reviewed everything we have."

As if on cue, Jon entered the room, but didn't interrupt our conversation.

I explained my tardiness. "I visited my mom's gravesite with my grandparents this morning. I don't know why she wanted to be buried in Bemidji—she hated going back home."

Serena shared, "People want to go back to where they were raised for different reasons. Sometimes it's for family and sometimes it's because they feel something was left unresolved that they need to work through."

Jon interjected, "Kind of like soldiers going back to Vietnam."

"Which was it for you two?" Immediately after the words left my lips, I regretted it—*not my business!*

Instead of being insulted, Serena softened. "For me, it was a little of both."

Jon said warmly, "It's simple. When you love somebody enough, you go where they go. The best place I've ever been was by Serena's side."

She stepped into him and gave him a loving kiss.

As quickly as she had softened, Serena disengaged from Jon and returned to business with no segue. "We have Blaze's cell phone records. He hasn't made a call since the night he disappeared on August 22, 2017. His last call was to Gunner Black. According to the timeline we've pieced together, this would have been prior to leaving Legends Bar. We also have Blaze's report from the VA. In 1992, he was shot in the hip in Iraq. He received a prescription for Oxycodone, which he filled without interruption, aside from when he was incarcerated. He hasn't refilled his prescription since August of 2017."

Twenty years old and both of my biological parents might be dead. I asked Jon, "What are your thoughts?"

"It concerns me, because I think he was dependent on his Oxys. And even if he wasn't, he knew the street value. It would suggest Blaze met his end but, last night, Connie

Berg believed he was outside her home. I contacted Paula Fineday—a BCA investigator—she'll run the footprint I got through Soulmate, so we'll know the exact size and make of the shoe. We need to keep collecting data until we know with certainty. I'm going to take a look at Keith Stewart's house in Eagles Landing tonight. I don't know if it's related, but I'd like to see what's going on there."

"Is this the guy who trafficked my mom?"

"Looks like it."

I eagerly offered, "You *have* to take me along. My mom was there with Blaze. I have to see it."

Jon wore his reluctance like a neon sign.

I tempered the whine I could hear rising in my voice as I tried again, "I need to do something other than watch Greg suffer every night."

He warned, "I won't be getting home until after midnight. And I will be trespassing. I'm not breaking and entering or taking anything, but I will be wandering onto his property."

"I'm okay with that," I told a half-truth. "I'm up late, anyway."

Serena seemed to have the final say. "An extra set of eyes could be helpful. But here's the deal—you have to stay here, tonight. I don't want you driving three hours home after midnight. We have an extra bed downstairs I'll make up for you. You'll have your own bathroom."

Jon explained, "We have a king sized bed set up in the basement for the nights it storms. Instead of going down in the basement and wondering when it's safe to go back upstairs, we all just go downstairs and sleep."

The Fredericks drove a hard bargain. Resigned, I called my grandparents. They weren't wild about it, but I am twenty, so Grandma just gave me her *ways I could catch COVID in a friend's home* scenarios and, after I listened patiently, I bid her goodnight.

She didn't hang up right away. Grandma waited quietly and I eventually asked, "Is there something else?" I thought it was sad that someone who so desperately needed to hear, *I love you,* had such difficulty saying it. I finally told her, "I love you, Grandma." I made her wait, sometimes, because she never said it first. I needed to be kinder.

She quickly said, "Love ya," and hung up.

It was the best I was gonna get.

## 10:00 P.M., EAGLES LANDING, ST. AUGUSTA

As IS COMMON FOR SPRING IN Minnesota, it was a chilly night; thankfully, Serena sent an extra jacket for me. After driving through a pretty typical rural town, we were suddenly winding through acres of million-dollar homes with horseshoe driveways and large, meticulously manicured lawns lined with perfectly-spaced landscape lighting. The lights cast haunting shadows onto the street.

I thought out loud, "What *is* this place? What do these people do for a living?"

"Eagles Landing. Most are large business owners or doctors."

As my memory banks were kicked into action, I told Jon, "Wait a minute—I've *been* here before. My mom brought me to a house party in this area when I was a teenager. I remember being in awe of the Henkemeyer's home. They owned a lot of property around St. Cloud and were super nice."

Jon said, "Stewart's home is hidden on the edge of this development. It's surrounded by woods to ensure privacy."

He parked down the road from Stewart's house. The estates were large and dimly lit; there were no streetlights, so the sparkling stars in the clear night sky, light years away, appeared almost close enough to touch.

While I was thrilled to be along, I was uncomfortable about the trespassing piece. I said, "Jon, I hope you're not offended by this question. As someone who protected the law just last year, how do you justify violating it now?"

"I was a public servant last year. This year, I'm not. Look, if you're uncomfortable with trespassing, stay back."

I wanted to be a social worker whose morality was never questioned. Still, I'd been offered an out and I wasn't turning back.

Registering my apprehension, he gave me a kind grin and challenged me. "A man was charged with abusing a twelve-year-old he met online. Once he was released from incarceration, he was ordered to stay off of the internet and to maintain sobriety. His probation officer suspected he was setting up another child, so she found a way to use his Soberlink device to identify the presence of any internet devices in his apartment. She found a hidden phone and discovered he was set to meet an eleven-year-old child at a park that same night. The man was arrested. The child was saved. The Soberlink device *is* legal, but adding spyware to it was illegal. Should she have violated the law to save that child?"

It was an impossible conundrum. I wanted to say, *Yes!* But in the larger interest of protecting privacy, said, "I guess—no, if it was illegal."

Jon replied, "That's what most people say, until they deal with their first missing child."

I didn't know where to land. "It's a hard call."

"Here's where I draw the line. When someone abuses the basic rights of another, I have a right to check up on him. I'm not breaking into his house—just observing from outside."

We were now walking into the shadows at the edge of Keith Stewart's property.

Jon looked hard at me. "If you're still in, we're going to walk through the woods rather than down his long driveway. I'm sure he has security cameras all along the drive."

My curiosity was killing me. I had to see Keith Stewart.

The algid air had the feel of a meat locker. An owl could be heard hooting questions in the distance. Twigs and dried leaves snapped too loudly beneath our feet, each crackle causing me to tense. I would have been scared to death to take this walk alone at night, but Jon's steady strength and determination reassured me.

As soon as I saw the large entryway, I flashed to Mom driving us right up to this house. Without saying a word, she abruptly wheeled around the horseshoe driveway and left. I wish I knew what she was thinking that night. I remembered rambling on about my teen worries, while she sat in silence.

Jon and I crouched down and watched steam rise off the heated pool. He handed me his night vision goggles so I could get a better look. A teenaged girl swam about in a bright white bikini, constantly looking up to the second floor patio, her expression expectant, as if she was seeking approval.

A man with thick, silver hair stood on the balcony, overdressed in a white, button-down dress shirt with the tails hanging out over shiny, metallic-blue dress pants. I hated him at first glance. "Is that Keith Stewart?"

"Yes."

There he stood, cock of the walk, ogling the young girl below.

"She's Native," I observed quietly. I wondered what Moki would say about that. She probably wasn't even old enough to have a driver's license.

A sleek car came cruising up the driveway and we ducked slightly to remain out of view.

Jon whispered, "That's an Alfa Romeo Spider, four cylinder. It's an Italian sports car."

The stats were lost on me. "It looks expensive."

"My guess would be in the ninety-thousand dollar range."

The car eased to a stop in front of the house. A dark-haired man in his mid-forties stepped out, all business-looking; he tossed his suit jacket back into his car. Stewart appeared at the door, his shirt now tucked in, to greet his guest. The two disappeared inside.

Jon waved for me to follow and whispered, "Let's head back by the pool."

From the backside of the house, a second adolescent girl—this one wearing a blush-colored bikini, with thick golden hair draped down her back—escorted the business-man outside. Arm in arm, she walked him to the edge of the pool, surreptitiously looking up toward the balcony.

Stewart stepped out on the second floor patio sipping on an iced cocktail. He motioned the Native girl to get out of the pool. She ascended with the grace of a gazelle. The girl was stunning. Her lithe body was sleek and her long, blue-black hair cascaded beyond her waist.

Like Vanna White pointing out a new letter, the golden blonde directed the men's gaze to her Native counterpart. *She was just a girl.* Clearly accustomed to being on display, the Native beauty turned in a slow circle. Even from our distance, I could see the wet girl shivering and, as if in sympathy, felt goosebumps surfacing across my own skin. I imagined Mom's terror when she was sent, as a girl, to gratify a brute like Blaze. In contrast to my skin's chill, my blood began to boil. It infuriated me. I didn't care if we were trespassing, anymore. I wanted to see arrests.

Stewart disappeared into the home and the guest continued to leer at the girls as they conversed. He directed them to place their hands behind their backs and then on their hips, to pose for him. He took another sip of his drink and then told them to turn around, spread their legs, and bend over.

*What a pig.* Couldn't he see the Native girl was freezing? He didn't care.

When they stood, *le cochon,* as they say in France, or *the filthy swine,* as Grandpa would say, directed the blonde to French kiss the Native girl.

Jon whispered, "I'm going to run and get the car. I want to get the police here while the businessman is still present. We need to be gone. You stay put—I'll pull up close to the driveway and come to get you." Stealth-like, he slipped away.

A minute later, the front door of the home opened and three Doberman pinschers, barking furiously, made a beeline for me. I could've run, but they quickly made ground. I was dead meat.

I found the nearest tree with low branches and frantically began climbing. In my hurry, my foot lost its support and my shinbone scraped hard on the bark. I waved my arm blindly until I connected with another branch and gripped it fiercely to avoid falling. I repositioned my foot and fought my way up higher.

Within seconds, the devil dogs were below me, snarling and pacing.

I squeezed the swaying limb with everything I had, hoping it would maintain my weight. I could feel it bending. If I fell, those domesticated wolves would turn me into mincemeat. *Jon, where are you?*

The Spider's engine revved up and the machine tore out of the driveway. A low baritone voice emerged from beneath me, "Well, what do we have here?" He ordered the dogs, "Cerberus! Sit!" Their butts dropped obediently and they silently froze in place. He ordered me in the same manner, "Down!"

I also complied. It wasn't lost on me that, in Greek mythology, Cerberus was the three-headed watchdog who kept the dead from escaping hell.

Stewart looked at me scornfully, as if I was some pitiful creature. "You cost me some business, girl. I had an important meeting tonight."

He took my chin into his right hand and studied my face with a pocket light. I could see a skull and crossbones on the face of his ring. "Where have I seen you before?"

I said in my best naïve, girly tone, "I'm *so* sorry. The Henkemeyers are friends of my parents. We were at their house for a dinner tonight. They said you had this beautiful, heated pool. I got bored and thought I'd check it out." I pulled a pouty face and begged, "Please don't have me arrested for trespassing."

In a low hum, the Dobermans angrily expressed displeasure, muscles rippling under their sleek coats. Stewart scratched his chin as he contemplated my story. "Maybe." He gave my body a careful onceover, as he walked around me.

*Maybe what?* That wasn't an answer. If my mom was alive, she'd have torn him apart for leering at me.

"Maybe," he said again, "we should head over to the Henkemeyers' and hash this out." He slinked uncomfortably close to me. If he was trying to intimidate me, it was working.

I whined, "They've been so kind to us. Please don't tell them I was here."

The beasts' growls escalated.

Stewart turned to his guard dogs and roared, "Cerberus—stop!" They hushed on cue, but their lips continued to curl back, revealing fangs I didn't want to see up close. Stewart reached into his pocket.

*Oh, shit!* I took a step back.

He pulled out a business card, "Alright—but next time, call ahead of time and I'll give you a personal tour." His smooth baritone crooned, "*Only* you. That's how you can make it up to me. Bring your suit—or not."

In feigned appreciation, I eagerly nodded. He was so creepy.

Stewart reached for my hand.

I pretended not to notice. Instead, I squeezed the card like it was gold, waved it toward him, and started jogging away, yelling, "I've got to get back."

Jon's car was just out of Stewart's sight in shadows at the end of the driveway. I pulled open the passenger door, but was surprised to find it empty. The driver's door swung open. Startled, I bit back a scream.

Jon quickly entered, started the car, and drove away.

Trying to calm my rattled nerves, I asked, "Where were you?"

"I was only ten feet away. You were handling it so well, I decided not to intervene. I was afraid the dogs gave me away, but Stewart ordered them to stand down. It's better for us if he doesn't know you're working with an investigator. Nice work, Harper."

Adrenaline was pumping through my veins a hundred miles an hour. I could feel my heartbeat in my throat. "Did you call the police?"

Jon paused, "Not yet. I need to think about it. I won't tonight, because I don't want Stewart thinking you reported it. The guest must have been spooked when he realized the dogs had found an intruder, and decided to bolt."

"But the girls are still there."

Jon was clearly bothered. "I know. When the second man was there, we could've reported what appeared to be a transaction. What would we tell them, now? Two underage girls kissed by this guy's pool?"

I sputtered, "So, it was all for *nothing*?"

Jon reassured me, "This was a good night of surveillance. We have a pretty good idea of what's going on here."

I tried to recall anything useful that came out of my time alone with the letch. "Stewart wears a skull ring."

"That may prove to be an important piece of the puzzle." He looked uncertain, then noted, "But I don't see Stewart giving Blaze a beating, unless Blaze was drunk and Stewart had a guy holding Blaze in place."

"I agree. Stewart's too slick." I could picture his under-age servant standing behind him with a warm, wet towel, so after he hit Blaze, Stewart could immediately wash his hands.

Deep in thought, Jon was silent for a moment, before sharing, "Harper, you might be the key to shutting down Stewart's little shop of horrors. He's been running this show with his henchman, Zig Ziegler, for two decades."

I asked, "So, how am I the answer?"

"The charges Blaze avoided occurred in 1998, but they weren't officially dropped until 1999, which is also when he slept with your mom. With the blackmail, Stewart avoided charges, but they both threw Zig under the bus and Zig did over a dozen years in prison. I'd bet the house that Zig wasn't aware of Blaze and Stewart's agreement."

Jon was basically suggesting the event that led to my birth could be used to drive a rift between Zig and Stewart. Neither of us had any more to say about it for the time being. I finally asked if he minded if I called Greg, to just watch him sleep for a bit. By observing his affection for Serena, I knew he'd understand.

I was soon gazing at Greg, lying feebly in bed. He managed to say, "Hi," and then told me I should be home. He said he was feeling a little better today, but I wasn't so sure. He snuggled back under the covers and fell asleep. I felt a little foolish, since the phone was supported upright by one of the folds in the blanket, but I just watched.

A nurse's aide stepped into the room and checked his vitals. I was pleased to see how gently she handled him.

Greg mumbled to the aide, "I was FaceTiming," then closed his eyes again.

His phone had been knocked under Greg's dinner tray, but was still propped where I could see him, but she couldn't see the phone.

The nurse leaned over and kissed him on the forehead. *Okay, that's going a little too far.* To my horror, as she smoothed his hair off his forehead, she asked softly, "Have you told her yet that you got COVID from sleeping with me?"

His eyes remained closed.

She added sadly, "I bet you haven't . . ."

# 19

*Sam Stone was alone when he popped his last balloon*
*Climbing walls while sitting in a chair*
*He played his last request*
*While the room smelled just like death*
*With an overdose hovering in the air*
*But life had lost its fun*
*There was nothing to be done*
*But trade his house that he bought on the GI bill*
*For a flag-draped casket on a local hero's hill*
*There's a hole in daddy's arm where all the money goes*
*Jesus Christ died for nothin' I suppose*
*Little pitchers have big ears*
*Don't stop to count the years*
*Sweet songs never last too long on broken radios*
—JOHN PRINE, *SAM STONE*

## JON FREDERICK

2:30 P.M., SUNDAY, MAY 3, 2020
BUCKMAN PRAIRIES, 83RD STREET,
TOWNSHIP ROAD 328, BUCKMAN

Serena performed a reading at her uncle's funeral yesterday morning. We visited at a safe distance outside the church, before returning home. When in the middle of pandemic, there were lots of funerals; however, you only dared attend a few.

The death toll numbers I'm giving you are real people who were loved and cherished. Today, we found out that Judy

Riley, an important part of our Pierz community, was dying. Judy went out of her way to do kind acts for others, even though the recipients often never discovered the origin of their good fortune. She would ask someone to give another a good deal, because the person was struggling. We were losing people who simply couldn't be replaced. Serena and I vowed to treasure the intersections of time we have with the people we love. It was all we had. We decided to spend the entire day enjoying our children.

At least, that was the plan.

BY MID-AFTERNOON, BCA INVESTIGATOR, PAULA Fineday, called and asked me to meet her in a rural area, between Buckman and Royalton, referred to by the locals as Buckman Prairies. Specifically, to a part of the Prairies called *Peterson Pines*. Two high school students working on a project for their botany class had come across a body.

The warm, sunny morning had developed into a humid and ominously overcast afternoon. Among the acres of towering pines were occasional, *Keep Out* signs, posted on their trunks, assaulting the natural beauty of the ancient trees. I was now enveloped on a narrow gravel road, comprised of sand so deep and soft, if I slowed down, I'd get stuck. There were no houses or structures in this area, just untamed wilderness. A sign along the treacherous stretch warned, "Low Maintenance Road, Travel at Your Own Risk." Decades ago, the isolation of Buckman Prairies made it a popular party place for teenagers.

When I came over a hill, I saw the death squad was out in full force. The gravel path was lined with Morrison County Sheriff's SUVs, a coroner's vehicle, and BCA agents' unmarked cars.

I pulled to the side of the road and was soon approached by Paula.

"Deputies have been here since early this morning," she informed me. "It appears we are looking at Randy Vogel's body. This man had a prosthetic left foot, with the words 'Kohe Mondi' written on it, as did Randy. The Kohe Mondi is a mountain peak in the Kulan Valley. Randy was awarded the Purple Heart after he was wounded in action in Afghanistan. He was a father and a war hero. But he was also an addict. Randy disappeared shortly before he was supposed to testify against Billy Blaze. Rumor has it you are on the hunt for Blaze. His disappearance has to be related to Vogel's death. What do you have for me?"

I believed in helping law enforcement and Paula was a trusted colleague, so I shared, "Gunner Black had a physical altercation with Blaze in August of 2017. Blaze hasn't been seen nor heard from since that night and Black won't talk to me."

# 20

*An old man sleeps with his conscience at night*
*Young men sleep with their dreams*
*While the mentally ill sit perfectly still*
*And live through life's in-betweens*
—JOHN PRINE, THE LATE JOHN GARFIELD BLUES

# JON FREDERICK

1:45 P.M., FRIDAY, MAY 8, 2020
LITTLE FALLS BAKERY AND DELI,
121 BROADWAY E., LITTLE FALLS

I called the Stearns County Sheriff's Department and reported my suspicion that Keith Stewart was trafficking a couple adolescent girls. In order to avoid putting a bullseye on Harper—being Stewart had confronted her that night—I waited almost a week before reporting my concerns. When law enforcement checked it out, both girls denied any questionable activity. They claimed Stewart was a philanthropist who was helping with their career searches. The deputy left me with, "Knowing something is happening isn't the same as being able to prove it." I decided to focus on my search for Blaze for the time being.

I caught a break this morning, when Tony Shileto called from the St. Gabriel's Medical Center in Little Falls, to tell me Mara Berrara was sharing the same waiting room. He gave her my card and we set up a meeting for this afternoon. I was leery, as Tony warned me she wasn't "firing on all cylinders."

Mara and I met at the Little Falls Bakery and Deli to discuss Billy Blaze. I bought us each a mocha and Mara a chocolate whoopie pie, while I went with an apple turnover. We sat on the street bench, at opposite ends, so we could ditch our masks.

The emptiness in Mara's eyes reminded me of a once-warm home that had gradually been abandoned with the departure of each child. She searched the recesses of her brain for a memory, "The last time I saw Billy was last October. We had Thanksgiving together."

That surprised me. "You spent Thanksgiving together? In October?" I began to question her recall. "From what I've read, Blaze hadn't been seen since August of 2017."

"We celebrated early," she explained, "because Billy was going to Florida." With a blank stare, Mara appeared to be reliving a distant memory. "I had that turkey marinating in brine for a day and it was perfect. I made cranberries boiled in orange juice and cornbread dressing. The whole day was perfect!" A moment of happiness glistened in her eyes. "But the bad days with Billy were disastrous. He never ended up leaving and, by the time actual Thanksgiving rolled around, he had reverted back to the old, nasty Billy, and I had to get a no-contact order against him." Suddenly, her demeanor sank into despair.

While I didn't doubt the veracity of her statement, I questioned the timeframe. Mara didn't seem totally aware. I asked, "Are you okay?"

She nodded lethargically.

"From what I read, you received the Order for Protection in August of 2003."

Mara gave me a vacant look, "Is that right?"

"Yes. You were granted the OFP when you filed for divorce."

As if she was barely hanging on, Mara reached across the bench; her bony fingers took my hand and squeezed. "It must have been 2003, then—sorry. We only had one Thanksgiving together." She waved to a young man who had been observing us from a distance and he jogged to her.

The man asked, "Mara, what do you need?"

She gestured for him to talk to me, "Tell the man."

I realized the man was a personal care attendant. He told me, "Mara suffers from multi infarct dementia. She's had a series of strokes that affect her memory."

Mara asked, "What happened to Billy?"

"He disappeared."

She emitted crazy laughter, "Well good riddance. How long ago?"

"In 2017."

Mara eyed her whoopie pie with longing.

"Go ahead and eat it."

She raised the pie to her mouth, but then stopped and, with lucid confidence said, "You know Billy's dead."

"What makes you say that?"

She held the pie inches away, "Billy's like a tornado. All you have to do is turn on the news to see where he's at. You might go months without hearing about a tornado, but not years. If you haven't heard about him for three years . . ." She shrugged without emotion and took a satisfying bite out of her pie.

# 21

*There's a backwards old town that's often remembered*
*So many times that my memories are worn*
—JOHN PRINE, *PARADISE*

## JON FREDERICK

10:05 P.M., FRIDAY, MAY 8, 2020
PIERZ

It was Friday night, which basically meant nothing in the COVID era. Nothing was open; nobody was going anywhere. Harper hadn't been back since learning of Greg's infidelity. When we returned to my place, that night, I told Serena how the news was broken to Harper. In classic Serena manner, she spent a couple hours comforting Harper before coming to bed. Harper was gone by the time we got up the next morning.

Tonight, I rubbed Serena's feet as we watched the news. The New York Times reported that St. Cloud, Minnesota, was the epicenter for the spread of COVID-19 in the United States. Morrison County, where I resided, now had its first confirmed case. Statewide, we were at a new daily record, again (+617 new cases).

If this wasn't enough, Serena had been out of sorts since she first started interviewing people involved in this case. She was always loving but, romantically, had been uncharacteristically hot and cold. The cold was the bad part. More significantly, I worried about her. Perhaps I was discombobulated, too. It was easier to take someone else's inventory. There were so many victims in this case and at least one killer. Serena closed her eyes and, half asleep, enjoyed a deep rub of her legs. Respecting her need to quietly self-meditate, I mulled over the case.

If Blaze was dead, as Mara suggested, who was stalking Connie Berg? Maybe a better question was, if Blaze was dead, why pretend he was alive? Despite all of their resources, the DEA had no luck finding him. With the information I had gathered from the cold case box, I created a list of names of people who had motive to kill Billy Blaze. This was an important task since, with the vast majority of solved cold cases, the killer's name was found in the file. Typically, you were scrambling to find names for the list. I had more than forty suspects.

It finally registered. It was Friday night! I set Serena's feet aside and stood up.

Puzzled, she opened her eyes, "What are you doing?"

"I'm going to Connie Berg's."

"This late?"

"Mara Berrara was married to Blaze. She knew him better than anybody—and Mara believes he's dead. Still, someone's showing up at Connie's on Friday nights."

"So, who's stalking Connie?"

"I don't know. If someone's trying to blame Randy's murder on Blaze, it would be a good time for him to make another appearance."

11:15 P.M., RIVERSIDE DRIVE SOUTHEAST,
ST. CLOUD

MY PHONE BUZZED AND, SEEING IT was Connie Berg, I immediately picked it up.

She shared, "He's back."

"I'm only a couple minutes away. Call the police and stay inside."

A fog crept up from the mighty Mississippi River, misting over the street around Connie's home. The streets of this urban neighborhood were lined with parked cars, due to the limited parking in the area, but all were abandoned for the night. I parked in her neighbor's driveway and quietly made my way around Connie's house. My adrenaline raced as I moved from one dark corner of her yard to the next. I searched the bushes. Nothing.

I called Connie and had her come to the door to make sure she was safe. She told me, "He disappeared right after I called."

There had been a dozen unsuccessful attempts by police to find Connie's night stalker over the past three years. The river walk was fifty feet below her home and hidden by tree cover. I watched Connie lock the door, and then jogged down to the river bank. If the night stalker took the trail along the river, rather than walking through the neighborhood, he could avoid being spotted by squad cars. I'd bet officers didn't abandon their vehicles to make that walk.

At night, the waterfront in any city is dangerous. Anyone walking along the river's edge in tonight's thick fog must have found a way to overcome their fear of dying. A person just thirty feet away was invisible.

I headed north on the trail, toward the heart of St. Cloud, thinking this would be the most likely direction the interloper would travel. As I jogged the path, the cool mist dampened my face and adrenaline coursed through my veins. After about fifty yards, I saw a dark figure walking ahead. Had I finally found Billy Blaze? The experience was dreamlike, as if I'd stepped into an old black and white movie about Jack the Ripper.

I followed at a distance that kept him just visible, but still allowed me to slip back into the fog if he turned. This stocky man wasn't big enough to be Billy Blaze. If this was the man who killed Randy Vogel, he wouldn't think twice about killing me. In the back of my head, Serena's voice was urging me, *Just come home.*

The man stopped for a moment and looked back.

I quickly ducked back into the cover of fog. I waited, heart pounding as my internal fight or flight alarms sounded.

I heard a couple steps coming toward me.

*Do I confront him, or run?* It was safe to assume he was armed.

The footsteps stopped, and then trailed away once more.

I waited a few more seconds before continuing my pursuit.

The wind picked up and howled along the river bank. The footsteps were no longer audible, so I cautiously searched the fog for movement. *Had I lost him? Was he lying in wait for me?* I crouched down and found the breeze had opened up a space below the fog, a couple feet off the ground, where I could see clearly. I could see his legs walking away from me, still on the trail.

I matched his pace and his silhouette slowly came into view as he approached the city. The man walked Riverside Drive, under the bridge beneath Division Street, until he reached the urban city lights of East St. Germain Street. His outline was now visible in the haze of the overcast, damp night.

He stopped for a moment and looked back.

I crouched behind a parked car.

The man waited as I patiently kept his figure in sight through the car's windows.

Apparently satisfied he wasn't being followed, he headed east.

I watched him enter a home on 13ᵗʰ Avenue North in St. Cloud. I was familiar with this address. It was the home of Gunner Black. It wasn't a coincidence that Gunner, in his conversation with Harper, commented that there were people who said Blaze was alive—Connie Berg, for one.

# 22

*The coal company came with the world's largest shovel*
*And they tortured the timber and stripped all the land*
*They dug for their coal 'til the land was forsaken*
*Then they wrote it all down as the progress of man*
*Daddy, won't you take me back to Muhlenberg County*
*Down by the Green River where paradise lay*
*Well, I'm sorry, my son, but you're too late in asking*
*Mister Peabody's coal train has hauled it away*
—JOHN PRINE, *PARADISE*

## JON FREDERICK

10:30 A.M., MONDAY, MAY 11, 2020
BUREAU OF CRIMINAL APPREHENSION,
101 11TH AVENUE NORTH, ST. CLOUD

Paula Fineday called to ask if I wanted to sit on the other side of the glass when she interviewed Randy Vogel's former partner, Andri Clark.

Andri had just turned thirty-three. She was a wiry woman of both African and European descent, with dark skin and red, frizzy hair. Her race was significant simply because there weren't many nonwhite people in Blaze's circle. Andri was in constant motion, restlessness oozing from every pore. She sat in the gray interview room, her hands tucked in the pouch of her faded green, hooded sweatshirt. The pocket jumped steadily, as if occupied by a business of ferrets.

Her voice was laced with bitterness and pain. "I *told* the cops Blaze was going kill Randy."

Paula said, "Tell me about Blaze."

"Racist prick. He wouldn't even acknowledge me. Pretended to be Randy's friend, just to keep him using. Randy had two weeks clean before he disappeared. He came to me and cuddled every night, begging me to stay with him. Randy has a son and a daughter. He wanted to be sober for them."

Paula suggested calmly, "What was your last conversation with Randy about?"

"He called me from work on August 10, 2017, and told me he had to work overtime. We had tickets for *An Evening with Herbie Hancock* at the Minnesota Zoo on Friday, August 11."

Paula gave her a blank look.

Andri challenged, "Oh, c'mon, you must have heard of Chameleon by Hancock?"

"No."

"Hancock's a music legend," she explained. "Anyway, Randy knew how much it meant to me. He wouldn't have missed it. I later discovered he got a call from a woman, just before he called me, and he'd lied to me about the overtime."

Paula tapped her pen on her notepad. "Who was the woman?"

Andri leaned forward, clasping her busy hands together in front of her. "I'd love to know." She fidgeted with agitation in the hard plastic chair. "Randy was an Afghanistan war veteran. He cared about people, but he couldn't get the monkey off his back." She paused, "Look, I have no illusions about Randy. He struggled, but he was trying. I know what happened. Blaze got a woman to lure Randy somewhere and killed him."

Paula shared, "It appears Randy overdosed on fentanyl."

Andri adamantly stated, "He didn't use fentanyl. He wouldn't even use heroin—fentanyl was a death wish. Randy was slipped some laced meth," she stabbed a finger at Paula. "He wasn't available to testify and Blaze never got convicted. It's so obvious, Scooby Doo could solve it."

"Billy Blaze was in jail when Randy disappeared."

"Well, whatever. You *know* Blaze orchestrated it. The fact that he was in jail, itself, should have told you he was setting up an alibi. Blaze always bailed out . . ."

AFTER ANDRI LEFT, I JOINED PAULA in her office to discuss the interview. She sat behind her desk and told me, "It is difficult to explain how Randy leaves work and ends up overdosing in the middle of the wilderness, thirty miles away from his car."

I asked, "Where was his car?"

"The Toys R Us parking lot. The store had closed months earlier."

"So, the killer was familiar with St. Cloud and knew there would be no video footage in that parking lot."

Paula questioned, "Who do you think killed Randy?"

"I like Andri's theory—that it was someone working with Blaze, but he has vanished into thin air. Connie Berg's been reporting Blaze is stalking her at night. She called me and I followed the stalker all the way from Connie's neighborhood to his home on East St. Germain. It turned out to be Gunner Black."

"Do you think Gunner may have killed Blaze?"

"He seems invested in making people believe Blaze is alive."

Paula pointed her ballpoint at me, "Thank you for your help, but the BCA is taking this case over now . . ."

11:15 P.M., PIERZ

SERENA'S LEGS FELT PARTICULARLY WARM WHEN I rubbed them tonight. Deprivation had a way of messing with your brain. When hungry, I paid particular attention to food. Since

Serena told me we needed to avoid making love for a bit, I couldn't stop thinking about her. Work was the aniphrodisiac or, in other words, a force that blunted and quelled the libido.

I shared, "In the search of Gunner Black's home, the BCA found the shoes that left the prints outside of Connie's window. Gunner claimed they belong to Blaze, but wouldn't say any more about him. Paula said they'll test DNA from the shoes. This could prove Gunner's been wearing them."

Serena didn't appear to be especially interested in my news, but for the simple sake of responding, murmured, "Hmmm."

As I rubbed her smooth, sensuous legs, all the way up to her upper thigh, I felt the heat of a teenager who knows his only option is to keep the lid on his carnal desires. After I had finished her massage, I washed the lotion from my hands and returned to sitting by her on the couch.

With a sudden and mischievous grin Serena aggressively straddled me and plunged her fingers into my hair, eagerly directing my mouth to her sultry lips. We kissed, first softly and then with urgent desire. Her hips tilted and rocked against me and I removed her nightshirt. My lips, against the soft smoothness of her body—my hand gliding through the brunette curls that rained down her bare back—luscious. She slid down and slipped off my briefs and, with a throaty moan, demanded, "Look at me."

Serena lay back on the carpet, now warmed by our fireplace. I removed what was left of her nightwear and stared into her scintillating green eyes as she waited in anticipation. She pulled me up into a warm caress, demanding, "My brain can't escape when you keep your eyes locked on mine."

The intensifying heat between us was a force that could no longer be denied . . .

# 23

*Give my feet to the footloose*
*Careless, fancy free*
*Give my knees to the needy*
*Don't pull that stuff on me*
*Hand me down my walking cane*
*It's a sin to tell a lie*
*Send my mouth way down south*
*And kiss my ass goodbye*
—JOHN PRINE, *PLEASE DON'T BURY ME*

## PETE ROLFZEN

7:00 A.M., TUESDAY, MAY 12, 2020
KABEKONA TOWNSHIP,
PAUL BUNYAN STATE FOREST

It was a beautiful day in May—a perfect day to grab my Henry Lever Action .22, shoot some squirrels for supper, and scout out a new area for deer hunting. A trip down this abandoned logging path filled me with the same kind of excitement that exploring the Minnesota wilderness had given me as a small boy. It brought back memories of my Native, childhood friend, Omar Espeseth, and what he had taught me about scouting, hunting, and trapping.

May showers had the leaves budding. The morning sun-light radiated through naked branches, as the forest's canopy of leaves had yet to develop. Climbing each new bluff offered the prospect of adventure, just ahead. I was alert when traversing new terrain to the possible presence of old traps and snares left by fur hunters who had long abandoned the forest.

The smells and sounds of a forest were indescribable. You could feel the presence of the animals and hear the sounds they made when you were infringing on their territory. The birds were chirping, alerting other creatures of my presence. From my crow's nest view of the forest, I could see I was north of Kabekona Corner, but south of Kenny Lake. I wasn't traveling much further north, as there was a large bog a hundred feet beyond the hill.

A sand hill crane glided over. *Ribeye in the sky.* Cranes were a protected species in most of Minnesota, but not here. Best grilled rare so it didn't toughen up. Unfortunately, I had the wrong rifle along. *Preemies are delivered by a stork, but big babies need a crane*—a little grandfather humor.

As I walked along, I became aware of a different smell in the air. It was a scent that corrupted the natural bouquet of the forest. The odor of decay reminded me of the resurgence of timber wolves in the area and put me on guard; a wolf may have killed a deer.

Morbid curiosity drew me toward the source of the intrusion. The stench intensified as I moved west. Scanning the ground in front me, I caught sight of the edge of a beige-colored tarp sticking out of the dirt. You don't see straight lines in nature, so manmade products stood out. This was no timber wolf kill.

I found a large stick and tried using it to ease the edge of the tarp further up, but it was ensnared. I put on my gloves and, with both hands, gave it a big tug; it didn't budge. I braced my feet and, with one last, hard yank, the ground broke and I tumbled backward, still clutching the tarp's edge. Rotting skull and dark hair rose from the dirt, and the carcass was unearthed as I continued my backward trajectory. I stared at the find in shock, my brain trying to compute what my eyes were seeing. The carrion of a human toppled forward, face first—if you could call what I was seeing a face—it dropped to the dirt at my feet, revealing what was once a shoulder tattoo, stained into the tarp.

Holy shit, I wasn't expecting the Grim Reaper . . .

# 24

*Something, somewhere, somehow took my Linda by the hand*
*And secretly decoded her sacred wedding band*
*For when the moon shines down upon our happy, humble home*
*Her inner space gets tortured by some outer space unknown*
*Now I ain't seen no saucers 'cept the ones upon the shelf*
*And if I ever seen one, I'd keep it to myself*
*For if there is some life out there beyond this life on earth*
*Linda must have gone out there and got her money's worth*
—JOHN PRINE, *LINDA GOES TO MARS*

## HARPER ROWE

11:35 A.M., FRIDAY, MAY 15, 2020
BIRCHMONDT DRIVE NORTHEAST,
WEST SIDE OF LAKE BEMIDJI, BEMIDJI

Jon shared with me that Billy Blaze was dead and his body was found only eighteen miles south of Bemidji—where my mom was raised. Highway 71 South takes you from my grandparents' home to the site of Blaze's body.

Last night, I dreamed my mom had taken me to visit Billy Blaze, one last time. She didn't like the way he was holding me and he was making comments that, someday, a man like him would be using me, like he used her. After all, "The apple doesn't fall far from the tree." Mom brought me out to the car but, somehow, I was still able to watch her return to the house, take a handgun out of the kitchen drawer, turn, and fire. *Did my mom dump the body on her way home? Jon said people tend to discard bodies in places where they have some familiarity.*

The good news was Greg was recovering. The bad news was *I wasn't.* I tried to convince myself it was an unusual circumstance—he was working extra shifts and was lonely. My efforts to minimize his behavior couldn't dissuade my encroaching pain and anger. That *aide* was still talking to him, face-to-face, while Greg was quarantined away from me.

I knew I'd been difficult lately, with Mom's death and all. Greg was apologetic for the affair. He repeatedly told me he loved me and needed me. What cut the deepest was the fear of losing another person who made me happy. The floor had dropped out from beneath me and I felt enervated to the point of being feeble—and meaningless.

Yesterday was a record, again, for new coronavirus cases in Minnesota (+786). We were still on the rise and it wasn't ending soon. A week ago, Morrison County, where Jon and Serena lived, had its first confirmed case. Now it had nine.

And Moki had simply stopped answering my calls and emails.

Grandma knocked, stepped through the open door of my bedroom, and announced, "There's someone at the front door for you."

As I walked with her to the door, she said so seriously, "Don't go anywhere with him. It's not safe."

Alarmed, I asked, "Who is it?"

"An Indian."

I laughed at the absurdity of this, in the midst of all my worries, and dramatically clutched at my imaginary pearls. "Not an *Indian!*"

Grandma didn't know how to take my reaction, so I slipped my TOMS on and stepped outside, happier than I expected, to see Moki. After being greeted by a blast of cold air, I asked him to hang on and stepped back in to grab my winter jacket. *Holy crap!* It was twenty degrees colder than yesterday, with temps now in the thirties.

Once back outside, I confronted Moki, "What are you doing here? You ignore me for three days, and then just show up at my *house?*"

He was not happy. "Do you know where I've been?" Moki asked angrily. "I've been on a seventy-two-hour hold in the Hubbard County Jail, as a suspect in your *father's* murder. This is all because I showed you where I found that damn billfold. They held me for as long as they could without formally charging me. I have no idea where I stand with my college instructors."

He stalked toward his car, glancing back at me. "Do you want to go for a drive? I'm starving. I could go for some takeout."

"I shouldn't go anywhere. Wait—they locked you up?"

He threw his hands in the air. "Well, far be it from me to inconvenience you. I've been eating dry cheese sandwiches in jail for the past three days but, by all means, go back inside to your fluffy, safe, *white* world."

His emphasis on my ethnicity cut deeply and reminded me of our differences. I hadn't seen him this agitated and I wasn't sure how to respond. My grandparents would tell me to run.

Moki planted himself at his driver's side of his car and threw me a look that was as challenging as it was beseeching. When I stood frozen and speechless, he shook his head sadly and pulled open the door.

He was about to leave when I shook myself out of my self-absorbed shock and shouted, "Wait! Let me get my purse . . ."

WE PICKED UP SOME THAI FOOD at Tara Bemidji, which I insisted was my treat. I felt terrible—I dragged him into this awful mess. Following my suggestion, Moki drove around the north shore of Lake Bemidji and into the serenity of the state forest.

I hadn't considered that Moki likely had his fill of state forests with me, until he sarcastically uttered, "You got another body hidden?"

"I am so sorry." Feeling defeated and drained of energy, I said, "I swear, I can't do anything right, anymore. Just bring me home."

Finally, Moki's icy expression thawed, "That was supposed to be a joke."

That's all it took—the damn burst. I dumped everything—that Greg had cheated on me; that I loved Greg, but didn't trust him; that I missed my mom like nobody's business; how much I hated that I was lying to my dad by looking for Blaze behind his back; how sickening it was to learn my biological father was a complete ass who impregnated my mom when she was sex-trafficked. I wrapped it all up by spilling how I was now being blackmailed, with my own sexting, to help solve this horrible sperm donor's murder.

Moki stopped eating and was now a quiet observer of my verbal stampede of misery. After he handed me all of our napkins to wipe away my tears, he finally broke his silence, "You win."

Confused, I blew my nose before responding, "What do you mean?"

"I thought being the prime suspect in a murder and three days in jail was bad, but losing your mom, being cheated on, and blackmailed has to supersede it. Okay—what if you stop looking for Blaze's killer? You don't have to, Harper. It's not your job."

"And have everyone I know see the sexts?"

"What are you worried about? Greg's seen you. Your family will forgive you. And everyone else has a billion other nude photos to look at on the internet. Yours will soon be meaningless."

It was time for brutal honesty. "Even to friends like you?"

Caught off guard, his eyebrows knitted together. "Honestly, no. But only because they were never intended for me."

I explained my angst. "Every time we're talking on the phone, I'll wonder, *Does he have that laptop open? Is he looking at me?* I know you're a decent guy. Maybe I'm just being paranoid. I feel so exposed."

We were at a standstill. Moki was a beautiful friend, but I was in love with Greg.

Suddenly, Moki got out of the car and set his lunch on the floor in the backseat. He opened his backpack and retrieved his laptop. He walked with it to the shore of Lake Bemidji.

I stepped out of the car and called after him, "What are you *doing?*"

He turned back to me, "Fuck the internet and everyone on it."

He spun like a track and field disk thrower and his laptop spiraled like a flying saucer headed to outer space, until it finally jettisoned and splashed into the lake. He turned to me and bowed. "There. Now you don't have to worry about it . . ."

# 25

*I know a guy who's got a lot to lose*
*He's . . . kinda confused*
*He's got muscles in his head that've never been used*
*He thinks he owns half this town*
*He starts drinkin' heavy, gets a big red nose*
*Beats his old lady with a rubber hose*
*Then he takes her out to dinner and buys her new clothes*
*That's the way that the world goes 'round*
*—JOHN PRINE, THAT'S THE WAY THE WORLD*
*GOES ROUND*

## JON FREDERICK

10:00 A.M, SATURDAY, MAY 16, 2020
BUREAU OF CRIMINAL APPREHENSION OFFICE,
BRAINERD

Paula invited me to her office to sit in on a Zoom interview with Phoenix Blaze, provided I continued to share information with her. Paula had permission from the Minnesota Correctional Facility at Oak Park Heights to conduct this interview via the internet, with Billy Blaze's gang-affiliated son. She asked questions while I sat off-screen. Her cellphone sat like a beacon on the table in front of her, allowing me to text her additional questions.

Phoenix couldn't see me; from my innocuous location, I watched him escorted into the prison's interview room in shackles. He was wearing a standard, prison-issued orange jumpsuit. Phoenix had short dark hair and was muscular, like

170

his father, but also bore darker features from his Mexican heritage. Blaze reportedly stood a little over six feet tall; Phoenix's stats showed him to be around five foot ten.

He callously made light of his father's death. "Well you know *I* didn't kill him." He waved to the prison walls. "I have a solid alibi, with hundreds of witnesses."

Paula dispassionately gave him credit for staying out of trouble in prison.

Phoenix laughed, "I know to stay away from the hooch in this place. They keep an eye on all the fruit, because it's the easiest to turn into alcohol. The guys here are stuck making it with catsup and barbecue sauce." He mimicked a dramatic gag. "They dip bread in it to add the yeast. It's terrible. One thing I got from ol' Billy is if you're going to lose your mind, only do it with the good stuff."

Paula informed him, "You will not be prosecuted for anything addressed in this interview, so be honest. The entire purpose of our meeting is to gather information on your father's homicide."

Phoenix nodded, distrust leaking from his eyes like tears.

Paula asked, "Did your dad use meth?"

"My *dad*," Phoenix cachinnated. "What a joke! Everyone called him Blaze—including me. He was more like a guy I might have met in prison. We shared war stories and a few drinks when our paths crossed. And, to answer your question, he wasn't a meth addict. Instant asshole—just add tequila. Tequila and Oxys for pops."

I texted Paula.

She seemed surprised by my question, but asked it anyway, "Did he sell meth?"

Phoenix hesitated before clarifying, "No charges, right?"

"No charges."

"Dear old Dad bought about seven thousand dollars' worth of meth, a week, from me to sell . . ."

I considered the timeline. Blaze's money supply dried up in 2015, because Phoenix went to prison. Blaze seemed to have money again in the months before he died, suggesting he foundd a new supplier.

2:30 P.M.
BELTRAMI COUNTY MEDICAL EXAMINER
& CORONER'S OFFICE
1300 ANNE STREET NORTHWEST, BEMIDJI

AFTER THE INTERVIEW WAS FINISHED, PAULA granted me permission to speak to the medical examiner. To my relief, Dr. Amaya Ho had been called in by the BCA. She and I had worked a number of cases together, when I was with the bureau, and we had established a good working relationship. I made the two-plus hour drive to Bemidji to meet with her.

Before I could enter her office, I donned the N95 respirator mask she had delivered to my car. We would start by sitting in the conference room going over pictures, rather than standing over the body. We'd save that treat for the very end.

Amaya casually greeted me, "Good to see you, again. Paula tells me we're sharing information, here."

"I always appreciate your help, Amaya. You're the best in the business."

Without preamble, she dealt me a series of pictures with the flair of a skilled poker player—and the dead eyes to match. The photos started with portions of a body hanging out of a light brown tarp, wrapped with rope, and ended with the cadaver on a slab in the lab.

Dr. Ho didn't waste time, which was part of the reason we worked so well together. She explained, "Billy Blaze didn't die where he was buried. He was transported in the tarp and buried in the forest, close to a logging road. Blaze has likely been dead since he disappeared in August of 2017, although he could have died in September or October, and we wouldn't be able to decipher the difference. Changes in weather can affect the process of decay over such a long period of time. As far as the cause of death, he was shot in the forehead and the front of the neck, with a Smith and Wesson nine-millimeter handgun. One of the bullets was still in his skull. There was a trail of blood from his forehead to the back of his skull, suggesting he was supine when shot."

I recalled that Blaze had stolen a Smith and Wesson nine-millimeter, along with a cache of weapons from a home, back in 1999. The first scenario that came to mind was the gun that killed Blaze was conveniently in the home for his killer to use.

Dr. Ho held a magnifying glass to a close-up on the entrance wound on Blaze's neck. She asked, "Do you see the small feather?"

Trying for a moment of humor, I said, "He was holding a chicken when he was shot."

With no expression, Amaya informed me, "A goose feather. He was most likely sleeping or passed out when he was shot."

This suggested Blaze was murdered after the argument with Gunner, rather than during the course of it. I commented, "I didn't see any shoes. Was he wearing shoes?"

"No. Barefoot." She continued succinctly, "There was a study done in New Zealand that found you are better off getting shot naked than with clothes on."

"I'll try to remember that the next time I'm being shot at."

She gave me a fraction of a twinkle in her eyes. "Every item a bullet strikes flattens the bullet a little, making it more lethal."

"Please tell me you have DNA."

"The elements are hard on DNA. Most of it is rendered useless within weeks."

"So, the stories of DNA being discovered and used after a million years are exaggerated?"

Amaya clarified, "Under ideal conditions, frozen solid, or stored permanently in an airtight resin, it could be used for up to a million years. But we're talking about a body buried in a shallow grave, in a boggy area."

I implored, "Amaya, I really need your help, here. I still have about twenty suspects and I can't talk to any of them, face-to-face, with COVID restrictions. Many of the suspects already have DNA profiles in our records, as a result of past criminal charges."

The mask made Amaya's reaction even more difficult to read than her usual mirthless responses. "I can't guarantee you anything." She went back to the picture of the rope. "That rope is made of polypropylene, which is used for water sports, because it seals out moisture. It's possible that, when the killer tied the knot, sweat was sealed in the knot and I could extract some DNA, but it's a complicated process. Since the texture of a rope is porous, the DNA isn't concentrated in one spot. I'd use an M-Vac to suck the DNA into a filter and this would give me enough of a concentration to test the filter."

"What are the odds you'll find something?"

"About fifty-fifty. Killers sweat. It depends on how tightly the knot sealed the DNA. It will be weeks before I have the results."

"Please call me as soon as you have something . . ."

# 26

## SERENA FREDERICK

### 2:30 P.M., SATURDAY, MAY 16, 2020
### PIERZ

Thirty people died from COVID-19 in Minnesota, yesterday, tying the record for the most losses in a single day. I sat down for a FaceTime call with Trisha Lake.

She looked much better than when I last visited with her. While still pale, her skin was no longer ashen. Her bruised eye had healed and the swelling of her lip had receded. Dark roots were still progressing beneath her bleach blonde hair. Trisha's face was free of makeup and she looked healthier. She was living in a halfway house and participating in outpatient chemical dependency treatment, through Recovery Plus, since her release from the St. Cloud Hospital. She was in the honeymoon phase of therapy, basking in the revelations of her newly-found knowledge and excited to share it.

After I updated her with the meager information I had about Blaze's death, Trisha shared her purpose. "I have concerns about your marriage to Jon. I know he rescued me from Carlos, but when I look back, he was *crazy*." She rotated her finger next to her temple with big eyes. "I'm not going to get him into any trouble, unless you want me to report him—glass houses and all."

I bristled at her comment. While I understood the saying that people in glass houses shouldn't cast stones, she wound up to shatter my home with what she believed to be granite revelations. She didn't understand my house wasn't fragile—it was a fortress of hard-earned love. I told her, "Jon and I are doing fine."

Trisha was persistent, "Are you, really? Because I saw a man full of rage enter my house and then he said very little during the three-hour drive to St. Cloud." She allowed a pause, then said, "Let me pose some questions. Has Jon treated you like you're special—like you are the only possible one for him?"

"Yes."

"Has he told you, and only you, about his own history of abuse?"

"Yes."

"You're his soulmate, right? Only *you* can fix him. This is how it always starts. They develop your trust." Trisha went on, "Has he made you feel like you're the dominant one in the relationship, when the truth is, he just does what he wants?"

Jon had continued to work as an investigator, when I was working through my trauma, even though I didn't want him to. At the same time, I handled our finances. Walls of the imaginary fortress trembled briefly. Unsure where this was going, I answered, "I don't know. Maybe."

She raised an eyebrow, as if validated by my hesitation. Trisha continued, "Tell me about times he's been angry. What does he do?"

"He doesn't talk. One time, he was so angry he didn't talk to me for days."

"Doesn't that seem manipulative?"

I didn't bother to tell her Jon had just found out I'd slept with his best friend, before we were together, and was frustrated I hadn't told him. At the time, he wasn't sure if he could get over it, so he wanted to break up. Instead, I simply said, "Yes, but it hasn't happened since we've been married."

Since Jon no longer had a formal work shift, he got up with the kids so I could get twenty more minutes of sleep every morning. He started my tea water. We always consulted each other before making major decisions and I'd never felt my opinion wasn't valued. He never badmouthed me to anyone. When we were at a gathering, he turned and acknowledged me anytime I entered a room. He massaged my feet every night. I sighed inwardly. I had no complaints.

Trisha interrupted my thoughts, "C'mon girl, you've *got* to see it. The rage I saw in Jon's eyes that night—*crazy scary.* Has he ever killed anyone?"

I didn't answer. I didn't need to. It was in the process of keeping a man from killing me, years ago.

"Yeah," Trisha said, hanging on my every expression and ready to twist it, so it would be clear from her vantage point. "Somehow, that doesn't surprise me. They always get away with it, don't they?" She appealed to me, "Honey, you need to heed my advice. I've felt the hollow echo of hopelessness—the scary reality that no one's coming to help. You accept the degradation just to survive. You need to develop an escape plan . . ."

As she went on, I thought about how Jon had the same history many abusers had, but instead, became a kind and loving man. I guess it always came down to individual choices, didn't it? I had to focus on the information I needed from Trisha. When I had an opening, I asked, "How do you know all of this?"

"Abusive men. Therapy. College. Life. It's finally starting to sink in. There's no happy ending in this for me. That night Jon showed up? I had abandoned everything—even God. I just wanted it over."

"I'm so glad you're recovering, Trisha. You never deserved that—no one does." I wanted to comfort her, but I had investigative work to do. I didn't love earning her trust to just glean information; it wasn't my nature, but there we were. "Was Billy Blaze abusive to you, too?"

"No, not physically, anyway. He made it clear to everyone—nobody lays a hand on me."

"How was he emotionally abusive?"

Trisha waved an indifferent hand, "Just the shit he said and did." The flash of pain in her eyes was there and gone so fast, I wasn't sure it had happened. She recovered quickly and continued, "There was this girl, Cayenne."

"Cayenne Tiller?" Cayenne was the young woman on her knees in front of Blaze outside of Perkins and the woman he was caught doing dog-style on the trunk of a car in a parking lot.

"Yeah." She looked taken aback at my quick reply, but continued, "She was a hardcore addict. Billy would make her do sexual things in public for drugs. Stuff like making her blow him in the living room when he and Gunner were watching TV. He'd laugh and say, 'I'm helping her hit rock bottom.' I'd told him, 'You can't be doing that kind of crap, anymore. What will people think of *me?*'"

"That's sad." I cringed at her self-absorbed concerns. Never mind what was happening with Cayenne.

Trisha paused, "And sometimes, after she was done, he'd tell her he was out of drugs and lock her out of the house. She'd stand on the porch yelling, but what are the cops going to do? Arrest Billy for not giving her drugs?" I thought I saw a flash of compassion in her features, but it was also gone as quickly. She puffed up, "But I put a stop to that."

I glanced down at my notes. It was no use telling her that, based on the timeline we had from the murder book, she hadn't. "Whatever happened to Cayenne?"

"She overdosed on meth about a month before Billy disappeared."

This was close to the last time Cayenne was standing on Blaze and Gunner's porch, disturbing the peace. I changed tactics. "Does Gunner still talk to you?"

Trisha was quiet for a moment. "We haven't spoken for a while, but yeah, he would, if I asked. I've tried to leave that part of my life behind me."

Knowing Gunner wasn't going to talk to us, I appealed to her, "I could really use your help with this investigation into Billy's death."

For the first time, a genuine smile crept across her face. "It's been a while since someone asked me for help."

"I've created a list of suspects. Would you mind running them by Gunner to see what he has to say about them?"

Trisha paused. Finally, she offered, "I promise to do this for you, if you promise to have an escape plan the next time we talk. I don't know if you realize what you're asking."

"What do you mean by that?"

Trisha dismissed my question. "Never mind. Something good has to come out of this."

# 27

*Down through the years*
*Many men have yearned for freedom*
*Some found it only on the open road*
*So many tears of blood have fell around us*
*'Cause you can't always do what you are told*
—JOHN PRINE, *THE HOBO SONG*

## HARPER ROWE

7:30 P.M., SATURDAY, MAY 16, 2020
TALON DRIVE, EAGLES LANDING, ST. AUGUSTA

I turned off of Majestic Drive onto Talon, toward Keith Stewart's home. I'd bet he didn't have many eight-year-old Impalas pulling into his driveway. I, on the other hand, had a kaleidoscope of butterflies in my stomach, warning of the dread I felt taking Stewart up on his invitation. I had to see where my mom had been and, after my previous visit to Stewart's nest of inequity, the presence and actions of girls only a couple years older than my little brothers had disturbed me to no end. I'd lamented to Moki my concerns and, when I mentioned one of the girls was Native, he enlisted himself to help.

The weather was a surprising 63 degrees today, spring boarding from the dive it took in temperature yesterday. We had a simple rescue plan. I would drop Moki off down the road; he would hang close and call the police once I located the girls.

His stories of the countless missing Native females strengthened my resolve. This was a separate task from finding Blaze's killer, so we didn't see the need to inform Jon and Serena.

Before departing company, Moki squeezed my hand. "Be safe. Just hit my number and I'm coming. You don't have to say anything."

I nodded. I had given him my can of mace. He would get as close as he could, until he heard the dogs barking, and then bail. If they caught up to him, Moki would rely on the mace. *Simple is good, right?*

I left the Imp in gear. I didn't know if it was my dead mother, or instinct, but a prickling sensation needled down my spine and I began to chicken out. I so wished I would've listened to my instincts. Keith was out to greet me before I could abort the mission and pull away.

He was slicked out in a Tommy Bahama shirt, khaki shorts, and sandals. His hair was crunchy-looking, slathered off his face with pomade that clearly promised, even if he walked through a hurricane, it would remain entirely undisturbed. I took a quick inventory of the yard, but didn't see or hear any dogs.

Keith took my hand and guided me out of my car, which might have been a chivalrous gesture, if I didn't find him so revolting. His eyes traveled slowly and unapologetically over my sundress, making me feel naked. A carnivorous smirk emerged across his BOTOXed face as he escorted me into his home.

The entryway was bigger than my bedroom, with a gleaming marble floor and a high ceiling from which a chandelier dripped with shimmering crystals. We passed under an ornate archway into a kitchen that looked almost too pristine to even consider dirtying up with food. A plate of cheese and fruit was displayed artistically on the glossy, agate black countertop. The chocolate strawberries looked divine, but I didn't trust him enough to risk eating one. I politely declined the offerings. Keith then gave me a tour of his home, going on and on ostentatiously about the places he'd visited in Europe. The opulent mansion featured the spacious bathrooms and bedrooms only seen in movies. There were two bedrooms we didn't enter; I assumed this was where the girls hid out.

When the tour finished, we sat on a curved, sectional sable Giovanni Italian sofa set, facing a large fireplace. Having a mom who was a buyer for Macy's taught me to be keenly aware of *expensive.* Conspicuous consumption was the best term to describe Keith's buying habits—spending lavishly to enhance one's prestige.

Keith asked, "Who are your parents?"

"I live with my dad, Jeremy Goddard. My mom's dead. I didn't really know her." That was sort of true. I added, "My dad works for Central Lakes College in Brainerd."

He narrowed his eyes. "Didn't you tell me you were with your *parents,*" he dragged out the word, "at the Henkemeyer's house, last time you were here?"

*Shit!* My brain scrambled for an answer. I was so scared my eyes filled with tears. "I said the Henkemeyers were friends of my parents—and they were. I was with my dad." I sniffed emotionally, fanning my face with stiff fingers for added drama.

Keith gave me a disingenuous smile, as if this was to be comforting. He trod on, "The name, Goddard, doesn't ring a bell, but you sure look familiar."

When he slid closer, I jumped up and asked, "Do I get to see the pool?"

"Slip into your swimsuit and let's have a firsthand look."

After grabbing my bag from the car, Keith guided me to a guest room. I could hear the tinkle of ice against crystal as he mixed a drink in the next room.

I hadn't thought this through. From what I'd learned, he was likely recording me, so I scanned the four walls, trying to guess where I'd find the most privacy. There clearly weren't any hidden cameras in the glass of the large window facing the yard. I did a quick survey out the window and, with no one in sight, I faced the window and changed as close as I could to it. I'd have rather briefly exposed to Moki than have Stewart see my naked body.

Knowing a swim would probably be expected, I'd brought along my cobalt blue one-piece, in an effort to cover as much of myself as possible. I saw Keith exit the house below me in only a Speedo. *Yuck.* I cringed at the sight. He strutted around the pool without a modicum of insecurity, then dove into the water. I wondered if his spray tan would survive the harsh pool chemicals.

I bolted to the two rooms he didn't show me and knocked quietly on the doors of each. No answer. I tried opening them, but they were locked. Desperately, I shook the knobs hard and pressed my mouth to the small gaps between the frames of each, calling softly, "Hey, are you okay? I'm here to help you."

My pleas were met with frustrating silence. Knowing I was out of time, I finally abandoned my effort and went to the pool. Maybe the girls were out there. I'd have to be careful what I shared with Keith, as I couldn't afford to get caught in another lie.

Keith was the only one in the pool. Joe Cocker's *You Can Leave Your Hat On* played in the background as I walked cautiously to the edge. Mom used to say it was the "sexiest song ever," as she danced around, cooking Jeremy au gratin potatoes. The song would forever be tainted in my memories, now.

Keith swam over and reached for my hand, like I needed guidance walking down the steps into the water. It wasn't long before I discovered my fear of being caught in a lie was unwarranted, as Keith was fine just talking about himself. I was starting to grasp Serena's description of narcissism. I spent thirty minutes paddling away to avoid contact with him, as he continually invaded my personal space.

This game was exhausting. I finally propped myself on my elbows on the ledge of the deep end and, as Keith closed in, I told him with phony graciousness, "Thank you, but I need to go. You have a beautiful home and I absolutely *love* the tiled pool," I gushed, for good measure. "It's a work of art."

Satisfied with my approval, he said, "You're a work of art, yourself, doll. And a bit of an exhibitionist—I don't mind *that* at all."

I wasn't sure I could keep reacting appropriately to these revelations. I choked, "I'm sorry. I didn't see anyone out here."

Keith gave a lecherous grin, "You don't need to apologize. How about if we find a nice bottle of Pinot Noir and return to the fireplace?"

He inched closer into my personal bubble. I could feel his warm breath on my face as he brushed the back of his hand across my stomach. Revulsion tightened my abs. I dove down and kicked hard to escape being groped. Once under, I feared if he fathomed why I was here, he would hold me under and drown me. Panicky, I quickly swam toward the other end of the pool and scrambled up and out onto the pool deck.

Relieved to be out of the danger zone, I tilted my head and squeezed the chlorinated water out of my hair. I looked down at him. "I'm sorry, but I do need to go. Can I get a raincheck on that Pinot?"

He chortled at my skittishness and remained immersed, making no moves to get out of the water.

With a quick wave, I hurried back into the house. I rushed to the first locked room and knocked again. "Please answer. I can help you. I've only got a minute."

There was no response. I heard the swish of a sliding door as Keith entered downstairs.

I frantically yanked on the locked door, one more time.

I scurried to the second door and pressed my cheek against it, urging into the door frame, "I can help you. Please let me."

The door swung open and I tumbled into the broad chest of a beastly man who filled the doorframe. As I regained my balance and stepped back, I immediately recognized him from his mugshot. It was Riezig Ziegler. I took in his full, red face, pock-marked like he had a bad trip through puberty. His small, bluish-grey eyes were creased between thick eyelids and chubby cheeks, even as his physique looked hard as a bulldozer. He wore his auburn hair shaved on the sides and longer on the top, like some white version of Mr. T., without the bling. Thanks to his sleeveless t-shirt, I was able to see his arms, which reminded me of sausages about to erupt from their casings. His arms were tattooed with creepy mythological scenes. His right bicep featured a hooded, faceless man standing in a boat on a dark sea. The left bicep was a blonde woman with flowers in her hair and features much like my own, but her eyes were missing, as if rolled back in death. Riezig towered over me—easily six and a half feet tall.

The giant's squinty eyes stared intently at me, while he thundered, "Exactly *how* are you going to help me?"

At a loss for words, I swallowed hard. I came up with the best lie I could manufacture, while terror threatened to shut me down completely. "We were going to give Keith a surprise."

Seeing I was scared out of my wits, he said, "Calm down, Blondie. I'm just the help—psychopomp, by trade."

He studied me with familiarity, escalating my anxiety. I'd never seen him in person before—I would've remembered. I'd taken Greek mythology. Psychopomps were deities who escorted souls into the afterlife. This giant scared the hell out of me.

Zig turned sideways, giving me a clear view of the room behind him. A wolf pelt was splayed out on the table, with a brush and a bucket of soapy water next to it. More significantly, there were TV screens on the walls that displayed the goings-on in the bedrooms. Pretending I didn't notice, I said, "I'm sorry for bothering you."

He smiled, "Blondie, if you don't want to be referred for my services, I'd suggest you vamoose." He gave me a gentle shove backward and quietly closed the door.

When I turned, I had no time to register my relief, as Keith was right on me, wearing an open silky robe over his Speedo. He had me cornered in the hall and didn't look happy. He eyed me skeptically. "Are you looking for someone?"

"No. I didn't expect my room to be locked. I need my clothes."

His voice was now deadpan. "You dressed in the first bedroom." He hooked a thumb toward the room down the hall.

When I jigged to the left, he put out his arm and blocked my exit.

Trying for innocence, I giggled, "My dad says I could get lost in the bed of a pickup truck." Terrified, I ducked under his arm and squeezed my body through the space. This was no time for me to be passive. I hurried to the bedroom and pulled the door shut behind me, leaning against it for a second, collecting my erratic breaths.

Cameras be damned. I peeled my wet suit off and changed into my dry clothes, then rushed downstairs. I didn't want to give Keith time to review a recording of my efforts in the hallway.

As I hit the landing, he was right on my tail. "Why the sudden hurry?"

I turned, "I'm *so sorry,*" I gushed. "I'm staying with my grandmother tonight and I just remembered her aide won't be there to get her ready for bed." I rabbited toward the door. I needed to get out of this house.

Keith smiled with insincere approval. "That's very considerate." His expression turned smarmy. "There's nothing better than a girl who enjoys pleasing others."

Despite his casual response, he stayed right on my heels. He attempted to cut me off before I exited, but I yanked the solid oak entry door open, the doorknob banging into him. He grimaced as I twittered, "Sorry!" and hurried outside.

I reached the Imp and dropped gratefully into its worn and familiar interior. As I put the car in gear, Keith stepped out and held his drink up, toasting me.

After nearly peeling out of the driveway, I pulled over as soon as I was safely away from the house of horrors. As I gulped in deep breaths and swallowed my heart back to where it was intended to be, I texted Moki and he quickly emerged from the woods and ran to my car. I was so relieved to see him, I immediately flung myself into his arms, COVID be damned. I let him hold me tightly for a beat, taking in his calm and strength like a sponge, then pushed him away and threw the Imp back into gear. "That was crazy! Let's get the hell out of here!"

Moki was breathing hard and his forehead was shiny with sweat. "What the hell happened in there? You're shaking! Did you find the girls?"

"No." I sighed dejectedly.

"The way you tore out of the driveway had me worried you were going to leave without me." He laughed nervously and caught his breath. "I wonder if the girls are still here. Looking through windows from my vantage point, I didn't see anyone, other than Keith and you." He suddenly flushed with embarrassment. I realized he had seen me changing.

"That was for you," I winked. "And I would never leave you behind. You're too important to me."

He was so flustered that, for once, he was at a loss for words.

We were both quiet, mired in disappointment as we made our way out of the estates. About half a mile down the road, we spotted the Native girl flanked by three Dobermans.

I slowed down.

Moki asked, "Is that her?"

"Yes." I couldn't believe our good fortune.

Excited, Moki said, "We may save her, yet. Let me go talk to her."

Determined, but cautious, he got out of the car and approached her.

I powered down my window to listen as he introduced himself. "Hi. I'm Moki Hunter."

The girl's voice was hard. She warned, "If you take one step closer, these dogs will tear you to shreds." The dogs growled deeply as their bodies tensed into attack mode.

Moki stopped. "I have no intention of hurting you. I know what's going on and I'm—we're—here to rescue you." He gestured toward my car and said, "Hop in."

With a simple wave of her hand, the dogs relaxed and sat quietly. The young beauty planted a defiant hand on her hip. "What makes you think I want to be *rescued*?"

Dumbfounded, Moki looked back to me, and then asked, "Where's the blonde?"

Somewhat surprised, she said, "Shopping—she's leaving for L.A. on Sunday."

I ran to his side and told her, "Stewart did the same thing to my mom twenty years ago. This can only end badly for you."

There was toughness to her beauty. She scoffed, "And where am I going to go? Back to juvie or the rez? No, thank you."

Moki was hurt, but said, "I don't know where you're from, but you don't have to go back there."

"I'm a victim of ICWA," she pronounced it *ick-wah*. "I can't be removed from parents without approval from the Tribe, even though my house is a twenty-four-seven party. I run away to get a safe night's sleep, but I'm always brought back."

I knew she was referring to the Indian and Child Welfare Act.

Moki said, "The Act is intended to protect our culture."

I interrupted, placing a cautioning hand on his chest. "She's right."

He turned to me, eyes fiery. "What are you talking about?"

"When she runs, they put her in juvenile detention and, to get out of juvie, she has to go to a Native family. If there isn't one and there's no documented abuse, she's probably going home."

The girl nodded and her features flattened to stone. "I'm not going back."

Seeing Moki's confusion, I explained, "Let's assume there is the same percentage of decent parents of every race. The U.S. is only two percent Native. So, if she goes to lockup, what do you think the odds are that the next good family available to take her is going to be Native?"

She finished the sentence for me, "Almost zero. So, I sit in juvie until I agree to go home."

Moki turned to me, "How do you know this?"

"I'm a social work major."

He growled under his breath, "You're not helping."

"I'm sorry." I wouldn't want to go to juvie with COVID rampant in Minnesota right now, either.

Still, he wasn't giving up. "Stewart's using you."

She didn't flinch. "Of *course* he is," she said in the voice of a much-older woman. "At least this time I'm getting something out of it. Next month, I'm walking away with a nice savings."

It seemed too good to be true, which meant it probably wasn't. I wanted her to question Stewart's promises, so I asked, "Is the savings account in your name?"

She shifted her weight back and forth from one leg to the other. "Not yet. But he's turning the account over to me when I turn sixteen." She appeared a little concerned over revealing her age, but she was a tough nut to crack. "Look," she warned, "if you turn Stewart in, I'm denying everything and I'm running away the first opportunity I get. I'll end up working for a pimp. Right now, I have an end date, so please leave it alone."

Bewildered, Moki and I futilely searched in silence for an argument. My brain still felt fried from my close calls back at the house.

Moki pleaded, "You deserve so much better than being used by these overpaid douches."

I added, "There's a place called Terebinth in St. Cloud that takes in sex workers, until their lives are in a good place."

She rolled her eyes, "Sex worker, huh? *Everyone* pays for sex, one way or another." She turned to Moki and gestured toward me. "How much does she cost you?"

"A couple meals, a laptop, three days in jail, and a semester of college. But we don't have sex."

The girl started laughing. "I should be rescuing *you*." She signaled the dogs to start walking. "I'm going home."

She reached in her pocket and pulled out a brand new cellphone. The Samsung Galaxy S20 had only been out a couple months and she already had one. It must have been part of the *fast life* image Stewart portrayed of her.

In a sultry tone, she told Moki, "Give me your number."

To my surprise, he gave it to her.

With a flirtatious wink, she said to Moki, "We'll talk," and sauntered on her way, three attack dogs lolling at her heels, no longer interested in us.

Disheartened, I turned to him. "I'm sorry. I never meant to cost you—"

He sullenly interrupted me. "Don't—this isn't about you."

Without another word, we climbed into my car and headed back to Cass Lake.

I was ashamed of my self-centeredness and everything it had cost this kind young man. Something I said had created a rift between us—I *felt* it. He was collecting his thoughts and didn't want me interrupting with my feeble apologies. I owed him that much.

It was torture, having such a good friend angry with me. After five miles of tense silence, Moki softened and asked me to pull over.

He reached for my hand and I gave it to him as he tried to explain. "I just had a chance to save a girl of my blood, and I didn't." He rubbed the top of my hand gently before letting go, then turned to face me. "I need to explain the significance of the ICWA. From 1860 until 1978, Native children were taken from their families and placed in boarding schools all across the United States. Children as young as four were taken from their families on every reservation in Minnesota."

"Was there a school in Bemidji?"

He nodded. "The Beltrami County School was in Ponemah, by Red Lake. But Indian children from Cass Lake were often placed hundreds of miles from home, in Pipestone or Morris, so they couldn't run away and return to their families. The schools were run military style. The children attended classes in the mornings and were forced to perform back-breaking labor in the afternoons. Their long hair was cut short and they were required to wear uniforms—any of the clothing native to their culture was prohibited. The intent was to condition these children, who were essentially kidnapped, into abandoning their culture. My nookomis—grandmother—used to say, 'The Christians held our heads under the water until we seen the light.' It was all in the name of assimilation—so they would fit nicely into white society. In reality, they forcefully ripped culture and traditions away from our Native children." He hung his head in defeat.

"I can't imagine." It was all I had to offer. I couldn't wrap my mind around this; it was too horrific.

Moki's expression was that of pure anguish. An unexpected lump gathered in my throat. He searched my eyes for understanding. "Of course you can't imagine—how could you? If the kids in the school spoke in their native language, their mouths were washed out with lye soap. There were harsh punishments and rampant sexual abuse. Many of the schools had cells to detain unruly students. Each school also had its own graveyard for kids who died from accidents or diseases, like smallpox. Do you have any idea how deadly smallpox was?"

I shook my head, ashamed of my ignorance.

"Smallpox killed ninety percent of Natives. And these poor kids were often buried at the school before their parents even knew they were dead."

My heart sank.

Moki was progressively working himself up, as he continued, "Native parents were promised if they allowed their children to go to the boarding schools, they would be provided food, medicine, and clothing. Some were desperate enough to comply. Think about the impact of four consecutive generations of children growing up without family. The Indian Welfare Act of 1978 was put in place to allow us to maintain our culture. It finally allowed tribes to determine what happened to our children. It should be a basic right; it's a damn small concession for the damage done."

"Moki, this is so terrible. I have no words. I should've just shut up and let you handle it."

He continued, "It doesn't stop there; it brings us to today. After these children aged out of the boarding schools, they were dumped back on the reservations. Many were left without a sense of identity—of belonging. Are they Christian? Are they Native? Can they be both? Many turned to alcohol and drugs, like people do with trauma." He turned toward the passenger window, but his thoughts remained with me. "I don't expect you to understand. They say it takes seven generations to undo trauma to any culture or community. This isn't going away any time soon. I just want to do what I can to help in the here and now."

I respectfully remained silent.

After several minutes, his vexation had deflated. He shook his head dismally. "Nothing you said, or I said, was changing that girl's mind." He groaned, "I wanted to beg her not to be their stereotype. I wanted to tell her, 'You are so much better than what they made you.'"

I felt incredible shame, even though I personally was never a part of the brutal subjugation. We criticized Romania for creating so many orphans, but failed to talk about the damage we did to families, right here. I told Moki, "This is why I'm going into social work. I know I'm ignorant about so many things, but I want to keep learning—and help."

Somehow, a smile managed to crease his lips. He said, "Your kind heart is a tangible force. I feel it. I long to grasp it."

Moki had completely abandoned his frustration with me. I asked, "Why the sudden change?"

"It's not your fault. You and I are the same—hoping to someday make a difference." He added, "My dad would say, 'Okay, you tried one time and it didn't work. Indians would have never invented the suspension bridge if they would've quit when the first rope broke.' We'll return. This isn't over."

I lovingly squeezed his arm, "I love that you're so positive . . ."

11:30 P.M., FRIDAY, MAY 15, 2020
BIRCHMONDT DRIVE NORTHEAST,
WEST SIDE OF LAKE BEMIDJI, BEMIDJI

I SPENT THE EVENING READING EVERYTHING I could find on the Indian boarding schools. It reminded me of Nazi Germany—Federal agents busting into homes and removing small children from their parents. A piece of history that didn't get much attention was that many holocaust survivors were terrible parents. They were more likely to ignore their children's emotional needs. In their efforts to make their children tough, their parents left them with insecure attachments and, basically, sad. They never recovered from their traumas. I saw the Civilization Fund Act of 1819, which led to boarding schools in the U.S., as an attempt at cultural genocide. *God forgive us!*

My night ended with reading this quote from one of the boarding school workers:

> *The parents had a great love for their children and the little ones were very fond of their parents. It was heart-breaking for the children to leave their homes even though it might be a poor hut. Many tears are shed on the first days of school because of homesickness.*

After reading this, like so many Native children, I cried myself to sleep.

# 28

*One of these days, one of these nights*
*You'll take off your hat and they'll read you your rights*
*You'll wanna get high every time you feel low*
*Hey, Queen Isabella stay away from that fella*
*He'll just get you into trouble, you know?*
*They came here by boat and they came here by plane*
*They blistered their hands and they burned out their brain*
*All dreaming a dream, that'll never come true . . .*
*It don't make much sense*
*That common sense don't make no sense no more*
—JOHN PRINE, COMMON SENSE

# KHARON

## 8:30 P.M. SATURDAY, MAY 16, 2020
## HIGHWAY 6, BOWSTRING

Kharon is a ferryman of Hades, who escorts souls from earth to the afterlife. My role is not to judge or to bury; it's simply to start them on their journeys.

I love cruising Highway 6 at night—headlights bouncing off tar and illuminating black ditches. It reminds me of a submarine on a voyage through the dark depths at the bottom of the ocean. Once I get north of Deer River, I might not see another vehicle for the rest of the drive.

My current passenger, Lilly from Pengilly, won't shut up. Fourteen years old and she understands the world perfectly.

I was her age when I had my first sexual encounter. After my parents divorced, Dad kept me and Mom took the girls.

Once they split, that chasm was never crossed, even for the kids' sake. Dad pulled me out of school at age fourteen to help him run his auto salvage yard. His girlfriend's sister insisted I was home-schooled. Her wisdom was my only salvation. I appreciated her willingness to share her excitement of her literature courses. As for Dad's girlfriend, I woke one night to that drunk pig giving me a blow job. I felt incredible shame for years. When I finally worked up the courage to tell my dad, he laughed, and said, "I'm the one who suggested it." They say that kind of stuff traumatizes—bull shit. I told my dad, "Your girl is like Walmart—serves a purpose, but I wouldn't brag about being in her." I turned, walked out the door, and never looked back. I worked at the meat packing plant in Long Prairie, until crossing paths with Keith Stewart in the Red Carpet bar.

Lilly blathers on, "L.A., baby! Keith's printing out my flight itinerary as we speak. How's a girl going to get a rich, *Pretty Woman* guy in St. Augusta? Where would he even take me on a shopping spree—Augusta Auto Body or J&S Excavating?"

"Augusta Auto Body has eco-friendly paint."

With a childish giggle, she says, "Big priority for a hooker. How does that go? 'The squeaky wheel gets the oil?' Tomorrow, I turn over a new leaf. I'm out of cow country for good. My goal is to never see a sign that says *Meat Raffle* ever again.' "

The squeaky wheel gets something. Just because you've got that monkey off your back, doesn't mean the circus has left town. I can't stop thinking about Harper Rowe. I've seen the video of her lying in bed—at least a dozen times. Mark my word, Harper, one day, we will share this ride.

Lilly touches up her already over-done makeup one last time in the visor mirror, as she murmurs her mantra, "Nothing makes a woman more beautiful than the belief that she is beautiful." Feeling she has achieved perfection, she flips the visor back up and asks, "Who's the lucky man tonight?"

I grin, "One last adventure, with a man of distinction at a lake cabin, and then you're done."

She gazes out my truck's passenger window into the darkness. "I don't see any houses around here."

I take out my billfold and set three hundred-dollar bills, one after the other, on the dash. "Do you want to earn some spending money?"

She can't take her eyes off the cash. "I can't have intercourse before I meet my mark."

"Of course. I'm just looking for some road head." I know her better than she knows herself.

Lilly pretends to carefully consider this. It's her way of making the john feel special. "Okay, but don't mess up my makeup."

"If you bite me, I'll kill you. You understand?"

"No worries. I don't know what you did to Nitika, but she couldn't talk for a week after."

"You know how moody she is—she just didn't want to talk to you. Have you ever heard of irrumatio?"

"No. What is it?"

"I'll show you in a minute. For three hundred dollars, you need to lose the clothes."

With no lights visible in any direction, Lilly says, "Okay. It's a good idea anyway, to keep them clean . . ."

WHILE THREE HUNDRED BUCKS MIGHT seem like a lot, think about what I save on dinners, movies, and gifts. And the reality is, tonight isn't costing me a cent. While I never cared much for Billy Blaze, he was right about one thing. You get a driver's license to race a car and you get a wedding license to ride a lover. Anything else you want to do with her, you can do, and people don't seem to mind.

After she's workin' it, I tap the brakes and put my truck in park in the middle of the road.

She looks up for a moment and I tell her, "Remember—no

biting." Let's see if I can pull this off before we have any travelers cruising our direction.

I grab her head and begin slamming it hard into my lap. Rough elation—ecstasy and needling agony entwined—irrumatio. Just the way I like it.

She chokes and gags and attempts to push herself back, but Lilly can't overcome my brute force. The more she fights the harder I get. I grip her thick, golden blonde mane and use my elbow on her back as leverage to keep her under control. For a moment, I imagine I'm holding Harper's hair.

WHEN I FINISH, LILLY'S ENRAGED. SHE swears a blue streak as she flies back against the passenger door, hoarsely yelling, "Prick!" She pulls the mirror back down and looks at her lips, which are now swollen. Her upper lip is bleeding. As she quickly dresses, she warns, "You are so dead."

Talk about the pot calling the kettle black.

She grabs her cell phone and stares intently at the screen waiting for the call to go through. In her annoyingly childish tone, she rants, "Wait till Keith hears this. He knows my value. You're nothing! Just a big stupid ball of muscle. Even Nitty calls you *the beast.*"

I slide the wire garrote out of the door panel and wrap my hands around the wooden handles. I slip the wire over her head and tighten. Lilly doesn't have a lot to say, now.

She drops the phone and attempts to grab the wire with both hands. She manages to land her feet on the dash and pushes toward me. It's a valiant effort, I'll give her that, but once that wire's around the neck, it's over.

Lilly never quite figures out that there is no date. Keith was the one who asked me to shut her up. We give them free reign, provided they respect our privacy. Lilly posted selfies taken at Keith's home. The consequence for violating that understanding is severe.

*Okay, how long do you squeeze to get them to pass out and not die?*

Her body goes limp, and then I catch lights approaching in the rearview mirror. I give her one last tug, and quickly push her to the floor. I put my truck in drive. I get no rush from putting her down, beyond the comfort of her silence. She already served her purpose, far as I'm concerned.

An SUV races by my Silverado and red taillights gradually disappear into the night.

Okay, back to my golden blonde. I feel for a pulse. *Shit. She's dead. I was hoping to have her one more time at the cabin, before escorting her to the afterlife. Well, Lilly, those not worthy never cross over. They remain in the black water.*

# 29

*"Will you still see me tomorrow?"*
*"No, I got too much to do."*
*Well, a question ain't really a question*
*If you know the answer too*
—JOHN PRINE, *FAR FROM ME*

## HARPER ROWE

8:20 A.M, SUNDAY, MAY 17, 2020
BIRCHMONDT DRIVE NORTHEAST,
WEST SIDE OF LAKE BEMIDJI, BEMIDJI

Cold and gloomy raindrops wept down my bedroom window this May morning. Greg and I had a nice heart-to-heart last night. I told him everything, as I should have from the onset of this entire adventure. He suggested I turn to Jon for help with the blackmail and then step away from all of it. He apologized once again for forgetting what was really important to him. I did, too. Greg wanted me to be safe and he felt this meant me staying away from Moki. I was going to respect this, but for a different reason. I didn't feel Moki was a threat to my health, but I found myself struggling with feelings for him, while still loving Greg. It wasn't fair to Greg for me to continue communicating with Moki.

In my grief and loneliness, I took advantage of Moki's kind-heartedness and made a mess out of his life. He was a great friend at a difficult time, and now I needed to let him go.

When I finally went downstairs for breakfast, my grandparents quickly scurried out of the kitchen, leaving me sitting at the kitchen table with my dad. That was never a good sign. An envelope sat on the table, dated May 12, 2020, in Mom's perfect, cursive handwriting. The date certainly confused me, as she had been dead for two months, now.

With a stern, but concerned expression, Jeremy revealed, "Greg called me. I know I haven't been the best dad, but Blaze is dead now, so I'm all you've got . . ."

"Blaze was never my dad," I corrected.

As he went on and on, I wanted to strangle Greg. He had told Dad everything!

I countered, "Maybe I wouldn't have dug this all up if you or mom would've been honest with me."

Dumbfounded, Jeremy said, "I *am* honest with you."

"Really? Mom went to Billy Blaze's home with me when I was two. Did you know about that?"

"I know now."

I hurtfully spat, "As far as I know, Mom's still dead, so this can't be new information."

Jeremy glanced down, "Actually, it is. When your mom was quarantined, she wrote me a box of letters. Some are kind notes, others are things she never told me. Her instructions were to read one a day, for a year," his eyes teared up, "and then move on. I don't know that I'll be able to do that." He cleared his throat, "A letter this week revealed the visits." He pushed the envelope toward me. "This is an example of one of those letters."

I could hear my mom's voice, as I read:

*When I was eighteen, Billy Blaze offered me money to see his daughter. I'm ashamed that I accepted. The first visit lasted two hours and went fine, although I made sure I was at Harper's side every second. During the second visit, people were walking in and out and, once I realized we were in a drug house, I scooped Harper up and left. Harper never had contact with him again. Billy liked the idea of having a properly raised daughter, but he had no interest in parenting beyond being seen with Harper. He followed me to the car, bellowing with rage, "It hasn't been two hours!" I told him to keep his money and drove away. I know you must wonder why. It was careless. All I can say is, I was young and naïve, and I needed money. I learned that sometimes you're better off going hungry. Please know—there was absolutely no romantic interest in Blaze and no physical contact between us other than the one night Harper was conceived. And that shameful, degrading night was the worst of my life. I was so scared. I was manipulated by Stewart, but felt guilty over my role in manipulating Blaze, too. After meeting Billy again, I had no more guilt. He and Stewart are both psychopaths. Harper is evidence that love is stronger than psychopathy. Harper is pure love and my greatest gift from God. But Jeremy—you're right up there!*

I could only smile. It was easy to forget that Mom was once a young, uncertain woman, too.

Dad shattered my peace. "Did you ever consider that Kali could've killed Blaze? I loved your mom, but just the mention of Blaze brought about a fury in her that was hard to be around."

I'd already toyed with the idea, but ultimately determined the notion was absurd. Mom could never have killed anyone. I knew that with all my heart. "Why would she—eighteen years later?"

Jeremy said, "In 2017, we were notified that Blaze had signed papers giving you power of attorney over his affairs when you turned eighteen. Kali was furious. She spoke to an attorney and there was nothing we could do to stop it. She insisted she was going to give him a piece of her mind. I warned her not to, even made her promise me she wouldn't, but she did. I don't remember the exact date, but now that I look back at the date they're saying Blaze disappeared, it was right around that time."

"What happened?"

"She told me no one was home. Kali seemed to come to terms with it and moved on. But looking back now, what if he *was* home? What if he tried forcing something on her?"

Blaze's body was discovered only eighteen miles south of Bemidji. I wondered out loud, "Do you think there's a confession in the letters? You still have six months' worth to read."

Jeremy put his foot down, "I'm not reading ahead. I promised one a day. If it was up to me, I'd read them all, every day, but I gave your mother my word."

In melodic pain, I keened, "Don't read ahead." I sunk into my chair. "I guess we'll just wait and see. Please share anything related to me, with me."

"I intend to. When I finish, you can read them all."

We sat quietly as I reflected on everything Jeremy had said. How would Mom move the body? Blaze was a big guy. I had to ask, "Dad, did *you* kill him? I swear, I won't tell a soul, because I know you would have only done it in the context of protecting Mom."

Jeremy sighed, "No, Harper. I never met Blaze—alive or dead." Resigned, he said, "I shouldn't have even insinuated Kali did, either. I just want you safe. You could end up being trafficked. I'm a Marine. I know dangerous people and you're messing with dangerous people."

"I'm too old for Stewart's trafficking scheme."

"How do you know?"

"He's blackmailing people. The age of consent for sexual

behavior is sixteen in Minnesota, so he looks for girls just younger than that."

Jeremy pled, "Please, Harp, let somebody else solve this; you're not *trained* for this. If you want to be a homicide investigator, fine, but learn to do it right, first. A mistake could cost you your life."

He was right. I had put my life in jeopardy. Mom was smart enough to realize she was in over her head and bailed. I needed to follow her lead. I promised, "I will go to Pierz today and tell the Fredericks I'm done."

Jeremy came to me and hugged me, "Thank you! I love you, Harper. I can't lose you, too."

JON AND SERENA HAD BEEN SO KIND to me. I wanted to break the news face-to-face. After driving an hour south on Highway 371, the rain stopped and the sun found its way through the clouds. I felt Mom's warmth and love. I felt better about my life and I was more determined than ever to leave this investigation. *Margo, just do whatever you're going to do!*

11:45 A.M., PIERZ

JON FREDERICK AND A LANKY MAN with long blonde hair were in his backyard, building elevated garden boxes, when I pulled in the driveway. Jon introduced his brother, Vic, when I stepped out of my car.

I nodded and told Vic, "I'm Harper Rowe."

He scratched his head, "There's a famous person with your name."

I offered, "Harper Rowe is the DC comics Batman sidekick, or maybe Harper Lee of *To Kill a Mockingbird.*"

"No." Vic brightened. "Oh yeah! Mike Rowe of *Dirty Jobs.*"

He reached out his hand, but I told him, "We probably shouldn't shake hands, per coronavirus recommendations."

Serena had shared with me that Jon's brother, Vic, struggled with mental illness.

Jon informed me he and Vic were just talking about the case. He smiled at his brother. "So, your theory is they built a catapult large enough to launch a body, thirty-five miles in the air, unnoticed in the Toys R Us parking lot, and Randy Vogel randomly landed in Buckman Prairies."

Vic replied with a noncommittal shrug, "Could happen."

Jon shared, "I've built catapults in physics. You'd need to create some sort of chain reaction to have this much power. Even so, I don't like the odds."

He argued, "The odds are fifty-fifty. Either they did, or they didn't."

Jon suppressed a laugh and glanced in my direction.

With unrestrained curiosity, Vic turned to me, "What are you doing here?"

He seemed harmless enough, so I shared his candor. "Jon and Serena are helping me find the abusive man who impregnated my mother."

He pondered, "So he knocked her up and down. I'm lucky. I'm living with Leda. People warned me about her, because her last couple boyfriends are pushing up daisies, but she's the most caring woman. Last night, I woke up and she was holding a pillow over my head—to protect me from the virus."

I wasn't sure how to respond but Jon laughed, so I assumed it was a joke.

Jon said, "Let me put the tools away so I can watch the kids," and walked away.

I told Vic, "I'm trying to get my life in order, so I need to talk to Jon or Serena alone, for a bit."

Vic commented, "I need to get all my ducks in one basket, myself."

"Isn't it in a row?"

Vic replied, "No. You're a Rowe. I'm a Frederick. Are you in a relationship? I'm not hitting on you—I'm with Leda. Just have some advice, if you are."

I smiled, "Sort of."

Vic made a chopping motion with his hand as he spoke, "Jon taught me that talking about sex is like dressing."

I thought for a minute and responded, "Either get it on, or put it off?"

"No, I mean turkey dressing."

I couldn't help but laugh and wondered where this was going.

Vic continued, "If you want it, you just say so."

I teased, "And if you're too salty, you ruin it."

He nodded in agreement and added with a grin, "I yam what I yam."

Serena came walking out of the house with her two children and rescued me. Little Nora smiled up at me and said, "You sure have pretty hair."

"Thank you. I love the rainbow on your shirt."

Jon had now returned. Serena told him, "If you want to take over with Nora and Jackson, I'll talk to Harper." She nodded toward Jon and Vic, "It's hard to have a serious conversation when these two get together."

As I entered the command center with Serena, Vic walked away, singing, *"People say I've got a thinkin' problem. That ain't no reason to stop . . ."*

I TOLD SERENA ABOUT MARGO MILLER blackmailing me to keep me working on the investigation, but held back on my visit to Keith Stewart's home. I tearfully pleaded, "Margo has a ravenous desire to find Blaze's killer, but I just want out. I need to finish college and look for a job. I can't do this."

She comforted me and said, "You're out. Jon will handle Margo and we'll make sure you won't be blackmailed."

# 30

*He's got more balls than a big brass monkey*
*A whacked-out weirdo and a love bugged junkie*
*Sly as a fox, crazy as a loon*
*Payday comes and he's a-howlin' at the moon*
*He's my baby, I don't mean maybe*
*I'm never gonna let him go*
—JOHN PRINE, IN SPITE OF OURSELVES

## JON FREDERICK

4:45 P.M., MONDAY, MAY 18, 2020
ST. CLOUD HOSPITAL,
1406 SIXTH AVENUE NORTH, ST. CLOUD

I was leaning against Margo Miller's black Mercedes Benz when her shift ended at work. I was immediately struck by her wicked beauty as she approached me. Margo looked expensive. Of course she had a Benz. She walked confidently on impractical heels, hands in the pockets of a black trench coat, belted snugly around a narrow waist. Her blood red lipstick and makeup looked like she'd stepped out of modeling shoot, accentuating dark, hard eyes. The raven-haired shrew was berating some poor soul on her phone. Her appearance gave me a different feel than my previous thoughts of Harper having a philanthropic benefactor.

She stopped in front of me and raised a disapproving eyebrow, flicking a finger toward her car, where I was leaning against it, gesturing that I get off the merchandise.

I introduced myself, "I'm Jon Frederick."

Margo eyed me coldly. "I know who you are."

She was about to pocket her cellphone when I commented, "Nice phone. Gunmetal gray?"

She remarked with annoyance, "Nothing's gunmetal gray, anymore. It's not politically correct. It's a cosmic gray, Samsung Galaxy S20 Plus—the top rated cellphone today."

I asked, "Tough day of work?"

"A guy coded during a routine surgery and we lost him." Her voice and facial expression were completely devoid of sentiment.

"I'm sorry."

She added callously, "I can't say I knew him. I just hate losing." With key fob in hand, Margo popped the locks of her car and said, "I imagine you want to talk. Harper wasn't supposed to tell you about me."

I interrupted, "She didn't."

"How did you figure it out?"

"You bought Blaze his Corvette."

Margo reluctantly acknowledged, "Money flowed through Billy like water through a screen. He gave me the cash and I filled out the paperwork. He also paid for Gunner's house, but he let Gunner own it, provided Gunner took care of it. Billy felt paperwork was a waste of his time."

"I want Harper out of the investigation. At this point, worrying about her safety is more of a hindrance. I can still have her sign releases as needed."

"Okay. But I still want her to pay you. It gives me a little bit of a cushion from being publicly associated with Billy. We didn't hide our relationship, but we also didn't advertise it. Billy was my guilty pleasure."

I added, "And you're deleting the sexts of Harper and Greg."

With a sinful grin, she agreed, "Alright." She added

without remorse, "I did what I needed to do. We all do—for the ones we love."

I wasn't going to argue with her, as I didn't want her to get angry and back out. Instead, I asked, "Why did you pick me?"

"You were fired for killing Kaiko Kane and you never apologized for it. You take care of business."

I didn't particularly like her answer, but there was no point in correcting her. Kane was about to kill a woman when I shot him in the leg. Technically, I didn't kill him. The medic in the ambulance administered the wrong medication and that killed him. But I did put him in that ambulance. Kane put me in the predicament of either shooting him or letting him commit murder. I didn't regret my choice. I apologized when I was sorry.

Margo became wistful. "I miss Billy. Have you ever read *Faust*, by von Goethe?"

"Yes. He sold his soul to the devil."

"Sometimes I wonder if Billy did. Like Faust, he got what he wanted, but it all turned to hell on earth." She gritted her teeth, "I need this solved."

"You could help me by answering some questions about people involved in this case. Tell me about Gwyneth Porter."

Margo laughed wickedly, "She was pitiful. I introduced her to Billy when we were at a Fab Five concert at Pioneer Place and she apparently decided she wanted some of him, too. She must have slipped him her number and they got together a couple times." She added quickly, "Billy and I were kindred spirits. My next encounter with Gwyneth was a few months later, in June of 2017. I was with Billy at the Dancing With Our Stars charity event at St. Benedicts College. You and Serena should check it out. Local dancers work with community members to master a dance. It's great entertainment. Anyway, it was a beautiful summer night so, during intermission, we stepped out of Escher Auditorium. Billy and I were sharing a passionate kiss when Gwyneth came running at us, whining, 'Billy, I love you! Take me away with you!' It was *embarrassing*," she said with disgust. "Her husband was twenty feet behind her. It was so pathetic. Billy pulled me tighter and we turned and walked away. She just fell to her knees bawling." Margo smiled with cold satisfaction, "Billy and I had a good laugh on Gwyneth."

"Do you think Gwyneth or her husband could have killed Billy?"

She stared straight ahead for a minute. "It seems like a longshot. They were a spoiled and naïve duo. She was attracted to the *bad boy*, for a bit. Gwyneth struggled getting over Billy. He had to physically throw her off his property in July." She pondered this further. "It's funny, but I'd forgotten about her. Maybe," she contemplated. "Now, that would be a twist."

Margo ordered, "Find out for me. The year Billy and I toured Europe was the best year of my life. I could go anywhere in the world and never be afraid with Billy. When we were together, I had his undevoted attention."

I was going to correct her and say, *I think you meant undivided*, but un-devoted was probably a better choice of words.

"Wasn't Billy going to marry Trisha Lake?"

Accusing eyes snapped to mine, "Who suggested that?"

"Trisha."

"Wishful thinking on her part," she snarled. "I never heard a word about it."

Why would Trisha lie about this? My instinct was she was telling the truth. Margo might have killed Blaze if she'd known, but the news hadn't been delivered to her yet, which again supported my belief that she hadn't killed Blaze.

Nonplussed, Margo continued, "I want to find the bastard who took him from me. Billy was one of a kind."

I wanted to believe this, but I think Trisha proved you could always find another misogynist. I asked, "You didn't fear for your life?"

"Never."

"Even after he stabbed Randy Vogel with a screwdriver and Vogel disappeared before his court appearance?"

Margo laughed, "Billy didn't kill Randy. Randy was a wounded war vet who received a lot of sympathy from women in the trailer park. Some jealous guy obviously didn't appreciate it. But I'm not paying you to solve Randy's murder. I couldn't care less about that two-bit snitch."

"Randy Vogel wasn't a snitch. That much I have verified."

She looked like she wanted to ask me to identify the snitch, but restrained herself.

"Blaze's abuse of women didn't bother you?"

"Drama mamas," she scoffed, eyes rolling to Heaven. "I wouldn't believe any of them. That's why I need someone like you sorting out the truth."

"Do you think Gunner Black could have killed Blaze?"

"No. Gunner was the parasite and Blaze was the host. Gunner was calling around looking for him the morning after Billy disappeared. He'd check in with me, periodically, to see if I'd heard from him."

While checking on the whereabouts of the victim would be a great cover, killers rarely did that. "How about Keith Stewart?"

"Who?"

"The guy Blaze was selling meth for."

That comment caught Margo by surprise. "You're good. No chance. Blaze made Stewart a fortune. Blaze collected hard on drug debts—beatings, shots fired into your house. People wouldn't press charges because they didn't want to have to explain why Billy came after them. Don't waste any time on Stewart. I can't stand that pedophile, but he didn't kill Billy."

"Hebophile is the correct term for guys who are obsessed with pubescent girls."

"I don't care what kind of 'file he is. They should *file* off his little dick for being such a pig. A real woman would break him."

5:30 P.M.
625 RIVERSIDE DRIVE NORTHEAST,
ST. CLOUD

MY NEXT CALL WAS TO GWYNETH Porter. She agreed to meet me in Wilson Park, along the Mississippi River, provided I wore a mask and remained six feet from her as we spoke.

Gwyneth was in her early fifties, with stylish silver hair. In contrast to Margo, she was attractive in a softer sense. Her makeup was understated, matching her overall minimalist appearance. She wore a crisp white blouse and charcoal slacks, with sensible flats. Gwyneth's tailored red leather jacket was the only part of her look that suggested there was more beneath her practical surface. She insisted we both stand facing the river, like spies in an old movie. Fortunately, there was no one close, so speaking in normal tones wasn't an issue.

She fidgeted nervously with her hands as she spoke. It was difficult to understand her through her black mask, but I listened carefully. "I didn't tell my husband I'm meeting with you. I want to answer all of your questions and have this over with, so you don't come to my home for answers. Falling in love with Billy was the most shameful and sinful thing I've ever done."

"What was the attraction?"

She asked, "What?"

I removed my mask and repeated the question. We were six feet away and not facing each other. It felt safe.

"Yeah, this isn't going to work." She followed suit, pulling her mask under her chin. "Everybody I knew was so polite and respectful, and here comes along this handsome brute of a man, and he wanted *me*. Even though I was married and had a couple kids, he just wanted *me*—Gwyneth. He didn't care what I did or didn't do. There was no disappointing him. He convinced me that every negative aspect of my life was somebody else's fault. No pressure. I just felt free. He gave me permission to abandon all of my responsibilities, with no judgment."

"I heard about your encounter with Blaze at St. Benedict's College."

Gwyneth flushed deeply. "That was the absolute lowest point in my life. I completely humiliated myself and Larry—my husband. Blaze just walked away with that smug little—" she stopped herself. "Larry left me kneeling on the sidewalk bawling and I don't blame him. A compassionate Bennie finally gave me a ride home. I almost lost everything."

"You still went to Blaze's home."

"Yeah—that was embarrassing, too, but at least I had no family there to witness it. Billy wouldn't let me in the house. He physically dragged me off of his porch to the road and threw me to the tar, like roadkill. His last words to me were, 'I'm done with you.' Looking back, it was telling. It wasn't, 'We're over,' or 'I'm over you.' It was, 'Game over.' I was destroyed. And there stood Margo, looking out the window, laughing like the sophomanic she is."

"Sophomaniac?"

"Someone who believes she has superior intelligence."

I remarked, "I'm obviously not one."

Gwyneth woefully went on, "And you want to hear how stupid I was? That *still* wasn't enough. I drove back three more times, but never got out of the car. There was a blue Taurus in the driveway that belonged to some blonde. It finally registered. Billy had conquered and moved on to new territory. That's what it's really about for him. He chases professional women until they commit wholeheartedly to him, and then they're trash—even disgusting to him. My only consolation was knowing he was cheating on Margo, too. She plunged her tongue down his throat that night after she noticed it bothered me to see Billy with her. Margo was right there with him, vicariously living through his badass adventures."

Trisha Lake drove a blue Taurus. I asked, "Do you remember the date of your last visit?"

Her sadness morphed into a smirk as she remarked, "You're really taking me to task on this. I don't remember. It was three years ago."

I reminded her, "Think hard. If you want our discussions to be over in one interview, I need details now."

Gwyneth massaged her temples, as if trying to physically conjure information she'd long since buried. "It was a Tuesday. I remember I watched *Fear the Walking Dead* when I returned home; I watched my recordings every Tuesday night. I didn't have the kids that night."

"What month?"

"August 2017—mid-August. It was a muggy night."

"How did you get over Blaze?"

"I came face-to-face with haunting, life-ending despair. Larry asked me to move out. The kids stayed with him, because I didn't want to uproot them until I had my head straight. One night, I decided to kill myself, so downed a handful of pills. I apparently called Larry before I passed out and he called nine-one-one."

"Where did you get the drugs?"

She laughed bitterly, "I guess it's not going to get him into trouble, now. Billy had given me some Oxys to help me sleep at night—when we were still in *lust*."

I gave her credit for her willingness to honestly address incredibly shameful choices. "Are you okay?"

"Now I am. Initially, I had distortions. I went through this period of claiming to be an enlightened, emancipated woman—putting on this act like my marriage was suffocating my true potential. But the truth is, Larry didn't stand in my way. I already was a successful financial partner. I got arrogant and took advantage of his trust. After Larry left, I cried every night, knowing in my heart, I wanted to go back to being a family. I love Larry. It took humility, therapy, and marriage encounters to get my family back."

"Do you think Larry could have killed Blaze?"

"No. He was so hurt, but he's a devout, Christian man. He just turned his back on both of us and walked away. When I saw him with another woman, I fully realized I'd made a terrible mistake. Once you have kids, you get into a routine where you're so focused on taking care of them, you forget about all the things that brought you and your partner together. I never pursued a divorce, because I knew if I went to court and said I left to try to be with Billy Blaze, I would never see my kids again. Deep down, I think a healthy part of me always knew I wanted my family back. My affair with Billy is my fault. But when I look back, I swear, he was the devil. He made it all look so appealing, as he tore my life apart . . ."

I appreciated her candor. In typical, coronavirus style, we didn't hug or shake hands. We both kind of nodded at each other and departed. Even though the timeline worked, I didn't see Gwyneth or Larry as possible suspects. Gwyneth internalized her problems and became self-destructive rather than acting out aggressively. Larry turned the other cheek and walked away.

I was just down the hill from Connie Berg's home, so decided to give her a call.

Connie said, "I can't believe Billy's dead. So, who's stalking me?"

I asked, "Has the stalker been back since Blaze's body was discovered?"

She paused and answered, "No. Not that I'm aware of."

"I don't believe anyone's stalking you. I think Gunner Black wanted people to believe Blaze was still alive and your reports prevented an investigation into his disappearance."

# 31

*It got so hot, last night, I swear you could hardly breathe*
*Heat lightning burnt the sky, like alcohol*
*I sat on the porch without my shoes and*
*I watched the cars roll by*
*As the headlights raced to the corner of the kitchen wall*
*Mama dear, your boy is here*
*Far across the sea*
*Waiting for that sacred core*
*That burns inside of me*
*And I feel a storm*
*All wet and warm*
*Not ten miles away*
—JOHN PRINE, MEXICAN HOME

# SERENA FREDERICK

### 1:30 P.M., TUESDAY, MAY 19, 2020
### PIERZ

I hated that my past victimization still haunted me. It was years ago and he's dead. *Please let me go.* I decided to start my work by calling one of the least likely suspects left on the list and hopefully eliminating her. I needed to tone down my intrusive flashbacks. One day I was telling Jon I just won't be able to be sexual for a bit, and the next day, I was tearing his clothes off. I appreciated his willingness to follow my lead. It would get better. I'd been through this before.

I managed to get in touch with Nellie Ellison and she agreed to chat via Zoom.

When her image flashed on the screen, I could see Nellie was a character. I liked her on sight. In her early sixties, her pink scalp showed a bit through her thinning, obviously-dyed red hair. Nellie was boldly dressed in a flamboyant array of colors—her deep green tunic, embroidered with bright oranges and golds, blended nicely with the audacious yellow armchair in which she casually kicked back. It all somehow worked. She was a beautiful menagerie of colors and personality. A pair of leopard print glasses hung on a string of brightly-colored beads around her neck. She squinted into the camera before perching cat-eyed spectacles on her nose.

After introductions, I shared with her that Jon and I were looking into Billy Blaze's death. Nellie was a firecracker. She said, "I met Billy at the Quarry in Waite Park. It had a reputation for drug parties, but I talked a friend into taking me there."

"That was gutsy."

"And there was Billy, diving off the thirty-foot granite formations into the water. It was pure desire on my part and, when he learned I had money, Billy lusted for me, too. Did you know we were both characters in the Old Maid card game? Billy Blaze was a fireman and Nurse Nellie—well, you can guess. It wasn't a suggestion that I be breastfed."

Ignoring the reference, I told her, "It's such a joy to finally converse with someone who doesn't see herself as a victim of Blaze."

Nellie threw her head back and cackled, "Women love to hear me talk about using Blaze. Finally, a woman snares a guy a dozen years younger and ruts the hell out of the boar." She dropped a green olive in the glass of beer sitting on the table in front of her and said excitedly, "Watch this!" The olive sank to the bottom.

It was not particularly impressive. I asked, "So, why did Billy threaten your daughter?"

Her voice cracked, "For telling the truth. My daughter is about Margo Miller's age. Margo had Billy with her and her uppity friends at the Guthrie Theatre. Linda approached them, and said, 'Oh, so you're the next, now that my mom's done with him.'"

"How long were you and Billy together?"

"I've always been together—Billy's *never* been together. So what would you call that?"

"I mean—"

She interrupted with a wave of her hand, gold bangles around her wrist clinking against each other. "I know what you mean, girl. I guess that would be from the time he got out of prison in 2015 until he landed a new gig in early 2017. Billy wanted me when he needed money, so I made him work for it. I had no illusions of Billy. He was using me and I was using him. I couldn't stand listening to the narcissistic bastard. I mean, flattering lies are nice for a while, but when you know they're insincere, it's insulting. Finally, I told him, 'Just shut up. When we're alone, don't talk.'" She chuckled to herself, "It was a performance-based reward system."

Nellie pointed back to the olive. "This is what I call the poor man's lava lamp."

*Was there a rich man's lava lamp?*

The olive rose back to the top of the glass and then sunk again. Nellie explained, "Because of the salt in the olive, it collects bubbles on the bottom of the glass and floats to the top. Once at the top, the bubbles burst and it sinks back to the bottom. It can go on and on."

*Assuming you didn't actually drink the beer.* It occurred to me the olive's journey was not unlike Billy Blaze's. I was trying to think of a nice way to say this. "So Blaze was basically your," I cleared my throat, "escort?"

"I prefer *sex worker*. When I wouldn't give him money upfront, he got drunk and busted up all of my gnomes. The

Great Gnome Massacre of 2016." She reminisced, "He wasn't a cheap lay, but I don't regret it. The story itself is worth the investment. Wouldn't you just love tell a man with a perfectly sculpted body to just 'shut up and do what I say'? That's what money buys you."

"Was he ever abusive?"

Nellie shook her head, "Not to me—he knew better. Don't bite the hand that feeds you, right? But apparently, he was to everybody else in St. Cloud. Billy had a knack for judging how far he could push everyone. For me, it was *not an inch.*" She punctuated this, holding up her thumb and forefinger, displaying hot pink nails and rings on every finger. "It was all about the Benjamins for Billy. His motto was, *Anything worth doing is worth doing for money.*"

"So what was his new gig?"

"We didn't *talk,*" she smirked. "Probably drugs. It's where guys like him always end up. Billy wasn't *totally* amoral," Nellie noted. "I don't know that he ever killed anyone." She thought for a moment. "To be honest, I think he preferred that people continued to suffer . . ."

8:45 P.M.

I'D BEEN PUTTING OFF CALLING TRISHA again. I felt like I could get more information from her, if I continued to go along with her assumption that Jon was abusive to me, but I didn't like misleading her. I promised her that, after I put the kids to bed, we'd FaceTime.

Trisha looked hungover. In a hoarse voice, she whispered, "Are you in a room by yourself, with the door closed?"

"Yes."

She leaned in too closely to the camera, ordering, "Tell me your escape plan."

"If I remember correctly, you were going to talk to Gunner Black for me, first."

Trisha rubbed her forehead clumsily with the back of her hand, "I did." She slurred, "You'd better appreciate what I've done for you."

Concerned, I asked, "Trisha, what did you do?"

"Gave up my sobriety. Got Gunner to throw away over two years of recovery."

"I didn't ask you to do that." I felt terrible.

"I want this solved as bad as you do. The only way I could get him to talk was to suggest we destroy one last bottle of 1800 Anejo tequila." Trisha propped her chin in her hand, appearing to need the support to keep from tipping into the screen. "Blaze sent Gunner to the liquor store every day, to buy him a bottle of 1800—at forty dollars a pop."

That explained a lot. People have said, over and over, that Blaze was an ass when he drank tequila—and he drank tequila every day. "Did he ever think about just buying a case?"

Trisha chuckled, "Too much of a commitment for him."

I reasoned, "An adult without discipline is like a two-year-old, minus the cuteness and potential." While I meant the comment for Blaze, I realized Trisha may have internalized it. I quickly added, "I hope you never give up your sobriety again, for anything. I should never have asked you to talk to Gunner. I'm so sorry."

"It's okay. I needed this. It made me realize how I'd glorified Billy since I left him. He never really forced sex, but it was a given that I'd just consent. After all, I was staying with him and not paying rent. He was buying all my cocaine."

"Did he deal cocaine?"

"Nah, just meth." Trisha ground the heel of her hand into her eye, rubbing furiously and smearing makeup into an ashen mess on the side of her face. "It's funny, because I was telling myself he took the risk of buying cocaine for me because he loved me *that* much. Funny not funny. Gunner reminded me Billy loved to make people dependent on him. If he wouldn't have gotten me the cocaine, I would've moved on. Billy destroyed all of us," she said sadly. "Gunner also reminded me of how Billy threatened to hurt my son if I didn't marry him."

So, Gunner knew Blaze wanted to marry Trisha, but it never got back to Margo. I tried to give Trisha some credit. "But still, you had the strength to leave him."

"I did manage that."

Before I could respond, she continued, "I was going with a friend to L.A., because she was going to be on Judge Judy and I wanted to spend some time with my daughter, Saffron."

I let her ramble for a while, even though I wasn't particularly interested in how the Judge Judy case ended.

"When my friend said to Judge Judy, 'I'm here for the pain and suffering,' Judy responded, 'Yours or mine?' Judy also told her, 'Um is not an answer.' You have to admit she's damn funny."

I interjected, "What do you think about Margo Miller?"

"Ugh!" Trisha threw up her hands and said theatrically, "I thought Margo was my ticket out. I knew Billy was screwing her, but it didn't matter—I was leaving. That's why I was so shocked when he insisted we get married. Gunner's explanation that Billy wanted me to run his drug money made perfect sense. As his wife, I couldn't be forced to testify against him and Margo would never touch drug money. She didn't *need* it," she dragged out *need* like six vowels were added to the word. "And now that Billy was making a ton of money with Stewart, he wasn't going to *need* Margo." Trisha chuckled sloppily at her remark.

"So, you were supposed to be his drug mule. But instead of delivering the drugs, you delivered the drug money."

Trisha sadly nodded into her palm until her chin slipped out of her hand. She nearly bounced her face off the table in front of her. Unfazed, she continued, "Yeah."

Getting back to gathering evidence, I asked, "So, what did Gunner say about the list of suspects?"

"Nothing, at first. But he's an easy drunk," she giggled. "By the end of the night, he swore he didn't kill Billy, but he knows who did. He wouldn't give 'em up, but he said the name you're looking for is on that list."

I clarified, "Did he say the *person* is on the list, or the *name* is on the list?"

"He said the *name*. Now, let's hear about that safety plan . . ."

# 32

*The sun can play tricks*
*With your eyes on the highway*
*The moon can lay sideways*
*Till the ocean stands still*
*But a person can't tell*
*His best friend he loves him*
*Till time has stopped breathing*
*You're alone on the hill*
—JOHN PRINE, *HE WAS IN HEAVEN*
*BEFORE HE DIED*

# HARPER ROWE

10:30 P.M., FRIDAY, MAY 22, 2020
BIRCHMONDT DRIVE NORTHEAST,
WEST SIDE OF LAKE BEMIDJI, BEMIDJI

The bad news on the Coronavirus kept pouring in. Yesterday, there were thirty-two recorded COVID-19 deaths in Minnesota—another new record. I received an email from Margo Miller tonight.

> *Harper,*
> *I want you to know I would have never made your personal pictures public. I loved your dad and Billy would have hated me for doing so. I hope you can forgive me for the threat and understand I acted out of love for Billy. I don't completely understand your relationship with*

*Greg, and I have no intention to meddle further into it.
However, out of respect for our common bond, I thought
I'd share something I got out of Greg's email. Greg and
Shawna have been getting together since shortly after he
started his practicum. Billy would've wanted me to act on
your behalf, so I forwarded some emails to Greg's super-
visor, and Shawna was subsequently transferred to the
St. Cloud Hospital. This didn't end their relationship,
as I had hoped. They still have a standing date, every
Saturday night at 8:00 p.m. They get together to watch
Game of Thrones. Shawna is renting a house three blocks
north of the Mississippi Bridge, on North Benton Drive
in Sauk Rapids. It's only about a mile from the hospital.
Let me know if I can be of any further assistance to you.
Sincerely,
Margo*

Getting painful information about my lover, from an enemy,
was right up there on the *Things that piss me off* list. I immediately called Greg. "I don't want you talking to Shawna anymore."

He listened patiently and calmed me, finally explaining, "Okay, Shawna and I were together a number of times.
But Scout's honor, nothing has happened since I told you
it ended."

Like the devil on the internet, raunchy images were
racing through my head. "I need to know exactly what you
did with her."

I could hear Greg blow out a long exhale. "No good
would come of it."

"Honesty would be good."

Greg offered, "Use your imagination. Basically everything."

"What does that mean? Bondage? Threesomes? Donkeys?"

"Don't be ridiculous. Everything we do."

That hurt. I had to ask, "And more?"

"Maybe tried what you're not comfortable with—look, this is stupid."

His response might have been at the top of my aforementioned list. Jerk!

He cleared his throat. "Look Harp, I love you! I'm just trying to survive, here. I'm putting my life on the line for the good of humanity. I was there for you and I need you to be here for me. I need you. I need to know I have someone, outside of my crazy work, who loves me. And I'll be that guy for you. We'll have our work lives, where we both bring hope to a struggling world, and then escape to our private lives in each other's arms."

I felt like I'd been stabbed in the heart. I wanted to say, *I don't plan on sleeping with my coworkers.* In spite of it all, I didn't want to lose Greg. I felt defeated and so incredibly needy.

When I didn't respond, he asked, "What do you want me to do?"

The words came out angrier than intended, "Stop talking to Shawna!"

"I promise you Harp, I'll never risk losing you again. Talk about karma reigning down on me. I got COVID-19. I constantly worry about losing you. I hurt you—the best part of my life."

"I feel sick. Do you know how humiliating it is to love someone who's screwing somebody else?"

"I'm sorry, Harp. Truly sorry."

In my heart, I knew he was, but I wasn't ready to forgive him. I willed myself to say something kind. "If we could just have a moment together, you'd understand how much you mean to me. I'm sorry I can't be there for you."

Greg responded, "Don't apologize. I should have told you all of it, right away. I was afraid you'd leave me. I can't lose you. I was overwhelmed with the pressure of saving lives at work and I was lonely. It was so stupid. Please, forgive me . . ."

2:30 A.M., SATURDAY, MAY 23, 2020
BIRCHMONDT DRIVE NORTHEAST,
WEST SIDE OF LAKE BEMIDJI, BEMIDJI

*PLEASE GOD, JUST LET ME GET SOME sleep.* Racing thoughts
of Greg and Shawna tortured me and now a storm was rumbling through. I'd had it. Instead of waiting for Grandma to
come into my room and order me downstairs to wait out the
storm, I grabbed my pillow and retreated to the basement.
My grandparents didn't go downstairs because Grandpa
had a bad hip and Grandma said, "If we get trapped in a
storm, we're goin' together." The *plus* was it was cool and
dark, down there. A nightlight offered a small stream of
light emanating from the bathroom at the other end of the
basement. The *minus* was that the couch sagged, but my bed
wasn't working tonight, anyway.

I hated that wolf bitch, Margo, but she was right about Greg
being more involved with Shawna than he initially revealed. I
was tempted to go and check on Greg next Saturday night.

I could hear footsteps above me. Grandpa must be up.
God bless him, Grandpa was a great provider, but he was an
emotional and financial curmudgeon. Mom used to joke that
he was so tight he looked over his glasses, instead of through
them, so he didn't wear them out. He never told anyone he
loved them; he didn't feel it was necessary. He would say,
"Don't I provide a roof over your head?" No wonder Grandma
hungered for the words.

# 33

*The search light in the big yard*
*Swings round with the gun*
*And spotlights the snowflakes*
*Like the dust in the sun*
*It's Christmas in prison*
*There'll be music tonight*
*I'll probably get homesick*
*I love you*
*Goodnight*
*Wait awhile eternity*
*Old Mother Nature's got nothing on me*
—JOHN PRINE, CHRISTMAS IN PRISON

# KHARON

2:40 A.M., SATURDAY, MAY 23, 2020
BIRCHMONDT DRIVE NORTHEAST,
WEST SIDE OF LAKE BEMIDJI, BEMIDJI

I place a GPS tracker on the frame of Harper's ugly gray Impala and carefully walk around the house, considering my next move. *What am I going to do with this girl?*

The rumbling storm presents the perfect opportunity for an undetected break-in. When the downpour begins, I walk around the Rowe house, pushing up on windows. *Pay dirt!* An unlocked porch window slides open quietly.

The home is completely dark. Garrote in hand, I make my way down the hall. I open a bedroom door a crack, to see the grandparents sound asleep. Should I do them now, or wait? For the time being, I leave them breathing.

I don't want to merely kill Harper. Eros, in Greek lore was a fiery and dangerous form of sexual passion. Eros is what I need from Harper.

I make my way up the steps. Only one room has a closed door; the remaining rooms are unoccupied. I carefully turn the knob and open the door. The bed has been slept in, but it's empty. I sit on the edge and feel it. The sheets are still warm. Harper is here, somewhere. I flash a penlight on and search the room, to no avail. There's a picture of Harper with flowers in her hair, in a wheat field. I slide it out of its frame to keep as a souvenir. There are some shots of a yuppie-looking guy on the wall and a picture of a young, Native chef on the nightstand. But Persephone needs a god.

I make my way downstairs. I notice sets of keys hanging by a note board and decide to help myself to a pair. I am about to give up, when the basement door creaks. Isaac Newton's first law of motion: Objects in motion stay in motion, while an object at rest stays at rest. Cupboards and doors in old houses have a position of evenness they ultimately settle into. This door had been knocked out of it, but had creaked back into its place of rest. I wonder if it's recently been opened.

# 34

*Day time*
*Makes me wonder why you left me*
*Night time*
*Makes me wonder what I said*
*Next time*
*Are the words I'd like to plan on*
*The last time*
*Was the only thing you said*
—JOHN PRINE, *BLUE UMBRELLA*

## HARPER ROWE

2:48 A.M., SATURDAY, MAY 23, 2020
BIRCHMONDT DRIVE NORTHEAST,
WEST SIDE OF LAKE BEMIDJI, BEMIDJI

The footsteps above didn't sound like Grandpa, as he had a bit of a limp. They were too heavy to be my ninety-pound grandma's. Maybe I was just being hyper-alert. I so wished Greg was here—he always seemed to know what to do. *What was Keith Stewart going to do now that he'd seen me trying to rescue those girls?*

The footfalls padded heavily down the basement steps. My heartbeat quickened and my instincts shrieked at me to hide. I almost called out to Grandpa, but stopped myself. I wasn't taking any chances. I quickly assessed my options.

I'd been helping Grandma clean out a crawl space under the steps. I abandoned the couch and quietly slipped under the steps. Holding my breath, I carefully pulled boxes in front of me and a mothball smelling quilt over me. I could hear someone walking around the basement. *What is he looking for?*

The steps approached my hiding place. A flash of light burst in my direction and the intruder stopped. I couldn't even breathe. *Please Grandpa, if that's you, just say something.*

# 35

*And I dream of her always*
*Even when I don't dream*
*Her name's on my tongue*
*Her blood's in my vein*
—JOHN PRINE, *CHRISTMAS IN PRISON*

## KHARON

2:50 A.M., SATURDAY, MAY 23, 2020
BIRCHMONDT DRIVE NORTHEAST,
WEST SIDE OF LAKE BEMIDJI, BEMIDJI

I creep cautiously down the steps. Stewart told me Harper rushed back home to care for her grandmother. What would a girl like her do to spare her grandmother's life? Quid pro quo. Screw Stewart—tonight, I'm taking what I want. I lick my lips in anticipation. Her body type is exactly in my wheelhouse and I can't get the warm feel of her sheets out of my head. The video of her, topless, in bed runs through my brain in an endless loop. I'm going to have her. I'm not going to put a ring on her finger, but I'll put a tag on her toe.

The only light in the basement comes from a night-light in the bathroom. I use my cellphone light and scan the basement. A blanket and pillow lay abandoned on the couch.

I make my way to it and quickly look behind it. Nothing. *Where is she?*

The boxes piled by the steps capture my curiosity. Could Harper and those nice, long legs hide behind these boxes? It doesn't seem like it.

# 36

*If you lie like a rug*
*And you don't give a damn*
*You're never gonna be*
*As happy as a clam*
*I'm sitting in a hotel*
*Trying to write a song*
*My head is just as empty*
*As the day is long*
*Why it's clear as a bell*
*I should have gone to school*
*I'd be wise as an owl*
*Instead of stubborn as a mule*
*—JOHN PRINE, IT'S A BIG OLD*
*GOOFY WORLD*

## HARPER ROWE

2:40 A.M., SATURDAY, MAY 23, 2020
BIRCHMONDT DRIVE NORTHEAST,
WEST SIDE OF LAKE BEMIDJI, BEMIDJI

The light crept to me like a rising flood and then suddenly stopped at the boxes. The tail of my loose-fitting night-shirt was partially visible. It was too late to try and move it.

It might have only been minutes, but it felt like hours before the footsteps moved on. After one more, slow walk through the basement, the intruder eventually headed back upstairs.

I wasn't moving.

6:30 A.M.

I WOKE TO GRANDMA SHAKING ME. "Cripes on a cracker, girl, what's gotten into you? You're sleeping in the crawl space!"

I crawled out and gave her a hug. "I love you, Grandma. Always remember that."

With relief she said, "I love you, too, crazy girl. First, I couldn't find my house key, and then I find you down here. Heavenly days, tell me what is going on with you."

"Grandma, I need some sleep, or nothing I say will make sense."

She sternly told me, "Okay but we're talking later."

# 37

*A Mocca man in a wigwam sitting on a reservation*
*With a big black hole in the belly of his soul*
*Waiting on an explanation*
*While the white man sits on his fat can*
*And takes pictures of the Navajo*
*Every time he clicks his Kodak pics*
*He steals a little bit of soul*
—JOHN PRINE, *PICTURE SHOW*

## HARPER ROWE

### 5:30 P.M., SATURDAY, MAY 23, 2020
### CASS LAKE, LEECH LAKE RESERVATION

Moki invited me to dinner and I eagerly accepted the opportunity to escape. *Sorry, Grandma.* Was I a terrible person? I hoped not. I loved Greg, but I was struggling with his infidelity.

Moki served pumpkin soup that had the warmth and feel of sitting around a bonfire on a fall evening. It was silky, creamy, a little spicy, and amazing. The sugar pie pumpkin was enhanced with maple syrup, cinnamon, garlic and onion, and the flavors all melded nicely. The soup was topped with pepitas, which added the perfect texture.

Moki's parents were caring professionals who welcomed me with some wariness, but kindness nonetheless. His eighteen-year-old brother and thirteen-year-old sister teased him, a little, about having a dinner date with his family, but they were also kind to me.

Moki's sister, Kimi, taunted, "Maybe we could all go to a movie together for your second date."

Honestly, I think she would've loved it.

Moki corrected her, "This isn't a date. I simply asked a friend to dinner . . ."

After the decadent meal, he and I sat together on the back steps.

I nudged his shoulder with mine. "You have a great family. Kimi is observant. No matter what I tell myself—this does feel a little like a date."

Strands of his dark hair swept across his face with the breeze. "And still, you're here." With a shy glance, he asked, "What are you going to do about Greg?"

"I don't know," I told him honestly. "I'm going to give myself some time to think about it, now that I've finished spring semester and stopped searching for Blaze."

"Maybe I'm wrong," he suggested carefully, "but I think you have an image of Greg that's more loveable than the reality of him."

I argued, "I have to consider that he got caught up in unusual circumstances—with the pandemic and all."

Moki looked like he wanted to say something, but sat quietly.

I finally demanded, "What."

"Was it *that* unusual? I mean, the pandemic's unusual, but won't Greg always be working long shifts if he's going to be a nurse?"

I had nothing to say to that. Instead, I pulled a folded letter out of my pocket. "My dad scanned this to me. He has letters from my mom with the instructions to open one, every day, for a year."

Moki eagerly looked on as I read the letter.

*Dear Jeremy,*
*I love you and I want you to smile for me today. I think*
*Billy Blaze is dead. Despite your protests, I went to visit*
*him on August 18, 2017. His friend, Gunner, answered*
*the door with a battered face and told me, "You don't*
*have to worry about Blaze, anymore. Don't come back."*
*He closed the door and that was that. Against your*
*wishes, I left a safe and loving home for a dangerous*
*and evil altercation. I don't know what happened, but I*
*was fortunate to just miss it. I think I'm better off not*
*knowing. In the Bible, Peter wrote in verse 4:15, "Let*
*none of you suffer as a murderer, a thief, an evildoer,*
*or a meddler." A woman named Margo contacted me*
*when Harper was 18. I warned Margo to never contact*
*me or Harper, ever again. While I never wished ill on*
*anyone, I appreciate being done with Blaze. You gave me*
*my dream life, Jeremy! After August 18, 2017, I never*
*risked losing that precious gift again.*
*Love, Kal.*

I held the page to my chest for a moment, before I put the letter back away.

I told Moki with all sincerity, "You should know, I hope to become a professional meddler—as a social worker. I'll be asked to investigate suspected child abuse."

He smiled, "These children need someone to meddle. You'll be a hero to them."

As I considered this, we could hear his parents talking inside the house.

His father was saying, "I like Winona, too, but pushing a date on Moki is one way to make him hate her. To borrow a term from our son, Harper is just an *amuse-bouche*. When he's done with his appetizers, he'll find his way to the entrée."

Moki was about to get up and go to him when I put my hand on his shoulder. "It's okay."

He shook his head in embarrassment. "I don't view dating like it's a tasting menu. I've never met anyone like you. Winona's an Anishinaabe woman my mother thinks would be perfect for me. She's nice, but she's not you."

I should have encouraged him to go out with her, but I didn't want him to. Instead, I took his hand, "I like you, too, Moki—it's why I've been staying away." I squeezed his hand tightly. "Greg's been good to me for a long time."

He looked at our joined hands. "You look for Blaze, who's a complete ass, date Greg who cheats on you, but stay away from me, who you like. So—*that's* what white people do."

I laughed, "It *is* what we do. We pray decent people will always be there for us and let jerks wear us down. Speaking of race, anybody warn you about inviting a white woman to dinner, whose mother died of a killer disease? White folks don't exactly have a great disease history with Natives."

He looked away, suggesting it did come up, then countered, "You didn't even tell your family about me."

"I told my dad. He liked the idea of having a chef in the family—but said it's my call."

Moki grinned, "I guess I didn't tell my grandparents about you, either. And, by the way—you don't owe me a laptop. It's not your fault I was tossed in jail and dropped from my classes. If I wouldn't have used Blaze's credit card, I wouldn't be in this mess." He looked at me with concern. "By now, Keith Stewart has reviewed his cameras, so he knows you tried to go into that locked bedroom. You need to be careful. I was in Bemidji last night and drove by your grandparents' home. There was a silver truck a couple houses down from yours, with what looked like a big man sitting in it. There was also a silver truck at Stewart's the night we were there."

If he was trying to scare the hell out of me, he succeeded.

"I don't mind you checking on me, I'm just not ready to let go of Greg. He was with me through my mom's passing." That ended conversation for a bit. My life was sinking into a dark place and I was helpless in stopping its descent. The course was set and unchangeable. My eyes prickled with tears. "Would you mind giving me a ride home?"

Moki answered with a question. "Do you mind if I hug you?"

I melted into his arms as he held me. It felt so right, I clung to him. I finally pulled his chin to mine and we kissed.

The door behind us swung open and his mother marched out. "Your sister wants to know if it's safe for her to come out and talk."

I said, "Sure," as Moki simultaneously said, "No."

Kimi came out, anyway, and pulled up a chair directly across from us.

It was probably best. I swore I'd stop talking to him and here I was kissing him. Right now, Moki was my best friend. I found myself resting my head on his shoulder as Kimi excitedly went on and on about the drama of being thirteen. *Was I a terrible person?*

Moki and I drove by Teal's Grocery as we left Cass Lake. There was something about night in unfamiliar community that brought an eerie excitement and I wasn't ready for my time with him to end. I said, "Once we're out of town, I want you to pull down a side road."

His amorous smile reflected more uncertainty than confidence. I loved that about Moki.

I explained, "I don't want to worry about my grandparents watching when I kiss you goodnight."

We drove down narrow, Little Wolf Lake Road, and parked on the shore of the lake. In a matter of seconds we were passionately kissing with our bodies as close as the center console would allow.

# 38

*Feelings are strange*
*Especially when they come true*
*And I had a feeling you'd be leaving soon*
*So I tried to rearrange all my emotions*
*But they seem the same, no matter what I do*
*A blue umbrella rests upon my shoulder*
*To hide the pain, while the rain makes up my mind*
*My feet are wet from thinking this thing over*
*And it's been so long since I felt the warm sunshine*
*Just give me one good reason*
*And I promise I won't ask you any more*
—JOHN PRINE, *BLUE UMBRELLA*

## HARPER ROWE

### 6:30 P.M., SUNDAY, MAY 24, 2020
### BIRCHMONDT DRIVE NORTHEAST,
### WEST SIDE OF LAKE BEMIDJI, BEMIDJI

Yesterday, once again, was a new Minnesota daily record for new coronavirus cases (+927). It was also a new daily record for coronavirus deaths in Minnesota, with thirty-three. I wondered how many relationships died yesterday, as well. I didn't regret parking with Moki by the lake last night. As steamy as it was, our bodies never fully crossed the console. Regardless of what Greg did, I needed to feel good about myself. Even if nothing went further with Moki and me, last night was delicious.

I'd been telling myself all day that I was better than some insecure girl who needed to immediately get back at her boyfriend, or go check on him, but maybe I wasn't. Greg said he wasn't spending time with Shawna outside of work and I should've just accepted it. After all, I wasn't exactly an angel, myself. I reminded myself that the tip I received was from a woman who once tried to blackmail me. But I needed to put gas in my car, which I put off until early evening. Before exiting the gas station, I thoroughly searched for a silver truck, but thank God, there was none around. As if in a fugue state, I found myself driving south on Highway 71, toward Sauk Rapids. I told myself I was just being assertive. It was what my mom would do.

### 8:55 P.M., NORTH BENTON DRIVE, SAUK RAPIDS

I WASN'T FAMILIAR WITH SAUK RAPIDS, so I ended up anxiously driving around for a bit. *What am I doing?* Butterflies fluttered in my stomach and I felt a light-headedness as I turned North on Benton Drive. Sure enough, there was Greg's car, parked in front of a small house. *Now what?* I parked around the corner by a blue tin building to hide my car. Power Equipment Plus was closed for the evening, so leaving my car in their lot shouldn't have offended anyone.

It was cool and overcast. The sun had set a half hour ago—two hours into my two and a half hour drive. Darkness was good, as it would provide me some cover. I slowly made my way around the metal building and walked to the house through the back alley. *Here goes!* I walked along the small beige house, briefly glancing in curtain-covered windows, until I was peeking in the corner of the large picture window in front. There were Greg and Shawna, innocently enough eating pizza and watching a large screen television. *Liar!* Shawna was closest to me. They both appeared to be engrossed in the show, commenting to each other periodically about something that had occurred on screen. I waited for them to make amorous eyes at each other, but they sat vigilantly straight up, stoically focused on the screen. If Greg and I were watching the show together, we'd almost be on top of each other.

Greg and I needed to have a serious conversation. I bitterly recalled the Saturday nights I begged him to talk and he couldn't find the time. More importantly, he was still lying to me. He wasn't the man I fantasized him to be and that was disheartening. Greg had been good for me in many ways. I leaned heavily on him when Mom died and he kept me upright. He was my rock. But his notion that I was his shining light outside of work never sat well with me. My man was going to be part of me, and I part of him, even when we were separated—not just someone I visited when my work day was over.

It started to drizzle, so I headed back into the alley. Greg and I were over. Another bridge burned. My memories were filled with melancholic nostalgia of our relationship as I meandered back to my car. Honestly, there was part of me that felt a sense of relief—as if deep down, I kind of hoped I'd find Greg with Shawna.

I was pulled back to reality when I saw a silver pick-up sitting behind the tin building. I hadn't heard it pull in. On pins and needles, I strained my senses—nothing. The truck was empty. I peered in every direction, ready to bolt at any moment, but I couldn't see anyone. As I turned the corner around the blue building, I bumped right into a colossal man. Before his familiarity registered, my instincts already turned my body to run. I barely made it a step before I was yanked backwards by the cold metal of a wire biting into my neck. I clawed desperately with both hands to loosen it. I wasn't getting any air. My own nails scraped into my flesh as I tried to get ahold of the wire, but soon the edges of my vision blurred. An inky mist took over and I fully descended into the darkness.

# 39

*I couldn't care less if she never came back*
*I was gonna leave her anyway*
*And all the good times that we shared*
*Don't mean a thing today*
*Say sour grapes*
*You can laugh and stare*
*Say sour grapes*
*But I don't care*
—JOHN PRINE, *SOUR GRAPES*

## HARPER ROWE

11:45 P.M., SUNDAY, MAY 24, 2020
TALON DRIVE, EAGLES LANDING, ST. AUGUSTA

When I came to, I was lying across the bench seat of a pickup. I tenderly explored the skin around my neck. It was burning, hot with pain, but the wire had thankfully been removed. I realized with horror that I'd been garroted; I didn't even know how I was alive. I became aware of another sensation that was soothing, until I realized Zig was running his hands through my hair. I slapped at his hands and quickly sat up, as I pushed him away.

He pulled into Keith Stewart's driveway. I pleaded, "You can't take me in there. He's going to kill me."

Zig put the truck in park and shut it off. He calmly replied, "He's not going to kill you, but you're going to have to take one for the team."

I immediately understood that I was going to be raped. It was time to share Jon's theory. "Did you know Stewart blackmailed my dad to avoid the charges that you went to prison for?"

The creepily-tattooed psychopomp dismissed the suggestion. "I doubt it."

I taunted him by agreeing, "Yeah, Stewart would never use a fifteen-year-old girl like my mom to get out of charges. And I'm sure he'd never let a good friend like you get sent, just to save his own skin. Sorry for even suggesting it."

Zig directed, "Shut up!" and hopped out of the truck. He pulled me out of his Silverado, dragged me inside, and turned me over to Stewart. Keith directed me to sit on the couch.

The huge Kharon called Zig stood a few feet away from me with the Native girl, casually twirling the garrote around his thick index finger. I pleaded with my eyes to the girl to help me, but she returned my look with dispassion. Keith walked to Zig and muttered something to him I couldn't hear.

I was privy to Zig's response, as he wasn't concerned if I overheard. "I want her. I don't ask for a lot."

Keith looked back at me and said, "Zig—you can't."

Zig responded, "Boss, we need to talk. Or let me have her then we can forget about talking."

As panic flooded through my system, the Native girl bent down as if to check on me and quickly whispered, "Choose me." I stared after her in confusion.

Keith ordered the girl to her room and Zig stood solid, waiting. He licked his lips in anticipation.

A few seconds with that man could be the death of me. I'd heard stories about sadists who'd rape and torture their victims. My skin crawled with the unnerving feeling of being covered by insects.

"I know who you are, *Harper Rowe*," Keith said with annoyance. He ran his tongue across his teeth and sucked through them. He had a kernel of something he was trying to dislodge. "Why did you come to my home?"

"I had to see where my mom had been."

Keith used his pinky finger to dab something off his tongue and inspected it, as he pondered my response. He finally asked, "What exactly is your plan?"

"I don't have one. I haven't told anyone."

Keith let me sit while he strolled to his wet bar, pouring a drink in a crystal glass. He swirled it around and took a sip, then turned to me, pointing over the top of the glass. "I am an open-minded man. Let me lay out your options. I have a nice cozy fireplace in my bedroom. We could slip your rain-drizzled clothes off, warm up by the fire, and have a night of enjoyable, consenting sex."

I asked, "Or?"

With a salacious sneer, he added, "Or, you could give me some lesbian action with my Indian girl." Unconcerned over my choice, his eyes narrowed as he took another drink.

Both sounded disgusting. Keith was a letch and the fact that my other option was a girl, rather than a man or woman, was odious. While I had nothing against lesbians, it wasn't my thing. I tried to reason with him. "I haven't done anything to you. I'd like to forget I was ever here."

Keith nodded. "Maybe. But I need some insurance. I can obtain that by having a video for safe keeping of you with an underage girl, or of you consenting to sex with me. The latter makes any statement you'd make against me unbelievable. No one would accept you were aware that I was trafficking underage girls, and then went and had consenting sex with me. They would assume it was just the bitter words of a spurned lover." He paused, "I hope you appreciate that I'm giving you options, rather than taking your life."

I choked out, "I'll go with the girl."

When I was escorted into the bedroom, the girl was waiting for me, wearing violet lingerie. Before Keith left us, he gave me a departing piece of advice. "If this doesn't get rolling right away, you will soon have a very nasty, and quite large Kharon teaching you both a lesson."

These men all fantasized about being the personification of evil. If Zig was the Kharon and Stewart's dogs were Cerberus, Stewart had to see himself as the tempter or Hades. It was all so foreign to the loving kindness in which I was nurtured.

After the door closed, I could hear the lock clicking in place from the outside. I quickly scanned the room. Dad would say, *Think like a soldier*. There were three solid walls and a large window overlooking the pool—but the window didn't open. *Who builds a house with no fire escape in the guest bedroom? Keith Stewart*. There was a dresser, a vanity set with a stool, and a closet with sliding mirrored doors. I had no resources. While that stool might hold a frail teen girl, it would be worthless as a weapon. I could hear Jeremy's voice, saying, *There's always something*.

The girl was soon at my side. She brushed my cheek with her palm. "My name's Nitika." She kissed my cheek and instructed, "We'll take it nice and slow."

I softly responded, "I'm not into this."

She smiled as if I had told her something seductive. She pulled me close, "It's just a *job* for me—life or death for you," she hissed, while keeping her face neutral. "We're buying time." She stepped back and, exuding sexuality moaned, "I would like that too—but not right away."

Her movements were as smooth as a well-trained temptress. I wanted to say, *Okay psycho girl, pull yourself together*.

She kissed my lips, but I didn't respond. I felt nothing. There was no *I kissed a girl and I liked it*. She tugged at my shirt and I resisted. I screamed inside my head, *Think! Find a way!*

Nitika sauntered in front of a wall, her eyes guiding me to the location of a small lens, as she spoke, "We'll start with a body rub. Strip down to your underwear and lie face-down on the bed."

When I didn't respond, she spoke quietly through a fake smile, "Keep it moving or he'll turn you over to the beast."

As if on cue, someone was unlocking the door.

She quickly whispered, "I'm trying to save you. When Zig takes 'em, they don't come back."

It finally registered. This girl was putting her welfare at risk by trying to save me. I gently touched her cheek and peered into her eyes. "Thank you." There was no erotic passion between us. But there was the tender gratitude I could offer a girl who risked everything for my survival. Putting my trust in a fifteen-year-old prostitute, I started pulling my shirt over my head.

Keith peered in, saw what I was doing, and stepped back out again.

As soon as the door locked, I pulled my shirt back on. I whispered to Nitika, "Distract him."

She stepped toward the lens and slowly let lingerie fall to the floor.

I raced to the closet and yanked out the wardrobe rod, sending hangers of clothes toppling to the floor. Like a warrior with a spear, I ran at the large window and smashed the pole's end through the glass.

I could hear Stewart frantically working at unlocking the door.

Holding the pole like a javelin, I cleared the shards of glass.

I climbed on the ledge of the window. Stewart raced toward me.

Just before he could grasp me, I jumped.

I remembered thinking if I landed on the cement, I'd break a leg. The worst possible outcome would be hitting the edge of the pool and breaking my back. But I made it—I splashed hard into the pool—parachuting to the bottom, bubbles surrounding me like I'd been submerged in a glass of 7-Up. Energized by my success, I swam back to the top. When my head surfaced, everything was dark.

# 40

*Her father was a failure*
*Her mother was a comfort*
*To a doctor and lawyer and an Indian Chief*
*Her shirt ran out of buttons . . .*
*The bank took away her diploma*
*Locked it up inside of a chest*
*She moved away to Oklahoma*
*And got a tattoo on the side of her breast . . .*
*Headlights flashing, caught her skirt in the wind*
*Yonder comes a truck, drove by two men*
*Shotgun man leaned out, and said do you want*
*to take a ride?*
*Out in the pale moonlight*
*Help me somebody*
—JOHN PRINE, DOWN BY THE SIDE OF THE ROAD

## JON FREDERICK

12:30 A.M., MONDAY, MAY 25, 2020
TALON DRIVE, EAGLES LANDING, ST. AUGUSTA

I pulled over down the road from Stewart's driveway. A brief discussion took place between BCA Supervisor, Paula Fineday, and Wally, the fifty-year-old investigator who had taken my former job. His age could be a plus, if he was a police officer who recently moved into the field, or a minus, if he was a problematic employee who periodically got shuffled around the state rather than fired.

He told Paula, "I want it on record that I'm not comfort-able having a non-agency employee directing this operation."

Paula reminded him, "Duly noted. *I* am directing this operation, Wally. My order is to take the guidance of Jon Frederick as *my* word, until notified otherwise. Jon was my best field agent last year, and he is the only one who has a clue of both the layout and of what is going on, here."

The agent wasn't happy, but he acquiesced with a reluc-tant nod.

We were soon joined by employees from Xcel Energy and St. Cloud Animal Control. Like a magnet pulling resources from throughout the county, squad cars quietly rolled in my direction. I asked some of the deputies to spread out on the edge of the property and others to wait in their vehicles. I had St. Augusta police officers and animal control join me at the end of the driveway.

A large, boulder of a man, flanked by three Dobermans, came walking toward us down the driveway. I recognized him as Riezig Ziegler, or "Zig." The guard dogs growled and, with the command, "Cerberus!" they fell silent.

I quietly told animal control, "Tranquilize the dogs if he cuts them loose on us." I then told the Xcel engineer, "Cut the power to the house." I directed Zig, "Please put your hands in the air."

Zig pointed directly at me and the dogs sped toward us like they were shot out of a cannon.

When the first Doberman was hit, Zig went for his cell phone. I quickly ordered, "Tase him!" I couldn't have him warn-ing Stewart of our arrival. An electrified hiss cut through the night and Zig tipped over, as if someone had swiped his feet out from under him. His eyes were wide and incredulous. He strug-gled to a knee to get back up. I nodded to a second officer. The hiss sounded again and, after a mumbled litany of swearing, he was down and out. I told an officer to cuff him when he was able.

Paula asked scornfully, "Was that necessary?"

"I couldn't have him warning Stewart. Harper's life is at stake. We know he kidnapped her and he might be a killer. We have no idea what we're facing. I needed him immobilized."

The home went black and I joined an officer in his squad, as patrol cars rolled into the driveway.

The front door was rammed open and we were greeted by Keith Stewart holding a flashlight, yelling, "You have the wrong house! What the hell are you doing?"

Paula emerged from the shadows and stepped up to his face. "Special Agent Paula Fineday, BCA," she announced, holding out her badge. "We have information indicating Harper Rowe is being held here against her will and we have a warrant to search your home."

Keith yelled, "I can guarantee you, she's not in my house. Let me speak to my attorney, before you do anything!"

Paula turned to an officer and said, "Cuff him."

I waved on the officers with the battering ram and Maglites to follow me into the house.

The first bedroom door we busted open featured extensive video equipment, now black due to the power outage.

When the second door gave way, we spotlighted an adolescent girl in a t-shirt and distressed jeans, patiently waiting for us, safely on the bed. The Native girl had called Moki when she saw the guard carrying Harper into the home. Moki called me.

I ran to the busted window to see Harper drenched, but fully clothed, standing next to a police officer by the pool. The officer was wrapping her jacket around Harper. Harper looked up at me and smiled. Relief washed over me as I waved her in to join us.

The Native girl didn't have a lot to say, but did give us her name—Nitika. I fetched Harper a large towel and Nitika found her some dry clothes. Once Harper was dressed, Paula and I returned to question the duo, sitting next to each other on the bed.

Harper gave her entire account of what had transpired, while Nitika quietly observed. Harper ended by questioning, "How did they know where to find me? I didn't even know I was going to Shawna's home until the last minute. Do you think Margo's in on this?"

"I think they had a GPS tracker on your car."

Keith Stewart could be heard in the hall, telling officers, "I don't know the combination to the safe. You'll have to get it from my lawyer." Keith now stood in the doorway in hand-cuffs shouting, "Nitty, don't say a word!"

Paula directed the officers, "Get him out of here!"

Keith arrogantly countered, "You may as well release me, because I guarantee you, I will not be convicted of anything. I have too much—on too many people."

I asked Nitika, "Are you okay?"

She nodded.

As they escorted Stewart away, I told her, "Thank you for calling Moki. You may have saved Harper's life."

The hardened adolescent studied me skeptically and maintained her reverent silence.

Paula told her, "We are going to have you meet with a Sexual Assault Nurse Examiner at the St. Cloud Hospital. The acronym is SANE, so if they say, here is your SANE nurse, you will know what they are talking about. We will have you stay at Terebinth tonight, as they have got great people to talk to. I doubt they can keep you, because you are a juvenile, but we will have you stay there until we find a placement that is suitable for you."

The fact that Paula was also Native seemed to bring the girl some solace, as she finally spoke. "Are they going to do a rape kit?"

"Yes."

She looked beyond Paula and said quietly, "Okay."

Harper asked her, "Did Keith have sex with you before I got here?"

The girl had resumed her silent deliberation, but responded with an almost imperceptible but affirmative nod.

Disgusted, Harper uttered, "Ugh! That sick . . ." She then turned to Nitika, "Thank you! I am sorry for everything you've been through. I owe you. I'm so grateful to you! Do you mind if I give you a hug?"

The girl tolerated it, but didn't seem to need it like Harper did. Still, it seemed to soften her.

# 41

*The day will soon be over*
*And evening will be gone*
*No more gems to be gathered*
*So let us all press on*
*When Jesus comes to claim us*
*And says it is enough*
*The diamonds will be shining*
*No longer in the rough*
—John Prine, *Diamonds in the Rough*

## JON FREDERICK

10:30 A.M., TUESDAY, MAY 26, 2020
BUREAU OF CRIMINAL APPREHENSION,
101 11ᵀᴴ AVENUE NORTH, ST. CLOUD

Yesterday was, once again, a state record for new coronavirus cases in a day (+841).

Paula Fineday called me into her office to pick my brain for any additional information on the homicides.

She shared, "Late last night, the officer sitting guard on Keith Stewart's home was called down the street to perform CPR on a boy who had been pulled from a pool. The call turned out to be a prank. When he returned to Stewart's driveway, there was an explosion in the house so severe the ground shook. He then watched the home burst into flames.

Our CSI crew discovered an acetylene torch had been burning under the safe up to the point of the explosion. While the acetylene did not cause the explosion, it helped open up the safe and made the contents vulnerable to destruction. The person, or persons, responsible knew exactly what they were doing. They did not need the contents of the safe. They wanted to make sure the contents were destroyed. Keith Stewart and his accomplice, Riezig Ziegler, were released from jail two hours later."

Paula exhaled a tired breath. "The Native girl's last name is Brown. Nitika means *stone angel*. She is still refusing to make a statement against Stewart, but we have DNA, and Nitika acknowledged she only had intercourse with one person yesterday. Thanks to your shutting the power off, we have videos of Keith Stewart being sexual with her, not just yesterday, but also on five previous occasions. We also have Stewart with an underage blonde, but we have not identified her yet. So, right now, Stewart is facing five counts of Criminal Sexual Conduct in the Third Degree for having intercourse with an underage girl, and for kidnapping—although our evidence for the kidnapping charge is not particularly strong."

"Harper was at his home, with garrote marks around her neck."

"Zig isn't talking and Stewart's spinning quite a tale. He's saying Billy Blaze was the girl's father and she was conceived at a party at that very home. He's claiming Harper showed up with the marks on her neck, trying to get some revenge. We never found the garrote."

"What's his explanation for her leap out the window?"

Paula shared, "He has none. Harper admitted she had previously visited his home on her own accord. And Nitika is not making any statements against Stewart. Any theories about that?"

"Harper told me Nitika believes she's going to get some

money from Stewart. Now that he's facing charges, I think her odds of a payoff have improved."

Paula agreed, "Stewart is going to be charged, but her silence can keep others from being prosecuted."

I asked, "Were they able to find clips of anyone else with Nitika on the hard drive?"

"No. It had been recently replaced. The old hard drive was in the safe. The heat generated by that fire roasted all of the electronics and recordings in his safe. This explosion was done by a professional. We may never know who it was. The prank call was untraceable."

It deeply bothered me that we'd no longer have an opportunity to identify all the young girls and prosecute the people who had solicited them.

Paula drummed her fingers on the desktop, waiting for me to respond. I didn't. She finally offered, "It is not all doom and gloom. Regardless of whom he knows, Stewart is not getting out of this. We have high quality videos for evidence." She added, "And, I found a Native couple who will keep Nitika safe until this is all sorted out. If they can blow up a home this efficiently, they could come after her."

She inserted a flash drive into her laptop. "On the remaining hard drive, there is a woman who comes to Stewart's house the day after we discovered Randy Vogel's body. She doesn't meet with Stewart. Instead, she meets with his sidekick, Zig. They go into a room with no video coverage, so it is not particularly useful."

I sat up, "Do you mind if I take a look?"

Paula fast forwarded as she told me, "Brunette. Professional. Decent looking." She stopped.

And there she was—"Margo Miller."

Paula asked, "How is she related to all of this?

"She was Billy Blaze's lover. Tell me what you have on Zig."

"Riezig Ziegler? He did some serious time from the end of 1998 to 2013 for trafficking meth, but has no charges, since."

Zig's sentence fit into place perfectly. "I believe Billy Blaze turned state's evidence on someone at the end of 1998 to get an Aggravated Assault charge dropped. And Blaze was found beaten in an alley in late May of 2013."

Paula shuffled through papers. "Riezig—or the guy you call Zig—was released from the Minnesota Correctional Facility in Lino Lakes on May 6, 2013."

Stewart had blackmailed Blaze to avoid prison. But Blaze had money once again, before he died. I thought about Stewart's skull ring and the marks on Blaze's face. Stewart hit Blaze for Zig's sake, then he came back and hired Blaze to sell drugs. I'd bet anything that Zig never knew Stewart blackmailed Blaze out of his charges, while he let Zig take the fall and sit in prison for thirteen years.

Paula continued, "So Riezig had motive for the murder of Billy Blaze. Now we need to figure out where Blaze was murdered." Paula reorganized the reports on her desk. "I appreciate all of your help, but this homicide investigation belongs to the BCA. Prosecuting Keith Stewart will be delicate. I cannot have you interfering. And by the way, turn over your list of suspects in the Billy Blaze murder and we will begin DNA testing. I will have Wally get DNA samples from everyone who is not already in the system. Dr. Ho suggested you have an extensive list, so he will be busy."

I thought to myself, *And a guarantee from Gunner that the killer is on that list.* I had no issue with giving her the names. Paula had resources I couldn't access, like the ability to search Gunner Black's house. I shared, "Gunner Black claims he knows who killed Blaze, but he's not giving it up."

Paula added, "Gunner could have let Zig know Blaze was passed out at his home. We will get a search warrant for Gunner's house . . ."

# 42

*If dreams were lightning*
*And thunder was desire*
*This old house would've burned down*
*A long time ago*
*Make me an angel*
*That flies from Montgomery*
*Make me a poster*
*Of an old rodeo*
*Just give me one thing*
*That I can hold onto*
*Come to believe in this livin'*
*Is just a hard way to go*
—JOHN PRINE, *ANGEL FROM MONTGOMERY*

## SERENA FREDERICK

2:30 P.M., TUESDAY, MAY 26, 2020
PIERZ

Four Minneapolis police officers were fired yesterday, after African American, George Floyd, was killed during an arrest. He was suspected of buying cigarettes with counterfeit money. It was a ridiculous allegation to die for. Most people who passed counterfeit money weren't aware that it was counterfeit—they received it from another source. A veteran officer kneeled on Mr. Floyd's neck for eight minutes and forty-six seconds, while George gasped, "I can't breathe." George was unresponsive when the ambulance arrived.

Riots had started in Minneapolis. Stores were robbed empty; an independent bookstore was burned to rubble. Windows were broken out of local businesses, squad cars vandalized, and this was just the beginning. I was rethinking my attempts to get Jon back into the BCA. This certainly wasn't the time for it. There had also been thirty-three deaths in Minnesota yesterday, as a result of the coronavirus. Another new daily record.

Hopelessness triggered flashbacks for me. Jon wanted me to take a break from the case, but the day's events in Minnesota were so nauseating, I had to work. It was hard working an investigation with someone you loved. I wouldn't have told anyone, other than Jon, about how my work had sparked physical reactions to my own past trauma. I just shut up and went to work.

I sent a FaceTime call through to Trisha. I understood her. There was a shaming adrenaline rush in victimization and, when you were struggling, you felt a self-destructive impulse to trigger it. I'd felt it, too. Therapy put stoppers in my brain that reminded me, *That's not who I am. Don't go there.* Victimization tainted your ability to recognize *safe* people. I didn't live as a victim. I lived as a warrior. I knew it would come up and, when it did, I'd have to fight it.

I was glad to see Trisha looking a little brighter. She said, "I saw the doctor today and he won't give me any more benzos for my anxiety. I have to stick with the SSRIs, which I guess are okay—as long as I don't have a partner complaining about my lack of a sex drive. If I had to guess, I'd say the doc was gay."

"Did you have to guess?"

She laughed, "I just meant some people's orientation is more obvious than others. It doesn't concern me. My head is a dangerous place right now and the meds are the force field keeping my mortifying shame at bay. Okay, smartass, why'd you call?"

"Do you think Keith Stewart killed Billy Blaze?"

Trisha balked, "No. Absolutely not. I'd love to see Keith in prison, but he had no reason to kill Billy. How has Stewart managed to get by with destroying girls' lives for decades? I don't believe he's ever had any consequences."

"Blaze sent Stewart's right-hand man to prison for five years."

Stunned, she offered, "So that's why Billy had me deliver the money. I thought he trusted me, but he was just afraid he was being set up."

"Why was Blaze paying Stewart?"

"Billy was selling drugs for him. Stewart wasn't wild about Billy, but Billy could move drugs. Stewart never would have killed him—Billy was his cash cow."

"How about Zig? Could he have killed Billy? Blaze sent him to prison."

"No," Trisha laughed. "Zig and Blaze puffed up like peacocks around each other, but didn't make a peep. I was there when Stewart made it clear that the past is in the past. If either made even a gesture toward the other, he was off the payroll. And they abided. No one dared interfere with the cash flow."

I paused, "Can I ask you a very personal question?"

With a low chuckle, Trisha said, "I've asked you to leave your husband. Told you disgusting things that happened to me as a child. You asked me to sleep with Gunner to get information."

Taken aback, I stammered, "I—I never expected you to sleep with him. I would never ask that of you. You *slept* with him?"

Trisha snickered, "Talking has never been my forte, doll. Regardless, I think it's safe to say we're at the point of asking personal questions. Give me a little of your rape story, first. I need to know you're in this with me, not just interrogating me."

I squeezed my hands into fists and forced it out, "A man broke into my home and attempted to anally rape me, years ago."

"Attempted? We call that denial in my groups."

I suddenly flashed back to his weight on me—trying to gasp for air. "Okay—I was raped. I guess I meant he didn't *penetrate* me."

Trisha waited for me to continue. When I didn't, she asked in a barely audible voice, "What scared him off?" She compassionately experienced the trauma with me.

I shuddered at the memory as I revealed, "I had a brutal, physical fight with him and, after my head was struck hard, I started violently throwing up. It grossed him out and he left."

Trisha questioned, "What is it with rapists and anal sex?"

"I think it's about inflicting pain and basically making you do things you don't like." I had to change the topic to maintain my composure. "Did you go to a crack house with Robert Johnson and Billy Blaze?"

"How the hell do you know that?" Trisha considered, "Rob bragged to you about sleeping with me, didn't he? Look, if you're not interested in him, you have my permission to pass along my number." She paused, "Rob is a nice guy, but he isn't the guy for you. You should talk to NJ. He's not into any of the drug stuff. Loved me unconditionally, I just didn't feel it. Love sucks. Wouldn't you love to have a redo with some lovers?"

"There was one guy that, years ago, I misread. He became kind of a jerk for a while, but ended up becoming a *nice* guy. Well, nice-*ish*, anyway." I shook the thoughts of Clay free and teased, "So you were involved with MJ—Michael Jordan?"

"He should be so lucky! Noah Johnson. NJ. I'll call him for you. I owe him one."

"Trisha, I'm married!"

"Yeah, to a psychopath."

### 11:30 P.M., PIERZ

I DIDN'T KNOW WHY I FELT I absolutely needed to pick up green tea tonight. I think I needed to get out of the house and, knowing there was a Coborn's open, even if it was in Sartell, gave me a reason to go for a drive. The store was quiet. I went to the tea and coffee aisle, number seven, and ran into Clay Roberts. Like a lion, Clay was musclebound and had a thick mane of blonde hair. After some small talk, Clay invited me to stop on my way out of town to see his home, which he had just finished remodeling. I was wide awake and knew everyone would be sleeping when I returned home, so I thought I wasn't taking time from anyone.

I remember being nervous as I stepped into the beautiful home. I was embarrassed—I was *married*, for God's sake. Clay indicated he'd been alone for some time. I admired the detail he put into making every aspect of his home warm and inviting. When I realized I had stepped into the master bedroom, I stopped and said, "I need to go."

Clay approached me and I looked up into his hazel eyes as he kissed me. I tried backing away, but stepped back into the wall. I can't explain why, but I kissed him back. It became more comfortable and I rationalized that I'd already kissed him, so I guessed it was okay if it lasted a little. I seemed to hunger for him and, as we passionately enjoyed our embrace, my jeans were unbuttoned . . . So warm and wet and tender—his kiss.

AND NOW I WAS LYING IN bed, sweating and ashamed. *Why?* I'd stayed home for weeks. I went out once and threw everything away. I loved Jon. I loved my family. Jon would be awake waiting for me. Clay was with Hani.

I looked over at the muscular man lying next to me and he was sleeping. Better yet, he was Jon. I had never left home. The conversations I'd had with Trisha, combined with my own past trauma, led me to this shameful and weirdly arousing nightmare. It was a nightmare I used to have years ago, before I became a survivor. I had no desire to be with Clay and he never assaulted me. But I was ashamed of having been with him, in the past, and had learned that all of our shame gets mixed together when we're anxious.

I took my t-shirt off and lay across Jon's chest.

He stirred, "Are you alright?"

"Yeah." The battle between good and evil lies in the heart of every person. Everyone involved in this case had the potential to make loving, or hurtful, choices—just as I did. Discussing trauma still messed with my head. But I was not destroying my life, or the people I loved, over it. I just needed to pay attention when the self-destruct light came on, and not push it.

It didn't take long for Jon's body to respond to my touch. I'd made a decision that, anytime my dreams go there, I'd turn it into something positive for my marriage.

# 43

*You come home late and you come home early*
*You come on big when you're feeling small*
*You come home straight and you come home curly*
*Sometimes you don't come home at all*
*So what in the world's come over you*
*What in heaven's name have you done*
*You've broken the speed of the sound of loneliness*
*You're out there running just to be on the run*
*—John Prine, The Speed of the Sound*
*of Loneliness*

## JON FREDERICK

12:25 P.M., FRIDAY, MAY 29, 2020
ST CLOUD HOSPITAL
1406 6TH AVENUE NORTH, ST. CLOUD

The riots spread from Minneapolis to St. Paul last night. The Third Precinct building was abandoned by police, taken over by rioters, and burned down. Target closed twelve stores in Minneapolis and St. Paul, in the interest of protecting their employees. Dozens of small, minority-owned businesses were looted and burned. I felt badly for all of the small business owners, trying to wait out the coronavirus shutdown, who were now shutting down due to the damage. Rioters apparently believed that destroying innocent peoples' businesses was necessary retribution for the ridiculous killing of George Floyd. The argument that violence and destruction was what needed to happen to get people to listen was the same argument I heard from assaultive men in domestic abuse cases. Martin Luther King Jr. was right, when he warned, "Hate begets hate. Violence begets violence."

A white pawnshop owner shot and killed an African American man who broke into his store with a group of people that ransacked the place. The story is one of the looters had a gun and the owner fired into a crowd. Neither the business owner, nor any of the witnesses, were cooperating with the police. The crime scene and cameras were all destroyed. There would be no charges. A man lost his life. *For what?*

To their credit, African American leaders were speaking up against the rioting. Change was necessary and we were badly in need of creative solutions.

People had a right to be frustrated. Good would eventually rise up from the peaceful protests, but today was distressing. While we'd exhausted our police force putting out fires, calls to respond to rapes and domestic abuse weren't being answered promptly. The immediate fallout would be Minneapolis police would back off in their community presence and, over the next several months, there would be a sharp increase in murders and thefts. And to top it off, once again, we reached a new record, yesterday—thirty-five coronavirus deaths in Minnesota.

I met with Margo Miller outside the St. Cloud Hospital, during her lunch break, to share everything I had regarding the search for Billy Blaze's killer. We social distanced, each standing on one side of her Mercedes. I handed her a sheet of paper across the hood and told her, "One of these eight people killed Billy Blaze."

Margo snatched greedily at the page and studied the list of suspects:

Keith Stewart—blackmailer and drug supplier;

Riezig Ziegler—Stewart's henchman;

Cheryl Wicklin—victim of rape;

Gunner Black—victim of assault and partner in crime;

Rachel West—(Gunner Black's daughter) victim of
  threats from Blaze as a child, teenager, and an adult;

Deb Zion—(Blaze's half-sister) victim of theft and
  threats;

Trisha Lake—lover;

Margo Miller—lover.


Margo chided, "I see I made the list, but you didn't include obvious suspects, like Connie Berg or Kali Rowe."

"Connie Berg believed Blaze was still stalking her, until his body was unearthed. We had Trisha present our list of suspects to Gunner Black and Gunner claimed the killer was on the list. Kali wasn't on that list. I also don't believe Deb Zion is involved."

She commented, "You really whittled this down."

"The BCA is going after Keith Stewart and Gunner Black. If it's one of them, the BCA has a better chance of proving it than I do. I think Gunner knows who killed Blaze. I want that thought to steer the ship for a bit."

Margo looked over the names again and peered up at me. "There are a lot of women on this list."

"The murder weapon was nine-millimeter Smith and Wesson MP Shield, which has been the most popular handgun for women for years." Testing Margo's reaction, I noted, "Gwyneth felt you purposely kissed Blaze passionately in front of her."

"Asserting my dominance." Margo smiled like the Cheshire cat from Alice in Wonderland. "Dominance hierarchies have existed longer than humans. Like animals, we posture to eliminate the competition for the desired sire."

"Despot."

She smirked, "No, just proving to be the fittest. Maybe despot if she continued to fight, but she cowered soon enough. You don't have Gwyneth on the list."

"Too soft-hearted."

"*Pliant* is a better word." Margo handed me the list back, "You have not disappointed."

"I honestly don't believe you killed Blaze."

Satisfied with this, she ordered, "Find the killer and let me be the first to know when you do."

# 44

*Somebody said they saw me*
*Swinging the world by the tail*
*Bouncing over a white cloud*
*Killing the Blues*
*Now, you ask me just to leave you*
*To go out on my own and get what I need to*
*I don't need to find what I already have*
—JOHN PRINE, *KILLING THE BLUES*

# JON FREDERICK

6:45 P.M., SATURDAY, MAY 30, 2020
EAST LAKE STREET, MINNEAPOLIS

I had hoped to close the Blaze homicide tonight, but the case needed to be set aside for the time being. Moki was in trouble. Harper sat next to me in my Taurus as we hurried to Minneapolis. At 8:00 p.m., the major highways around Minneapolis and St. Paul were being closed to prevent rioters from setting fires throughout the metro, so we'd need to be in and out quickly.

Harper explained, "I received a call from Native elder, Chimalis Bena—she said Moki's in danger. Chimalis owns a restaurant called the Blue Pheasant on Lake Street in Minneapolis. When Moki was in school, he used to cook some nights for her, to help her out. She called him this morning and told him that rioters were just down the block and she's afraid she's going to lose everything." Harper expressed, "When Chimalas called me from Moki's phone, it finally made sense."

"What are you talking about?"

"Moki and I had a nice long talk, last night. I told him I was going to break up with Greg and, when the night ended, we were perfectly in sync. But this morning, he called and told me he didn't want to see me today and he didn't know when he'd be available. It was so unlike him. I had a feeling he was going to do something dangerous and he was afraid I'd follow him. I told him not to go after Stewart by himself. He promised he wouldn't."

"Migizi Communications, a Native American youth center, has been set ablaze in Minneapolis. It's half a block from the Minneapolis Third Precinct, which was also torched last night. Are you sure he's at the Blue Pheasant?"

Harper saddened. "Yes. What does *migizi* mean?"

"Eagle."

I had worked a homicide in this area with the Minneapolis PD last year, when I was with the BCA. When I turned onto Lake Street, a traffic cop waved for me to roll down my window. He recognized me and gestured me through. I didn't mention I was no longer with the BCA.

WHEN WE ARRIVED, MOKI WAS STANDING in front of the Blue Pheasant, trying to push people back, while looters smashed windows and stole items. A broken sign that once advertised, *Special: Tweed Kettle Salmon,* lay in pieces next to him. A mixed-race group of rioters taunted him, while a Native elder sat sadly in the shade, behind him.

I found a parking spot out of the way, between a burned out minivan and neon orange construction cones. As I scanned the area cautiously before getting out, Harper stated the obvious, "This is bad."

I reached over to the glove compartment and removed my handgun, tucking it in the back of my jeans when I stood up. The good news was nobody was yielding a weapon, yet. The bad news was this place likely had lot of sharp knives and dishes that could potentially soon be airborne.

As we approached, Moki, was yelling, "Do you know how long Chimalis worked and saved to open this restaurant?" He paced back and forth, making certain to always protect an elderly woman I presumed was Chimalis. In contrast to Moki's agitated state, she sat stony-eyed on the restaurant's steps, a screen door swaying from one hinge behind her. Chimalis's salt and pepper hair was pulled into a long braid that fell over her stooped back. She wore a once-white apron that reflected the stains of a thousand, lovingly-prepared meals. Her long fingers rubbed busily over the backs of her hands—the only sign she was in distress. Chimalis's watchful and wise eyes slid smoothly across the crowd and landed on us as we got closer to Moki.

Moki pointed at people in the crowd like a TV evangelist calling out sinners. "Stop trashing it! This is all she has."

A white woman commented coldly, "That's what insurance is for."

Moki wasn't backing down, "Insurance is not going to cover the extent of this damage. All of these places are underinsured. How are you going to replace the pictures of her ancestors?"

A black man shouted, "It's what needs to happen to create change!"

Moki took a step toward him, "*This* is what has changed. Chimalis had a restaurant. Now she has nothing. She cannot rebuild. She maxed out all of her resources to start this place. All she has left is the debt and the cost of cleanup. So, thank you," he waved his arms in the air at the entire mob, "all you assholes!"

Bottles immediately rocketed toward Moki and he was struck in the head. I moved between him and the crowd, yelling, "Back off!" It was all I could do to hold Moki back from going after his attackers.

Harper stepped in to help and Moki stopped struggling.

Surprised, he grumbled, "You are not supposed to be here."

Harper and I guided him back as the group surged forward.

As a white person, I had difficulty understanding the logic of the white people in the crowd. A white cop murdered an African American man. Now, as a white person, you were going to go in and destroy a Native woman's restaurant? Didn't that make you just like the abusive cop?

The tide turned when a striking black woman, recognizable to most, pushed through the crowd and stood next to Chimalis, who was now on her feet. News reporter, Jada Anderson, took the elder's hand and, in a gesture of solidarity, held it high.

I had called Jada on the way to the restaurant, but wasn't sure if she'd be able to take a break from her reporting to help us out. I knew I didn't have the ability to stop this. Jada elected not to bring the camera crew, as she was afraid attention would escalate the situation. It was a gutsy of her to come alone. Like pale bookends, Harper and I joined hands with Jada and Chimalis.

Grumbling obscenities, the crowd moved on to the next business.

Still fuming, Moki asked Jada, "How can they destroy their own neighborhood?"

"They're not from here," she explained. "Some are outstate idiots who claim to be part of something without doing the work. Many of these rioters aren't even from Minnesota. Don't believe they're all on the side of Black Lives Matter. Rioters distract from the root issues." Jada changed her tone, "Don't forget the Minneapolis Police Department brought this on. The union protects officers that should be fired and the department has dragged its feet in addressing racial issues. They were given funding to train officers that went unused. Add in the Minneapolis PD's failure to even respond to complaints about racism and it's not surprising we are here."

The bruise over Moki's eye was starting to swell.

Harper told him, "Let me see if I can find some ice."

Moki lamented to all of us, "It breaks my heart for Chimalis. We had a couple people from school coming over to help the Blue Pheasant out and keep it afloat. We were all busy, but we gave away our time—and, after today, it means nothing."

I pointed out, "You volunteered your time for Chimalis. That means something."

He still hadn't calmed down. After surveying the damage, Moki turned his anger toward Jada, "It hasn't been any easier for Natives, but we don't destroy cities. It's possible to be heard without all the destructive drama."

Jada turned her chin up like she'd fought off a slow punch. She stepped into his face, "There comes a time when silence is betrayal. Do you know who said that?"

Moki replied, "No."

"Learn. And look up the Freeway Phantom. A killer of six black girls in the early seventies. A highway worker found one of the girls, dead in the ditch, and called the police. One week later, the body of that black girl was still there. The police still hadn't responded. All of the forensic evidence for the murders was destroyed and the case was never solved. They did discover a seventh African American homicide victim named Angela Barnes, but they determined her case wasn't related to the others. Angela was just fourteen years old. Do you know how she died?"

Moki softly uttered, "No, I don't."

Jada tapped her forefinger against his chest. "She had been raped, sodomized, and murdered by two white cops. While all these black girls were being murdered, two white girls, the Lyon sisters, were abducted in the same area. The disappearance of those white girls was one of the highest profiled cases ever, and their case was in the headlines until it was solved. And that's why we scream, Black Lives Matter! We've just had enough!"

Sufficiently chastised, Moki humbly remained silent. Harper had retrieved a semi-cold bag of peas from a damaged freezer and he applied it to his head.

Jada directed us. "I need to get back to my crew and you need to get the hell out of here." She turned to Chimalis, "Do you have a place to stay?"

Without emotion, she answered, "If they help me clear a path to my door, I can stay here. I live above the restaurant."

"You shouldn't stay here," Jada said with concern. "This isn't over."

Moki went to Chimalis, "Come and stay with my family for a couple days."

Harper offered, "Tell me what you need and I'll crawl over the rubble and pack for you."

Chimalis nodded with stoic appreciation. She and Harper disappeared into what was left of the restaurant.

Jada approached me and gave me a peck on the cheek. She said softly, "I mean it. Get them out of here. Tonight could be bad, according to what we're picking up online."

"Thank you, Jada. Take care of yourself. You know as well as I do that the white survivalists are out here, too."

"Too well." She gave me a sad smile. "Now, I need to go rescue the next gallant in distress."

Moki watched her walk away. "Isn't she a newscaster?"

"Yes, and a great person. Jada just kept you from taking a severe beating. When you calm down, I'll expect that you'll apologize to her."

Moki asked, "What was I supposed to do?"

"Pick up Chimalis and leave. If it wouldn't be for her calling us, your epitaph would've read, 'He gave his life for a tweed kettle salmon special.'"

Still frustrated, he turned to me, "Can I ask you a question about the Freeway Phantom? If they never solved the murders, how do they know the cops didn't do all of them?"

"The cops had alibis for the others and the victims had African American male body hair on them. Don't lose sight of her point. The investigation disrespected the importance of those girls' lives. And this is the exact lack of respect that's haunting people right now. This is a moment where we all need to be very careful of our choices."

As we walked back to the entrance of the Blue Pheasant to check on Harper and Chimalis, they met in us in the doorway. Chimalis's necessities were thrown into bags slung over each of their shoulders.

I told Moki, out of earshot of Harper and the elder, "I would bet this isn't the worst thing Chimalis has been through."

His eyes blazed as he argued, "She had *hope*. That's lost now."

"So, help her get it back. Chimalis can work through this. My family had to file for bankruptcy when I was a kid—it was humiliating. It's shaming and embarrassing to tell people you can't pay them back, I know. But it's survivable."

As Harper joined us, Moki turned on a heel and stalked angrily back into the remains of the restaurant. Harper stood motionless, watching his back with confusion, holding his sopping bag of peas.

# 45

*I bumped into the Saviour*
*and He said pardon me*
*I said Jesus you look tired*
*He said Jesus so do you*
—JOHN PRINE, *EVERYBODY*

## HARPER ROWE

10:00 A.M., TUESDAY, JUNE 2, 2020,
BIRCHMONDT DRIVE NORTHEAST,
WEST SIDE OF LAKE BEMIDJI, BEMIDJI

It was time to have a difficult conversation with Greg. There were few things more gut-wrenching than ending a long-term relationship. The *mum effect* referred to our reluctance to talk about bad things—such as acceptance that there was no happy ending for Greg and me. So much had happened since I'd seen Greg watching *Game of Thrones* with Shawna, the conversation felt anticlimactic.

Before I could tell him it was over, Greg commandeered the conversation. "I've spent some time with Shawna, but please hear me out. COVID-19 causes a lethal form of respiratory distress in which oxygen levels plunge and breathing becomes impossible without a ventilator. The ventilator delivers oxygen to the lungs with the hope of buying time while the body heals. So, we face a difficult balance with ventilation—too much oxygen causes lung damage and too little damages the brain and kidneys. I'm getting good at finding the perfect balance, but people still die. And then, when I look out the window, I see Minneapolis and St. Paul burning all around us, from rioting. It's depressing. So I've gone to Shawna's to mindlessly watch TV for a couple hours. That's it."

I wanted to ask if they had sex, but did it make a difference, at this point? Before I could speak, he went on, "Look, I know you like this Moki guy. And I haven't been there for you. I'd love to hate him, but I imagine he's a great guy. If he desires you, he's got exquisite taste. I just picture myself some night, a decade from now, maybe picking up takeout and running into you. We're going to look at each other and wish we would have never let *us* go. We have this moment—this very moment—to keep that from happening."

The memory of Greg holding me when my mom died, when I could barely stand, prevented me from responding.

As if reading my heart, he added, "I still wonder, sometimes, how would Kali Rowe handle this? Your mom was classy and moral—decisive. Everything a person should aspire to be."

I would never date another man who knew my mom. I sighed and said, "Okay." I didn't have to make the decision right in that moment.

But I did it, anyway. "Greg, I need to end our relationship. I appreciate your help through some terrible times and respect your willingness to put your life on the line to help others. But it's over, for me. I'll mail back your items."

"Don't bother." He was hurt. "I'm not trying to be a jerk. Rioters burned down the post office and I don't know when I'll receive mail, again. Harp, there has to be something I can do. I'll do *anything*."

I forced out through tears, "No . . ."

It wasn't the closure I would have preferred, but it was over. I burned that bridge. Mom was right. Greg always sang her praises, especially when I was trying to hold him accountable. I didn't want to come to resent hearing about my mom. Still, part of me wondered if I'd done the right thing.

My phone buzzed. *Come on, Greg—please.* This was hard enough; I didn't want to keep rehashing it.

Barely audible, a man's voice garbled, "Call it off."

I didn't recognize the number. I pushed my volume button up and pressed my phone harder against my ear. "Who is this?"

"Gunner," he croaked. "I didn't kill Blaze. But if you don't call it off, they're killin' me."

I sat up. "Gunner Black?"

"Yeah."

"Why would someone kill you?"

"Because I know who killed your father." He went into a coughing spree and was swearing when he came back on. "Last night, he busted my ribs—my nose. Next time, it's my neck. I have a daughter—like you—who hopes to marry someday. She wants me at her side to walk her down the aisle. It's one last thing you can do for Billy. He wouldn't want me talkin'. Just call 'em off."

The line went dead.

# 46

*Where are the bootstraps*
*To lift myself up?*
*Where is the well*
*Where I once filled my cup?*
*Where does this sorrow*
*All turn into joy?*
*And where oh where, is the sleepy eyed boy?*
—JOHN PRINE, SLEEPY EYED BOY

## JON FREDERICK

11:35 A.M., TUESDAY, JUNE 2, 2020
13ᵗʰ AVENUE NORTH, ST. CLOUD

After Receiving a call from Harper, I immediately drove to Gunner Black's home. I pulled on a pair of gloves and hooked the bands of my mask on each ear. His door was unlocked, so I let myself in. Trepidation tried to slow my legs, but I pushed through the ransacked home and found Gunner, curled into a bloody heap on the living room floor.

Scarlet splatters had dried across his too-pale face and crusted heavy into his thick, handlebar mustache. Gunner's thinning, oily hair was pulled into a ponytail and the strands that were knocked loose were matted. He struggled as I carefully helped him to his feet. He hoisted his Wranglers back in place under his substantial belly and tucked his faded black,

AC/DC t-shirt back into his pants. Despite his gruff exterior, his eyes were reflective of a sad heart. I tore off a pile of paper towels in the kitchen and wet them, then handed them to him.

Gunner made his misery clear as he pushed my hands off his arm, grumbling, "I can do it. You've done enough—you're gonna get me killed." He swiped roughly under his nose as he said, "I need some air," and led me out of his house to the backyard.

We sat in battered wooden chairs by a rusty fire ring. *Imagine the crimes that had been contemplated in these seats.*

Gunner's hot air deflated visibly as he slumped forward, resting his elbows on his knees. He spoke to the ground, "For the most part, I've been sober since 2017. I hate the man I was back then. I know I asked for all this shit. I started it."

"How?"

He grunted, "You haven't figured it out? Billy fuckin' took advantage of everybody, but if you dished any of it back, there was hell to pay. It started when I slept with Connie Berg. She was the first. Hell, they were all pretty decent and she wasn't the only one who sought solace from me when Blaze was tearin' her down. I told Connie not to tell him—but she did. He went nuts. Beat her, tore apart her store, even tried to kill himself, by first trying to OD and then jumpin' out of my movin' car. Blaze loved Connie. He didn't give a damn about anything after that."

"So, he got you back by telling your daughter he had an affair with your wife."

"Yeah, although he *did* have an affair with my wife. I guess *he* started it. But to be honest, I wasn't aware of it when I slept with Connie. Blaze was impulsive about drinkin' and sex, but if he had dirt on you, he could hold onto that for years. And when you were at your lowest point, he'd announce it to the world." Gunner eyed me under a pair of thick eyebrows, cocking one up as he challenged me, "What do you think happened to Darko Dice?"

I patiently waited for him to continue.

"They were at a biker party and Darko made fun of the way Blaze said somethin'. Blaze was all tequila'd up. He announced that Dice had a charge for molesting a boy two decades earlier. Darko had told Blaze about it one night when they were commiseratin'. Blaze gave the gang Darko's real name and told them they could look up his picture on the sex offender registry. Dice went home and blew his brains out." Gunner gazed off into the distance. "If I had any sense of morality, back then, I would have killed Blaze myself. But I didn't—and I regret it. He was the opposite of Midas—everything he touched turned to shit. I don't blame the killer."

I leaned in and asked, "Was he angry that you were home when he and Trisha returned from jazz night?"

He scoffed, "Jazz night—jazz is what you get when you push a blues band down a flight of stairs." Gunner kicked a rock away with his black leather boot. "Blaze was pissed and I was home. Two separate things."

"What was he angry about?"

He gingerly touched his damaged nose. "Did he need a reason?"

I took a shot. "His proposal to Trisha didn't go well."

Gunner looked away.

"Who killed Billy Blaze?"

He shook his head, "I can't—"

"But you know with certainty."

He nodded his head, looking over the oxidized edges of the fire ring, but clearly far away.

I pleaded, "You've got to give me something, man—I'm trying to save your life."

I nearly missed his quiet response. "I heard the shots."

Blaze had proposed to Trisha. Gunner knew about it, but Margo did not. Rachel West was called to save Gunner. Blaze's killer could only be one of two people. It was a simple case, once you scraped off all the hate. I was on a roll, so I kept pressing, "Did you kill Randy Vogel?"

With a crooked finger, he pointed at me and swore, "I didn't kill *anybody!* Even as a drunk, I never crossed that line. Billy Blaze never directly killed anyone, either. He was jacked when he heard Vogel was off the grid. Dead people don't buy drugs."

I considered, "Blaze thought he could turn Vogel to testify on his behalf. Why didn't he bail out? He could've prevented it."

"Margo was in charge of that. When she refused to bail him out, that was the beginning of the end for her."

"You know who killed Vogel."

"I have my suspicions."

"The BCA will be here before the night's over. Last chance. Who killed Randy?"

He challenged, "Who didn't want Blaze sitting in prison?"

I could think of two people. "Margo Miller. Keith Stewart." And neither was with Billy Blaze on his last night.

Gunner stared at me without saying a word.

It seemed impossible, but the murders of Billy Blaze and Randy Vogel weren't related. I responded, "Keith strikes me as a guy who generally doesn't get his hands dirty."

"I'm sure he didn't do it himself."

"So, you're thinking his muscle man, Zig, did the deed."

"Zig loved it when Stewart called him Kharon—Hades's ferryman."

According to Greek mythos, Kharon walked beside a soul in her dreams, as he guided her to the afterlife. Hades was not only the God of the Underworld; he was also the Giver of Wealth. Stewart and Zig thought very highly of themselves.

Gunner stared at me. "I'm not sayin' *anybody* did it. I honestly don't know. You asked me my suspicions."

He was shutting down. "Whoever beat you is going to kill you, if you don't turn him in. I need a name."

At that moment, BCA agents infiltrated the backyard, announcing, "Gunner Black, you're under arrest for the murder of Billy Blaze."

Gunner's last words were, "You said it."

Shortly after I told Margo Miller that Gunner knew who killed Blaze, Zig showed up to beat the answer out of him. But even facing death, Gunner didn't give it up. Who did Gunner care for that much?

ON MY WAY HOME, I RECEIVED the call I'd been waiting for, from Dr. Amaya Ho.

I answered by telling her, "Please tell me you pulled some DNA off that rope."

Amaya dryly repeated, "I pulled DNA off of that rope."

"Seriously?"

Amaya cracked, "When's the last time we joked around?"

I thought, *never*. "And you compared it to everyone on the list of suspects?"

"I have. There is no match."

"That's impossible—Rachel West, Trisha Lake, Gunner Black, Zig Ziegler, Keith Stewart, Margo Miller—it has to be one of them."

"No match." Amaya reminded me, "DNA doesn't lie . . ."

# 47

*Sabu was sad the whole tour stunk*
*The airlines lost the elephant's trunk*
*The roadies got the rabies and the scabies and the flu*
*They were low on morale, but they was high on . . .*
—John Prine, *Sabu Visits the Twin Cities Alone*

## JON FREDERICK

12:30 P.M., THURSDAY, JUNE 4, 2020
111 13TH AVENUE NORTH, ST. CLOUD

The riots in the Twin Cities ended after the National Guard moved in, full force. The manner in which they ended the looting and destruction, in one night, was impressive. This week had been the lowest number of COVID-19 increases in Minnesota in a month. They kept telling us COVID could hit like a hurricane come fall, but for the moment, we were on a downhill slope and that was good.

Bars and restaurants were reopening this week. Owners were scrambling to create outside seating where they previously had none. They were appealing to wait staff to return to work, but it was a tough sell. On top of unemployment benefits, they were given an additional $600 a week because of COVID. The irony was that some people were making so much money, not working, they no longer qualified for medical assistance.

Despite positive events in the state, this case sucked. When I told Serena the DNA on the rope wrapped around Blaze's tarp-entombed body didn't match anyone on our list, she went to our bedroom and cried. Serena had been through gut-wrenching agony in her interviews on this case and we were back to step one. Dr. Ho was able to tell me the DNA on the rope came from a man of European ancestry—basically, a white guy. The man who tied that rope wasn't on our radar. It didn't make any sense.

I spent the morning at home, playing with our kids. No matter how dismally I failed, time with Nora and Jackson lifted my heart. It *meant* something.

Serena had a determined look in her eye when she joined the kids and me for lunch. When we got a minute alone, she told me, "Ignore the DNA results."

Surprised, I asked, "Why?"

"You're the one who's always telling me that, ninety-nine percent of the time, the killer's name is in the murder book. We've been through the murder book and we've shortened the list to six people. I know you think I'm too emotionally invested, but I can *feel* it." She implored, "We're close—trust me. Maybe there's just a weird explanation for the DNA on the rope . . ."

I CALLED PAULA FINEDAY AND TOLD her Gunner Black admitted hearing the shots that killed Blaze. Mid-afternoon, Paula invited me to take a look inside Gunner's house. The BCA had completed their search. I met her outside; we both donned our masks as we left our cars and converged on the driveway. She didn't greet me—Paula wasn't one for frivolous conversation. She merely nodded at me, then turned and strode to the front door.

As we walked through the weathered, two-bedroom home, Paula revealed, "I grilled Gunner Black and he just sat and stared at me. Did not say one word." When I didn't respond, she looked at me deadpan. "Kind of like that."

I finally said, "Dr. Ho said Blaze was lying supine when he was shot."

"She thought the shooter was sitting next to him."

I thought out loud, "If Blaze was lying down, he was probably in the living room or a bedroom." I carefully studied the floor and the walls in both bedrooms. Both were carpeted with painted walls. There was no indication the walls had been patched to cover a bullet hole.

Paula knew what I was looking for. "Wally had the same thought. He had the bedroom floors cleared and even pulled the carpet up. There were no bullet holes."

I walked into the storage room.

Paula's boots clacked as she followed me across the hardwood floor. The walls of the storage room had recently been paneled. A slovenly pile of opened boxes spilled over each other on a rug against one wall. The BCA had clearly already torn through them. It was a pet peeve of mine when investigators destructively ransacked homes, for two reasons. Somebody had to clean it up and they might have destroyed evidence someone would later want to revisit.

I asked, "Is Wally the one who went through the boxes?"

Paula nodded, "He is thorough, but messy."

"This room bothers me." It was larger than the two bedrooms and had windows.

"What are you thinking?"

"It would be my first pick for a bedroom and you can bet Blaze had his pick. This paneling is relatively new. Do you know of anyone who's paneled a room in the last three years? Or even the last decade?"

Paula pointed to a wall, "I'd put the head of the bed on this wall."

With nothing further said, we got to work, moving boxes to the middle of the room.

I went to my car and grabbed a crowbar I kept in the trunk. I returned and we began ripping paneling off with determination. As the first five-foot wide panel came off, the wall behind it was finished and painted a dirty blue.

As the second panel came loose, there it was. A bullet-sized hole, plastered over on the wall. I took out my pocket knife but Paula reminded me, "You are not BCA."

In some weird Freudian display of power, she then pulled a large hunting knife out of her bag and began carving into the wall until she could get ahold of the bullet.

As she worked, I remarked, "Yours is bigger."

Without emotion she said, "Never forget it."

Paula rolled the bullet around in her gloved hand, carefully studying it. "There is no blood or tissue on it. This shot missed." After dropping it into an evidence bag, she went over the scenario. "Okay, Blaze and Trisha come home from the bar. An argument ensues. Gunner calls his daughter, Rachel West, to pick him up. Blaze insults Gunner's ex. Blaze breaks Gunner's nose, but then lets him reset it. Gunner returns home the next morning. Blaze is never seen alive again."

It has always bothered me that Blaze was shot in the neck. Who would shoot someone, likely passed out, in the neck? After considering Dr. Ho's forensic report, I told Paula, "If the bullet we found missed, and there was a bullet in his head, the bullet that went through his neck is still unaccounted for."

"The neighbors never heard shots?"

I remembered the goose feather in Blaze's wound. I walked into an adjacent bedroom and returned with a down-filled pillow.

Paula smiled as she made the connection. "Gunner used the pillow as a silencer. This explains how he managed to miss him at such a close range."

"I don't know that Gunner killed Blaze. I know Zig didn't kill Blaze." Anyone who killed him out of anger would have looked him directly in the face. The pillow suggested the killer was afraid of Blaze. I asked, "So, where's the bullet that went through Blaze's neck?"

We pulled up the braided rug. One of the slats in the wood floor had clearly been replaced, as its gleam was outstanding among the more worn boards.

Paula's mouth screwed into what was as close to a satisfied grin as we were gonna get. "Time for me to have another conversation with Gunner . . ."

I STEPPED OUTSIDE AND CALLED SERENA with the news. "We now know where Blaze died and that he probably died after that last argument at Gunner's house."

She reminded me, "You thought the shooter was a woman, because of the gun."

"I still do. I know it seems obvious, but I don't see Gunner killing Blaze. He felt Blaze's vengeance was justified—that's why he let Blaze reset his nose. Gunner was covering for someone."

Serena softly interjected, "Someone he loved. Whatever happened to Gunner's ex-wife?"

"She died from cancer two years before Blaze disappeared."

"Blaze really was an ass—degrading Gunner over a deceased loved one."

"Something really pushed Blaze over the edge that night."

She asked, "Who was Gunner dating at the time?"

"It wasn't someone Gunner was dating."

Serena interrupted, "You don't think Blaze slept with Rachel."

"No, I think Gunner slept with someone Blaze was sleeping with. All I have right now is a theory. We need evidence. Gunner's in custody, so he's safe, for now."

# 48

*Night has fallen*
*I've said the things I did*
*The only baby sleeping*
*Is when I was a kid*
*Do you remember*
*When you were my friend?*
*That's the way I'd like things*
*Just like way back then*
—John Prine, *Way Back Then*

## SERENA FREDERICK

### 1:45 P.M., THURSDAY, JUNE 4, 2020
### PIERZ

Over 670 Businesses were damaged by the rioting in Minneapolis and St. Paul. Peaceful protesters were fired upon with rubber bullets and injured. I imagined the agony of worrying if your son had a taillight burned out on his car, he might not come home. We all loved our children. It was truly unbearable.

With a heavy heart, I called Gunner Black's daughter, Rachel West. The arrest of her father offered a new opportunity to enlist her cooperation.

When she finally answered, Rachel was agitated. "My dad's just been arrested. Why should I talk to you?"

"Because I don't believe he's guilty."

She hung up.

My phone trilled immediately with an incoming call. She called me back on FaceTime. "If we're going to talk, I need to see you."

Rachel was in her mid-twenties and quite striking. She appeared pretty stocky, but her simple black, deep v-neck tee complimented her curves. Her dark hair, punctuated with shots of burgundy, fell over her shoulders—bangs fringed across her forehead and layers framed her round face. Her makeup highlighted expressive, dark eyes. Stylish, large-framed glasses reflected a muted news show playing in front of her.

Eager to speak, Rachel said, "Dad has been telling me not to talk to anybody, but I've got nothing to hide and it's not helping." She propped her phone in front of her and adjusted herself in an overstuffed chair, folding plump arms across her chest. This movement pushed her bosom up from her v-neck, revealing edges of a tattoo I couldn't discern.

"I can understand you're in an impossible position, Rachel. I appreciate your willingness to talk to me. May I ask—could you go over what happened on the last night you saw Blaze?"

"Okay. My dad called me to come get him. I didn't know exactly what to expect, but not much surprised me with those two. When I got there, my dad and Blaze were going at it like they always did. I never liked Blaze and that night confirmed my reasons why. He was trying to throw my dad out of his home—a house my dad *owned*." Her eyes flashed with angry fire. "And Dad was just conceding. Whatever went on between them, before I got there, was bad enough he had to call me to pick him up *right now*."

"What happened after you arrived?"

"Blaze blocked the door and wouldn't let us leave until we heard him out—and he got nasty." She grimaced at the memory. "He was going on about the sexual stuff he did with my mom when my parents were still married. We loved Mom—and we'd lost her to cancer. And there was Blaze, emotionally stabbing us to death. He was with my mom long before he and my dad were friends, although honestly, I don't know that it would have made a difference. Blaze was able to describe my parents' bedroom and my mother's body, in detail. I lost it—I slapped him and told him to just shut up."

I could see it; not sure I'd have done anything different. "How did Blaze react?"

"He wasn't fazed for a second. He laughed in my face and became even more graphic about the way my mom would plea-sure him—really sick stuff. My dad charged at him, but Blaze was ready. He cocked back and punched him, hard, breaking his nose. Dad was laid out on the floor, bleeding, and I tended to him. I wanted to call the police, but my dad wouldn't let me. Blaze reset Dad's nose and we left. I told them, 'You're both crazy!' That was the last night my dad drank."

I didn't feel it was my role to mention Gunner's relapse with Trisha. Instead, I asked, "Do you think your dad killed Billy Blaze?"

"No. Absolutely not. He was with me until noon the next day. I walked into the house with him and called out for Blaze, to make sure it was safe. Nobody answered. If he was home, he would have hollered, 'Shut up, bitch!' Billy Blaze was evil. When I look back at that night, it was insane. Blaze loved to provoke people. He'd make a gun with his thumb and forefinger," she demonstrated the gesture, "and pull the trigger at cops while driving down the road."

Jon had left me a note with an odd question for Rachel. I asked, "Where was Gunner Black on Tuesday night, the night before the argument?"

Puzzled, she responded, "At home. But Blaze was gone that night. Texas Hold 'Em on Tuesdays, at Shooter's Saloon. He never missed it."

"And you're sure your father was home? This was three years ago," I reminded her.

"Yeah, I'm sure—he got a DWI Monday night, so I called to see how he was doing. He seemed to be in a surprisingly good mood, so the Wednesday call was a shocker."

Rachel shut the muted TV off before she continued, "My mom and I had some hard conversations before she died. When she told Blaze she'd left Dad, she thought he would be ecstatic. Instead, he beat her, raped her, and then asked her, 'What makes you think I'd ever settle for a cheating whore like you?' He ruined her life and it felt like she gave up. I didn't tell my mom I knew about the affair. It's a horrible secret to hold."

I sighed with empathy—I couldn't imagine. "I'm so sorry. That sounds terrible. Are you okay?"

With a wistful smile, Rachel said, "Yeah, I think so. Thanks for asking." She wiped away a tear with the heel of her hand. "Let's get back to saving my dad."

"Fair enough. Where was Trisha Lake while all of the arguing was going on?"

Rachel tapped a bright blue acrylic fingernail against her full, burgundy-stained lips. "That's a good question. Trish was there when I arrived. When the argument got heated, she bailed. I don't remember exactly when. And Blaze was on his usual rant. *She can stick it up her* blah, blah, blah. *Trisha's a* blah, blah, blah *bitch*." She mimed a puppet on her hand with each blah. "I'd heard his incessant whining about women so often, it was just noise. And that's why he had to talk about my mom. He knew that would get to me." A flicker of defeat twitched at the side of her mouth.

"Was Trisha ever violent?"

"No. Never. Blaze was still on the chase with her, so he was nice to her face. I got my jabs into him, but it was nothing like the onslaught of evil he hurtled at me. When he told me Trisha was going to be his trophy wife, I told him he must not have won first place—maybe consolation. Blaze hated me, simply because I helped people who struggled. I was the antithesis of Billy Blaze."

"Did you ever talk to Trisha again?"

"No—wait, I did, once. She called me and told me I needed to clean up the blood from Dad's nose being busted. My dad had already offered to clean it up. I think Trish was freaked out about having to go back there after she heard about their brawl."

"When did she call you? Was it that night?"

Rachel pondered, "I don't remember. It was three years ago, as you said. It could've been that night or even the next. It didn't mean anything to me, at the time. I was done with Blaze, and I, for damn sure, wasn't going to clean up after him."

Jon quietly entered the room. I knew he was being kind, but I didn't need him checking up on me.

I asked Rachel, "Did you ever think about killing him? Blaze?"

She let out a one-syllable, bright and boisterous laugh. "Yeah. Because my dad lived with him, I've had to take shit from Blaze since I was little. He ruined my mom and made my dad his whipping boy. Addiction kept my dad tethered to Blaze. But I wasn't the one who sent the Grim Reaper to Hell. I have to admit, though," her eyes twinkled, "I was in a good mood when I heard they found his body." She covered her mouth to suppress a smile, even as it was evident in her expression. "My dad's relationship with Blaze was bizarre. The morning after the brawl, I asked him what needed to happen for him to get sober. It cost him his marriage, and then he allowed that pig, Blaze, to repeatedly degrade him. I told him I'd had it. I was never picking him up again. Maybe he could tolerate the people he loved being humiliated, but I couldn't—and wouldn't. So, he got sober, but he still left notes on the door for Blaze, stating he was welcome."

She had me thinking. "Does Gunner think you killed Blaze?"

Rachel laughed quietly. "He asked me, quickly followed by, 'Don't tell me.' I swore to him I hadn't killed Billy, but I am happy he's dead. People started to heal when that monster got his."

Jon took my phone and turned the screen on himself. "I just walked in. Hi Rachel—I'm Jon Frederick and I'm assisting Serena with this investigation. Sorry to intrude, but would you mind if I asked a question? You might have some helpful information without realizing it."

She nodded with trepidation.

"Who paneled Blaze's bedroom?"

Rachel looked confused, clearly not what she was expecting. She said slowly, "Dad insisted on doing it on his own. He needed to be busy when he first got sober. My dad wanted no interruptions until he was done. We hardly even spoke during that time. Why?"

"Did you hear gunshots as you were leaving?"

Flabbergasted, she said, "Umm—I don't know. It sounds crazy, but it wasn't unusual for Blaze to fire a gun in the house when he was raging. I'd just heard my mom had done the most disgusting things you could think of, with a man I hated with all the malice in my soul. I watched him bust my dad's nose, and then reset it! I was in shock. I just don't remember."

I slid close to Jon and whispered to him, "You're getting off track."

Without a word, he handed over the phone. Jon wrote on the notepad in front of me, *It's off track, but we need her to corroborate our version of what occurred.*

I urged Rachel, "I need to know exactly what Blaze said about Trisha."

"It's disgusting."

"It's important," I countered.

Rachel quietly ruminated for a minute. "I said something like, 'Do you think your date likes hearing about you banging my mother?' He said, 'If she doesn't like it she can take a broom handle and shove it up her—'"

I cut her off, "That's all I needed to hear." There was the trauma bond—the connection to her own past victimization that had the potential to unleash her rage. "I think I can help your dad, here. I'm sorry, but we need to go . . ."

# 49

*It's a mighty mean and a dreadful sorrow*
*That crossed the evil line today*
*How can you ask about tomorrow*
*When we ain't got one word to say*
*So what in the world's come over you*
*What in heaven's name have you done*
*You've broken the speed of the sound of loneliness*
*You're out there running just to be on the run*
—JOHN PRINE, *SPEED OF THE SOUND OF LONELINESS*

## SERENA FREDERICK

2:30 P.M., THURSDAY, JUNE 4, 2020
BUREAU OF CRIMINAL APPREHENSION,
101 11ᵗᴴ AVENUE NORTH, ST. CLOUD

I lifted my blouse and Paula Fineday attached a small micro-phone to the front strap of my bra. Jon stayed out of her way, but reading my husband's face, I knew he was anxious about this.

Paula instructed, "We will test the mic when we get out in the parking lot. Agents will be following and ready to step in at any time. All you need to do is say, 'Taurus,' and we will swoop in."

I nodded, "Okay." I kept my hair down, hoping it would add to camouflaging any sign of the wire. I nervously smoothed it over the front of my shirt.

Paula commented, "I still think Gunner Black killed Blaze. Blaze punched him in the face and had an affair with his wife. Rubbed it in his daughter's face."

Jon argued with her, "I think Serena's on the right track, here. Rachel West said Trisha called her and asked her to clean up the blood. If Trisha was gone before the argument got heated, how would she have known about the blood?"

We knew Blaze neither made nor received any phone calls after he returned home that night. I pointed out, "Gunner didn't have time to kill Blaze. He left with his daughter, with a busted nose. When she returned him home the next day, Blaze was gone. I think Gunner set this whole scenario in motion."

Paula questioned, "How so?"

"I believe he slept with Trisha Lake the night before. I have a witness who saw her car at the house. Gunner was home and Blaze wasn't."

I added, "That would be a severe narcissistic injury to Blaze."

Jon told Paula, "I'll drive Trisha along the path she traveled that night. I think our best chance to keep her talking is to trigger memories."

Still overwhelmed with the thought that Trisha could have killed Blaze, my brain was itching to remember a name from past conversations with her. Michael Jordan came to mind, but I knew that wasn't right. It was bugging me, though. Was it NJ?

Paula was nothing if not observant. She watched me closely, as I kept fiddling with my hair, and attempted to reassure me. "We have put a GPS tracker on your car, Serena, so we do not need to be right on your tail. We will be there in seconds. Try not to worry. Ask Jon—I have a great track record."

I could feel Jon evaluating my ability to pull this off. He gave me an encouraging smile, then turned to Paula. "If Trisha admits to killing Blaze, take her into custody. Margo is vain and vengeful. If she had Zig give Gunner a beat-down, she wants more than incarceration for Blaze's killer."

Paula took it all in, in her usual, expressionless manner. "Anything else I should know before we do this?"

I blurted out, "Noah Johnson!"

Confused, both Paula and Jon's heads swiveled toward me. Paula asked, "What?"

"Trisha mentioned that she owes Noah Johnson a big favor. You might want to see if his DNA matches what was found on the rope . . ."

### 1:10 P.M.
### HESTER PARK, 1020 6ᵀᴴ STREET NORTH, ST. CLOUD

JON AND I MET TRISHA LAKE at a small park just south of the St. Cloud Hospital, along the Mississippi River. We watched as she paced the sidewalk and nervously spun the charm bracelet around her wrist, like the wheel of fortune, hoping for something other than BANKRUPT.

Jon asked, "What does Trisha always say when you ask her about Blaze?"

When I didn't respond, he reminded me, "*I left him* and didn't see him again after that night. It's true. She left him in the woods."

I whispered, "I feel for Trisha. She had such a terrible start."

Jon didn't have the same benevolence. "I have a hard time with people who abandon their kids and then, later, expect them to be there as needed. Trisha battles between gloating in the superficial charm she receives from men and her painful feelings of worthlessness. Where does she find value? She hasn't done anything meaningful. She didn't raise her kids; she hasn't maintained work."

I compassionately argued, "Maybe with the right guidance, things would have been different."

He studied me for a moment and apologized, "I'm sorry. My judgment was harsh. I feel like she intentionally turned a blind eye to Blaze's abusive behavior. But, who am I to judge anybody?"

I squeezed his hand, and then stepped out to open the back door for Trisha.

Before she reached the car, my phone chirruped with a text from Paula that read, *We just picked up Noah Johnson in Cold Spring. His first response was, 'I've been waiting for this day.'*

I joined Trisha in the back seat.

She twisted toward me as she got comfortable and cocked an eyebrow. "Why did you bring Jon?"

From the driver's seat, Jon glanced at us in the review mirror and told Trisha, "You were the last one to see Billy Blaze alive. Noah Johnson is now cooperating with the investigation."

Trisha gasped and her back stiffened in fear.

I squeezed her forearm briefly and told her, "I am so sorry we have to have this conversation, but I'd rather be the one who talked to you about this. I've always felt you were a good person in a terrible situation. I still do." As we passed by the Place of Hope Ministries on 9th Avenue, I conceded, "I'm a terrible investigator. I feel like you've been trying to confess to me, but I didn't want to hear it."

Trisha exhaled years of pent up shame. "I've been faking smiles for so long, I don't know what my real emotions are, anymore. But I was honest with you. Every time you brought up a new suspect, I told you it wasn't him."

3:05 P.M.

111 13TH AVENUE NORTH, ST. CLOUD

JON DROVE US TO GUNNER BLACK'S home. After he parked, he asked Trisha, "Do you want to go inside?"

She shook her head. "It's not necessary. I've relived it enough in my head."

I told her, "They've found a bullet in the wall of Blaze's old bedroom, which matches the bullet in his skull."

Trisha sighed, "It has to be such a relief for Noah. I've wanted to talk about this, but never had the courage. He was just a nice guy—trying to help a woman who felt trapped."

I suggested, "Blaze's rage wasn't about Gunner being home. It was about your sleeping with Gunner."

Trisha bumped my shoulder. "Well, look who's not afraid of personal comments anymore?" She shared, "Billy proposed to me over a mic in front of the whole damn bar. I had to say yes. I know it sounds crazy, but you have to do crazy things to survive with Billy. If he wanted you, you were *his*, until you made him not want you. On the way home, I played my trump card. If he knew I'd slept with Gunner, he would never marry me. So, I told him. I prayed Gunner wouldn't be home, but—" Her words trailed off. "Gunner opened my eyes when we killed that bottle of tequila together a few weeks ago. Billy just wanted me to run his drug money."

Jon asked, "Do you think Keith Stewart had a hand in Randy Vogel's murder?"

Trisha clearly didn't want to talk to Jon, but rushed out the words, "We didn't talk about Randy. Billy made it clear if anyone asked about Randy Vogel, you can bet they're wearing a wire. I wasn't going to be accused of being a rat. It cost Randy his life."

My nerve endings felt electric, with a wire now resting against my bare skin. Jon caught my glare in the rearview mirror and immediately understood I wanted him to stop talking.

With a slight nod, he turned on Highway 10 and headed north.

I took the lead once again. "Okay, Billy proposed and you told him you slept with Gunner. What happened next?"

"He went ballistic. Gunner called his daughter, but Billy was on the rampage and wouldn't let Gunner leave. I went and laid down on Billy's bed." She gazed out the window at the protesters in front of Planned Parenthood on East St. Germain Street, as she reflected, "The luster had worn off of my infatuation with Billy. At first, he was a modern-day outlaw; he bought me all the cocaine I wanted—a never-ending party."

Jon was taking us to Highway 10. I took her hand in both of mine, in an effort to support her. This poor woman was unloading it all, even though it could cost her life in prison.

She brought herself back to task. "I could hear everything from the bedroom. Billy was telling Rachel about the sexual acts he made her mother perform. Licking his—" she cut herself off. "It felt so incestuous. And it was so disgustingly detailed, it made my skin crawl. I think I started flashing back."

I asked, "Did they know you had retreated to the bedroom?"

"They thought I left, but leaving didn't feel right. Gunner warned me not to tell Billy we hooked up. He waited for us to get home that night, because he was afraid if I told, Billy might kill me. Gunner took the brunt of Billy's rage to save my life. When I heard Billy say something about shoving a broomstick in me, I just went into a trance." She whispered, "Have you ever had a broomstick shoved—"

I softly told her, "No," and patted her hand gently to comfort her. "Did Billy?"

"No. But I shared with him that it was how I was molested, as a young girl. Knowing that, why would he even *say* that about me?"

Because it was what Billy Blaze did. In Trisha's case, he set fire to a past trauma bond of hers.

Trisha continued, "I walked out to my car. I don't know how long I sat there and cried. Billy was still going to make

me marry him and he then threatened to hurt my son, if I
didn't! My body tightened over and over as I thought about
that broomstick. I couldn't see a way out. Billy had given me a
handgun for protection that I kept in the glove compartment.
When I finally walked back in, everyone was gone. Billy was
standing by the bed when I came in the doorway. The first
shot caught him dead to rights. I added two more for good
measure." She softly shared, "I can shoot."

I glanced at Jon. We both knew Billy was lying on his
back. It was fairly common for people to try to save face, even
in confessions. I asked, "Are you sure Blaze was standing?"

She realized I knew she was lying and quickly changed
her story. "Like a coward, he laid on the bed and begged for
his life."

I doubted it, but I wasn't going to argue.

Jon mouthed in the rearview mirror, "Let it go."

We were now in Royalton.

Trisha yelled to Jon, "Turn right before the 10 Spot!"

He drove east on Centre Street, passed Linda's Bar and
Muyre's Motors.

When we drove onto the Platte River Bridge, Trisha
said, "Stop."

Jon pulled over next to the wooden McGonagle Park
sign, on the other side of the bridge.

Trees with fresh, chartreuse leaves bowed over the small
river in reverence.

We stood on the bridge facing south. Trisha shared, "Here's
where I threw the gun out. I was in such a weird state. We
pulled into Royalton and I panicked. I needed to get rid of the
gun. I told Noah to stop here and I tossed it into the river.
It's crazy when I look back—I had a dead body in the *trunk*."

A car drove by us over the bridge.

"It was dead quiet that night," she continued, as if from
another place. "It must have been about three-thirty in the

morning. Noah had to guide me back to the car." She stared directly into my eyes. "Do you understand why I shot him?"

I felt emotionally exhausted. "I do. No more abuse."

Trisha grasped desperately at my hand. "Don't sell yourself short, hon. You're the reason this case is now solved."

*I got her to confess. What else should I be asking?* Feeling lightheaded, I braced my foot on the bottom rail of the bridge and leaned forward. If I was working with anyone other than Jon, they might have viewed it as a relaxed and composed gesture.

Jon, however, recognized my behavior as unnatural. He immediately stepped in and asked Trisha, "At what point did you connect with Noah, that night?"

Trance-like, she steadfastly gazed out over the river, watching the relentless power of the surging water headed toward an inevitable destination.

She finally spoke. "After I shot Billy, I remember sitting on the bed, holding this bloody pillow. My only thought, at the time, was *I can't let this blood run all over.* I had a tarp in my trunk. It was all I could do to drag Billy off the bed onto the tarp." She turned to me to explain, "I knew I couldn't move that body. And then I thought of Noah. He told me he'd do anything for me. So I called him and told him he needed to come to me—it's bad. I made him promise no police. Noah assumed Billy beat me. When he arrived, he was shaken by the scene. He said, 'I'll help you, but when we're done, you can never call me again.' I told him we'd bury Blaze in Paul Bunyan State Forest."

Jon asked, "Why there?"

Trisha told us, "I grew up in Park Rapids. We used to go hiking on the forest's trails, so I was familiar with them. I remember frantically digging that hole for Billy's grave. Noah finally pulled me out of it, repeating, 'That's enough.'"

Trisha leaned forward and gripped the top bridge rail with both hands. "I came back to Minnesota to confess, but when I talked to the old crew, one person after another said if Billy was murdered, we ought to give the killer a reward." She looked at me imploringly, "I swear I can still smell his blood in the trunk of my car. I gave myself one last night out on the town before I went to the police station. And that's when Carlos Tavares convinced me I could start over with him." She gazed after the moving river and then looked directly at me. "But I *didn't* start over, did I? I just let the current take me down the same path."

The unmarked car that had been trailing us zoomed in with lights ablaze. Paula and two BCA agents stepped out and Paula told Jon and me, "We will take over."

Trisha didn't fight or argue; rather, she straightened her posture, shook her hair away from her face, and held her head high. She offered her hands to be cuffed and, when she looked at me, there was a hard mixture of pride and resignation in her eyes. She was assisted into the backseat of the unmarked squad car.

A chill ran up my spine as I caught her eyes, now entombed in the past. As she was carted away, I went to Jon for an embrace. He wrapped his strong arms around me and my body trembled.

I thought out loud, "I had to delve into my own past trauma to gain Trisha's trust and, once I had earned it, I used it to prosecute her. It feels so vile."

Breathing me in, Jon shared, "That is the unfortunate role of an investigator. We're not the judges. We clarify what happened."

I'D NEVER FORGET STANDING ON THAT bridge and squeezing him tight. I was sad, but gradually, I felt lighter. I'd been sharing deep, personal thoughts with a murderer; a part of me sensed the sin and agonized over it. But the demon I'd been battling left with Trisha. I defeated my demons; she still carried hers.

We returned home and relieved my parents from their babysitting duties. Jon drew me a bath and got the kids ready for bed. Once they were tucked in, I joined my husband in the bedroom. There was much to be said for the compassion a deeply intimate relationship fostered. I felt like being pampered and, with little said, I let that happen. A warm blanket would have been fine, but I let Jon run with his desire to help me attain peaceful tranquility. A blanket draped over our comforter and a pile of towels, warmed in the dryer, rested at the foot of the bed. I stripped, laid face down and closed my eyes. With warm lotion, he slowly worked the muscles loose from my neck to my toes. As he finished each area, he rubbed the lotion off with a hot wet towel, and then covered the area with a warm dry towel. I fell into a deep sleep.

# 50

*Broken hearts and dirty windows*
*Make life difficult to see*
*That's why last night and this morning*
*Always look the same to me . . .*
*Memories, they can't be boughten*
*They can't be won at carnivals for free*
*It took me years*
*To get those souvenirs*
*And I don't know how they slipped away from me*
—JOHN PRINE, SOUVENIRS

## HARPER ROWE

7:45 P.M., SUNDAY, JUNE 6, 2020
1012 HAVEN ROAD, LITTLE FALLS

It was a beautiful, still night. The warm temperatures promised the arrival of summer. Donning our first pairs of shorts of the season, Moki and I stopped at the Dairy Queen in Little Falls. Then, with our treats, we walked across the street and down the road, to the railroad bridge. I sat on the edge of the bridge, my feet dangling out twenty-five feet above the water, while Moki walked the bridge.

I needed to end the craziness that had become my life. As much as I savored his company, Moki and I were not okay, in my book. An unfinished conversation hovered around us like the Mayfly tentatively touching on my hand. I stretched my fingers out, but it steadfastly stayed put. The fly was harmless, but it would continue to bother me until I dealt with it. The lifespan of my issue with Moki was short-lived, but it needed addressing. I blew the insect gently off my skin. It bothered me that he faked ending our friendship, so I wouldn't interfere with his effort to help Chimalis.

Moki sensed my earnest resolve and slid down to join me on the side girder.

I told him, "Don't protect me from the truth. It's an insult."

"I didn't want you to get hurt."

"Greg treated me like an ornament. I'm not fragile and I won't be with a man who treats me like I am. Just know, if you do that again, you're ending us."

"It was my battle to fight." He waved half-heartedly at another Mayfly, affording him the opportunity to avoid eye contact with me.

"And you thought a social work major, someone with training in addressing social issues, would really be a hindrance."

He said nothing.

I continued, "Your anger didn't accomplish anything, Moki. In a sense, it wasn't any different than the people who trashed Chimalis's restaurant. They felt an injustice and acted out. You felt an injustice and you were ready to beat somebody up over it." He didn't need a lecture from me. I reached over and took his hand. "You could've been killed."

"What is life?" He asked with exasperation. "The flash of a firefly in the night. The breath of a buffalo in winter. The shadow that runs across the grass and loses itself in the sunset. Those are the words of a Blackfoot Chief, Sahpo Muxika."

"I love the imagery," I sighed. I offered a smile and agreed, "Life *is* fleeting. But it's hard to commit to a man who is okay being dead tomorrow."

Moki turned sharply toward me. "I have no death wish, Harper, but as a Christian, don't you believe there are things more important than life?"

"I do." It was why I admired my dad's involvement in the military. Jeremy made that commitment for all of us.

He asked, "What are you thinking about?"

"Burning bridges."

"Please—give me another chance."

I took his hand. "I'm not saying goodbye. I'm cleaning house—clarifying what I have that's worth saving and burning the rest."

"Burning bridges was a white man's strategy," he mused. "Generals burned bridges after crossing them to eliminate the possibility of retreat. Cortez burned his ships in his conquest of Mexico, so the men would have to either conquer or die." Lost in his thoughts, Moki continued, "He defeated us in 1519, but Spain was so racist, at the time, they wouldn't accept offspring who weren't one hundred percent Spanish. Generations of single men were sent to America, to fight a war they ultimately lost to Mexicans—people who were a combination of Native Americans and Spaniards. With the help of their Spanish ancestors, the Natives took it back in 1810."

I noted, "I'm not starting anything on fire. I'm speaking in idiomatic terms."

Moki let go a small chuckle. "Well, I'm an idiot. Idiomatic should be my native tongue."

"An idiom is to speak in terms that are not literal—figuratively speaking."

"That was a joke," he clarified. "I get it. You're destroying connections to your past."

I leaned affectionately into him. We sat in comfortable silence, with no need for words. This was a new experience for me. I didn't feel the need to fill the quiet with my ramblings. After a time, I said, "I can't help thinking about George Floyd and Minneapolis. It angers me that the officer kneeled on his neck."

"Me, too."

I hesitated, but decided to get it all off my chest. "They say I'm not capable of understanding, because I'm white."

Moki said, reluctantly, "Some of that is true."

"I know." I paused, collecting my thoughts. "But does that make me less than human? People used to say, 'You can't vote because you're black or a woman. You can't understand politics.' I guess my point is, *teach me*. If I'm not capable of comprehending injustice, why would you even want to spend time with me?"

Moki stared toward the setting sun. "This is what I know. I'm happiest when I'm with you. As far as the rest—I guess we'll see." Carefully, he asked, "What's your first thought when you see a news story involving a reservation?"

"Tragedy. Sadness for the choices made by my race and your race."

"What choices did we make?"

"I interned in social work in Cass County last year. I worked with a fifteen-year-old girl who was raped by three men on the reservation, near Cass Lake. When they were done, one of the Natives took a broken bottle and cut across her body from her left shoulder to her right hip, leaving a thick scar to serve as a constant reminder that she was powerless to impede their desires. The girl turned all the names over to the tribal police, but no one was charged. They said she was too wasted to be a legitimate witness."

Moki blew out a long breath. "There's a lot of work that needs to be done."

"And I'm up for it. Maybe it's my white privilege coming out, but I think the message is wrong. If they keep telling white people they can't understand, without helping them see why this is so, people are just going to give up, rather than help."

"Do you have any positive thoughts about reservations?"

"I have a cousin who was born on White Earth reservation. My aunt—my white aunt—was eight months along and was on her last solo adventure, before she hunkered down at home. She was always adventurous, so was on her way to see the source of the Mississippi, by Lake Itasca, when she went into labor. Two Native women found her, distressed, by the side of the road, and helped my aunt deliver her baby in their Native home. There is no greater time of vulnerability than childbirth. I would have loved to see those women teaming up and working together—speaking a universal language. That's the kind of person I hope to be."

Moki smiled. "I love your tender heart."

"In many ways, we're the same, Moki. I smile every time I drive onto a reservation now, because I think of you."

His caramel eyes drank in the beauty of the sunset with me. Moki's swinging, anxious leg was loveable. Like I was so important, he needed to be nervous about what he said. I took his hand and quietly shared the orange and red-hued horizon with him.

"I'm sorry for dumping this all on you." I put my hand on his bicep. "The stereotypical white person regurgitating the little she knows about racial issues to her only non-white friend."

He laughed, "I'm not beyond heaping racial matters on you. We both feel safe to share hard conversations and that says something great about us."

Hypnotized by the warm sun, I finally said, "I like the way I feel when I'm with you. I can relax and it's so much easier to open your heart when you're relaxed."

He held my palm to his lips and kissed it. I felt his warm breath as he spoke, "You make me feel good about who I am and what I do. You appreciate the thought I put into everything I make. When I tell someone I'm a chef, they ask if I know Bobby Flay or Giada. And then they start talking about them. If you're a plumber, people don't ask, 'Do you know Mario and Luigi?' You—you just focus on me."

I took in his boyish grin. Losing my mom taught me to remember moments like this. I was at peace—blissful—thankful for this experience, with this kind man. There might never be another moment like this, again.

I hated to taint our peace, but had to share my dire news, "Listen, the BCA wants me to talk to Margo Miller."

I felt his body tense. "Please don't," Moki warned. "They found your biological father. They've found the woman who murdered him. You've given enough."

I implored, "I can help solve a *murder*. They think Margo set a man up to be killed, with the help of a man Nitika called Zig. Her exact words were, 'When underage girls leave with him, they don't return.'" My hand traveled unconsciously to my neck, "I could have been one of his victims, too. If I can help have him arrested, I need to. Margo feels we have some sort of bond and the BCA wants to take advantage of it." I reminded him, "Didn't you just say some things are more important than life?"

Moki was trapped and he knew it. The best he could do was ask, "What do Jon and Serena say about it?"

"They tried to talk me out of it, but I'm doing it." I looked into his eyes and said firmly, "And I need you to respect my choice, Moki."

He wasn't happy about it, but said, "Okay, but it won't keep me from worrying."

"I'll take it." I smiled openly, with my heart painted all over my face. It was time to change the topic. "So, what's next for us?"

Moki smiled back, "Spend every second we can together."

I teased, "Maybe we should write a tacky romance novel together."

He played along. "Alright, but you've gotta help me get started, here."

I decided to tease him with something scandalous. In tones straight from a Hallmark movie, I said melodically, "There she lay, like an open diary on the bed, waiting for an entry."

Moki choked a little on his laughter. "That was good! How about, 'He was so aroused in her presence, he found himself stocking up on eye drops. He couldn't even blink. All the extra skin was gone.'"

I groaned dramatically, "That's *terrible!* Okay, scratch that idea. How about if we just have an amazing romance?"

His leg swung a bit faster as he said, "I don't know what I'm doing. I'm learning as I go."

"That's the best. If we want to have a love greater than typical, we need to be brave enough to create it together, rather than relying on conventional wisdom."

# 51

*I know that you're sad*
*I know that you're lonely*
*You lie awake 'till way past when*
*I want you to know that I'm leaving you only*
*'Cause I might not get the chance again*
*I'm cold and I'm tired and I can't stop coughing*
*Long enough to tell you all of the news*
*I'd like to tell you that I'll see you more often*
*But often is a word I seldom use*
—JOHN PRINE, *OFTEN IS A WORD I SELDOM USE*

## HARPER ROWE

### 1:00 P.M., THURSDAY, JULY 16, 2020
### BCA OFFICE, ST. CLOUD

I had the utmost respect for Paula Fineday. She understood people. Trisha Lake wanted to apologize to me in person for killing my father. It didn't mean much to me to hear it, but Paula broke the visitation rules and convinced me to visit with Trisha, face-to-face—or, rather, mask-to-mask. Paula believed Margo wanted to avenge Blaze's murder and Paula was using me to set Margo up. I guess that was Paula's job.

For six consecutive weeks, I'd visited Trisha at the Minnesota Correctional Facility in Shakopee. I was escorted in while prisoners were moving to the dining area, or to *rec*, so much of the population would see me waiting in a visitation room. It was spine-chilling to know many of the women glaring at me were killers, and all were going to be in a cage for years.

Paula directed me to never initiate a conversation about the visits with Trisha, when Margo called to check in on me, warning me someone inside would eventually get the word out to Margo.

My conversations with Margo were being recorded by the BCA. With Paula's guidance on how to respond, Margo and I were now *buds*. Her request to meet in person, today, at Caribou Coffee, suggested something serious was going down.

Jon met with me at the BCA office in St. Cloud, before I met up with Margo. He asked to visit with Paula in her office alone, first, while I waited in the lobby. Even though the door was closed, I could hear Jon saying, "Margo doesn't take betrayal lightly. You're going to get her killed."

Paula retorted harshly, "Keep your voice down. I will handle this . . ." and then I couldn't hear more.

I was too naïve to give much consideration to the concerns. I put blind faith in the BCA. It was a decision that would prove to be fateful.

Instead, I ignored the discussion and texted Moki, "Rendezvous tomorrow in Bemidji—lunch at high noon. Arrive early if you want it to taste good." My grandparents traveled to Rothsay for the Prairie Days celebration. Every year, they had their picture taken in front of the *World's Largest Prairie Chicken*. That clucker was thirteen feet high and weighed 9000 pounds. It would be late by the time I got back to Bemidji, but tomorrow, Moki and I would have all day and night.

He texted back, "Stocking up on eye drops—kidding. Be careful, hon."

"Love you, Moki." I hit *send* with no regrets.

Jon and Paula stepped out of the office. The tension etched into their faces was enough to tell me they were both were dissatisfied with the conclusion.

Paula said tersely, "Okay—show time . . ."

### 2:30 P.M., CARIBOU COFFEE
### 4101 WEST DIVISION STREET, ST. CLOUD

MARGO WAS WAITING FOR ME OUTSIDE of Caribou. I wasn't sure why she was carrying a white garbage bag, but assumed I'd soon find out.

She cautiously scanned the parking lot and asked, "Why did you go to Keith Stewart's house?"

My hand instinctively covered my throat. "I was kidnapped and brought there."

Her eyes met mine. "I mean, the first couple times."

I realized Margo either spoke to Stewart or Zig Ziegler. "I wanted to see where my mom had been."

"Who called the cops?"

"I don't know. I didn't. I didn't even have my phone; it was still in my car."

She nodded in approval and we walked into the coffee shop.

Margo ordered a nitro campfire mocha on ice, while I ordered a dark chocolate hot mocha. She confidently smiled and paid for both. While we waited, Margo whispered, "Let's step into the bathroom."

Confused by the request I cautiously followed her. I stopped in front of the one-stall bathroom and said, "I can wait."

Margo glared into my eyes, "You're coming in with me."

She locked the door behind us and shook open the garbage bag. "Put your cell phone, wallet, earrings, jewelry, and bra in the bag."

"Bra—*really?* I'm not dressed for braless."

She sneered, "You're fine. We'll just be in my car talking."

I was about to pull my bra off through my sleeve when she stopped me. "You're undressing and re-covering. I need to know you're not wearing a wire. Who knows what the BCA can do with underwire these days?"

I chided her, "Are you kidding? I'm no Kylee Jenner, but I've never been accused of buying my bras from the Bureau of Criminal Apprehension before."

She wasn't kidding. I removed and replaced clothing, dropping my belongings, as requested, into the bag. At that moment, I was so thankful Jon told Paula she couldn't put a wire on me. I warned Margo, "I'm hoping this is a one-time thing. I have no desire to be strip-searched every time we talk."

All business, she informed me, "Once we're at the car, you're going to give me your shoes and socks, and I'm placing the bag in an insulated container in the trunk."

When we returned to the counter to pick up our beverages, Margo purposely grabbed my mocha, felt the heat and smiled, "I'm sorry, I guess that's yours."

I couldn't read Margo and my heart was racing.

Once seated in her Mercedes, she told me, "I'm sorry for the cloak and dagger routine. I just had to make sure. What do you think about Trisha Lake?"

"I don't think much about her." Needing to appear sincere, I forced out, "She killed my dad. She can't undo that, no matter how sorry she is. I've visited her, trying to understand, but she just comes across as weak and pathetic."

With sudden anger, Margo snapped, "She's not getting away with it."

"She's facing murder charges. I don't know what else we can do about it—it's over."

"It isn't over until I say it's over. Do they search you when you visit Trisha?"

"No. They did at first, but not anymore."

"How closely do you come in contact with her?"

"She reaches across the table and holds my hands, like I'm her daughter. It's gross. If it wasn't for your request to maintain the visits, I wouldn't even go there."

Margo smiled. "Good work. Is she depressed?"

"Very despondent. She thought her kids would visit her, but they haven't."

She looked around. "I hope that jezebel is miserable."

Margo started her car and drove through the Crossroads parking lot, across the street to the Westside Liquor parking lot. Satisfied we weren't being followed or listened to, she handed me a small plastic packet with a white substance in it. "Draw the word *coke* in her hand with your finger and slide this into her hand."

I didn't want to appear too eager, so I resisted. "I don't want to end up sharing a cell with Trisha."

Margo assured me, "This will never come back on you. The cops will say they searched you, because they're supposed to. And where are you going to get fentanyl? All you have to do is deny it and they will never find the source. Have you ever heard of a prison purse?"

"No."

"It's your vagina or anus. It's how most drugs get into jail or prison. Drugs are rampant enough, where they can't trace the origin to any one visitor." She studied me for a moment before continuing. "Your dad left you thirty-five thousand dollars. Once you pull this off, I'll tell you how to access it. That's a pretty awesome payoff for holding hands."

"Okay." I hesitated, and then admitted, "I'm nervous. Have you ever done this before?"

She grinned, "How do you think I got rid of Cayenne Tiller? I told that skinny bitch to stay away from Billy. She said, 'I can't, I need the drugs.' I offered to take care of her and handed her a packet just like this. Told her it was meth.

And that was the end of Cayenne. I donated money to have her cremated. Evidence gone, plus Cayenne got to smoke up one last time—at the crematorium."

I pressed further, "Didn't Randy Vogel die of a fentanyl overdose?"

A realization washed over Margo that shed me in a different light. Furious, she smashed my mocha cup into my chest. She held her hand out. "Give it back or I'm tearing you apart with my bare hands."

I messed up. It was one too many questions. I was in good shape, but I wasn't about to take on a raging forty-year-old woman. I could feel my face flush as I handed her back the plastic baggie.

"Get out!"

I quickly stepped out and asked, "Could you pop the trunk so I can grab my stuff?"

Margo spat at me, "Fuck off. Your dad was never a snitch."

As law enforcement sped in, Margo peeled out.

The chase was on . . .

# 52

*Father forgive us for what we must do*
*You forgive us and we'll forgive you*
*We'll forgive each other 'till we both turn blue*
*Then we'll whistle and go fishing in heaven*
—JOHN PRINE, *FISH AND WHISTLE*

# JON FREDERICK

3:15 P.M., THURSDAY, JULY 16, 2020
HIGHWAY 15, ST. CLOUD

Margo Miller hightailed it out of the Westside Liquor parking lot and turned north onto Highway 15 for three miles, before she stopped and, with law enforcement hot on her tail, suddenly pulled over on the Mississippi Bridge. She was standing on the bridge when officers caught up to her.

I had picked up Harper and was following at a distance. She had my binoculars and was watching from the passenger seat. "Do you think she's going to jump?"

"No. I think she just dropped that bag of fentanyl in the Mississippi."

Harper announced, "Paula's yelling at her, but she's smiling."

"Margo's a long way from believing she's going to be prosecuted. She still doesn't know your conversation was recorded."

Harper rested the binoculars in her lap. "It was a great idea to have the microphone concealed in my mocha and handed to me. How did you get the mic to work in a hot liquid?"

I smiled, "It wasn't a liquid. I had the staff heat dry food and stuff it in the bottom of the cup to give it weight and heat."

Harper looked down at her shirt and muttered, "No mocha spilled on me." She queried, "What if Margo would have taken a sip?"

"Drink from your cup in the COVID era? It's too much of a social taboo."

My phone buzzed and I told Paula she was on the hands-free speaker.

Paula advised, "Please bring Harper to the BCA office. Thank you for your assistance, Jon, but you can go home. You know I would get a lot of heat from my supervisor if he knew I was working with you. If you can hear me, great job, Harper."

Harper responded, "Thank you!"

I asked, "How are you going to protect Harper?"

Paula shared, "Already have a plan in place."

I considered, "Are you going to give her clothes back? I hate to make her do a three-hour drive home barefoot."

Harper instinctively crossed her arms over her breasts.

Paula asked, "What did Margo touch?"

"She looked over my bra," Harper replied, "and I handed her my socks and shoes, but I was the one who dropped my wallet and phone in the bag."

Paula responded, "Stop at Target or somewhere and have her pick up a bra, socks and shoes, and whatever else she needs. The BCA will pick up the tab. I will get her phone and clutch back for her, but we will keep her clothes, for now, in case we need to pull prints off of them. Absolutely do *not* let her out of your sight, Jon. Bring her back to the office when you are done."

Once Paula was off the phone, Harper asked, "Should I try to find clothes like the ones Margo took?"

I warned Harper, "I think Margo's going to send a killer after you. We need your testimony to verify that she handed you a packet with a white substance in it. I believe Margo killed Randy Vogel to keep him from testifying. With that in mind, what would you buy?"

"The best sports bra and running shoes I can find."

"So that's what you're getting, on the BCA's tab. Riezig Ziegler's whereabouts have been unknown for a month and we don't know who Margo called during her little escapade, here. You need to be damn careful."

She questioned, "You told Paula earlier they didn't need my recording. How could they have prosecuted Margo without it?"

"I didn't want you to meet with Margo at all, because she's dangerous. I wanted the BCA to find another way. She has an android phone. If someone uses an android, investigators can work with Google and determine the exact location of her phone at any point in history. I believe her phone could place Margo at Buckman Prairies on the night Randy Vogel disappeared. It's circumstantial evidence, but with enough circumstantial evidence, you can still get a conviction."

When she didn't respond, I shared, "Paula felt they needed more evidence and she may be right."

Harper longingly gazed out the window at a young couple in an adjacent vehicle. I asked, "What's on your mind?"

"Guys always want to take care of me. Do I come across as that weak?"

"I would have made the same argument if Moki would have been in your place."

She argued, "You didn't have any trouble letting Serena wear a wire."

"Informed consent."

"What do you mean?"

I challenged her, "You're a social work major—you tell me."

Harper bobbed her head as she explained, "In social work, it asks the question, 'Does the person have enough information to make an informed decision?'"

"That's exactly what I'm talking about. You're twenty years old. How many investigations have you worked? Serena's thirty-three and has been helping me with investigations for years. She wore a wire with Trisha Lake, while I was seated in the same car with a loaded gun. You carried a mic into an encounter with a woman who may have committed a murder with a serial killer."

"Who do you think they killed?"

"I think Margo killed Randy Vogel with Zig's help. Randy received a call from an unidentified woman right before he disappeared and Margo would need help moving a body. While Zig is on Stewart's payroll, he has also received some payments from Margo."

"Do you really think Zig is a serial killer?"

"How many girls have been trafficked at Stewart's home over the last twenty years? I don't imagine they all escaped like your mother, yet no girls have ever made allegations . . ."

AFTER I DROPPED HARPER OFF AT the BCA office, I called Trisha's son, Baric.

Lacking sympathy for Trisha, he said, "I heard Mom confessed to killing Blaze. She finally did something right." He cleared his throat and emphasized, "I meant the *confession.*"

"I want you to know that Blaze threatened to hurt you and the threat bothered Trisha. It wasn't the sole reason she shot him, but it was part of it."

The comment left him silent for a moment, before he said, "I just want to be done with her drama."

"We don't get to pick our parents. Trisha isn't a terrible person. She isn't even a malicious person. She just makes too many decisions based on what will make her immediately happy."

Baric laughed, "That's for damn sure. She's driving down the road and barely sees past the end of the hood, while everybody's yelling 'Look out for the tree!' Will she ever see the light of day again?"

"I hope so, but she's in serious trouble. She's charged with second degree murder. Even though she was traumatized by Blaze, Trisha can't argue battered wife syndrome, since she's repeatedly stated he wasn't physically abusive to her. My guess is she'll serve fifteen to twenty years."

Baric countered, "Trisha was clearly under the influence of drugs that Blaze provided."

"Drug use isn't a mitigating factor, because she chose to use them."

Baric sputtered, "It's crazy. She's an abled-bodied adult who's gone her whole life without taking care of herself or her kids. And she still won't have to, will she?"

"I hear you, but understand it hasn't been an easy road for her. Trisha seems to gravitate toward manipulative people, so she needs healthy people to volunteer their time. Here's my two cents. I think you need to stop thinking of Trisha as a potential mother and see her as a hurting family member. It's in giving we receive, right?"

Resigned, Baric commented, "It is what it is. Thank you for the call. I'll set up a visit."

"That would be nice." Baric needed to stop worrying about the kind of woman Trisha has been and focus on the kind of man he was going to be. It was easy to be bitter, but kindness brought hope.

# 53

*The rain came down on the tin roof*
*Hardly a sound was left from the birthday party*
*The kitchen light fell asleep on the bedroom floor*
*Me and her were talking softer*
*Than all the time before I lost her*
*Her picture sat on top of a chest of drawers*
*One red rose in the Bible*
*Pressed between the Holy alphabet*
*Probably wouldn't believe you if you told me*
*But what I never knew I never will forget*
—JON PRINE, ONE RED ROSE

## JON FREDERICK

### 12:00 A.M., FRIDAY, JULY 17, 2020
### PIERZ

At midnight, my phone buzzed. I quickly grabbed it off the nightstand, hoping it wouldn't wake up Serena.

Moki Hunter gasped, "Harper's missing!"

I sat up. "When did you last speak to her?"

"About ten-thirty. She was almost home and was going to call me after she settled in. At eleven, I tried calling her, but there was no answer, so I drove here. Her car's in the driveway and the cop out front said she went inside. The back door was open, so we searched the house. She's gone.

Harper's cellphone and wallet were on the floor by the locked front door. It looked like they'd been dropped."

"Okay, get everyone you can on the road looking for a silver Chevy Silverado. I'll call the BCA and be there in two hours . . ."

# 54

*I love you so much, it hurts me*
*Darlin', that's why I'm so blue*
*I'm so afraid to go to bed at night*
*Afraid of losing you*
*I love you so much, it hurts me*
*And there's nothing I can do*
*I want to hold you, my dear, forever and ever*
*I love you so much, it hurts me so*
—JOHN PRINE, *I LOVE YOU SO MUCH IT*
*HURTS ME* (FLOYD TILLMAN ORIGINAL)

## JON FREDERICK

10:35 A.M., FRIDAY, JULY 17, 2020
FALLOW STREET, LUXEMBURG

Harper was nowhere to be found. After five hours on the road and a couple hours' sleep, Serena's parents took the kids while Serena and Moki went with me to St. Augusta. Prior to dropping off the grid, Riezig Ziegler had lived on Fallow Road in the small town of Luxemburg, fewer than two miles from Keith Stewart's home in St. Augusta. Zig, for the most part, had stayed off the radar, with only occasional stops at the Hayloft Bar.

Paula Fineday was waiting at the door of Zig's small rambler. This was a bad sign, as it indicated they weren't closing in on leads to Harper's whereabouts. The BCA had been through this home, weeks ago, and found nothing that helped them locate Zig.

Paula pointed to Moki, "Nothing personal, Moki, but Jon," she turned a hard stare at me, "you need to give me a reason he is here."

I felt badly for Moki. It was a matter of the degree of bad we were facing. The CSI crew found that Margo Miller had shared the sexting clip she possessed of Harper, with Zig. Based on my past work investigating sex crimes, Harper had likely been sexually assaulted and may be dead. Moki was heartbroken and I wanted to give him an opportunity to help.

I told Paula, "Moki's a hunter from northern Minnesota. He might see something here we'd overlook."

Moki asked, "Do you mind if I start in the kitchen?"

Paula nodded with slow reluctance and Moki left us.

Stolid and somber, she turned to me. "I know you think I messed up. Harper told me she was staying with someone. I never would have let her return home, alone. The Rowe home does not have a security camera, but we did see a Chevy Silverado on camera at a neighboring home, headed toward the Rowes' at about nine p.m." Paula gazed around the house, "I was not completely oblivious to the threat Riezig presented to Harper. Before she went home that night, I had an LPR mounted to an overpass on Highway 371 and on the side of the road on Highway 71, programmed to notify me if Zig's plates came up, but they never did."

Serena asked, "An LPR?"

Paula explained, "License Plate Reader. It puts the license plate of every vehicle that passes into a data system."

I postulated as to why this didn't work. "He was already there. Zig didn't have to drive north to find Harper, because he was hiding out somewhere north of your LPR."

Agreement twitched the corner of Paula's mouth. "Okay, so if he was north of Park Rapids and Walker, how do we find him? He is not using his credit cards. We sent his picture and truck description to every gas station, hotel, motel, and resort in the state. No good leads."

I said, "He's not in town. Someone would have reported him. And if he's not at a resort, he's hunkered down somewhere in the wilderness of northern Minnesota, between the Red River Valley and the Arrowhead region."

Moki walked out of the kitchen with a box in each hand, "He's on a lake." One of the boxes read *McCormick Beer Batter* and the other read *Shore Lunch Fish Breading.*

I told him, "Thank you, that's helpful."

Still discouraged, Moki said, "But not helpful enough."

He was right, but I didn't want to be the one who said it. "Let's keep looking."

Moki went back into the kitchen, as I went through drawers. It was clear Zig had emptied the place out. Serena was busying herself pulling up floor rugs, looking for trap doors, and pushing picture frames aside, looking for hidden safes. All of this felt futile, as we knew the BCA had already scoured the place.

I found the book, *Persephone,* in a coffee table drawer. The model on the cover bore a disturbing resemblance to Harper. When I paged through it, I found a loose picture of Harper pressed between the pages.

Paula noted my interest and asked, "What did you find?"

I showed her the picture. "Do you know who Persephone was?"

"No."

"According to Greek mythology, Hades kidnapped Persephone and brought her to hell, then made her his bride. Gunner said Stewart referred to Zig as Kharon. A Kharon in Greek mythology was a man who transported souls into the afterlife."

Paula grimaced. "This is not good, is it?"

"No. Guys with the Satan fetish always have the narcissistic need to be cruel."

"We need to find this sick bastard." Paula brainstormed, "Zig cut his GPS bracelet and disappeared shortly after his release from jail. Keith's GPS indicates he has been moving around the house, but he hasn't left home. Maybe if I could pull Keith Stewart back into custody, I could wring something out of him. Stewart has been hiding behind his attorney since he bailed out. Nitika disappeared two nights ago, but she took off on her own. She packed a bag, her purse, and phone, and left after the foster parents were asleep. She had made it clear she was not going to be testifying against anybody. I hope she did not contact Stewart. If so, Zig may have already disposed of her."

Serena called Moki back into the room. "Moki, you need to tell Paula about Nitika." She turned to Paula, "He called her on the drive here."

Moki was clearly debating how much he should reveal. Finally, he said, "Nitika's okay."

Paula said, "Where is she?"

He appeared to be holding back when he replied, "I don't know."

Paula surmised, "That is not true. Just tell me if she is in danger."

Adding some resentment about Harper's abduction, Moki stated, "She's safer than *you* can keep her."

This got me thinking. "What kind of a phone does Nitika have?"

Moki pled, "Please don't track her down."

"That's not my plan," I assured him. "I think we're all fine as long as she's safe."

Moki relented, "A brand new Samsung."

"I might have a new charge for Keith Stewart. Nitika's only fifteen years old. You need to be an adult to sign a contract to buy a phone. If it's a new phone—"

Paula cut me off, "Keith Stewart must have posed as her guardian, which is against the law—Falsely Impersonating

Another. Thank you." She immediately got on the phone and requested Keith Stewart be picked up on a new charge.

Moki asked, "Can I check out the garage?"

Paula nodded once. "Have at it. My agents have already been through it."

Serena suggested, "We should get Ziegler's license and truck description out and to anyone using DashCams in their vehicles in northern Minnesota. We could ask volunteers to help go through those videos. People want to help find her. I don't know that there are any tour buses going but, even with COVID, there *is* summer school. School buses have cameras."

Paula remarked, "Do you have any idea how many silver trucks there are in northern Minnesota? I have started going through the vehicle registration data. In Red Lake County, alone, there is one truck for every three people."

Moki came back in, holding a half empty garbage bag, looking like he just discovered gold. "Have you ever had this?" He was holding and empty container of *Busha Browne's Traditional Jerk Rub*.

I answered, "No."

"It's crazy good and addicting. There are three empty containers in the garbage. It's made in Jamaica. What if he's having it mailed to his new address?"

Wally called and Paula asked me to take it, since she was busy tracking down the Jamaican jerk rub.

Wally said, "We're at Stewart's. The floor looks like a slaughterhouse. The stench of blood is sickening, but there's no body. Blood is dried all over the floor. My guess—three days old."

If Zig did this, he did it a couple days before kidnapping Harper. I questioned, "I thought the GPS indicated Stewart has been moving about the house."

"It does—I don't get it."

I directed, "FaceTime me, so I can have a look."

Wally hung up. I wasn't sure he'd call back, but he did. When he scanned the room with his phone, I first saw an officer searching the home, plugging his nose. Then I saw the Dobermans scampering about.

I told Wally, "The GPS is on one of the dogs."

He remarked, "That's impossible. The system indicates it's always been on a live subject."

Suddenly, the officer shouted, "Behind the couch—it's a severed foot—all chewed up!" Hand clamped over his mouth, he ran outside.

Wally first showed the foot on camera, then switched over to a SAWZALL, covered with blood. With grave concern, he said, "The foot was severed when the victim was still alive. It's the only way you get all this blood pumped out."

To Wally, I said, "Someone cut off Stewart's foot and slipped the GPS onto the dog, to make it look like Stewart's alive."

He turned the phone back on his face and Wally shook his head. "Son of a bitch—you're right. It's on the dog. Even though his body's not here, I guarantee you Stewart is dead. There's a lot of blood, here. Tell Paula I'm turning this scene over to Stearns County and I'll be joining her."

It was typical for the BCA to turn the crime scene over to the local county. I had to put this morbid scene on the back burner and refocus on finding Harper. I was convinced Zig bled out Stewart. It's a practice used at meat packing plants to make meat kosher. I'm certain Zig had witnessed this done back when he worked at the plant in Long Prairie. The body would be subsequently less likely to spill blood when transferred.

WITH THE ASSISTANCE OF THE BCA, we discovered the Jamaican jerk rub wasn't being mailed to any private addresses in northern Minnesota, and there were only half a dozen stores, north of Walker, that sold it. One establishment stood out on the list—Hayslips Corner, in Talmoon. It was a small bar and the only place that had started purchasing the rub in the last month. The owner indicated a big, grey-eyed woodsman, who lived in the Chippewa National Forest, had asked him to order it. The woodsman met the description of an unshaven Riezig Ziegler.

Paula informed us, "If you want to help with the search, head to Hayslips Corner. I will have an agent there direct you." She left with lights ablaze and we took advantage of this like an Indy driver drafting, by following her lead (but at a safe distance).

# 55

*It was raining, it was cold*
*West Bethlehem was no place for a 12-year-old . . .*
*When he got there the cupboard was bare*
*Except for an old black man with a fishing rod*
*He said "Whatcha gonna be when you grow up?"*
*Jesus said, "God"*
*Oh my God, what have I gotten myself into . . .*
*They're gonna kill me mama, they don't like me bud*
*So Jesus went to Heaven*
*And he went there awful quick*
*All them people killed him*
*And he wasn't even sick*
—John Prine, Jesus, The Missing Years

## HARPER ROWE

(FOUR HOURS EARLIER)
6:35 A.M., FRIDAY, JULY 17, 2020
BIG TOO MUCH LAKE, BIG FORK

I t was early morning and the sun, blanketed in a red sky, glared through the curtain-less window. Matthew stated in the Bible, *Foul weather today, for the heaven is red and lowering.* The pragmatist version would be, "An advancing weather system at sunrise creates a red sky."

There were no lights and no bathroom in my one-room cabin—just one bare room with a woodstove, a bed, a wooden chair, and a table. I felt hungover, and I was naked and shivering. I was given a tranquilizer of some sort. I imagined Margo, as a surgical nurse, had no difficulty providing it for Zig. Beyond being stripped, it didn't feel like my body had been violated—yet. That was a good sign. My neck was sore from being squeezed and I could feel a raised ring around it where the garrote had been tightened.

My left wrist was handcuffed to the frame of the bed. I sat up and found my clothes by the side of the bed. With my foot, I swept them close and dressed, shoes and all, up to my waist. I knelt on the floor to get my sports bra clasped; with its adjustable Velcro straps, I was able to get it completely on. I gave up on my shirt, since the handcuff was an insurmountable obstacle.

Paula Fineday had provided me a police escort all the way to my grandparents' home, last night. I remembered waving to the cop out front while entering the house. When I turned to bolt the door, a wire was immediately tightened around my neck. I couldn't scream. My instinctive attempts to grab at it were useless. My last thought was, *not again . . .*

I had promised Paula that Moki would be waiting at home for me. But I was dirty and tired, and I just wanted to sleep. I felt a loving synchrony with Moki I never had with Greg, and I wanted to clean up, and be awake, when he arrived—this morning. *Sorry, Moki.* My vanity would be the end of me. It would break Dad's heart that I never called him and told him of my predicament. I didn't want him to worry; instead, I left him to grieve.

On the mattress next to me, a large indention indicated Zig had slept beside my passed out body. *Where was he now?* I was ready to run—except for that damn handcuff.

Through the large picture window, I could see the cabin was on a lake, but there were no signs of people or houses anywhere, at least from my vantage point. The lake was overgrown with brush and pine trees, butting up to the shore, as far as I could see. I could tell by the flora I was somewhere way the hell up in the wilderness of northern Minnesota. There was a pile of rusting wheels in the brush near the lake.

Zig came into view like a man with a mission. He pulled the camouflage tarp off a flat bass fishing boat, picked up the wheels, one at a time, and hauled them to the boat. The wheels looked heavy, even for him. And then I saw him pick up a chain and loop it through the wheels, making sure there were a couple feet of chain left at the end. That chain was intended to be the last belt I wore, and those wheels were to transport me to the bottom of this lake. *I'm dead.* He tied the boat to a tree and pushed it onto the lake.

I gave my room another quick onceover and realized this wasn't a place where someone vacationed; it was a death camp. I focused on my handcuff and the steel frame of the bed. The metal cuff was clamped around my wrist so tight, it dug into my skin. There was no way out.

With all my strength, I tried to yank my wrist through the cuff opening, even if it meant breaking every bone in my hand. I screamed through my bruised vocal chords, "HELP!!!" The bedframe bounced on the floor, revealing rusty specs of dried blood on the wall behind the bed. I could only imagine the horror someone else experienced here—and I couldn't break free.

Zig marched in and barked, "Stop!"

"HELP!!!"

He hauled off and punched me so hard in the temple, I fell back onto the bed. Stars swirled before my eyes compounded by bolts of pain. I wasn't completely unconscious, instead groggily dazed into submission. I closed my eyes to try to gather my bearings and slipped back into the darkness.

# 56

*Love gives*
*Love takes*
*It takes a lot of lucky breaks*
*Lucky strikes*
*Lucky stars*
*I don't know how I got this far . . .*
*You have your way*
*You have your doubts*
*The falling in*
*The falling out*
*A bridge is built*
*A bridge is burned*
*Till you reach the point of no return*
*Don't know where we're coming from*
*Or where we're going to*
—JOHN PRINE, *ALL THE WAY*

## JON FREDERICK

1:30 P.M., FRIDAY, JULY 17, 2020
HAYSLIPS CORNER, HIGHWAY 286, TALMOON

I called Jeremy Goddard and updated him regarding Harper's disappearance. The former Marine immediately went into soldier mode—no hysterics or drama, just a battery of hard, clipped questions, as he demanded the facts about his daughter. We arranged to meet at Hayslips Corner, just outside of Talmoon.

I called the Itasca County Sheriff's Department on the way and shared that four of us were headed to the Chippewa National Forest to look for Harper. Officer Rhonda Thorn agreed to meet us at Hayslips Corner, clarifying she meant the bar, informing me that the city of Talmoon was once called Hayslips Corner.

Hayslips was a dark, dive bar with a friendly owner. There was actually a small hole in the wall through which I could see directly outside. I had explained on the phone to Officer Thorn, earlier, that access to a boat would help tremendously in our search for an isolated lake cabin. It would simply take too long to drive the windy, gravel roads searching.

Wally, the BCA agent, marched into the bar and interrupted us. "I'm directing this search. If you want to help, there are plenty of lakes to search. I have a team scouring the Little Turtle Lake area." He ordered, "A couple of you drive around Jessie Lake, while the other two take Little Too Much Lake."

Officer Thorn pointed out, "You also have Little Jessie Lake and Big Too Much Lake in close proximity."

They must have been struggling with coming up with new lake names. I interjected, "The bartender thought the man took his Silverado north on Highway 6 when he left." I looked from one face to another and suggested, "Let's take a moment and think about this, first."

Wally scoffed, "I'm running this show! *You* just sit here and think about it. *We're* going to go find her." He barreled out the door.

Officer Thorn warned, "We have a flash storm with lots of lightning coming through here, but it should all be over in an hour."

I shook my head, "We can't afford to wait."

Jeremy looked at the map of the lakes area and said, "I'll head to Lake Little Too Much."

It was the first lake north of Little Turtle Lake on Highway 6. Without another word, Jeremy strode militantly out of the bar. He'd abandoned the gentle civilian disposition Harper spoke of and now carried the demeanor of a powerful man, with a straightened back and hard expression.

Serena had quietly observed the exchanges to this point. She finally spoke up, "I think it would make the most sense for me to stay here, where I have WiFi. I'll continue to contact people and businesses in the area, to see if anyone has noticed anything, and call with any new information."

I was glad she offered this, as I wanted her safe and was uncertain what we were going to encounter when we left the bar. I loved her and didn't want her confronting a powerful man who wouldn't hesitate to take a life. Back in the day, Zig had dropped Blaze to the tar with one punch, and Blaze was a force to be reckoned with.

Thorn said, "I have a boat docked at Big Too Much Lake access, as you requested. But I can't take it out until this storm blows over. We'd be a lightning rod out there on the lake."

Moki was frantic. "Do you understand that this guy's going to *kill* Harper?"

She repeated, "Like I said, the boat is docked, but *I* can't take it out. We have regulations. I might have left the keys in it." She gave us a pointed look. "I'll have to check when I'm done with my business in Talmoon."

Moki looked flatly at me, "I'll drive."

Officer Thorn directed, "Frederick, you're BCA. If someone *happened*," she emphasized, "to take the abandoned boat, it would be better if you did."

I nodded, not about to correct my current standing with the BCA.

Moki and I headed out before Thorn could change her mind.

As we drove to the public access, Moki questioned, "You're a BCA agent?"

"No. I used to be. I didn't want to lose the boat, so I opted not to say anything."

"There are thirteen hundred lakes in the Chippewa National Forest and a thousand miles of streams. Why do you think it's Lake Big Too Much?"

"A great couple I know, Zeke and Leatte, fish the northern lakes. I called and told them I think the guy's close to Hayslips Corner and they suggested I start here."

I didn't bother to tell him I had asked where a man could dump a body if he never wanted it found. They told me Big Too Much Lake was a huge, deep hole—ninety feet deep—surrounded by wilderness. Fifteen feet from shore was already fifteen feet deep and it was north of Hayslips Corner, on Highway 6.

# 57

*I remember everything*
*Things I can't forget*
*The way you turned and smiled at me*
*On the night we first met . . .*
*I've been down this road before*
*Alone as I can be*
*Careful not to let my past*
*Go sneaking up on me*
*Got no future in my happiness*
*Though regrets are very few*
*Sometimes a little tenderness*
*Was the best that I could do*
—JOHN PRINE, *I REMEMBER EVERYTHING*

## HARPER ROWE

(FOUR HOURS EARLIER)
9:30 A.M., FRIDAY, JULY 17, 2020
BIG TOO MUCH LAKE, BIG FORK

I woke up to Zig sitting over me, laughing in my face. "Yelling isn't going to do you any good. We're the only ones on the lake. No one for miles. I just don't like yelling."

I couldn't get my bearings on the time of day, as it had gotten dark outside. Lightning cracked and it began to rain. The clatter sounded like someone was dropping handfuls of marbles onto the tin roof of the cabin. The rain then stopped abruptly like the sky was just kidding.

I sat up slowly, inching away from him as I did. Waves of vertigo left me woozy as I tried to corral my galloping thoughts. "How long was I out?"

"Almost an hour. It's too much of a temptation to have you lying here and not touch you, so I checked my traps—no wolves today. Wolves have thin skin, so you need to get the fur off them as quickly as possible, or that hide will always smell."

He rambled on, like I would somehow be interested in these poor creatures being trapped and skinned. The subject matter already had me cringing—when he put his hand on my leg, I shriveled away from him. I gave my handcuffed arm an inconspicuous tug, hoping for some miraculous change in my entrapment. It was no use. I was still tethered to the bedframe.

He took in my appearance and chuckled. "Why'd you bother dressing?"

"It's what I do in the morning."

Zig went on, "Well, just so you know, I'm not one of those pervs who messes around with unconscious women." He then leered, his beady eyes scanning me more intently. "But you're not passed out anymore."

I was running out of time. My wrist ached from the hard yank I gave it earlier and my head throbbed from his assault. I allowed my body to curl inward, trying to appear submissive. "I'm no threat to you. I've never said a word against you."

Zig asked, "Have you ever heard of Persephone? She was beautiful, like you—and became Satan's bride."

I knew the tale. "Persephone was allowed to return home."

"Only temporarily—as you were when you left Stewart's."

"Again, and again, and again." According to the myth, we experience winter each year, when Persephone is forced to return to hell.

"See, that's where the myth fails. If I let you go now, you're not coming back." He attempted, awkwardly, to comfort me. "I appreciate you setting me straight about Stewart. Keith has been dealt with. I know you're not one of his whores, but you never should've set Margo up. Persephone went to hell after feuding with Aphrodite. There are consequences. I'm not wild about Margo, but Stewart's dead, so she's my boss, now."

I was incredulous and not interested in hiding it. "You're going to kill me to protect that wolf bitch?"

He laughed heartily. "That's a great name for her."

"Zig—you kept me *alive*. You could have killed me right away, but you didn't."

His breathing was becoming slow and heavy. "Honey, it's just business."

And then the realization of my fate sunk in. My bravado dissipated with my hope. When he was done with me in this bed, I was going to the bottom of the lake, chained to those wheels.

I tried again, "Since I'm not one of his whores, you need to give me time."

He sat by me on the bed and ran his calloused hand through my hair.

As I tried to pull my throbbing head away, I felt the sting of strands pulling out of my scalp.

His grip tightened on a handful of my locks and his face transformed to what I could only describe as vacant of humanity. He said, "Darlin', you're out of time." Zig pushed me hard onto my back and held me still by my neck, reminding me of the power he had over me.

Helpless, I felt hot tears trickling into my bruised scalp as he groped me. Pleading wasn't working. Submissiveness didn't, either. *Think like a soldier.*

As he clumsily tried to remove my bra—unsuccessfully—I tried a new tactic.

"Persephone was the Goddess of spring vegetation, right?"

Curiousity piqued, he stopped, "Yeah."

I could see he was a bit off guard. In the most seductive tone I could conjure up, I said, "Un-cuff me. Let me enjoy this."

He snorted through his nose and, with his weight on top of me, undid the cuff. I felt like I was being crushed.

"I'll give you a little space and you can slide your clothes off. Or, I could rip them off. I kinda like doing that."

I couldn't move my body enough to escape—I could barely breathe. I grunted, "Let's go outside."

Annoyed, he asked, "What?"

"Would a god have Persephone, the Goddess of Spring, in a grungy little bed, or in the wide open wilderness?"

He kissed me as he mulled it over. His overgrown scruff felt like steel wool against the tender skin around my lips. I clamped my teeth hard together, dreading the idea of his filthy tongue poking into my mouth. I didn't respond, but I didn't fight it, either, even as my instincts were screaming. He appeared to relax.

I pulled back and said, "Let me enjoy this fantasy with you, Zig—or do you prefer *Kharon?*" He brightened at the use of his fantasy name. "I've dreamt of having passionate sex in the rain. Can you at least give me that? I've never been a whore, but I'll be *your* whore—right now, if you'll grant me that."

It took him barely a moment to concede. I half expected him to pound on his chest like the gorilla he was. He rolled off of me, all the time carefully remaining between me and the door.

I bent down to grab my shirt.

Zig scoffed, "You won't need that."

I held my ground. "I've undressed outside, but never gone outside undressed."

He relented, "Whatever," and let me put my shirt on. Zig then gripped my sore wrist tightly and dragged me outside.

THE MOISTURE-LADEN CLOUDS WEREN'T READY to give up their next cache just yet, but were weakening. A thin mist thickened in the humidity, giving the stage of our ensuing battle a glossy sheen. I stood there in knee-high, wet grass, my wrist still locked in Zig's clutches.

Trying to buy time, I commented, "That's a big lake." Now that I could see the whole area, my earlier impression was confirmed. There was no sign of life—no homes, no well-groomed beaches. Just an untouched, isolated lake.

Zig chuckled, "Some would say, big—too much."

Heart hammering against my ribs, I scanned my surroundings. There was no driveway. Zig's four-wheel drive truck had left two strips of a worn-down path through the uncut grass, from the narrow gravel road. Unlike the myth, my mom wasn't dropping in to save me. I was on my own.

Zig read me like a thrift-store book; clearly, he was familiar with panic on a woman's face and reveled in it. Enjoying my overwhelming helplessness, he twisted the figurative knife, "Stewart said you were a bit of a freak—stripped right in front of a bare window." He chuckled in an insulting and gross manner, then added, "I must have watched that video Margo gave me of you, all snuggled in your bed, a hundred times. You need a little man-handling."

The fine mist had now condensed into a sprinkle.

Becoming impatient, Zig directed, "Okay, let's get to it before it starts pouring."

I stared at his huge bratwurst fingers, secured vice-like around my wrist. "I'll need my hand to undo the buttons on my shirt and jeans. And my shoes are too tight to kick off."

Making myself vulnerable, I closed my eyes and let the showers drizzle across my face.

I needed him to trust me—just for a moment. He let go and I started unbuttoning my shirt, screaming internally to my hands to stop shaking. With all the calm I could muster, I told him, "Undo your jeans and I'll start on my knees, right here in the meadow, in front of you."

With a lascivious grin, Zig asked, "Have you ever heard of irrumatio?"

I shook my head, but didn't ask. I didn't want to know.

"Say *ahh*. You're about to get a lesson."

When he started fumbling, eagerly, to unfasten the buttons on his jeans, I ran.

He bolted after me in pursuit. Zig was fast for a big man.

I sprinted to the road with desperate urgency. In a fraction of a second, I chose to take the road right instead of left—a decision that would have dire consequences.

Within one hundred yards, Zig closed in to an arm's reach.

My shoes slapped the dirt as I raced down the path. I ran the 400 in high school track and hoped, if I could stay out of his grip, I could outlast him. And then he caught my hair.

I jerked my head forward and let the hair rip, with indescribable pain, from my scalp. I couldn't control my cries but, determined, I once again pulled out of his reach.

I ran harder than ever, even when competing. My lungs burned and tightened. After almost a half a mile, the bastard finally slowed and, exhausted, I slowed with him, just enough to catch my breath.

In front of me was this path, butted by a lake and surrounded by wilderness. Off the path, there were lofty trees every ten feet, surrounded with thick underbrush. If I ran a hundred feet in this forest, I wouldn't find my way out, and the untouched density looked like it went on for miles.

I slowed some, to an easy trot, as I wanted Zig to believe he could catch me for a little longer. I needed to get him as far from his truck as possible. My only hope was that this path offered a way out and I'd find an exit before he'd have time to go back for it. For now, I needed him to keep chasing me on foot. It was my only chance.

We were both now half-walking and half-running. I was about thirty feet ahead of him.

Zig was sweating profusely and massaged his chest as he yelled, "Where do you think you're going?" He croaked out a laugh and wheezed as he gasped for breath. "You are one unlucky wench. You went the wrong way. This path eventually just ends and you're going to have to come back to me." He slowed, "Nobody lives on this lake."

I could have cried. The pathway was getting narrower and more overgrown, the further I trekked into it. Feeling without options, I started walking.

Zig aggressively advanced toward me.

I had no choice. Even as my body protested, I started running again. I had the cardio advantage, as long as I kept running. But if Zig got a grip on me, I was dead—I couldn't match his power.

I had to stick to the path, wherever it would take me. It had to lead to *something*. If I deviated from it, the unknowns in the woods would just be a longer death sentence.

And then I came to an impasse. With the recent rain in this area, running water surged over the sharp banks of the lake and poured off into a river in front of me. The runoff swelled over boulders and blocked the path. As my eyes followed the river, I could only conclude that, if it wasn't for bad luck, I'd have no luck at all. The creek started west, but then bent south, locking me in.

I could see Zig perspiring heavily as he trudged forward, closing the distance between us.

He sneered as I looked left and right, frozen in my tracks. "And now, you're mine. You can't escape, darlin'. And there's no way in hell you're gonna outswim me . . ."

# 58

*We are falling down*
*Down to the bottom of a hole in the ground*
*Smoke 'em if you got 'em*
*I'm so scared, I can hardly breathe*
*I may never see my sweetheart again*
—JOHN PRINE, *BOTTOMLESS LAKE*

## JON FREDERICK

(ONE HOUR LATER)
11:45 A.M., FRIDAY, JULY 17, 2020
BIG TOO MUCH LAKE, BIG FORK

Moki and I were out on the lake in the boat questionably acquired from Officer Thorn. We didn't have to look for the keys, as they were hanging from the ignition, hooked to a chain with a large red and white bobber.

I cringed with every thunderclap as lightning shot through the sky behind us. Despite the electrical drama, there was only a nominal measure of rain, which helped with visibility. We were able to get close to shore but, because of the thick brush, we had to move slowly to make certain we didn't miss anything.

Moki commiserated, "Zhawenim is the Anishinaabe word for expressing kindness. That's Harper. And she ends up being kidnapped by a mondo assasin." He added with sarcasm, "Chi Miigwetch to the BCA."

I'd heard Paula use the phrase before. It meant *big thank you.* "Don't waste your energy on anger when we still have time to save her. While Harper has her mother's wisdom and kindness, she also has Blaze's genes—and he was physically tough. There's a reason the police always responded to calls involving Blaze with at least two officers."

My phone chirped with Serena's ringtone. "Jon, I think I have something for you. An employee from the North Itasca Electric Coop told me there is a stretch north of Lake Big Too Much, through which power lines run, so a path has been cleared. He had to make a repair after a storm last week and noticed a truck had driven through the clearing. I don't know if it's anything, but I thought I'd share it. It could have just been some high school kids."

I hesitated, "Was it torn up, or a path?"

"It was a path."

"Did he see where it ended?"

"No, it went off into the woods, under the cover of trees."

"Okay—call Jeremy and give him the directions. Call me again if anything better comes up."

Moki interrupted, "Hey, there's a bass boat in the lake up ahead."

I told Serena, "We're on the northwest side of the lake and were going to shore."

"Be careful."

# 59

*Sadness leaks*
*Through tear-stained cheeks*
*From winos to dime store Jews . . .*
*For the life of me*
*I could not see*
*But I heard a brand new joke*
*Two men were standing on a bridge*
*One jumped and screamed, "You lose"*
*And just left the odd man holding*
*Those late John Garfield blues*
—JOHN PRINE, THE LATE JOHN GARFIELD BLUES

## HARPER ROWE

(40 MINUTES EARLIER)
11:05 A.M., FRIDAY, JULY 17, 2020
BIG TOO MUCH LAKE, BIG FORK

I hotfooted it into the river, shoes and all. The current was fast, so I planned to run along the creek bed until I had to swim. When my feet finally left the ground, my efforts to swim failed abysmally. The turbulent creek instantly took hold and rolled me; I protectively covered my already injured head to keep from cracking it open in the rapids. I managed to straighten my legs as I shot down the stream, feet first, to protect my body from the blow of a wicked-looking boulder I was approaching—too fast. Crack. My left foot hit the rock square, but twisted unnaturally on impact. Searing pain shot from sole to hip by the brutal blow. I bit back the howl threatening to give me away and pushed off hard, kicking myself sideways out of the rush. The river rejected me back toward the shore. It had enough of me.

My feet finally caught bottom and I trudged out, favoring my new injury. I couldn't cross this damn river. *God, give me a break.* Exhausted, I collapsed on the shore. My ankle was either badly sprained or broken. Deep inside, I felt Mom's presence urging me to *get up. Get Up. GET UP!*

I was expecting the beast's breath to be heaving down on me as I crawled to my knees. Then I saw him. And I laughed. *Himmel herrgott,* as Grandpa used to say—*God in Heaven!* Zig had beat the rapids and made it to the other side. He must've thought I crossed it.

He spotted me and dove back in. The brute began swimming toward me, his meaty arms pounding through the rushing water with ugly, but effective strokes. I wouldn't have long.

Now it was a race back. Zig must have driven to the cabin from the other direction. I had a bad wheel, but I also had a head start. With renewed energy, I was on my feet and fighting my way back to where we started. The rain had stopped and, because of the tree cover, the grass-covered path was barely wet. Sun beams lasered through the clouds, heating things back up. The humidity was so thick, I felt like I was breathing through gumbo.

Even though I was hobbling along, it took Zig a while to get close, again. He was still rubbing his left shoulder, but pursuing me as doggedly as ever. He was going to catch me.

When he closed the gap to within twenty feet, he dropped heavily to a knee and gasped, "Okay—you win. I'm having a heart attack. I'll let you go, but you have to promise me you'll send help. Without the truck, you're never getting out of here alive. I'll lay here, completely helpless."

I stopped and watched him roll to his back and drop the keys from his outstretched hand.

# 60

*Some humans ain't human*
*Some people ain't kind*
*You open up their hearts*
*And here's what you'll find*
*A few frozen pizzas*
*Some ice cubes with hair*
*A broken Popsicle*
*You don't wanna go there . . .*
*Have you ever noticed*
*When you're feeling really good*
*There's always a pigeon*
*That'll come shit on your hood?*
—JOHN PRINE, *SOME HUMANS AIN'T HUMAN*

## RIEZIG "ZIG" ZIEGLER, AKA KHARON

11:18 A.M., FRIDAY, JULY 17, 2020
BIG TOO MUCH LAKE, BIG FORK

That bony bitch thinks she's getting away from me. She's been just out of reach since we left the damn cabin. But it's only temporary. I can't wait to be done with her. I don't even care if I have her, at this point. It's time for her to cross the River Styx into the underworld.

I've felt a burn in my chest for the last half hour. I've got to stop eating all that spicy food. Growing up, mustard

350

for sausages was about as crazy as we got. Pretty sure my dad thought he was going a little crazy when he'd put salt on potatoes. I'm not my dad.

When Harper's within reach, I am going to clamp down on her and never let go.

She carefully creeps a couple feet closer and says, "You need to tell me what happened to the girls from Stewart's, first."

I put on an act of pain that could win me a Grammy. I groan, "Most just left on their own after Stewart was done with them. He bought them a bus ticket and we never heard from them again. Hell, he even made connections for them."

"In other words, he sold them to pimps." Hands on her bratty hips, she scoffs, "But some are dead."

*Oh, if you only knew, Princess.*

Through a clenched jaw, I order, "You need to get me help."

"Do I, though?" She screws up her face with sarcasm. I want to slap that smirk off her mouth so bad. She asks relentlessly, "How many are at the bottom of this lake?"

"Why do you even care?"

"My mom was one of those girls. She escaped. I want to know where the bodies are of the girls who weren't so lucky."

"I'm not the kind of guy who squeals." She's so out of her league and doesn't know it. I tell her, "Just get the keys and get going."

"Sit up, with your legs straight out and lean your weight back on your hands."

If she tries to kick me in the balls, I'm going to clamp down on her feet as soon as she steps between my legs. I slowly lean back as instructed and spread my legs. When she bends and starts to reach for the keys, I am going to lock her legs up with a death grip. Stupid bitch!

# 61

*Take it back, take it back*
*Oh no, you can't say that*
*All of my friends are not dead or in jail*
*Through rock and through stone*
*The black wind still moans . . .*
*Sweet revenge, sweet revenge*
*Will prevail without fail*
—JOHN PRINE, *SWEET REVENGE*

## HARPER ROWE

11:21 A.M., FRIDAY, JULY 17, 2020
BIG TOO MUCH LAKE, BIG FORK

I carefully stepped behind Zig as if I was just walking around him. If he wanted resuscitation—I'd give it to him. I put my weight on my bad ankle, for a second, and kicked him as hard as I could in the back of the head. CPR—social distance style.

"Ahhhh!" Zig clutched at his fat head and writhed in pain. His dark eyes gave me a menacing glare.

Landing a kick on his cerebellum meant it would be several minutes before he regained his balance.

I snarked, "You can blame it on my bad genes."

In agony, he growled, "Fucking bitch."

I stepped safely away and remarked, "The adjective part of that is presumptive and the noun part is environmentally induced. So I guess I'm an EIB—*environmentally induced bitch.* Just be lucky I'm walking away."

Zig managed to roll to his feet, but stumbled. This guy was an animal. He had to be hopped up on steroids or meth.

One thing I knew, for sure, was that serial killers were liars. He was tired of chasing me and thought he'd try lying in wait. So, I thought I'd use his play to help equalize my injured ankle. I needed to get some separation from him, but it wasn't going to last long. I hobbled away as fast as I was able, hot pain shooting from my ankle up my leg. The realization that I could no longer outrun him sank in.

The path curved ahead, so I'd be out of Zig's sight for a moment. Changing strategy, I ducked into the brush-covered woods. Through dense leaves, I watched him swear as he surged by, zig-zagging down the path, trying to catch his balance. Gave a new meaning to his nickname. Zig was afraid he'd lost me. It was nice to give my ankle some relief. Under the cover of brush, I crept along with the satisfaction that he was putting the distance between us. I would simply hide close to the path and hope someone would eventually find me.

I took a careful step, babying my ankle, and then heard, before I felt, a hard, metal snap. Jagged metal teeth bit into my already swollen leg and I wailed . . .

# 62

*My baby went away*
*Across the sea to an island*
*While the bridges brightly burned*
*So far away from my land*
*The valley of the unconcerned*
*I was walking down the road, man*
*Just looking at my shoes*
*When God sent me an angel*
*Just to chase away my blues*
*I saw a hundred thousand blackbirds*
*Flying through the sky*
*And they seemed to form a teardrop*
*From a black haired angel's eye*
*That tear fell all around me*
*And it washed my sins away*
—JOHN PRINE, *EVERYTHING IS COOL*

## JON FREDERICK

12:15 P.M., FRIDAY, JULY 17, 2020
LAKE BIG TOO MUCH, BIG FORK

Moki suddenly shouted, "There's his truck!" He hopped out of the boat, dredged through the water, and was on shore before I even cut the motor.

I wrestled my phone out of my pocket and tried to call for help, but I had no reception. We were now in a dead zone.

If you enjoyed this book, please post a brief comment on Amazon, or pass on the word...

Thank you for your kind support of my work!

www.frankweberauthor.com
www.facebook.com/frankweberauthor

The Silverado was parked in overgrown grass, next to a one-room cabin.

I ran the boat up on shore, jumped out, and drew my gun as we approached the cabin; I had it ready when we pushed open the door.

Moki stood stock-still, imagining the horrors Harper withstood while held captive. He looked to me with fear and fury. As he walked stiffly around the space, he reached toward the cuffs hanging from the bed frame.

I quickly warned, "Don't touch anything!" I gestured toward the door and stepped out.

Moki followed me outside. The brief shower had done us a favor. It was much easier to follow tracks in wet grass.

I pointed to a trampled footpath headed to the lake road. "It looks like they headed north. We'll stay on the path until we see a trail off of it."

# 63

*So its hurry! Hurry! Step right up*
*It's a matter of life or death*
*The sun is going down*
*And the moon is just holding its breath*
—JOHN PRINE, MEXICAN HOME

## HARPER ROWE

(40 MINUTES EARLIER)
11:35 A.M., FRIDAY, JULY 17, 2020
LAKE BIG TOO MUCH, BIG FORK

I fell to the ground, my body involuntarily curling up in excruciating pain. I clawed at the snare, trying desperately to pull the menacing teeth apart, but the rusted old trap wasn't having it. Yanking at the chain proved futile. It was anchored down like it was embedded in concrete.

I cursed myself for screaming, but it was water under the bridge, now. Okay—*stop and think*. How did hunters remove their death traps? I looked the contraption over carefully, my tears not subsiding. With shaky hands, I pressed the small levers on each side of the jaws and they mercifully released. As my leg came free, I nearly groaned with momentary relief.

As quickly as I was filled with elation, I looked up to see Zig standing over me with his lascivious grin. His foot blasted to my face before I could even raise my hands.

# 64

*The lonesome friends of science say*
*"This world will end most any day"*
*Well, if it does, then that's okay*
*'Cause I don't live here anyway*
*I live down deep inside my head*
*Where long ago I made my bed*
—John Prine, Lonesome Friends of Science

## RIEZIG "ZIG" ZIEGLER, AKA KHARON

11:35 A.M., FRIDAY, JULY 17, 2020
LAKE BIG TOO MUCH, BIG FORK

The path turns a corner ahead of me, so Harper is temporarily out of sight. When I turn the corner, she is gone, so I push myself to catch back up. My chest hurts and my body is getting worn down, but I'll catch her. I always do.

And then I hear a brief, piercing scream from behind me. Harper has become ensnared in one of my wolf traps. I relish the satisfaction of my prowess. I know exactly where she is.

It doesn't take long to locate her, as I marked the trees along the path close to my traps. I find her sitting on the ground, frantically pulling on the trap. The ecstasy I feel when my foot smashes into her face is indescribable. Persephone died at the hands of Kratos. Kratos was the personification of strength and he crushed her to death.

As I raise my foot a second time to smash her skull, the pain in my chest hits me like a spear. *Hell. I don't have time for this shit.* I fall . . .

# 65

*You wish you left your well-enough alone*
*When you got to hell to pay*
*Put the truth on layaway*
*And blame it on that ole' crazy bone . . .*
*If they knew what you were thinkin'*
*They'd run you out of Lincoln*
—JOHN PRINE, *EGG & DAUGHTER NITE, LINCOLN*
*NEBRASKA, 1967 (CRAZY BONE)*

## HARPER ROWE

### 11:55 A.M., FRIDAY, JULY 17, 2020
### LAKE BIG TOO MUCH, BIG FORK

I was reliving the same nightmare, once again coming to, unsure how long I'd been out of it. My face felt puffy and swollen, and I could only see through a small slit in my right eye. As my vision cleared, my first sight was Zig, crouched beside me on one knee.

He rubbed his chest hard with a hairy knuckle, as he warned me quietly, "There's a wolf close—I can hear him. You're going to want to get up and stay by my side." He put his hand out to me, but I didn't move. Zig continued with a weird light in his eyes, "He'll go for your neck first to kill you, and then feast on either your organs or your ass. The muscles in the arms and legs are eaten last."

I didn't know whether to believe him, but knew he'd kill me if I didn't cooperate. I carefully sat up.

Before my spinning head could adjust to the movement, a blur of dark fur streaked into my peripheral vision, as a black wolf pounced toward Zig. Protecting his throat, Zig jammed his forearm into the ebony beast's salivating jaws.

The wolf bit down hard and tore flesh away.

I couldn't make sense of what I was seeing; everything was happening faster than my rattled brain could track. Zig didn't hesitate. He punched the animal hard in the ribs and pushed it back. Zig stood, rivulets of blood now streaming down his left arm.

The wolf's low growl warned of an idling death machine. It was not going to be robbed of a fleshy meal.

Terrified, I scooted myself as far back into the brush as I could, while keeping an eye on the macabre scene.

Barely fazed by Zig's attempts, the wolf rebounded immediately. Zig tried to kick at it, but the predator was faster and stronger. A jaw loaded with razor-sharp teeth locked down Zig's leg.

Zig roared, "You're a dead bitch!" In a display of human strength I couldn't fathom, he somehow grabbed ahold of the crazed wolf's head and dug his thumbs into its eyes. The beast yelped in pain as Zig crabbed back and dropped next to me.

I had to turn away. I would be the winner's next target. Reluctantly, I squinted open my good eye, out of morbid curiosity as much as self-preservation. I could see that, like me, one of the wolf's eyes was damaged, but it could still see with the other, and was intently focused on us. The wolf hunkered down and paced patiently, just out of reach.

Zig said, "He's going to wait us out. He thinks we're too damaged to make it far."

Before I could formulate any kind of response, I heard movement behind me. I turned to see a second wolf crashing toward us in full sprint. This one wasn't waiting.

THE SECOND WOLF HAD SILVERY FUR that flashed like burnished aluminum. I instinctively crossed one arm over my neck and another across my head as it raced toward us.

To my surprise and relief, the sterling animal ran by us, going after the black, injured wolf lying in wait. The two were immediately in a snarling and horrific fight to the death. Breathless, I inched further backward, fascinated and sickened at the same time. Within two minutes, the black wolf lay dead with a crushed throat. I stared wordlessly at the carnage.

Zig's cackling laughter intruded on my contemplation. He got up and lumbered into the woods.

The silvery wolf seemed to study me for a moment. I was frozen in fear. I didn't dare breathe as our eyes locked. There was something human in the moment I would never be able to explain.

I didn't know if it was divine intervention or simply the smell of blood, but to my great relief, the argent killer pursued Zig.

After it took a few steps in Zig's direction, out of my sight, I heard the metallic snap of the jaws of that steel trap clamping down. I flinched, feeling the pain delivered as the wolf howled in agony.

Frantic and confused, I scrambled to my feet.

To my dismay, Zig limped out of the brush, triumphant. "I reset the trap when I heard the first wolf approaching."

Like a zombie, I dragged my injured leg as I stumbled away from him. I waved an exhausted hand at him.

Zig snorted, "You win," and he dropped like a ton of bricks to the ground.

I stopped and raised my eyes to Heaven, silently cursing the empathy my mom instilled in me. In defiance, I sighed heavily but didn't turn around.

He gasped as he told me, "Most wolves are killed by other wolves—not hunters. They can smell a wolf invading their territory from ten miles away."

Against my screaming instincts, I looked back.

He continued, "It's my heart." He studied his arm and ravaged leg, "Although I might bleed to death, first."

I moved back toward him, but remained at a safe distance.

Zig panted between jags of pain, "I didn't want to kill you. Hell, I would've married you. It's just a job and Margo pays well."

I had to know. "How many girls are in this lake?"

He sighed in resignation. "Just two."

I exclaimed, "Where are the rest? Stewart's been doing this for two decades."

"People didn't use to share their business with everyone." Zig coughed. "And even if they did—it wasn't until the last few years where people believed the stories trashy girls tell."

The world around me started spinning. Off balance and exhausted, I felt my body collapse against my will. It was all just too much. I settled into a bed of leaves and moss, and finally gave up. Green leaves looked so much brighter when contrasted against a dismal and angry gray sky.

# 66

*The dogs were barking*
*As the cars were parking*
*The loan sharks were sharking*
*The narcs were narcing . . .*
*In the parking lot by the forest preserve*
*The police had found two bodies in the woods . . .*
*Their faces had been horribly disfigured*
*By some sharp object*
*Saw it on the news*
*On the TV news*
*In a black and white video*
*You know what blood looks like*
*In a black and white video?*
*Shadows, that's exactly what it looks like*
*All the love we shared*
*Between her and me*
*Was slammed*
*Slammed up against the banks*
*Of Old Lake Marie*
*We were standing by peaceful waters*
—JOHN PRINE, *LAKE MARIE*

## JON FREDERICK

12:20 P.M., FRIDAY, JULY 17, 2020
LAKE BIG TOO MUCH, BIG FORK

Moki and I both heard a desperate wail in the distant woods. We broke into a sprint, but soon realized the cry was much further down the path than we initially thought. We were in the Chippewa National Forest, which had one of the largest populations of eagles in the U.S. The majestic birds of prey circled the sky north of us. We both knew this meant they were alert to the dead or wounded.

Moki bolted ahead of me, toward a pack of wolves surrounding a motionless body, lying on the ground. Seeing flaxen hair spilled across the deep green of the mossy earth, Moki cut loose a guttural scream at the wolves and they quickly scattered. He took Harper's face carefully in his hands and begged, "Harper! Please, say something."

When I caught up, Harper was out cold. I crouched and placed two fingers on the carotid artery in her neck. I was relieved to feel the thumping of life pulsing under her skin. The fine, porcelain features of her face were now bloated and bruised, suggesting she took a hell of a blow to the head.

Moki looked wildly around, finally landing his frenetic eyes on me, asking, "What *happened?*"

I shook my head. "I hope she'll be able to tell us." I advised, "We need to be careful with her. She may have a fractured skull. The inflammation of her face could be a good sign, as it can indicate the swelling is on the outside of her skull, rather than on her brain."

One of Harper's eyes was swollen shut; the other painstakingly fluttered open, just a fraction. She murmured, "The flash of a firefly in the night."

Tears streamed from Moki's eyes. "Stay with me, babe. I am not leaving. We are threads woven together. What happens to you happens to me."

Harper's confusion seemed to clear as she focused on Moki's face. "Who said that?"

He forced a grin. "I did."

Harper reached for him and he embraced her gently. "You need to stay still and rest. You're safe, now."

The rumbling of a truck disrupted the intimate moment, as it plowed down the path toward us. I drew my gun and stepped toward the noise, prepared to protect Harper and Moki.

To my relief, Jeremy's white truck came into view. The hemi engine was barely stopped when he was out and running toward Harper. Moki respectfully moved aside to allow Jeremy to see to his daughter. Jeremy dropped to his knees and spoke softly to Harper, carefully inspecting her injuries.

After determining she was stable, Jeremy stood up and directed, "We need to get her to a hospital."

I agreed and asked, "How bumpy was the drive?"

Jeremy glanced at the mud all over the side of his Dodge Ram pickup. "Jarring. It's not a ride I'd recommend for someone with a head injury. But it doesn't look like you can land a helicopter, here."

Moki had resumed his protective hovering around Harper, mindful not to hold her too closely, cradling her limp hand to his face and whispering words of encouragement. He interjected, "We have a boat."

After some discussion, we agreed to carefully carry Harper to the boat. Jeremy knew more about addressing her injuries than I, so I sent him and Moki off with Harper. When I informed them I was going back after Zig, both expressed concern for my lack of backup, but their focus was on Harper, as it should be.

With a heavy sigh, Jeremy tossed me his keys and I tossed him mine. I said a quick prayer for Harper, as the boat sped smoothly toward the public access where I'd parked my Explorer.

Zig was still here, somewhere, and I intended to find him. From the lakeshore, I could see the eagles were circling further down the path. I jogged back to Jeremy's truck and drove in the direction of the birds.

It wasn't long before I found the wolf pack surrounding another body. I laid on the horn and the beasts scampered off. As I jumped out of the truck, I could hear a lone wolf still whimpering in the woods, left behind and forgotten by its pack.

Zig was alive, but was a bit up, bloody mess. Gun back in my hand, I held it at my side and stood at a safe distance. I asked, "Where's your worst pain?"

"My heart," he groaned. "I got a bad heart."

I couldn't argue with that.

I told him, "Okay—I need to put a tourniquet on your left arm to stop the bleeding. I'll see what's in the truck."

After using a bungee cord to stop the blood flow in his left arm, I helped Zig to his feet and lugged him to the truck. I strained under his tremendous weight. As he was barely able to stand, I leaned him against the warm hood. In lieu of handcuffs, I wrapped a tie strap multiple times around his body, pinning his arms to his sides. I had him take a big step up and heaved him into the truck. Once the safety belt was fastened, Zig wasn't going anywhere.

The lone wolf howled again.

I asked, "What's the story with the wolf?"

Zig grunted, "I trapped one."

With gun in hand, I walked to the wolf. It gritted its teeth and growled as I approached. I fired a shot into the ground close to it, to assert my dominance, and it cowered to the ground. I bent down and freed its trapped foot. The beast hobbled meekly away.

When I returned to the truck, Zig grumbled, "Why the hell didn't you kill it?"

"Same reason I didn't kill you."

I started the truck and headed down the path.

Zig theorized, "You don't want the hassle of explaining it to everyone."

"That's another good reason. Let me just say this—when I start thinking it's okay for me to be the judge and jury, I have to question my thinking. If I didn't, we'd be the same, wouldn't we?"

# 67

*Well I'm thinking*
*I'm knowing*
*That I gotta be going*
*You know I hate to say so long*
*It gives me an ocean*
*Of mixed up emotion*
*I'll have to work it out in a song*
*I'm leaving a lot*
*For the little I got*
*But you know a lot*
*A little will do*
*And if you give me your love*
*I'll let it shine up above*
*And light my way back home to you*
*'Cause you got gold*
*Gold inside of you . . .*
*Well I got some*
*Gold inside me too*
—JOHN PRINE, *YOU'VE GOT GOLD*

## HARPER ROWE

6:00 P.M., THURSDAY, AUGUST 27, 2020
BIRCHMONDT DRIVE NORTHEAST,
WEST SIDE OF LAKE BEMIDJI, BEMIDJI

The Coronavirus cases in Minnesota continued to surge, breaking records on a daily basis. Today, we hit a yet another new record for the number of new cases in a single day (+1154).

It wasn't my grandparents' fault I no longer spent the night at their house. I was the one who brought a killer to their home. It was just too hard, knowing Zig had taken a photo from my bedroom. There had been a few nights I'd stayed at Moki's, sharing a bedroom with Kimi. I wasn't sure how his conversation about me had gone with his family, but I was now welcomed with open arms.

Zig's boot to my face resulted in an orbital fracture or, in other words, a crack in the bone by my eye socket. The swelling was down and the plum and greenish hues were fading away, but I still experienced some numbness in my face. After that steel-toed wallop, I'd lost consciousness; when I came to, I thought a dog was licking my face. It turned out to be a pack of wolves. I'll never know why they didn't bite me. I told myself that, like Persephone, I was rescued from hell by my mother. As I was mesmerized by fantasy and half-consciousness, a deep shriek cut through my haze and the wolves scattered.

And there stood Moki. A chef saved my life.

Moki gave me total credit for surviving, but I will never forget that he found me. He also saved Nitika, by finding her a nurturing and safe home. Moki was my hero! Even though my smile wasn't as full as it once was, I was happier than I'd ever been.

Zig survived, but would never fully recover from his massive heart attack. In addition, the tenderizing he took from the wolf pack did irreversible muscle damage. His once bombshell-like biceps were stripped to the bone, giving him that Popeye—before spinach—look.

While Zig was behind bars, Margo had found a high-priced attorney who managed to get her house arrest. Her newest accessory was a GPS tracker locked on her ankle, clarifying her whereabouts every second. Paula Fineday had an agent sitting outside her house, randomly checking in on Margo, to ensure she wouldn't disappear before the trial.

DAD AND MOKI WERE AT MY grandparents' with me, today, for a fried chicken dinner. We had gone through the story with my poor grandma and grandpa, so they could make sense out of what they were reading in the paper.

Grandma sniffed, "I'm glad you didn't keep any of Blaze's money. You don't need that kind of money."

I didn't respond. I didn't *need* his money, but I took it. Why shouldn't I be the one who decided what it would be used for? I gave it to Chimalis to help cover the damage to her restaurant insurance didn't cover. Moki shared that *Chimalis* is the Native word for bluebird. When he told her that Harper Rowe was *Bluebird* in the Batman series, she told me she'd call the restaurant "Bluebird" when it reopened. I thanked her, but told her she could call it whatever she wished.

It was fun to have some money to just let go of, for a good cause. Nitika was now living with Chimalis and assisting her with the renovations.

As I passed Grandpa the au gratin potatoes, he commented, "They say the truth sets us free, but does it? Are you happier now?" Deep thoughts from a generally quiet guy.

I was happy until 2020. I was now happy, again. The loss of my mom was brutal, but meeting Moki was wonderful. Finding out the truth about Mom just made me love her more. And, in the midst of all the chaos, I discovered I had a sister. We'd been corresponding online for three weeks. She was a couple years older and worked as a social worker in Morrison County. I told Grandpa, "I'm happy."

He said, "I've always said I hope my kids have the good sense to lie to me."

"Well, *I* can handle the truth," Grandma interrupted. "I know you haven't told me the entire truth. Tell me one more thing that you haven't dared to share with me."

Dad attempted to save me. "Harper's been through enough. She'll share on her own terms."

I reached under the table and took Moki's hand. "I guess there's one thing I can share, and then we relax and eat." I held a pregnant pause, simply to build up the anticipation, and then revealed, "Dad doesn't like au gratin potatoes."

Jeremy smiled and shook his head in embarrassment, knowing he had explaining to do.

Grandma passed the potatoes to him, "That's ridiculous. Of course he does."

After throwing Dad under the bus, I was rescued by the ring of the doorbell. Both Dad and Moki got up and rushed to the window, and then okayed me to answer the door. I knew they were being considerate, but this would need to end when Margo's court case was over.

I smiled as I answered the door, "Hi."

There she stood, at about five feet tall and with about thirty pounds on me. She had Blaze's black hair, but I had his long-legged stature. At five feet six inches, and 120 pounds, my body was more vulnerable to high-altitude winds.

Rachel West pulled her glasses off and studied my frame and light blonde hair. "We are damn near identical twins."

We both laughed. "You're a little early, but please join us for dinner."

She smiled, "Sounds like I'm right on time."

Rachel and I were going to be great friends, despite the fact that our commonality was that we were both conceived during a sexual assault, and we both hated Blaze for it. His only contribution to our wellbeing was the moment of conception. We were Disney princesses. We both had loving mothers, now deceased, and still had caring father figures. Our *dads* simply weren't blood-related. In my opinion, blood was overrated.

# 68

*Sally used to play with her hula hoops*
*Now she tells her problems to therapy groups*
*Grandpa's on the front lawn staring at a rake*
*Wondering if his marriage was a terrible mistake*
*I'm sitting on the front steps drinking orange crush*
*Wondering if it's possible for me to still blush . . .*
*From the bells of St Mary*
*To the Count of Monte Cristo*
*Nothing can stop . . .*
*The sins of Memphisto*
—JOHN PRINE, THE SINS OF MEMPHISTO

## TRISHA LAKE

8:05 P.M., AUGUST 27, 2020
MINNESOTA CORRECTIONAL FACILITY—SHAKOPEE

Legally, I couldn't have a cell phone, but a woman I didn't know well handed me a burner phone, and told me to expect a call from Margo Miller. I sat, waiting, in a cement-floored room in my orange jumpsuit and gawd-awful, leper white rubber slippers. The call came in.

Margo asked, "You know who this is, right? Don't say my name or this call ends."

"Yes, I know. Why do you need to talk to me?"

"Just a reminder to not to say a culpatory word about me. There is only one women's prison in Minnesota so, if I'm sent there because of you, I will make the rest of your feeble life hell."

"I'm not saying a word against you. I promise."

She revealed, "I like to take care of business ahead of time. With my plea deal, I'm still going to do time."

"I'm sorry I killed Billy," I offered lazily. "He just wouldn't let me go."

Margo cut me off, "Don't make excuses. That just pisses me off. And stop telling people Billy wanted to marry you. That's a bold-faced lie."

There was no point in arguing with her. Inwardly, I found satisfaction knowing Billy was going to dump Margo for me. He simply hadn't told her, yet.

She continued, "I've been wondering what Billy'd have done if you would have killed me? With that in mind, I've decided I'm not going to kill you."

"I don't know what that means, but thank you."

She bragged, "I'm a registered nurse. Do you have any idea how valuable that will make me in prison?"

I pondered, "I imagine quite valuable. Especially now, with COVID."

"I won't be able to technically work as a nurse, but you can bet they'll have me do as much as possible and sign off like they did the work. In return, I'll receive favors." Margo continued, "Looking at the pictures of the women in Shakopee, I don't have a lot of great options, so I want you to be my roommate. I'll make certain you're protected, so you can shower and walk about without fear. In return, you'll pick up snacks for me at the canteen and write personal letters I dictate—I'll just sign them. You'll keep our cell clean and, if I decide I need an orgasm, you'll make sure it happens. I'm not gay, but *years* is a long time. And," she emphasized, "you won't say a word to anyone about it."

I thought out loud, "So, basically, you're saying if I would've killed you, Billy would have used the hell out of me instead of killing me."

Margo laughed, "No doubt."

There was no escaping it. One abusive partner after another.

Margo picked up on my reticence, "Don't fret. You're pretty and quite good at pleasing others. I don't anticipate having to slap you around. It might be the best relationship you've ever had. But don't get sappy. This won't be an affair. You're just temporarily meeting a biological need for me. There will be no, *I can't do this because my feelings were hurt.* It's something you'll do in exchange for the opportunity to live—because you took my lover."

"And if I don't go along with it?"

"You're dead," she said bluntly. "So, how badly do you want to live?"

"Bad. I have to make something good out of all of this."

"See you later." She hung up.

Serena put her hand on my shoulder and said, "You were perfect, Trisha—so cool—you didn't even blush."

I took a deep breath and felt relief as I slowly blew it back out. "Margo was right. It does feel better to take care of things ahead of time." I turned to her with a grin, "And honey, all the blush has been fucked out of me."

Serena turned crimson.

Paula Fineday was sitting across from us, watching a SWAT raid on her cell phone. "The agents have entered Margo's home and now have possession of her burner phone. Terroristic threats and tampering with a witness just earned Margo time in Federal prison. I promised Harper I would get that *wolf bitch* incarcerated before her court date. Neither you nor Harper will ever have to worry about Margo, again."

Paula had discovered that Margo knew an inmate at the MCF— Shakopee, who was incarcerated for opiate distribution, and made a deal with that inmate for mentioning to Margo she could get me a phone. Being the controlling monster Margo was, she had to act. It was why she killed poor Cayenne, killed Randy even though he swore he'd never testify, and why she tried to kill me. Margo used to say, "It's not finished until I say it's finished"—not true anymore. I was done with her.

My mind had stopped racing since I'd been in prison. You had to wait for everything, so everything was slowed down to a snail's pace. I attended Bible study and sober support meetings. I wanted to be forgiven. Serena gave me some workbooks to help me process through my trauma. I hoped to be starting therapy, soon, but the therapist was busy in here.

If I could do it all over again, I would've told my grade school teachers, over and over again, what was happening at home. That was how long ago the change would have had to happen for my story to end any differently. I thought about Serena going out of her way to make sure I'd be okay in here.

*There are people who just want to make the world better. I think I'll spend more time with them.*

# 69

*He's just a small fry*
*A bit too gun shy*
*To have his heart touched without a glove*
*He looks at strangers as potential dangers*
*Trying to steal his aimless love*
*Love has no mind*
*It can't spell unkind*
*It's never seen a heart shaped like a Valentine*
*For if love knew him*
*It'd walk up to him*
*And introduce him to an aimless love*
—JOHN PRINE, *AIMLESS LOVE*

## SERENA FREDERICK

10:30 A.M., NOVEMBER 20, 2020
PIERZ

The prevalance of COVID-19 was sky-rocketing in Minnesota. Yesterday's news announced yet another new record of seventy-two deaths and 7863 new cases. But, by and large, we'd learned to mask up and enjoy the moments we had with loved ones.

Jackson was now able to say a few words, which always came out adorably in his chirpy, one-year-old tone. Jon had Jackson helping him make popcorn. While the corn popped, Jon poured a glass of orange juice, and then drizzled some pomegranate juice in it. He turned to me, "Did you know Jackson can say pomegranate, now?"

Jackson was smart, but it was absurd. "I don't think so."

He raised an eyebrow, "Do you want to bet?"

"Sure. If you win, you can have whatever you want."

Jon smiled, "We'll address that later. Okay Jackson, can you say pomegranate?"

Jackson gave me his cute smile and proudly said, "Yep."

My sweet boys shared high fives.

Jon was such a dork, sometimes—but I wouldn't want him any different.

The freedom I felt from finishing this case was exhilarating. I had helped with investigations before, but this was the first I'd taken on for our own private agency—Moon Finder. I named it this, because we took Nora and Jackson out to find the moon, every night. Sometimes it was hidden, but that was life. You lived to search another day.

I picked Jackson up and kissed him. "So, you can say pomegranate."

He repeated, "Yep."

"You are so smart." I turned to Jon, "We pulled it off. We solved our first case as a private agency."

"And sent our benefactor to prison."

Shakopee had the only state women's prison in Minnesota, but we did have a special place for those who attempted to tamper with witnesses. Margo was now housed at the Federal Correctional Institution in Waseca. Trisha was in the Minnesota Correctional Facility in Shakopee. Zig would never completely recover from his massive heart attack and needed to be placed in the infirmary at the Minnesota Correctional Facility in Faribault.

I felt Trisha's sentence of twenty-five years for Second Degree Murder was harsh, considering the circumstances, but it wasn't my call. The prosecutor argued that Blaze wasn't a threat to her at the time she shot him. Billy Blaze was always a threat. If that wasn't the case, why did police always respond with two or more officers? I guessed, with good time, Trisha would only serve seventeen years.

Jon asked, "Are you okay?"

"I'm great! Feeling like throwing my hands in the air and shouting in exhilarating joy! But I have to admit, I was so nervous I was in over my head, I was on the verge of throwing up every night."

"As private investigators, we're always in over our heads. Acceptance of that fact is important. Your interviews with Trisha were some of the hardest I've ever seen—but you managed them well."

"I feel fantastic," she beamed. "I proved to myself I can do this. I feel so light—so free. This work is intoxicating, isn't it?"

# 70

*Time was once just a clock to me*
*And life was just a book biography*
*Success was something you just had to be*
*And I would spend myself unknowingly*
*And you know that I could have me a million more friends*
*And all I'd have to lose is my point of view*
*But I had no idea what a good time would cost*
*'Til last night when I sat and talked with you*

*An apple will spoil if it's been abused*
*A candle disappears when it's been used*
*A rainbow may follow up a hurricane*
*And I can't leave forever on a train*
*You know that I'd survive if I never spoke again*
*And all I'd have to lose is my vanity*
*But I had no idea what a good time was called*
*'Til that night when you sat and talked with me*
—JOHN PRINE, *A GOOD TIME*

## JON FREDERICK

### 8:45 P.M., NOVEMBER 20, 2020
### PIERZ

When I finish a case, I consider what I could have done better. Even though I'd only seen Lilly for a moment, I tried to find scenarios that would have prevented the fourteen-year-old from being one of the bodies pulled from the depths of Lake Big Too Much. I called law enforcement and left them a tip, but the girls denied being trafficked when interviewed.

The Brainerd Diving School, a group that specializes in body retrieval, found three bodies chained to wheels at the bottom of the lake. One of those bodies was Lilly. It turned out Lilly wasn't from Pengilly, as Nitika believed. Instead, her legal name was Lilly Pengilly, and she was only fourteen years old. The BCA was still in the process of attempting to identify a second, African American teen. She may have been the girl Trisha saw at Stewart's, back in 2016. Tragically, almost half of all underage sex workers are African American. As a society, we need to offer better options for kids in both our inner cities and rural America.

The third body was missing a foot. This discovery of Keith Stewart's lifeless remains submerged in the murky depths of Lake Big Too Much, with the unfortunate young girls he so casually disposed of, was the essence of divine retribution for him. He wasn't the god he believed he was. The location and state of his body clarified that Zig had just as carelessly disposed of Stewart. Keith had taken a severe beating before his foot was severed.

It's more difficult to get people out of sex trafficking than you might think. The scenario involving Harper's mom is pretty typical of how teens get hooked in. Once in, they're often too ashamed and dependent to leave. In order to justify the behavior, a person needs to make a variety of concessions, which make them progressively more damaged. An inordinate number of violent killers had sex workers and strippers for mothers. A higher number had violent fathers.

Nitika is now living with Chimalis and helping out with the restaurant. Chimalis calls her "Tika" and Nitika now prefers to be addressed by her new moniker. Tika is not completely out of the life, yet. Paula discovered she is on a site called "Only Fans." This is a site created in 2016, which allows individuals to sell nude photos of themselves to "fans." While it's supposed to be restricted to adults, fourteen-year-olds have opened sites using IDs of people who look nothing like them, so it obviously isn't closely monitored. Selling nude selfies is an easy way to attract a dangerous stalker. Paula has taken Tika under her wing and has her involved in therapy. My hope is Tika sticks around long enough for it to take.

I THINK YOU HAVE TO BELIEVE in the unfathomable to make the world better. While I've seen the worst in people, I've also seen heartfelt gratitude from people who experienced incomprehensible oppression. Trisha Lake and Billy Blaze were once children like our Nora and Jackson. It was on me and Serena to keep our children safe and provide them the nurturing guidance they needed to be decent people.

Despite her past trauma, Serena is the kindest person I know. She is evidence there is an exodus, even from the darkest of times. I'll never forget speaking to Serena, as a teen, the first time after realizing I loved her. She sat comfortably close to me, on a metal chair at a graduation party, while friends filled the circle. The memory of what was said is now hazy, but her face remains in sharp focus. Glistening green eyes and luscious lips, gifting me with words I clung to. An incredible pressure to be kind, respectful, funny, and smart immediately weighed on me, but only the first two came easily. As she was making a point, Serena ever-so gently would place her hand on my forearm. It was no longer a fantasy; I'd just won the lottery.

LIFE CONTINUES TO CHALLENGE MY WISDOM. I find parables particularly helpful. Adam and Eve ate the forbidden fruit, after being charmed by a serpent. In the oldest versions of this story, the serpent is described as difficult to see. When I was young, I wondered why God put the snake in the Garden of Eden. The parable was intended to point out that evil is always present, because it is *in* us. After eating the forbidden fruit, Adam and Eve were *conscious*—they felt naked and unworthy to stand before God. The capability of sin was always present—unseen, but present. Once they realized we were all prone to temptation, they felt less safe. *The line between good and evil cuts through the heart of every person.* We are left to our own accord to determine the people we are going to be, which makes expressions of gratitude and grace even more amazing! We choose to express heartfelt kindness and love, despite our demons, and that makes it so much better.

I finish changing Jackson's diaper. Serena joins us, sharing, "Nora's in the music room with Legos. She told me she needs some 'privacy to focus'." Nora was imitating what we had told her when we worked on this case.

Serena teases, "I think I won our bet. I'm not so sure Jackson can say pomegranate."

"Okay. Ask me anything and I'll do it. Give me the worst job you want done and I'll do it with a smile." Kindness is money in the bank in a relationship.

She challenges, "How about clean the Explorer—including the car seats."

As I pick up Jackson, he says, "Pom gran." I raise him in the air in victory.

Serena shakes her head at me, laughing, and kisses me. Life is good!

## THE END